D0007601

THE FIRE WAKER

THE FIRE WAKER

BEN PASTOR

THOMAS DUNNE BOOKS
ST. MARTIN'S MINOTAUR ❧ NEW YORK

This is a work of fiction. All of the characters, organizations, and events portrayed in this novel are either products of the author's imagination or are used fictitiously.

THOMAS DUNNE BOOKS.
An imprint of St. Martin's Press.

www.thomasdunnebooks.com
www.minotaurbooks.com

Library of Congress Cataloging-in-Publication Data

Pastor, Ben, 1950–
    The fire waker : an Aelius Spartianus mystery / Ben Pastor.—1st ed.
        p. cm.
    ISBN-13: 978-0-312-35391-9
    ISBN-10: 0-312-35391-X
    1. Rome—History—Empire, 284–476—Fiction.   2. Miracle workers—Fiction.
I. Title.
    PS3566.A77525F57 2008
    813'.54—dc22

                                                            2007050683

First Edition: April 2008

10 9 8 7 6 5 4 3 2 1

To those who fight and suffer in wars
and against those who wage them

ACKNOWLEDGMENTS

My gratitude goes to many: among them, to the friends of the Archae-ological Museum at Biassono (Milan) for their generosity in sharing written and illustrative material on ancient Northern Italy; to Major General Giorgio Battisti, Italian Forces in Afganistan/ISAF, for his welcome advice and conversations on men at war; and, as always, to my agent Piergiorgio Nicolazzini, to Philip Patterson, and to Peter Wolverton and the whole crew at St. Martin's. Need I add that the episode of Aelius's generosity to the beggar was inspired by the life of the Press's namesake, a soldier and saint of ancient Pannonia?

PRINCIPAL CHARACTERS

Aelius Spartianus—imperial envoy, historian, and regimental commander

Agnus—known as *Pyrikaios*, or the *fire waker*, Christian healer

Casta—previously known as Annia Cincia, Christian deaconess

Curius Decimus—aristocrat, officer in the Palace Guard

Baruch ben Matthias—Jewish former freedom fighter, artist, and entrepreneur

Marcus Lupus—brickyard owner

Minucius Marcellus—judge in Mediolanum

Lucia Catula—his wife

Isaac—ben Matthias' son-in-law, Lupus's brickyard supervisor

Fulgentius Pennatus—brickyard owner

Sido—head of Mediolanum criminal police

Gallianus—army physician

Duco—Briton-born officer, Aelius's colleague

Frugi, Otho, Dexter and Sinister, Vivius Lucianus, Ulpius Domnius—Roman officers, members of Decimus's "Cato's Sodality"

Protasius—Judge Marcellus's secretary, a former Christian

Aristophanes—eunuch, imperial chamberlain

Justina—Aelius's mother

Belatusa—Aelius's sister

Barga, Gargilius—Aelius's brothers-in-law

Diocletian, Constantius, Galerius, Maximian—the joint emperors, or tetrarchs

Constantine—Constantius's son

Helena—former imperial concubine, Constantine's mother

Maxentius—Maximian's son

Anubina—Aelius's Egyptian former lover

Thermuthis—Egyptian brothel-keeper

Nihil enim extra totum est, non magis quam ultra finem
In fact, there's nothing beyond totality, nothing beyond the end
—Lucius Annaeus Seneca, *On the Happy Life*

...a mutable surface, where the eye never encounters a resting place, and is led to slide along a faint chiaroscuro, now and then interrupted by deep furrows, and circumscribed in a brusque and nearly brutal way by masses that represent hair and beard...
—R. Bianchi Bandinelli, "The Pain of Living," from
Rome: The End of Ancient Art

I

TINDER

1

B aruch ben Matthias to Commander Aelius Spartianus, greetings.

If I didn't know any better, this could be Vindobona or Intercisa rather than Confluentes: Army posts are all the same. By now I can find my way around with my eyes closed. One-third of a mile square, barracks right, command post left, officers' quarters swarming with deadly bored orderlies who'd sell their mother for a transfer. Even commanding officers are beginning to resemble one another; they all look like middle-aged troopers thickening at the waist.

Speaking of which, Commander, I met your two brothers-in-law at Castra ad Herculem on the Danube: quarts of beef on legs, if you allow me. No wonder you do not go often to family reunions. Were you aware that you are now an uncle to seven nephews and nieces?

I will not bore you with the details of my travels and endeavors in the past month. Suffice to say that I left Egypt shortly before you, and here I am. Business is good, as I have widened my artistic and commercial scope to include sculpted epitaphs (in prose and in verses, with and without portrait of the defunct). Otherwise, aside from the economy, the situation on the north-

eastern border is what you probably already know. There's no keeping aliens out, army or no army. For any three of them who are ferried back across the Danube, ten more sneak through by night. As long as an empire needs cheap labor, or ferry-men make a tidy living at the traffic, the matter of illegal settlement within the borders will stand.

But you are probably asking yourself the reason for my letter, so I come to the point. You may remember my daughter (the one whose cakes we ate at Antinoopolis when we met last year, and whose marriage was celebrated in Rome shortly thereafter). Her husband, Isaac, who is a German-born Jew, works as a supervisor in a brick factory south of here. Last week the owner of the brickworks, a man called Lupus, died of a malignant fever and, after all due ceremonies, was buried in the family plot. You may imagine my son-in-law's astonishment, Commander, upon returning to work this morning and finding Lupus at his desk, looking none the worse for his illness, death, and apparent resurrection. A fairy tale, you will say, or else Jewish exaggeration. None of it! My relative does not drink, unlike me he is an observant Jew unlikely to tell a lie, and besides, awe and fear struck all employees at the Figlinae Marci Lupi, to the extent that a couple of them took sick and several ran away swearing not to resume their work ever.

Now, of you—other than having fought against you nearly ten years ago—I know these things: that despite your barbarian origins you are educated, courageous, respectful of your gods but no more than it befits a high-ranking officer, and exceedingly curious. As a historian, you might be interested in recording that at the close of Our Lord Diocletian's reign (may he be preserved, etc., as the formula goes), a dead man was brought back to life in the province of Belgica Prima. As an investigator with imperial leeway to inquire, you might wish to discover just what took place at Noviomagus. All I can add to my report is—but you presume this surely—that Lupus is a Christian, prosecution against his kind not having progressed in this neck of the woods, according to our Caesar Constantius's (may the gods, etc.) tolerant view of the sect.

Keep in mind that I shall divide my time along the Rhine between Confluentes and a charming spot called Bingum, south of here. Will I ever get used to such silly city names? In Confluentes you'll find me one door down from the keg-maker Erminius. Best regards and farewell. P.S. I heard that Constantius's repudiated "wife" is not thrilled that her favorite son, Constantine, has made her a grandmother through Minervina. At half a century of age, Dame Helena keeps up more than appearances, being still as attractive to junior officers today as she was to Aelius Spartianus (so goes the gossip in the army camp) a few years ago. Do not worry, this letter is being hand-delivered by a trusted friend.

Written at Confluentes, north of Augusta Treverorum, Province of Belgica Prima, on 4 Kislev, Sunday, 19 November, day XIII before the Kalends of December.

SOUTH OF MOGONTIACUM, 20 NOVEMBER 304 C.E., MONDAY

Aelius read ben Matthias's letter last, after the concise, badly written one from his father, complaining of "my only son's three years worth of *absense* from home," and reporting his mother's "*anziety* that you *havent* yet taken a wife as you should." Despite having retired as a colonel of the Seniores Gentiliorum, the old man had felt no desire to educate himself beyond what was needed these days to build a career—although others had become emperor with less. As for Aelius's mother, she made sure to propose every six months a marriage prospect: soldiers' daughters, landowners' widows, or little girls who'd have years of growing up before they could share a bed.

Dropping his parents' letter in a box where others (each one practically identical to the rest) lay, Aelius was receiving a strange composite image of what his old enemy, the Jewish freedom fighter, had communicated. On one side was Helena, who'd seduced him when she

was exactly twice his age and left him lovesick like a calf, and on the
other, this absurd tale of a dead man reborn. True to the Christians'
fame as hard workers, Lupus was apparently unable to think of anything better than returning to the office after resurrection. It made
him simper, certain that ben Matthias was pulling his leg for whatever
reason, sarcastic atheist that he was. But the composite image had a
third side, hazy and lopsided, a sting to the heart: because Anubina
had borne him a daughter in Egypt seven years before and but for her
unwillingness to marry him after her husband's death, he could be
writing to his mother to quit looking for a wife.

To be sure, the efficiency of the postal service never ceased to amaze
him, yet couriers had been able to find him everywhere, even during
the eastern campaigns. Therefore it was only logical that mail would
reach him between Noviomagus and Mogontiacum (a few miles south
of the latter, in fact), it being known that he'd left Diocletian's summer
capital of Aspalatum nearly two weeks earlier, headed for Tergeste, and
from there, across four provinces, already come less than two days
from Constantius's capital city. He'd spent the night, ben Matthias was
right, in a place like every other, a stop on the side of the military road,
with its stable and tavern, salesmen of shoddy wares, and whatever
small industry typified the region. Here it was glassworks; farther
ahead it might be pottery, or leather.

The early morning filled with haze the spaces between hills beyond;
the straight road led into that haziness, and one could imagine any
landscape beneath it: surely Mogontiacum, where the road forked, and
then cultivated fields, fallow land bristling with the yellow weeds of
late autumn, interminable woods. The Other World, even, if what the
poets wrote was true, and constant mist is where the shades are
obliged to spend eternity.

The reason given by his parents for the letter was his upcoming
birthday, the thirtieth; but his father was wrong in saying he had not
been home in three years. It was four and a half, and as far as he was
concerned, Aelius felt no great need to go back.

When he mounted on horseback and rode out, heading to the

northwest, the haze had not yet lifted. It might be midday before
the sun burned it enough to leave the river land, the mountains across
the bank, and all details bare and exposed to view. For now, as he proceeded, the mist seemed to recede, yet if he glanced back he could see
that it closed behind him, too. How many times had he ridden
through the fog to battle, or back to camp, or away from camp. Fog
seemed always the same, but he'd cut through it in anticipation, or
mum fear, or exhaustion. The Other World had better not be like this,
or else it was desirable to return from it, as Lupus the brick-maker had
apparently done.

Carrying His Divinity's messages for Constantius meant that everywhere doors opened to him, and he had precedence over others waiting to go past checkpoints or manned bridges. He had, in fact, made
such comparatively good time from Aspalatum that he was a full day
early. Given that the complex ceremonial did not allow for an early call
any more than it tolerated lateness, there would be time to stop and see
ben Matthias at the army town of Bingum, three or four hours north
of Mogontiacum on the river road. It was where he headed now, expecting to reach it by noon.

Constantius he had met during a summer tour of duty at court in
Diocletian's eastern capital, Nicomedia, but not seen in the few inter-
vening years. One of the two vice-emperors groomed to take power
next May at Diocletian's and Maximian's expected resignation, he had
impressed Aelius as a solid general who had asked that staff officers
be presented to him after an army review. One by one he'd greeted
them, a massive, pale, bulge-eyed man with crooked thumbs who had
married his colleague Maximian's daughter and put away not—as
ben Matthias wrote—his first wife but his long-term concubine Helena.

It was a time, that summer, when Helena was as filled with hateful
resentment as any ambitious woman snubbed after climbing from ob-
scurity to privilege. That she had never been able to get Constantius to
marry her was her principal regret, but there it was. Aelius recalled
courtiers and priests taking turns at her side, at any one time seemingly

convincing her to embrace one lifestyle or another. The first time she
had let him into her bedroom she'd told him it might be the last, since
she was considering a religious life (she had not decided whether Jewish or Christian). The second, she'd informed him of his numerical
rank among her lovers. The third, she'd mentioned dreaming that she
would be a saint and altars would be raised to her. With the doltish
flattery of youth, Aelius had said that her bed was an altar already, as
far as he was concerned, and she'd given him special liberties that day.
Constantius knew, of course, as everything was known at his colleague's court. "Tickle her under her navel," he'd unexpectedly advised
him one morning at the baths, in good humor. "She loves *that*."

From the haze, as Aelius proceeded, on both sides of the road the
long walls of fortified farms appeared now and then, whitewashed or
brick red in the distance, with their avenues of pruned trees or hedges.
In that murkiness, serfs laboring to prepare the fields for winter, and
gray crows pricking the mist over them, all had the ghostly appearance
of beings from the Other World; or, if not of Hades, they reminded
him of battlefields once things were over and a commander paced
across them to recognize his dead and collect their cheap rings in a
satchel, for the families. Lupus the Christian, dead and buried—as
Christians did not believe in cremation—sealed presumably under a
monument appropriate to his state, had come back to life. Nonsense,
of course. But Aelius could not help thinking of friends and companions lost during the wars. Were they likely to walk back, to come toward him from the haze of death, and feel the flesh once more?

By and by—he had already crossed Mogontiacum's streets, where
one barely saw the point of one's nose—the sun burned away fog and
river mist. To the east, the great Rhine was revealed then, whenever the
road climbed enough to show its lucid waters braiding in the wake of
heavy vessels. They silently followed the current northward, to dock no
doubt at any of the ten and more cities between here and the ocean. Not
seafaring boats, but flat-bottomed barges carrying beer and wine, salted
pork, and whatever else the army marches on. A sharp odor of stubble
fires came from the fields, over whose expanse smoke idled in the

windless day; night patrols returned to camp in the distance, advancing in order along the tracks, invisible from here, that crisscrossed the land.

When civilian monuments and a number of military burials became more frequent along the river road, in a closer and closer crowd, Aelius knew he was approaching the next settlement. According to the milestone, Bingum, the town whose name made ben Matthias smile, lay only four miles away.

CONFLUENTES, PROVINCE OF BELGICA PRIMA
The mark on Lupus's bricks was, predictably, his namesake wolf's silhouette, with the letters EX FIG MA LUPI REN arranged around it in the hollow of a crescent. The triangular piece of fired clay, clean and unused, sat on the table of Baruch ben Matthias's well-lit, well-appointed workshop near the southern gate of town. Aelius studied it, his ear to the hollow sound of mallets pounding wood at the keg-maker's next door. "*Ex figlinis Marci Lupi*: from Marcus Lupus's brickworks. Don't tell me the REN stands for what I think, Baruch."

"It does: *renatus*, for 'reborn.'" Pouring wine into two paunchy green goblets, the painter observed, "I thought you were in Nicomedia and my letter would take weeks to reach you. But you must come from Aspalatum instead, and in a hurry." Aelius kept mum. "You understand that I am just setting up my franchises here, Commander," ben Matthias added, even though he hadn't been asked to justify his presence so far from home. "It isn't like I am permanently moving from Egypt to catch cold along this frontier."

"Well, I noticed that your toughs are traveling with you." Aelius smiled, refusing with a small wave of the hand the offer of wine from his former enemy.

"Toughs? They're not toughs, they're my sons and relatives. Besides, with all respect for imperial military organization, these long stretches of solitary road between posts and cities call for some precautions. Cutthroats are strewn all over the woodland. I see that—on the contrary—you still travel without an escort."

"Ah, that's where you're wrong. My horsemen are around."

Ben Matthias took a sip from one of the two goblets. "This year's vintage," he said, smacking his lips. "Not bad for a white wine." To his experienced eye, in the weeks since they had last met in Theo's spice shop at Antinoopolis, Aelius had been indoors or traveling in northern climates, as he'd entirely lost his tan. He was otherwise the same tall and agile cavalry officer ben Matthias had fought during the Rebellion, coming close to killing him. Armenia (or the worries of a career at court) had made him precociously gray-haired, and only because he was fair did the obvious contrast between young age and hoariness appear less strident. Signaling the semiofficial nature of his visit by not removing the northern frontier army cap known as a "Pannonian felt," a low, dark red cylinder worn by all ranks, he kept observing curiously the brick on the table.

"It's the first marked piece to come out of the brick factory after the resurrection, and you understand I couldn't pass it up," ben Matthias commented with merriment. "It's a matter of time before some Christian deacon or pious lady comes looking for it, and there'll be a bidding war to own a souvenir of the miracle. Just in case, I have ten more in the back room. If you need one to bring proof to Our Lord et cetera, we can agree on a fair price. I already told my son-in-law that you want to meet Marcus Lupus, so if you have time tonight, it can be arranged."

"Tonight I dine with the staff officers at court. What about tomorrow morning?"

"I'll see what I can do." Ben Matthias smirked in his beard. "Court, eh? Well, they do say the scent of power whets one's appetite. By the way, if I were you I'd also try to see the miracle worker. Otherwise it's like sitting in the audience of a magician without knowing the trick."

"Right. Who's he?"

"His Christian name is Agnus, better known among his own as Pyrikaios, the 'fire waker.'" Again ben Matthias had that look of spiteful amusement, although Aelius assumed that—for all his protestations of atheism—his Jewish sensitivity was offended by the claim that a human being could bring back to life another. "His followers swear that he has made the lame walk and the blind see in towns of Germania Superior and Inferior, but this time he beat all records of miracle working. They say he himself was amazed by his powers! Like all good stage magicians, our man has a female assistant, Casta by name, and I hear that in order to see him you have to make an appointment through her. Yes, yes, I know, I thought that, too: Only in a brothel do you set up an appointment through a woman. Well, what can I say? That's what I hear."

At a second offer, Aelius did accept the wine, a more than passable Moselle served without water added. "I suppose you also know how I may find her."

"Interesting that you should ask. She rooms at Augusta Treverorum with a group of old women, not far from Middle Gate, outside of which the Christians have one of their burial areas. The name of the alley is Solis et Lunae." Ben Matthias counted on his fingers, looking up. "First, second—no, third house from the left exiting town, with a painted garland across the front. See how good I can be, and charge you nothing? Why, no! What are you thinking? You offend me, Commander. I wouldn't *dream* of asking you to drop a word in my favor with Our Lord Constantius, even though there's such a competition for army commissions of tombstones and monuments, and we're all climbing on one another's backs to beat the others. It's enough for me to be able to claim that Commander Aelius Spartianus, *praefectus Alae Ursicianae* in the Persian campaign, His Divinity's official historian, has come to me for a fashionable headstone."

Aelius laughed at the outrageous proposal. "As long as you do not put it in writing on your shop sign, and make all due conjurations while you carve my likeness."

Augusta Treverorum, 21 November, Tuesday
Constantius's capital in the old Gallic province of Belgica Prima featured all the bureaucratic buildings expected of its rank, and naturally a noteworthy bridge on the Moselle. A gray city nonetheless, its dull-colored stones seemed to absorb what morning light came

through the clouds. It was one of those sunny moments in the midst of rain elsewhere, when open arches and columns assume the opacity of bone against the stormy sky, but white kerchiefs and white shawls on women's heads seem blinding. Aelius, due to meet the co-ruler for breakfast, was up early and did his waiting in true military form, straddling the floor with arms crossed, looking ahead.

Soon he was to see that despite his well-wishing official titles—Germanicus, Britannicus, Sarmaticus, Persicus Maximus, and more, some granted four times over—Flavius Valerius Constantius no longer looked Herculean or semidivine, far from it. He had aged greatly since the summer in Nicomedia, to the extent that Aelius had to guard himself from showing surprise when he was permitted to glance up at him. As if he were collapsing from within, the old man's stoutness had become flaccid; the handshake (exceptionally granted after the fairly abasing bows and greetings required by ceremonial these days) felt soft and damp, like a wet glove. Yet Constantius dressed his decay with enormous luxury—gold clasps the size of a child's hands, a fanciful uniform that one never saw in the field but only on painted walls of army shrines. "Aelius Bartarius's nephew," he said. "You favor him, especially around the eyes."

In his youth Constantius had soldiered with Aelius's uncle (incidentally Aelius's mother's first husband) and seen him fall in battle, as he recalled now, "in Germany, protecting the colors." That he had the real commander's gift of remembering his officers' names, he went on to prove. "And you're Aelius Spartus's son."

Considering he was to become one of the two principal rulers of the Empire in a matter of months, only because of that old friendship did he allow a face-to-face conversation. Still, Aelius had to be told specifically that he was to behave as though conversing with a superior in rank, not the lord of the world.

"And do look up, boy: I can't be talking to the crown of your head."

The room—not a throne hall, rather like an administrative office—was severe, even lacking in elegance. By the desk, for the imperial breakfast, a small table had been set with peeled boiled eggs, olives, bright red fish roe. Sitting heavily on a stool, Constantius prepared himself to eat. "Here." He motioned with a dainty knife for Aelius to step over. "Stand where I can see you as I talk."

Reports that he would have to cross over to Britain sooner or later and fight a major war were known to all. In fact, his regular seat these weeks was Gesoriacum, on the far shore to the northwest. "Trouble on the island's border, I'm sure you've heard," he said, and Aelius noticed there was something like a whistle that came from his chest when he spoke. "At times it seems that this goddamned Empire has nothing but borders, like a loaf of bread that is nothing but crust."

"Crust is tougher than crumb, Your Tranquillity."

"Is that supposed to make me feel better or worse?" Constantius bit through an egg, halving it. "Your poor uncle, I remember him well on the frontier south of here, when the barbarians caught us by surprise in the river mist. His last wish was that his young widow marry his brother. Being that a woman bears the imprint of the man who deflowered her, I want to hope that in a way you're a son to both men." Bits of sticky yolk curdled at the side of his mouth, and he did not bother to dab them off. "These foggy days I remember my dead friends better than those breathing around me. Men who never betrayed, those." Yes, Constantius had been all fat and muscle in Nicomedia. Now his neck hung with empty flesh, chin and mouth dominated the face, and his hands seemed too large for the meager wrists.

As if come to his next subject by a roundabout reasoning about betrayal, he added, "You notice that I manage to avoid religious strife in my piece of the imperial cake, crust or crumb. From the start, I met the heads of the local Christians and struck an agreement: You abide by His Divinity's first edict, give up or burn your books, quit practicing, make no trouble, and I will be merciful." Constantius looked at him directly, with his bulging, mud-colored eyes. "You haven't heard of any trouble made by the Christians hereabouts, have you?"

"None, sir," Aelius hastened to say. "Well—only the story of the brick-maker, but I am not certain one could term it trouble."

"It could become trouble." Difficult to judge how serious Constantius was in saying it. He'd been notorious for his humor in the past, much to the vexation of his imperial counterpart Diocletian, of whom it was said that "he'd been seen laughing only once, but the witness was a deaf and blind man." Constantius picked at his food, sucking rather than chewing it. With a long-handled, minute spoon he laid fish roe on the egg he had in hand, and was quick to lap it off when it threatened to slide down. "I can put up with healing and such, but this! Imagine if those executed by prosecution elsewhere in the Empire—the Christians, I mean—were to resurrect after crucifixion, beheading, and such. Not to speak of those sent to the arena: It'd be quite the spectacle seeing them come back alive in the belly of the animals that tore them to shreds. Would a leg activate in the paunch of a lion, and an arm in that of a panther? Would the limbs magically reunite being vomited out, or would we witness the birth of monsters, half beasts, half humans?"

"I think it's a tale, Your Tranquillity. Such claims have been made by charlatans before, many times. The fact remains that not even the legendary Pentheus came back to life after the enraged women lynched him."

Constantius dropped the argument afterward. He ate all that was on the table, pensively chewing on the blue-green olives and swallowing their stones. According to ceremonial, the official reply to His Divinity's message would be handed to his envoy in a sealed envelope by the head of the palace staff, the day after the meeting. What surprised Aelius, however, was that Constantius's first private question had not been about his son. For years Constantine had lived as a high-ranking hostage at Nicomedia by order of Diocletian, who had a farmer's good sense not to trust alliances without guarantees.

Perhaps His Divinity's message gave assurances about the young man's health and well-being. Perhaps not. Aelius fretted. Did Constantius wait to hear from him a spontaneous declaration, directly from his son's mouth? There had been none. Officially informed of Aelius's errand, Constantine sent no message for his father. He was biding his time, it seemed to those who knew him, spending a good part of the day in the gymnasium exercising as if the future were a great bodily struggle to which he would be called sooner rather than later. Like Maximian's own son Maxentius, his peer, he awaited the two emperors' abdication to see how the rich loaf of the Empire would be carved, and how close to the plate he would find himself.

So Aelius stood in silence, trying to think of a way he could convey a greeting from Constantine without blatantly inventing something.

"How's my son?" Finally Constantius capitulated. "Being his age and at court, I assume you saw something of each other in Nicomedia."

"He was well when I saw him last April, sir. As a new father, he'll be naturally taken with the pride of the occasion."

"You're right, yes. Is the child truly curly-haired?" A sudden spiteful turn of the lips made Constantius look sour, not at all accommodating. "Otherwise, why would he call him Crispus, instead of giving him my name?"

"I have not seen the boy. But since Lady Minervina is wavy-haired, it stands to reason—"

Rising suddenly from the stool, Constantius unsteadied the small table, so that plates clacked and slid across it, without falling. "All right, you may go." His hollow voice was not irritated, not exactly, and in fact the gesture bidding Aelius to leave had a forbearing tardiness. "Still working on imperial biographies, I hear. Which one now?"

The question caught the envoy while he backed toward the door, as required. "The life of Severus, Your Tranquillity."

"Septimius or Alexander?"

"Septimius Severus, the African."

"Hm." Constantius grunted. "Not a lucky one with his sons, either."

The night Aelius spent in Augusta Treverorum would be termed by ben Matthias "like any other," and to men who did not pay attention to details and hues, it might be so. Aelius rather disbelieved that a painter could be counted among them, so perhaps the Jew only played indifferent. Odors were diverse; street corners and stairwells breathed stench or perfume that readily would make an army man say, "Syria" or "Moesia," but not one *and* the other. Girls in the shade whispered similar things, but from time to time one's response—heightened urge, or irritation, or plain disgust—varied. Invited by a former colleague to share his quarters overlooking a crossroad, in the traveler's occasional insomnia, Aelius stood at the banister of a cramped balcony, catching only glimpses from the humid darkness below. Guards making their rounds, shaking the knockers to make sure doors were locked and safe. Running steps, the clacking sound of laden mules. He caught himself thinking, *How does a man supposed to have come back from the dead trust himself with going to bed, and confronting the scary night?*

The power of tales, amusingly told. Already he was fantasizing, as if the miracle had happened, and he'd have to report it to His Divinity in the most appropriate terms.

It would snow soon. Had he not been used to the cold of army camps ever since childhood, already Aelius would have had to resort to hooded capes and waterproof shawls as others did. He knew the season, the clean odor of winter winds on the way. There would be a mysterious moment when the fog lifted for good and one morning would be perfectly clear to the farthest horizon, and from the sky—soft and wet at first, small and so hard that one could not squeeze it between one's fingers—snow would begin falling. It was not that time yet, but a peculiar crispness in the night heralded its arrival.

In the morning, only the houses higher than three stories—not many, comparatively—emerged from the fog that covered the city. From the fourth floor, they looked like a scaly archipelago of roof tiles. The lively sounds of human activity below came disembodied to Aelius's ears, and once he left his friend's doorway and walked into the street, he thought that he was becoming a part of that crowd invisible from above. Actually the haze was suspended in midair, so that it formed an impalpable whitish roof, like a tent stretched in little folds. His Guardsmen, temporarily housed in the barracks adjoining the palace, were glad to be given a day off to rest or tour the town; two of them had women and children here, and were thrilled.

As for Marcus Lupus's clay beds and brick kilns, they stood outside the east gate and across the river, to the left of the military road in a place called At the Happy Diana. Riding in, the day before, Aelius had noticed the turnoff in a copse of oaks, with a bright red little roadside shrine to the goddess, and today he planned to check whether the cult statue or painting showed her indeed in a merry mood.

The sun had just risen when Aelius paced with his horse against the sleepy flow of merchants entering through the east end of town. Through the fortified archway, the haze took a fiery tinge between orange and madder, as if a conflagration were half seen, raging behind a woman's veil, or a sheet. At the gate, the soldiers saluted and let him through, and once outside Aelius wondered if they had even existed, so quickly the same haze closed behind him, canceling the gate and the walls and the head of the massive bridge across the Moselle. Nothing but the next stretch of the bridge and the rolling sound of water seemed to exist around him. A horseman coming from the opposite side did not cast a shadow but only a darker halo, where animal and man intercepted the flaming mist behind.

Curiosity was a historian's quality, although not the principal one; love of truth, Aelius thought, headed the list. One or the other, however, might be His Divinity's motivation for sending him out with the command of reporting on all notable incidents met on the way. It had been so in Egypt, where murder and conspiracy were what he'd stumbled on, at his own risk. Here—well, it was difficult to say. For now it came down to noting the state of the provinces visited, and in that sense miracles and portents did not fall under that rubric. But Lupus's "resurrection" could become trouble, as Constantius said, at a time when bloody prosecution across three-fourths of the Empire aimed to quash Christian superstition. In the African and Asian provinces the death penalty was handed down left and right against them, but there was no telling what rallying point for the beleaguered, testy Christians a man like the fire waker could turn out to be.

Impregnated with moisture, the small shrine at the Happy Diana turnoff had the color of live flesh. Under a worn eave, the little statue did not much exceed the size of a doll: Weather had smoothed it until the goddess's face had no features left but a button nose and the trace of a mouth laved into what could be a smile. Dry flowers and pebbles at her foot bespoke the passersbys' piety, although little crosses and other Christian scrawls had been scratched with a nail or the point of a knife on the niche's plaster.

Beyond, the brickworks were invisible in the mist. Only the high, reddish ledge from which the clay was obtained drifted in and out of sight, topped with a crown of young oaks that waited to be sacrificed to brick-making. The path, furrowed by deep wheel tracks, sieged by bushes, lay pockmarked with puddles. Water, Aelius noticed, trickled from the higher ground, and ice was already forming in the pools by the verge, where seldom carts passed. Among the trees, in the direction of the riverbank, one could make out a bivouac of makeshift tents, and bundles that no doubt were people sitting in their capes and covers. Aelius imagined they were believers or simply the curious who always flock when there is talk of a miraculous event. Still torpid with spending the night in the open, they barely stirred at the officer's passage. A woman among them glanced his way and covered her head.

This was the time of day when most manufacturers sent out their wares. On the military road (if Aelius looked back he could see the funerary monuments lining it vanish in the fog), oxcarts and mule trains moved along steadily. But from the *figlinae* ahead nothing seemed to proceed. Ben Matthias's son-in-law had his office in a small building near the kilns and would be waiting for him there, in order to introduce him to Lupus. Wondering whether by dint of long traveling he had possibly forgotten a holiday, Aelius gave no more thought to the absence of activity on the path until he heard the clatter and squelch of a single mount from the opposite side, and pulled the reins only so much as was needed to stop his own horse. The long ears of a mule and its patient shiny skull emerged first, then two men on its back; the pair, senior workers or overseers, wearing leather aprons, had the faces of anxiety, so that their greeting was hurried as the mounts brushed past each other on the narrow path

"Trouble at the brickworks?"

Aelius's dry question kept them from going off. They ogled him sideways, with faces low, as inferiors and—often—civilians did with men in authority. One of the two, red-nosed with the cold or recent weeping, answered, "Our master's dead."

"Yes, I *know* that." Aelius had to keep from smiling. "And come back to life, no?"

"No, he's dead again."

"When? How?"

"Oh, sir, Lupus's supervisor found him stiff in his bed when he went to wake him up this morning. Of course no one is touching him, just in case he could again—"

"Yes, God is merciful," the other began to say, but the first man elbowed him in the side, hushing him.

Aelius was not paying attention to Christian slips of the tongue. "In his bed, where? Not at the brickworks—"

"Yes, yes. Lupus's house is in town, but he was still weak, and when there is a big order to fill—you may be sure we were receiving requests from everywhere after the miracle—he stays at a little shack above the quarry hole. Why, he's there now, poor master. We're off to look for help."

That by "help" they meant Agnus was implicit. Aelius's first instinct was to follow them and see how the fire waker reacted to a failed miracle, but curiosity of another order won out, and he rode to the brickworks. There, ben Matthias's son-in-law Isaac, a hairy young man without as much as a cape on his shoulders, was scrambling from the foot of the cliff back to his office. A few words between them sufficed to inform Aelius that yes, the news was true, and that by taking a steep little lane at the right of the cliff it was possible to reach the shack where Lupus lay dead.

"Nothing has been touched in the room, Commander," Isaac added. "We thought it best. Poor Lupus—more's the shame, too. The army camp has just contracted a large order with us. They're enlarging the baths and infirmary, so the head surgeon came in person at daybreak, to check on the quality of the bricks. You'll find him at Lupus's bedside."

In fact, the officer at Lupus's bedside was as coolheaded and brusque an army surgeon as any Aelius had met. He confirmed the death, and testily shook his head to the suggestion that it had been a case of apparent death the first time around. "Yes, I know 'there are those who suffer from it,' and that it is 'like a deep, long faint.' With all respect, Commander, do not teach me my job. I am well aware of the weakness to which you refer, but in this case I can assure you, I have it from trusted colleagues that Marcus Lupus had died without a doubt back in September. You were not present, so you cannot pass judgment. Besides, you will agree with me that even reviving from a 'deep, long faint,' one scarcely has the strength necessary for removing the cover of the sarcophagus, forcing the mausoleum's door from within, and walking out. In the case of the gentleman you see lying here, statements were sworn that he reappeared in full health one week to the day after his demise. Yet the grave site was untouched. Even the flower garlands were still hanging in front of the doors as the relatives had placed them during the funeral."

Aelius looked at the dead man, whose stilled expression was of great surprise, as if something amazing hid above him in the rough ceiling. His appearance was remarkably *alive* otherwise, rosy and florid, unlike any other corpse the soldier had seen. "Well, then, maybe Lupus had a twin or a look-alike, who for whatever reason—I can think of a couple, both connected to money and property—found it in his interest to play the role of the reborn. Let's be serious, Head Physician. Was the mausoleum searched for proof of the body's absence?"

"They swear it was. Commander, I not only understand your skepticism: I fully share it." Big-mouthed, with the shadow of a blond mustache, the physician had a way of opening his eyes wide while he talked, to emphasize his point. "Yet, as a man who makes it his duty to study Nature and her phenomena, I must surrender to the evidence. In the face of the testimonials of my colleagues who witnessed the mausoleum's opening in the presence of officials, I have to say that Lupus did come back from the dead. Looks damn well for a corpse now, don't you think?"

Aelius ignored the comment. "*Come back from the dead.* Seriously! And why then has he gone back to them? Must we suppose he no longer liked it up here?" He had no wish to sound as acidic as he did, actually, but he felt between annoyance and disquiet. "Tell me, did you open the window coming in?"

"No. The Jew, the supervisor who found him, told me it was like that when he entered at daybreak. It was Lupus's habit not to lock it, apparently."

Marcus Lupus must have been well used to the weather. Coals in the brazier were long consumed, and through the partly open window on the side of the shack, the chill of morning flowed in as it did from the door. Glancing out of the window, Aelius saw that it looked on a steep cliff of shiny, friable clay, impossible to climb.

"The only sure sign that he ceased to breathe a number of hours ago," the surgeon observed from the bedside, "is that the stiffness of his limbs is beginning to ease. And I doubt it's because he is about to come back to life."

Aelius nodded, walking back to the foot of the bed. Distractedly, he stared at the coverlet thrown across that pink-faced dead; he felt the tight weave with middle finger and thumb, as if the cloth could give answers men could not. Why, even the surgeon's paleness was in excess of Lupus's; likely his own face looked whiter than the brick-maker's. "Does he have family, do you know?"

"As far as I can tell, only one brother and a sister-in-law. The Jew believes that as soon as they are informed of this, they'll hasten to send for the miracle worker, as they did the first time. You should have seen them weep with joy at the resurrection: You'd have never believed the brother stands to inherit everything, given that Lupus was childless."

"Maybe it was disappointment rather than joy that made them weep."

"You're cynical. At any rate, if I were in the brother's shoes, I'd let things stay as they are." But the surgeon was smirking, in the way physicians often make light of death, refusing to accept their powerlessness in the face of it. "I would suggest that he be cremated, in good Roman tradition," he added then, "but you know how these superstitious people are. You have to wonder why their god could not raise them from the dead if they lay in ashes."

"You seem to know more about it than I do. But, inheritance or not, Lupus had better lie in the state he is in now, or else we'll have hysteria in the streets from here to Judaea."

The surgeon nodded, screwing his face into a grimace. "I could make sure he is dead, at any rate. Drive a thin needle into his heart through the rib cage, for example. We would see then if that Pyrikaios, or whatever his name is, can really restart life's fire. But my oath as a physician forbids me to cause damage of any kind to a patient. Would you consider doing it yourself, if I handed you the needle?"

"Why, no. Absolutely not."

"Gentlemen." Isaac peered in from the door and, having caught the last exchange, knocked on the jamb to announce his presence. "Our workers returned from town to say they haven't been able to find Agnus thus far, but the family heard the news and wants to keep trying. We had lady visitors until late last night, and there's a number of them waiting to see Lupus, not to speak of people come from out of town. What should we do in the meantime?"

"Not keep the body here." The surgeon spoke meaningfully, looking at Aelius, who nodded. "If Lupus is to rise again, he can do so anywhere, even in an infirmary. Do let the family know, Supervisor, that the spoils can be collected at the legionary camp, care of Titus Gallianus, head physician."

Accompanying Aelius a few steps out of the shack, the surgeon said he would stay until a detail of troopers arrived to remove Lupus. "I want to be there this time, should Agnus show up to repeat the wonder. If you're still in town tonight, seek me at the military baths after sunset: I may have more to tell." From where they stood, past the intricacy of young oaks, the clearings in the fog revealed precipitous views of the country below, rich and wet; only the great river still flowed in a thick cocoon of vapors that followed its course northward. Familiar with the sight, Gallianus turned his back to it, while Aelius idled in admiration and sought to recognize this or that building in the city walls.

"You said 'wonder,' Head Physician. Why not 'trick'?"

"Well, magic is expressly forbidden to Christians." Gallianus shrugged. "Their dictate is that if your infant son is dying of disease and physicians have written him off, even in that case you are not allowed to seek incantations and faith healers. That you should rather let your son die. Crazy, isn't it? As a physician, you see, I am of two minds regarding that position. If the medical art can do no more, it is unlikely that anything else will. On the other hand, healing dreams are dreamed daily in the temples of Aesculapius, to whose divine care we are all entrusted as professionals. If any of my sons were ill unto death, I believe I would rush to the closest enchanter, or at least let my wife do it for me."

Aelius started down the steep track leading to the foot of the cliff. "The question remains. Philosophy and science teach us that a dead body suffers corruption and as such may not rise again. If it isn't a miracle, it is magic. I think it could be worthwhile discovering what the official position of the Christian clergy is regarding Agnus's doings."

"Good luck: They lie low these days. See you at the baths tonight."

Not before the afternoon would Constantius's reply to His Divinity come into Aelius's hands. This meant that he had time to set up an appointment with the fire waker, if he was available, and with that intention in mind he rode back from the brickworks. He tasted snow in the air, although the sky remained cloudless. As he crossed the bridge to town, the fog over the cold froth of the Moselle flowed above the water like a second, suspended river: It snowed in the mountains to the east and to the south, and the breeze tasted like frost.

The workers' yards on the bank, to the left once inside the south gate, were, according to ben Matthias, where the Solis et Lunae alley ran, short and blind, behind the shrine to the Sun and the Moon. Aelius found it without difficulty, and likewise the third house on the left, distinguishable from the others by the faded garland painted across the archway. The archway led to a flight of stairs. As for the garland, it might have portrayed flowers in the painter's intentions, but at present it resembled a link of pale brown sausages.

As a matter of fact, this was an island in the shipwrights' district, a limited strip of clothing stores, food stands, and glass shops owned by veterans, fastidiously clean. The narrow sidewalks were neat; everything bespoke the orderliness that army men carry into their civilian retirement. Even the brothels he'd eyed at the previous crossroad had freshly painted doors, with gilded phalluses sculpted in full relief above.

From across the street, the house revealed nothing; it had one high row of little windows, shuttered, and unless there was an inner court, darkness must reign inside them. When Aelius stepped over, a man sweeping in front of the shop next door looked his way. "Are you looking for someone, Commander?"

Christian or no (there were many Christians reported in town), the man stood with broom in hand on the doorstep, and everything in his posture indicated that he was ready, according to the answer, to make a sign to someone inside, who would in turn alert the dwellers. Aelius said, "No," but went in, and up the stairs. A small doorway, closed. The light from the street did not suffice to light the stairwell, and there was no judging if anyone was waiting on the other side of the panel, listening. Aelius knocked and said, "Official business, open up." Which he'd promised himself was the last thing he'd say, because it was so obtuse.

But the door did open. A girl of ten or so, serf or housemaid, stood before him with the silly face of children who have been instructed to act a certain way but forget when the time comes. "The ladies are not in" was all she put together. Behind her, Aelius made out an opening, like a passageway to an inner court. The odor of fresh whitewash came to his nostrils. When he stepped in, the little girl only moved aside, frowning as if trying to recall what she ought to be doing in this case.

A long room right and left, overlooking that inner court, went around the corners to continue to the sides. Aelius walked left, followed by the little servant, and saw that small rooms opened on the side walls. Some had drapes across their entrances; others did not, and revealed rooms ten feet square, with simple beds neatly made and nothing else. He'd seen jails in army camps look not appreciably different.

"Whom should I say?" The little girl remembered her orders, but there was no relying on her wakefulness. Aelius tossed a glance into the court below, paved and with potted plants laid in a cross pattern at the center. Instead of answering, he asked, "When do the ladies usually come back?"

"Before sunset, but now I don't know."

Naturally, if the shopkeeper below was a guardian of sorts, he'd have sent word already that a stranger had come looking—an officer, no less, with all that the army ever meant to sects at the edge of legality—and the inmates would stay away until the danger was past. Aelius left, but only to stop next door, where the sweeping man had cleaned all particles of dust from the same spot meanwhile.

"I am Aelius Spartianus, Caesar's envoy. This address was given to me so that I may inquire of a lady named Casta, supposed to live here with others. I have heard of the events surrounding Marcus Lupus of the brickworks and wish to have details."

The shop owner slowed down his sweeping. "Then it isn't Casta or the ladies you seek, but the miracle worker."

Aelius was beginning to lose his patience. "Yes, and I was told that one has to go through the woman called Casta."

"I'll tell her you came, Commander."

"No. You will tell her to call at my quarters in the Palace district, the house At the Silver Foot, before sunset, and to set up a time when I may meet this fire waker, as I hear he's called."

"Anything else?"

"Only this: Tell her that I have never seen a dead man come back to life, but then, I haven't seen a man being born, either, and do not discount the reality of birth because of it."

The shopkeeper did not seem impressed by the philosophical concession. He set the broom in the recess between the wall and the doorjamb, bristles up. "Their religion forbids men from entering the houses where consecrated women live."

"Well! I just entered, didn't I?" But, walking away, it came to Aelius that perhaps he had been able to enter because the women had moved elsewhere. It would explain the fresh whitewash, one little servant left behind, the spare, nearly empty cells.

"Baruch, you have to tell me more about these people, the fire waker and his assistant."

"I don't *have* to."

"Very well, I'll pay you."

"No. Say please. I love it when I'm asked nicely by a Roman officer." At noon, in a cozy room behind his latest franchise, ben Matthias measured his words as though sprinkling spice—an operation he was carrying out, in fact, over roast mutton. "First, a premise and a description of the man, Agnus. He is not at all what you would expect a holy character to look like. He's physically mediocre, which from an artist's point of view makes for the most impossible of sitters. Ugly folks, you know, are every bit as interesting to portray as handsome ones. Why, more so, even. Pretty people seldom have salient features to work on. Sage on yours, or not?"

"Sage, please."

"Pepper?"

"Yes."

"Older is better than younger (children are nearly impossible, they all resemble one another, like the greatly aged, and for the same reason: few or no teeth), dark is better than fair, skinny is better than fat. But I digress. Agnus is what I call a '*neither* sitter.' Neither this nor that. He's forty, maybe, and as far as color, weight, height, length of nose, and so on, draw a line where the middle is, and there you have it. Does not sport a beard—well, not quite, an inch's worth of hair on his face, if you call that a beard. Put a wig on him or dye his hair, he's the kind of character that changes completely if you change one detail. I haven't spoken to him, so I can't tell you about his voice, but I am ready to wager he has no appreciable accent, either. Hey, you *asked.*" Ben Matthias pointed at the plate in front of his guest. "How is it?"

"Very good. You should be a cook, if funerary art ever fails. What about her, this Casta woman?"

"Have never seen her."

"But what do you know about her? *Please.*"

Ben Matthias scratched his beard, chewing on his meat. Just as in Egypt, in his painter's workshop, he'd been all speckled with color and the hair on his chin bore flecks of green and red, here his new enterprise caused him to wear a thin veil of marble dust that in the light from the hearth turned at each movement into a storm of minute particles. "Gossip has it that she did not begin her life under that name."

"And what does that mean?" Aelius watched the whirlwind of marble dust rise from the Jew's clothes, twirl and fall. "Casta: 'pure, chaste.' Do you mean she adopted a new name—I know Christians do it—or that her lifestyle was once different from the present?"

"Some people say both. But then they also say that a good Pharisee changed both his name and his ways on the road to Damascus."

"Whatever, Baruch. Just tell me all you know, because I am aware you are enjoying this, and you ought to be paying me for letting you gossip about the Christians. Young, old—what else?"

"She's young and your type."

"Ah."

"But not what you think. Physically, she is—well, I remember Thermuthis, when she was your favorite redhead down in Egypt—nothing like Thermuthis. But she's elusive, like Thermuthis."

Aelius savored the well-cooked meat, giving himself time before answering. "Thermuthis is a brothel-keeper, Baruch. 'Elusive' may be a misnomer for her. And let us leave aside what my type ought to be in your judgment, as you haven't kept up with my changing tastes. Is this Casta simply a stage assistant to the magician, or may I expect to find out something worthwhile from her?"

"Some say she is the holy one of the two."

Sunset came and went, and no news of Casta. Two of Aelius's bodyguards reported no movement around the ladies' house: lights off, door closed. "It's not unusual," his host confirmed. "In order to feel safe, Christians keep moving." Satisfied that he would be informed if the woman presented herself at his quarters, Aelius went to the military baths, where Titus Gallianus was paying for a round of drinks after losing a ball game. He said readily that despite fierce resistance from the family—Agnus and his cohort apparently being still away— he had succeeded in obtaining Lupus's body, against promise not to dismember or incinerate it. "Which does not mean I would not perform an autopsy." When he walked with Aelius to the warm pool, he was still excited with his findings. "Serving on the eastern frontier, I have become used to seeing wounds of all kinds—that is my specialty. I can tell from where the scar is that the arrow you took in the chest could have killed you, and had you bleeding from the mouth two days at least."

"Three, damn ben Matthias and his rebels."

"Well, Lupus's case is entirely different. After closely examining the corpse from the outside and recognizing no signs of violence, I was ready to surrender to the idea that maybe the man had had a relapse of the violent fever that did him in to begin with. Only that floridness, Commander, those bright pink lips, gave me pause. So I waited until spots began to form at the extremities of his limbs—an unmistakable proof of decomposition beginning—to cut him up. Well! It was after I took a good look at his internal organs that I began to understand: stomach and muscles bright red, blood fluid and cherry-colored . . . My old anatomy teacher gave us an excellent lesson on the matter years ago."

Aelius slipped gratefully into the steaming water. "What was your conclusion?"

"That Lupus went back to the Elysian Fields not of his own accord but with a good dose of charcoal vapors as a helper."

"Despite the open window?"

"Ah—oh. Well, the murderer must have opened it afterward to let the poisonous air escape. Even though charcoal vapors are odorless, you'd soon know by vertigo and a headache if you stood in a room that hasn't been aired. Isaac the Jew claims that Lupus did not suffer the cold, seldom used braziers and such, and kept his window partly open. Apparently, he didn't even lock his door, as he kept nothing worth stealing in the shack."

Aelius had come to relax, but this was much better than growing torpid in the heat. "So he could have been surprised in his sleep. Wait a moment. There is—it's curious, very curious—another thing: Did you notice the coverlet, the edge of the coverlet?"

"Why, no." Gallianus went under and then emerged from the water again, rubbing his face with the joined hands. "What about it?"

"I assume there's clay everywhere in a brickyard. But it was dirt, bits of dirt, that I fingered on the cloth, as if the coverlet had been used—I don't know—maybe to seal the bottom of the door from the outside, to make sure the vapors would kill the man within. History has many examples of such murders by suffocation."

Gallianus pinched his short blond mustache to squeeze water from it. He agreed that yes, it could be done, and that in theory the killers could have waited outside for the time needed to stifle their victim and then replaced the coverlet on the bed, cracking the window to clear the air. "To this moment, I have neither informed Lupus's family of my findings nor spoken to others about them. Not knowing there's murder behind the case, at the brickyard and elsewhere in the town they already blame Agnus for failing in his resurrection, and it's better for him if he does not show up just now. Too bad, because I would dare him to bring the dead back to life after my autopsy. What have *you* heard?"

"A few things. Even though at a first glance the only ones to gain from Lupus's death are his relatives, I was able to ascertain that husband and wife were overnight guests of friends, and nowhere close to the brickyard when the man died. Never mind, it's my habit to ask about such things . . . Also, there is no night guardian, no watchdog near the kilns or the clay bed. Virtually anyone could come and go unnoticed, if he avoided the grove where the curious bivouacked in hopes of seeing the living dead."

Gallianus laughed. "So, you started snooping as well." He hauled himself out of the pool, and sat with his feet in the water. "I confess that this afternoon I became so restless that I went back to the brickyard with a couple of troopers, and until daylight failed us, we did seek footprints around the shack. But it's hopeless in a place where people come and go, it's bushy, and there's a risk of falling."

"A successful businessman might have had enemies in and out of the family." Aelius spoke while still in the water to his waist, his arms crossed over the edge of the bath. Over the pool, glancing up, he watched steam form a mist in the high-ceilinged hall and condense along the wall. In the dim light, the walls seemed to be weeping. "Did you know Lupus personally?"

"No. Last year he supplied bricks for some repairs at the camp, noticeably underbidding his competitors. That's why we thought of him when we decided to enlarge this building. But our army contract was a small one, so I doubt anyone would kill him because Lupus won the bid to sell us the wherewithal for an addition and new latrines. Since you have access to court, you may want to ask whether he had been approached for other, larger projects. There are new public buildings coming up all over the place. Augusta Treverorum—Treveri, we call it for short—is growing every which way. If Lupus won that sort of governmental bid, there's no telling what the competition might do."

Aelius did not have to go as far as asking at court. In fact, he did not have to go beyond the next room of the baths, a sort of informal officers' club, where civilian government workers often came for a drink or lunch. Before long, he learned that Marcus Lupus had been one of three brickworks owners who had entered a bid for a large contract, related to the building of a new tribunal and annexes. The other two bidders—businessmen from the frontier also, one based in Mogontiacum, the other north of Confluentes—had apparently lost by a hair.

"But you know, Commander," a talkative aging bureaucrat told him, "it is all in the game, eh?" Completely naked, he sat on a stool swinging his skinny legs and chewing on nut meats. "Someone has to win the bid, and Lupus did not always come up with the lowest one. But I can't understand why you call him a *successful* businessman. Successful, my foot! Before the publicity he received from his 'rebirth,' his brickyard was about to close, which explains the low bids. We're told he's dead once more. A shame, eh? These *miracles,* mighty short-lived, if you allow me the pun! If this were Egypt, I'd smell a rat in his sudden demise, but we live in the civilized world. If suppliers and merchants had to kill one another every time someone beats them to a fat contract, each of us would be reduced to baking his own bricks and raising his own herds of swine."

It was true enough. Aelius told himself that only because His Divinity had encouraged him to investigate those deaths in Egypt months earlier did he feel now that he ought to understand why a man about whom he knew nothing, other than the small detail that he had come back from the dead, had been suffocated in his own brickworks.

23 NOVEMBER, THURSDAY

Punctually, as Aelius expected, it snowed during the night. In the morning only a sprinkling whitened the roofs, and the daily traffic had already reduced to mush what had covered the streets. As often happens at the beginning of the cold season, the snowfall was followed by a rise in temperature, so that ice turned to rain, and this in turn gave way to a springlike day. But the birds flew south in large flocks, honking and calling in the night, and if one listened closely by the window sill, one could hear the flapping of large, tireless wings. *They go to Africa,* Aelius had told himself in the dark. *They go to Egypt. They will land along the great*

river, in the reeds and canes, among the papyrus plants. They will fly over
Anubina's little blue house. That her husband and her son by him died recently, I tell myself, is the reason why she wishes that we remain apart for
a time. She said so, but has no desire that I recognize the girl she bore me;
wishes to live off her embroidery business, and if she has an affectionate
reference, that is Thermuthis's brothel, where I met her. Thermuthis
promised me to look after her if needed, and to let me know in writing.

"They've cleared out. Skipped town. Picked up and left." Ben Matthias
sat comfortably in front of a marble slab, holding the chisel between
his dusty thumbs. "I love it when these things happen notwithstanding
imperial control, don't you?" He pretended not to notice Aelius's disgruntled countenance. "I heard they never stay more than a month in
any one place, like most itinerant preachers, although this time the fire
waker missed a great opportunity for an encore. There's no telling
when they left or where they're headed, although in my opinion they
would be fools to go out of the provinces under Constantius's rule. If
they step into Maximian's piece of the imperial patchwork, they're as
good as dead."

"Yes, well. Not that danger would stop them, necessarily. I've seen
Christians look for execution before." It was still early in the day, but
time for Aelius to continue his journey. He stood ready to go, and only
hope that the well-connected Jew could pass on more information had
brought him to the workshop.

"I assume it is not the news you wanted to hear, Commander, but it
solves your problem, all the same. The living dead is dead for good, the
miracle worker and his cohort are out of reach when they are most
needed, the relatives inherit the brickworks. I say, what if I came up
with death and rebirth to advertise my business? Gossip in town is
growing, as the eunuchs at court are spreading the word that Christian
magic is a fraud. Me, I'm leaving before moods and the weather get
worse. I have a little business in Italy."

"Whereabouts?"

"Mediolanum first, I think."

It was precisely where Aelius was bound next, to bring Diocletian's message to his co-ruler Maximian. Of course, he mentioned nothing in that regard, and as for ben Matthias, he let him think that on his part, too, there was nothing more to say. In fact, he waited until the officer stepped across the threshold to add, "I'll see you in Mediolanum," at once busying himself with the headstone in front of him against the wall, as if his knowledge of an imperial envoy's travel plans were incidental to his job.

FIRST LETTER FROM AELIUS SPARTIANUS TO DIOCLETIAN:

To Our Lord Emperor Caesar Gaius Aurelius Valerius Diocletian, Pius Felix invictus Augustus, grettings from your Aelius Spartianus.

Faithful to your recommendation, Domine, that I keep you informed of incidents encountered on the way to carrying out my duties in Augusta Treverorum, I must report something that took place after my successful meeting with His Tranquillity Constantius, Our Lord Maximian's Caesar. An odd occurrence of superstition ruffled for a time the Christian feathers in Belgica Prima, although there seem to be no lasting consequences due to the assassination of one of the players. A separate, detailed report of what I was able to gather regarding the incident is included in this mailing. As by Your Divinity's command, I am now readying to depart, bound for Our Lord Maximian's capital to continue my errand. Traveling on a cavalry mount and making use of relays, weather permitting me to travel across the mountain passes, I expect to be reaching Mediolanum in a week's time.

Observance of the imperial edict on maximum prices is to my judgment superior to what it was in Egypt. A sample of prices follows:

Gallic beer, 1 Italic sextarius. . . . .

. . . .

4 denarii

Hulled spelt, first quality, 1 army modius. . . . .

. . . .

95 denarii (1/20 below maximum price allowed)

Picture painter, daily wage with maintenance. . . . .

. . . .

150 denarii, although the man interviewed (Aelius did
not say it was ben Matthias) *swears by the fortune of Our
Lords Augusti and Our Lords Caesares that he can barely
recover his costs and begs that the limit be reviewed*

Butter, 1 Italic pound. . . . .

. . . .

*10 denarii (1/3 below maximum price, and it is of excel-
lent quality)*

    *Written at Augusta Treverorum, 23 November, day IX from
the Kalends of December, respectively in the IX and VIII year of
the consulates of Our Lords Diocletian and Maximian, also the
year 1057 since the foundation of the City of Rome.*

2

N otes by Aelius Spartianus:

En route from Augusta Treverorum to Mediolanum in Italia Annonaria. Fair weather for the season until Argentorate. Add here later regarding impressions skirting the forest that cost so many Roman lives three hundred years ago. Specifically: fat man from Arae Flaviae selling belt buckles and coins he says he found on the place of Varus's defeat; temptation to buy the steel and silver parade helmet he swore had belonged to one of Varus's cavalry officers. Farmers sowing wheat and barley in the protected nooks of the narrow valley toward Vindonissa. Snowfall in the night. Went back to buy the helmet.

Of the strange happenings in Treveri (as they call the city for short), this I have so far to work with: The army surgeon reports his colleagues' conviction that Lupus was truly dead before the fire waker brought him back, but he—Gallianus himself—was not present. Neither was he on the spot when the sepulcher was opened to ensure there was no tampering, or else that the revenant was Lupus in the flesh and not a look-alike. The brickyard at the Happy Diana was, according to the old

*bureaucrat, nearly bankrupt before the "miracle." Very interest-
ing. Isn't it logical to imagine that Lupus and the fire waker
worked out a deal profitable for both? A fake death, a false resurrection, but glory to the healer and commissions to the businessman. It does not solve the question of Lupus's murder, of
course. All I can say about it, for now, is that it was made to
seem like a natural death: something that all criminals worth
their salt would do anyway. Below is, as best I recall, the gist of
my final conversation with Isaac.*

*Isaac: "It was always the same procession. That day a leather
merchant came bringing a gift of expensive harness, in exchange
for permission to have any small object the fire waker touched
during his visits to Lupus. Even two cousins of the governor,
who study philosophy in Greece, asked to sit with Lupus. Matrons came together and separately with their servants. A crowd
you could not reckon brought pastries and wine for 'the miracle
man.' Sometimes we had to ask that they leave as politely as we
could, as it was getting dark already."*

*Spartianus: "Did you see Lupus alive and well after the
round of visits?"*

*Isaac: "Yes, of course. He told me he was going to bed early,
because there was much to do the day after."*

*Spartianus: "This 'crowd you could not reckon': Are you sure
all of them left the premises?"*

*Isaac: "Well, why wouldn't they?" But the supervisor's face
fell, as he answered his own question: namely, that one or more
in the crowd could have stayed behind unnoticed, to seal off Lupus's door and windows.*

*When I left the city, the magistrate was looking into the mur-
der on the strength of my deposition, and Gallianus's. Ben
Matthias's son-in-law and Lupus's brother will be called in to tes-
tify if they haven't been already, and they had better have both an
alibi and an alternative explanation to give. Matrons and gentlemen can be accounted for, but anonymous servants, no.*

Tidbits gathered along the border road: Agnus is a former teacher who spent time in Asia, where he was born, and Casta—no real name known—is a self-abasing lady from Laumellum who ministers to and cares for sick women, the sexes being rigidly separate among the Christians. She travels with Agnus but never rooms with him (not even in the same inn or house). A city administrator and itinerant judge in Brigantium thinks her wellborn by her speech. The couple was reported last summer here in Raetia, where according to reports "the lame walked and the blind saw." The judge, who has prosecuted a number of Christians, has it from reputable sources.

Tomorrow, having followed the Rhine practically to its springs, I will seek entrance by the pass known as the Golden Spike into Italy. I have been told of my good fortune, as often by this time of year the mountains are forbidding and one is stuck on either side of them, or else has to go around, adding weeks to his travel. The innkeeper maintains that as soon as the road begins to descend into Italy you can smell the fields and the richness of the land, and "tepid breezes rise from the plain to caress your face" (his poetic words). They had better, because— northerner that I am—riding for days in the rain and snow has lost its charm for me.

MEDIOLANUM, CAPITAL CITY OF ITALIA ANNONARIA,
30 NOVEMBER, THURSDAY

Maximian's new palace, Aelius had been told, was not aligned with the straight, perpendicular streets intersecting at the Mall square. Having entered Mediolanum through the westernmost gate, before long Aelius recognized at his right side the imperial quarters' thick, ornate mass alongside the racetrack's north-south direction. Not unusual for the seat of government to stand near a place of public entertainment: It was true even in Rome, where the Palatine Hill and its palaces formed a gigantic spectators' box above the Great Circus. Not unusual that the racetrack should be near the walls, either. What seemed an odd choice here, in terms of elementary safety, was that racetrack, imperial residence, and ramparts were fully contiguous. Hadn't barbarians attacked the walls no more than forty years before, nearly succeeding?

The short day was nearly over. In the shade, the waning light already stole details from the rows of river pebbles and bricks that ran, buried in mortar, along the endless blind surfaces; polygonal towers—the walls' and the circus's—loomed above. With the wind, an odor of mildew breathed in the street, undoubtedly from the small shops and houses where businesses generally thriving around horse-betting flourished. When Aelius turned back, he saw his Guardsmen ride by twos, visibly annoyed by the offers of services—carriers, muleteers, whores—inside the gate. Unlike their commander, they were bound across town to the new walled-in area added by Maximian to the northwest, which was reportedly large (one-third the size of the old city, they said) and sparsely populated, if one excluded the baths, the army compound, and the weapons factories.

In the tract between the gate and the palace complex, Aelius was stopped at roadblocks mostly manned by Pannonians. Once they knew his errand, they let him through. The last checkpoint, however, was less accommodating. Spaniards comprised it, led—unless he was mistaken—by officers from Hispania or Italia. His Guardsmen were not allowed to cross the line, and Aelius himself had to dismount, consign his sword, and wait in the windy street for someone to look at his credentials. Daylight closed like an eye. To his left, the circus's long wall cast a massive shadow, so that the street was captured by dusk already. Only the brick towers at the starting end, back toward the gate, stood bright red like torches in the sinking sun. Sparrows so small that from the distance they resembled a swarm of flies came and went from the towers, against a faultless blue sky.

"Nice view from up there." A voice caused Aelius to lower his eyes. He turned and looked at the spot, a few feet in front of him, where a beautifully appointed officer, his equal in rank, stood, the credentials in his outstretched hand. "From the top, Our Lord Maximian's mausoleum is visible straight ahead in the elm grove, and even the arena due south."

Aelius knew better than to assume that just because the papers had been handed back to him, permission was granted to proceed. So he nodded in a way meant to thank the officer for the information, useless as it was, and to greet him.

"Will you please follow me," the other said, not as a question but as a statement. "We have to go through the slightly uncomfortable ritual of checking you for weapons."

"I carry none, Commander."

"Well, Commander, we'll check you out anyway."

They walked into a narrow service door, leading to a diminutive room with slit windows, where even with the fiercest intentions one would have a hard time pulling a knife out of its sheath. Two soldiers frisked Aelius's chest, sides, and legs, and even bent down to make sure he did not carry a dirk stuck inside his boot. The officer stood outside, looking in, and when Aelius joined him again, he pretended not to notice his irritation. "This way, please."

Even though they were still outside the residence itself, armed guards were everywhere. Guardrooms, roofless passageways, and small courts formed a labyrinth impossible to negotiate without a guide. Aelius kept one step behind his peer, with the impression that such a convoluted arrangement was supposed to confuse a single attacker rather than a horde, the assassin rather than the barbarians. And he wondered then whether Maximian had not built his palace so close to the walls precisely to secure a quick way out of the city if necessary. After all, in the last one hundred years, if history told the truth, not one of twenty-seven official rulers and usurpers had died a natural death.

His companion looked at him sideways, not directly, with slight contempt or amusement that was difficult to gauge. He had neither introduced himself nor engaged Aelius in the usual army way, informal and meant to make a soldier feel everywhere one of the group. But when they finally entered a well-lit, wide corridor, he did say, as if searching his memory, "Aelius Spartianus—any relation to the Aelii of Hispania?"

Now Aelius knew the officer was mocking him, as it was highly un-likely that a man so obviously non-Roman, with such a barbaric last name, could be even distantly related to the deified Hadrian's imperial family. "No." He smiled back. "We're from Castra Martis on the Danube, but the excellent Aelii from Hispania owned us once. In a small but literal way, that's belonging to the family, isn't it?"

The officer laughed openly. He was a spare man, by Pannonian standards, sallow and dark-haired, with his hair a little long and thin-ning on top, sinewy arms, and an intense angry look. He was one of those men who look angry even when they laugh. "Manius Curius Decimus, from Rome." Shaking his head, he stepped ahead. "I will in-form the chamberlain of your arrival. Wait for me here."

Waiting was something Aelius was used to. Serving at headquarters and at court had educated him to the art of standing in antechambers for indefinite periods of time. He'd learned not to wonder, not to fret. Even when—as now—the delay was prolonged beyond a reasonable time, he kept his peace without yawning or pacing.

When Decimus finally returned, the last flicker of day had long gone. Wicks and torches had been lit in small niches and in brackets along the walls, and the increasingly rare sounds in the building meant offices were emptying themselves as officers and bureaucrats left for the night.

Maximian would not receive him. Not even the chamberlain would receive him. Aelius took the news without comment, revealing nothing by his behavior to the officer, whose duty might be to study his reac-tion. But he understood well enough it was because he carried a re-minder the co-ruler would not accept; His Divinity had warned him that such might be the case. "If he receives you but does not give you a message to bring back to me, all is well; he is merely cross at being re-minded we're abdicating. If he does not receive you but the chamber-lain walks out to pick up the message from your hands, things are still acceptable, as he's bound to read it. If not even the chamberlain agrees to see you, you are not to protest when you're invited to leave. Walk out with courtesy and send me a military dispatcher with the news in all haste. But as for yourself, do not leave Mediolanum at once. There's always gossip that filters through at court, and Italia is particularly prone to palace camarillas. If there's a chance, try to get to know the officer or officers who let you in, Aelius Spartianus. There's no telling what you might find out."

Decimus hardly seemed the type of aristocratic officer who lowers himself to engage in friendly chatter, much less gossip, and in fact his farewell three halls down was curt, nearly brusque. Only after leaving the palace and finding himself in the musty wind of the street did Aelius permit himself to be in a contrary mood.

Unlike Rome, Mediolanum was dark at night. Canals and sluices must run under the streets, judging by the sound of rolling water that came from manholes; it accounted for the odor of dampness, wet bricks, wet cement. Ever since crossing the Alps, Aelius had wondered at the lakes, the marshes, how the land north of the city was rich in rivers and irrigation ditches, still of a vibrant green despite the advanced season; such wealth of watercourses can make the fortune of a city at the same time that it eats at its foundations. Once out of the imperial complex, Aelius knew more or less where to go: keep east until he met the straight old street that with its perpendicular quartered the original colony. At the Mall, ease northeast out of the old city gate, seeking the recently added district beyond, inside Maximian's fortified new walls.

He'd come as far as a towering box-like structure, several stories high, before realizing that for all of his good sense of direction he'd gone off course and was—judging by the stench—probably much closer to the leather-making district than to the center of town. Governmental grain deposits faced him, enormous, blocking the night, and the pungent smell of animal skins stretched to cure came from obscure archways. Torches at a corner allowed him to read SORS FAUNI on a plaque, and that was all.

"I thought you would seek the army camp, Commander."

How is it that some voices, heard only once, become immediately recognizable? Aelius could see nothing in the dark at the end of the alley but knew who it was.

Decimus had followed him, or more likely he'd ridden ahead by shortcuts, so as to find himself waiting for Aelius in the narrow street. Only the glare from a doorway—eating place, brothel, or both—intervened between the two horsemen, but the second was invisible to the first. Thoughts raced to a roadblock and stopped, except for the certainty that Decimus had been sent to murder him, as he still carried in his saddlebag the message to Maximian from His Divinity. Aelius could kick himself for not having ordered his bodyguard to wait outside the palace to escort him, but recriminations served little now. Fleetingly a girl's naked leg, a round arm, like a vision, flashed across the doorway glare, without registering in Aelius's mind except to make him realize that he was about to die in front of a brothel.

"What's that, you're pulling your sword out of the sheath?" From the dark where his horse stood, Decimus reacted to the sleek sound of metal with such amusement as to seem to be struggling with laughter. "We're not on the Danube, Spartianus." He came, urging his horse one step forward with a click of his tongue, to the place where the light from the doorway showed him unarmed in the saddle. "It must be true what they say, that you can take the boy out of the borderland, but not the borderland out of the boy!" Although he wore no headdress in the cold night, Decimus was tightly wrapped in a cape so long that it partly covered his horse's saddle quilt. Pulling a weapon from under that bundle of cloth would be a feat.

Aelius felt a little silly, but still annoyed. "It may be. At the army school they taught me that officers are to make themselves recognizable to one another, sir."

"Don't be such a stick in the mud, Spartianus. Will you join me for dinner tomorrow night? I live in the southeast of town, not far from Porta Romana." Decimus grinned. "Ro-ma-na: what a beautiful sound. What can I say, the name of the gate alone makes me feel somehow less distant from *the* city. Make sure you bring nothing but your appetite.

I can't stand it when guests send ahead wines I do not care for, or venison I wouldn't put on the table."

"I haven't yet told you whether I wish to join you, Commander."

"But of course you must! No one ever turns my invitation down in Mediolanum."

Had it not been for His Divinity's encouragement to hear gossip, Aelius would have told Decimus that he might be in for his first refusal ever. As things were, he said he would come. The girl's leg swept again across the doorway, pink and agile. "But on one condition: that there be no more than three or four guests. I don't care for large dinners."

"I promise you there will be no more than one guest: yourself. Is that acceptable?"

Thanks to Decimus's directions ("one street down, right at the temple, and then follow the old walls to the first gate you meet"), Aelius was before long leaving the republican city limits. Minding to "bear right at the second street, as if you see the New Gate you've gone too far," he came to the cavalry barracks housing the regiment of five hundred men and horses known as the Maximiani Juniores, in what seemed to be a sparsely populated, dark lowland.

1 DECEMBER, FRIDAY

In the morning, he had to think twice to remember what he was doing in an army camp, and where the camp might be. He'd slept with the imperial message for Maximian in his belt, tight inside its tube-like envelope, so that hip and ribs ached with the chafing bulk of leather and metal prongs. Informing His Divinity of Maximian's refusal to receive him was a priority: Aelius's first care was to dispatch one of his men to Nicomedia; traveling nonstop, his own posthaste note could presumably reach Diocletian within a week. He was to await further instructions in Mediolanum, with the usual proviso that he spend part of the time doing historical research—that is, exploring the city's public and private archives for information on the lives of the ancient emperors, specifically Septimius Severus and his predecessor Didius Julianus (whose grandfather was born here), and taking minute notes on anything else worth reporting.

The day was clear. Only the canal beds and manholes had veils of haze, wispy and white. Judging by the number of cats prowling around the camp, rats, frogs, and who knows what other vermin must populate the unbuilt marshy spaces all around. From the walkway outside the tower room where he had slept, Aelius saw that what he'd taken the night before for weapons factories were actually army clothing manufactures, felt-making, dyeing, and sewing shops. Madder red capes hung to dry, with felt caps perched on top, formed a phantom parade across a lattice fence. Beyond the compound, past the city walls, rose a barrier of snowcapped mountains, the color of steel in the morning air; to the right of two pyramidal peaks, one overlapping on the other, there ran a longer massif like a crocodile's back. If he turned the corner (the wooden balcony surrounded the tower on three sides), he could look clear across the city in the diametrically opposite direction: There, the land grew flatter and greener, if possible, scored by brooks and roads leading to Ticinum and to Laumellum, where Casta was said to come from. Steel gray hills sealed the view far to the southwest.

Closer in, through the gate in the old walls, muleteers drove brick carts toward the new district's building sites—foundation holes bristling with stilts, stuck in the muddy earth like traps for wild animals, or defenses against cavalry attacks. The slow advance of the brick carts brought Lupus back to Aelius's mind; he was curious to hear from ben Matthias by letter, or in person eventually, about the murder case. Had the weeping relatives traced Agnus, and asked him to restore the life fire to the dead once more? Head surgeon Gallianus had promised he'd be on the spot if the attempt was made, "Because, by all that's good, if a corpse who's been stifled and cut open comes back to life, I want to see it, and hear the victim accuse his killers with my own ears." That the brick-maker still lay dead, Aelius was reasonably certain. As he contemplated the facts, he grew idly curious: How would public opinion have judged Lupus's death, if murder had not been revealed as its cause? Would the good people of Treveri take it in stride, or blame the fire waker for failing to keep Lupus's flame burning with life?

When something squat and gray scooted swiftly in front of the mule train, Aelius mistook it at first for an otter, but its motion betrayed it as a huge sewer rat, of the kind they impertinently called "of imperial size" along the Nile. *I'm still thinking of Egypt,* he told himself. *And considering that I didn't even want to return there last summer, that the land repels me as much as it attracts me, it has to be Anubina I'm thinking of.* Her white thighs, large and round at the top, tapering to a dancer's knees, came to his memory as he'd first seen them on the night he'd rented her from Thermuthis. It was just short of buying her off the brothel. "You might as well keep one at home, Aelius—it'd cost you less," Thermuthis had said. He had chosen Anubina out of three, because of those white thighs and her name: the name of the jackal-headed god of the dead, so sweetly incongruous for a castanets dancer. "She was a virgin until three months ago." Thermuthis had smiled from under the red sweep of her beautiful hair. "But I'm not charging you extra for it." He'd taken her along oddly ashamed, and that first night he'd sat with Anubina in his lap, embracing her, until they'd both fallen asleep.

Before leaving camp for the morning, in an offhand tone Aelius asked the officer of the day about Curius Decimus. He heard what he had already observed himself: proud, from a glorious and ancient family, well connected, bored with provincial life. Whether his colleague read a note of uncertainty in the question or not, he saw fit to add, "He doesn't like men, if that's what you're thinking. Decimus just comes across as a bit effete because it's an intellectual pose with him. Deems the lot of us boors and parvenus. Hell of a soldier, though. Did perfect wonders against the Picts and the Frankish pirates. He likes to invite people to dinner to find out things from them."

"And does he succeed?"

The officer of the day, a Briton full of freckles who must himself be related to those defeated Picts, raised his eyebrows. "Yes and no. Most often, as everybody suspects an official reason for the invitation, officers and politicians run at the mouth with the glory of Maximian and the Empire, hoping to benefit once their thoughts are reported."

"I see. And what is Decimus's real intent?"

"Intent? He does not have any intent. It's a *game* with him. If he were not old enough to be your father or mine, he'd still be playing with toys. Well, he's fifty, at least. Was married four times, and all he has to show for it is a daughter no one has ever seen. What else, let me see—His Tranquillity's former concubine Helena was his lover last winter, although they argued like cats and dogs."

Decimus, too? It seemed that everyone who had served at court in the East or the West had been Helena's lover at one time or another. Aelius knew how small such privilege in fact was, even though in Nicomedia he'd walked on a cloud during their weeks together. It only puzzled him that Decimus was not—by age or looks—the type of athletic youngster Helena prided herself on attracting.

"I have to come up with a password for the day." The Briton took advantage of the conversation. "Since you're a historian, give me one."

"How about 'Let's get to work,' Septimius Severus's imperial password?"

"A funny one, but it sounds good, thanks."

Until the lunch hour, Aelius stayed at the Mall, where thanks to his letters of presentation and rank he was given access to the city archives. Only because he wished to avoid seeming provincial did he not stop and stare at the monument to Brutus that sat under a bronze contraption in the middle of the square. But he did pass by slowly, looking at it. The bronze likeness of Caesar's murderer wore a periwig of verdigris, and the same blue-green patina formed something like muttonchops at the sides of the face. Slim columns held a roofed pediment over it, all in sheet bronze, and it was through rust holes that rain had dripped in to form incrustations. A scruffy dog was presently smelling one of the columns, with the intention no doubt to leave its own mark on history.

The bookseller whose shop opened just beyond, seeing that Aelius was headed his way, stepped back ceremoniously. "It's just because Brutus served as city governor, Commander, not because of what else he did." After the officer stepped inside, he added affably that each new imperial administration had considered removing the embarrassing monument. "But we're used to it in Mediolanum, and since the deified Augustus, he who was Caesar's heir, had the goodness to let us keep it where it was, it's bound to serve as traffic island and dog love-post for a long time to come."

Aelius had already stepped to the shelf where history volumes and sheepskin rolls lined up. He asked for the autobiography of Septimius Severus, Herodian's collected works, and "the pamphlets of a chronicler who goes by Aelius Maurus, but might have been the deified Hadrian's freedman Phlegon." Only Herodian's books were in stock, and when Aelius heard how much they sold for, he opened a small papyrus notebook to the page listing Diocletian's maximum prices for manuscripts. "His Divinity sells them for less."

"But they come from Greece, and there's freight."

"He's an imperial envoy, Nicanor. Did he mention it?" Decimus looked into the shop without walking in. Hatless, in the morning light he looked rather like a spiteful monkey. He replied to Aelius's nodded greeting with a flip of the hand, shaking his head at the bookseller. "Come, don't make us all look like money-grabbing Insubrians. Give him the Herodian works for the edict price, or he'll tell His Divinity on you. Commander, I'm off to my post at the Palace, but now that I happened to see you walk in here, I think I'll wait until you finish your shopping and give you directions to my place."

Aelius muttered, "Thank you," and without rushing completed the transaction.

Nicanor jotted down the other titles, promising that he'd secure them. "Anything else, Commander?"

"Yes. Any pamphlets or tracts you may have concerning miracle workers, wonders, and similar phenomena."

"I have Philostratus's *Life of Apollonius of Tyana,* just copied."

"No, I read that. Something more recent, about eastern cults, or even the Christian sect."

The bookseller grew rigid, as if a wooden board had come between his back and the clothes he wore. "We don't keep such *things* around here, sir." The reaching gesture he'd begun to make toward a higher shelf halted in midair. "I will bid you good morning, sir, and send word when the other titles come in."

Out of the corner of his eye, Aelius glimpsed his colleague's grin outside the shop. When he joined him, Decimus said in a not-so-low voice, "He has them, he has them. If it's Christian fairy tales you're looking for, you have to go to Nicanor after hours. Or do you really think we're burning all the Scriptures our policemen find in their raids? You should have asked him if he has your biography of Hadrian, Commander. It's a best seller in the city."

They walked together no more than a block, parting midway along the oldest north-south central avenue, where there was a private library Aelius meant to visit. Decimus insisted—and Aelius saw no reason not to listen—that before sundown he take a long, roundabout way to his house by Porta Romana. "Leave the city by the westernmost gate they call Porta Herculea, behind the baths, and take the lane due south. Never mind if it's a little smelly, as it is an area of bogs, and notwithstanding the canal upkeep, leaves rot in the low fields. Where three lanes fork, about sixteen hundred feet out, keep to the middle one till you join the road to Laus Pompeia and to Rome. There, hang a left and you'll see the portico. Once you pass through Porta Romana, my place will be immediately to your left. But make sure you start out when there's still plenty of daylight, to enjoy the tour. Very important."

Since Aelius seemed disinclined to say more than that he would do so, Decimus kept him from walking into the library by pronouncing his next words. "If you're waiting in town hoping that His Serenity Maximian will change his mind and receive you, you'll have time to get covered with verdigris and bird droppings like Brutus's monument. His chamberlain, the eunuch, had a hissy fit when I announced your arrival. Maximian could be heard shouting obscenities from two halls away, all if I overheard correctly related to the moral habits of your mother, and His Divinity's mother. Good thing you were three halls away."

Aelius kept a polite lack of involvement in his demeanor. Even weighing Decimus's words on the plates of truth and falsehood would result in a ruffled expression, so he did not place them on the scales at all. He turned to knock on the door facing him, as though the old paperwork he was about to view were more important than what he'd heard.

"How many hundred feet out of the walls before the lanes fork?" was all he asked.

Having reached Porta Romana with the sun sinking ahead, in a glory of etched details and gleaming roofs, Aelius was duly impressed with the rich colonnaded road he'd just ridden along. He'd read that Palmyra's streets were a veritable forest of marble shafts, but this was three times, at least, the length of the Asian city's. Decimus had stressed to him the magnificence of the two-mile portico, crowning the entrance into Mediolanum, of the road from Rome. Still, the odor of mildew wafted in the pinkish air, and twice already since taking the beautiful avenue, Aelius had crossed moss-choked lazy canals flowing south.

When Decimus said that he lived "hard by the walls," it was not an overstatement. The antiquity of the Curii's urban villa was proven by the fact that the first line of walls, built at the tail end of the Republic over three hundred years earlier, cut through one wing of it, mutilating an ample sitting room paved in black-and-white mosaic of a simple design.

"Refreshingly pre-Caesarian," was how Decimus described it as he welcomed his guest, simpering, "because Caesar made even our floorings more complicated."

In fact, the brutal city wall, bricks and stones without plaster, blocked the otherwise elegant room in the way a volcano stops its lava flow after destroying all it can. "This is as clear a symbol as I need to remind myself of governmental intrusion. Come, come, the better part is beyond the waiting room fish pond—I'm very proud of the fish pond, I designed it myself. There's a spring under the house, actually, so I thought I'd put it to good use rather than fighting it like my ancestors." He led his colleague through a sober hall painted black, with small yellow squares each representing a different freshwater fish. A glare that seemed to rise from the five-foot-square pond drew patterns like pale green stabs on the ceiling; something so unique and so novel that Aelius was not ashamed to show his wonder. Decimus's simper became a smile. "The bottom of the pond is glass, and when there's company I have lamps lit in the basement so that the reflection comes right through. Tell me it isn't beautiful."

"It's absolutely beautiful."

Giving Aelius time to admire the small fish darting in the shiny water, Decimus leaned against the wall with his arms folded. "Did you hear? Two men died in the grain depot last night: They stumbled in while they were checking the aeration of the storage bins and were strangled by an avalanche of wheat. It happened at the same time that you and I were chatting in front of that dreadful little whorehouse, just a block away. How close life and death can be, no? You pulling your sword out thinking me a murderer, the germ of life being shot into the harlots next door, those two mouthing their last in a sea of grain . . . It'd make me melancholy if it didn't make me laugh." In the next space, a cloakroom, a venerable old serf was waiting to take Aelius's cape but did not move until Decimus snapped his fingers. "I knew you would show up in a uniform, Commander Spartianus, albeit an elegant one. You people never know what civilian clothes to wear on private occasions."

You people may mean any of half a dozen unflattering things, all connoting class or national origin. Aelius chose not to reply. He had meant to appear the soldier rather than the imperial envoy: Because his host doubtlessly knew this, it was a *game* for him, as the Briton said. Without military clothing, on the other hand, Decimus seemed less impressive, and his relative smallness noticeable. At a time when applied embroideries—strips, squares, or ovals stitched in color—were the rage for civilian and army dress, his old-fashioned woolen tunic seemed singularly bare. Correctly Aelius judged it a way of distinguishing himself, rather than a sign of modesty. Gesturing toward a doorway to the dining room, Decimus glanced back, no differently than when he'd preceded Aelius through the palace's halls. When light struck his face sideways, mouth and nose jutted out like a clever animal's snout, and his shaven cheeks seemed carved by a strong finger into hollows, closely following the bone. In his vanity, he combed his hair to cover the balding top and temples, as one saw in the portraits of ancient Romans.

With a small wag of the head, he pointed to the cloakroom. "Nice brooch you had there. His Divinity's gift?"

The army cape clasp was something Aelius was proud of, Diocletian's personal token of appreciation after his mission in Egypt; but the amused way Decimus looked at it embarrassed him. "I'm sure you have a bigger and better one," he said, renouncing the contest.

Dinner was excellent, and such that Aelius described it in his notes as *delicacies spiced with questions, so cleverly and ambiguously put that I had to sieve each time the political implications, at the cost of seeming a yokel entrusted with official duties. Decimus is not one to be distracted, and if this inquisitiveness is simply a sport with him, he's overly taken with his toy.*

It was after they finished eating, and went to sit in a studio Decimus called the ancestors' room, that a chance to counter the flood of questions arose for Aelius. Because he chose to inquire about the application of anti-Christian laws in Mediolanum, his host made a short explosive noise, between a snort and a cough, as irritated women do at times.

"Why do you ask me about those annoying people? You cannot go past a courthouse or a theater without hearing them tried or thrown to the beasts, even though reports of their martyrdom—that's what they call it, unaware that such a concept of *witnessing* is not unknown to other philosophical traditions—are greatly exaggerated. Thanks to

Judge Marcellus and his turtle-speed justice, not half of those who should have their heads lopped do. I have nothing to do with Christians, as my preference is for gods who don't go around asking folks to die for them."

On three shelves, busts of the family members created a mute audience of men and women of different ages, some of them so closely resembling Decimus that Aelius could reconstruct through them his host's appearance as a youngster, and anticipate the looks of his old age. The headstone his own father had ordered years before on the frontier seemed crude in comparison, little resembling anyone but a roughly carved officer; only the name below it would identify it as Aelius Spartus's monument.

"Why do you ask?" Decimus urged him again, seated in front of the ancestral crowd.

Concisely Aelius reported the events surrounding Lupus's "first and second death," and his curiosity about Agnus the miracle worker. It seemed a harmless after-dinner conversation, likely to amuse his host. "I may be mistaken, but at Brigantium I came under the impression that the fire waker's acolyte is a woman originally from this region— Laumellum, I think."

Unexpectedly, Decimus's diverted glance grew rather narrow for an amicable get-together. Throughout the dinner, chatting at ease, he had been making small balls out of bread crumbs, rolling them between thumb and forefinger. Having idly brought one along from the dining room, he now squeezed it flat on the studio table. "You're either dumb or very clever, Commander Spartianus."

"I don't know what you mean. It's a civil question. If you do not wish to answer it, someone else in town will. I'm not aware Casta's identity is a state secret."

"A state secret, no. A source of some embarrassment to her native great city of Mediolanum, I'd have to say yes. What made you ask *me* is what puzzles me. I am nearly related to her. And I say 'nearly' because I am not sure how many degrees of kinship there are between us. She was married to one of the wealthiest landowners in Ticinum."

"I see."

Pacified by the comment's equanimity, Decimus relaxed once more. "Well, it makes a good story, and I haven't told it in a while. Why not." The bread was smoothed into a round ball again, about the size of those clay marbles boys play with. "The landowner—Pupienus, he was called—was an old man when he took her and, like all respectable old, wealthy husbands, had the good grace of leaving her a widow after a couple of years. There were no children from the marriage, so she inherited the whole property. Which made her very palatable to any male who could legitimately aspire to her hand: The city prefect wooed her to no avail, and so did Judge Marcellus's youngest son. Old man Pupienus was a traditionalist, a man after my own heart. She came from a family much along the same lines (it is not an accident that we are related), but had taken it into her head during her husband's last illness two years ago that holy men and miracle workers could do something for him."

"It was a love match between them, then."

"I don't see how, but I suppose so. The nymph Galatea was pursued by Polyphemus, and he was a one-eyed giant. At any rate, their Laumellum villa was for three months and more like Alexandria's harbor, with all sorts of characters coming and going, from all over the world. The old man in his sickbed was prayed over, incensed, fumigated, sprinkled with lustral water, given enemas, covered with amulets and sacred formulas. You name it, it was done. Then Agnus showed up. Not invited, mind you. It is unclear how it went. One morning he showed up on the doorstep, and next he was blathering his enchantments."

"Obviously Casta's husband did not live."

"Obviously, you say. But what is obvious is that the suffering he was undergoing before ceased after Agnus's visit, and the few days he lived afterward were as serene as Socrates's in his final imprisonment. I was present, so I can vouch for it. He died with a smile, discussing philosophy and Lucretius's theory of the atom." With the nail of his thumb, which he kept rather long, Decimus cut the crumb ball in two. "What you and I—or at least I—would say is that the illness had taken its course, and simply ran out of energy before the last flame was extinguished in the old man. Fact is that, one month to the day after the funeral, the woman you heard called Casta—which is not her name—renounced her immense wealth and kept for herself only a small suburban house outside Porta Ticinensis, by the arena, which she gave to the only servant she retained, her aged wet nurse. The next act of the drama saw her publicly giving away her clothes and jewels—jewels worth over five hundred thousand denarii—and becoming a Christian. This was two years ago, before the religious prosecution began. After telling one another that grief, or whatever it was, made her lose her mind, friends and gossipers thought no more of it."

Aelius had no specific reason but was beginning to feel an instinctive antipathy toward the miracle worker. "Interesting. Who was the recipient of the lady's wealth?"

"Why, the Christians themselves—their hierarchy, or church, as they call it. As unfortunate and untimely a choice as I can envision, given that within a few months the Christians' goods would be confiscated and end up in the government's coffers." Decimus tossed the minute crumb balls in the air, catching them one after the other. "So it was as if old man Pupienus had made the Emperor his heir, he who kept the letters of Brutus and Cassius in his library. There's more than irony in it."

Aelius spoke with his eyes on the portrait of the sole beautiful one among Decimus's foremothers. "I miss the connection between divesting herself of riches as she turned Christian and deciding to become Agnus's assistant. It's a leap." The marble image wore her hair in a tall beehive of curls above the forehead, as did the ladies in Titus's day, two hundred years earlier. Her face was so delicate, known somehow; calmness became sweet melancholy between the eyes and the mouth.

"Yes, it is." Quickly Decimus glanced back, to see where the guest's attention rested. "It puzzled us all that she would make such a choice, when she'd been used to giving orders rather than taking them. But, you see, at the time I was undergoing my third divorce, so I did not exactly have an interest in knowing what others did with their lives."

"Do you ever see her these days, or communicate with her?" Aelius was not sure why he was even asking. Mere curiosity, although the sight of the beautiful ancestress made his desire to know less disinterested; as if out of the five women represented, four were not decidedly ugly.

"With a *Christian*? No. We were hardly ever in touch before she changed her spiritual skin. Now she is probably in hiding. But I suppose that if you felt the overpowering need to meet her, wherever she is, you could take along a presentation letter from me. For the sake of kinship she may be disposed to receive you. Annia Cincia was a beauty once. For all I know, she may yet be one."

So, she is beautiful, or was. Her choice to serve an itinerant preacher, or whatever Agnus was, suddenly seemed more heroic than foolish. Aelius imagined Casta in her bare cell-like room in Treveri, perilously traveling snowy roads, mortifying her flesh—even defying the judges as he'd seen Christians do in Egypt, in the face of torture. It was intrigued, anxious thinking about a woman he might never meet, whom he supposed handsome like the marble lady in curls.

Decimus might have captured the flavor of that interest, and mentioned Casta's beauty on purpose to provoke him. "At court, we all heard of your sleuthing in Egypt, of the conspiracy that was discovered in the process. But now you tell me this tawdry story of stifling with charcoal. A dead brick-maker, Spartianus—who cares how it happened. A *murdered* brick-maker is only slightly more interesting. From the fire waker's point of view, it would have been better if this Lupus fellow had remained alive, but if he had to die, then murder is more acceptable, as it does not point to Agnus's failure. My advice, especially these days, is that you keep away from such a gullible group. For your own amusement, however, know that in Mediolanum live some of those who claim to have benefited from the wonder couple. Yes, they started their legerdemain here, before the government put a stop to such nonsense." Lazily Decimus tossed the minute crumb balls beyond Aelius's chair, like a boy purposely missing a target. "Come, let us speak about something more interesting than superstition."

Aelius fell neither for the sophistication nor for the casualness of the aristocrat sitting in front of him. *He is a man all external; there is nothing real about him. His culture and the beautiful objects in his house are also somehow void—facades covering nothing. And yet he is dangerous. I am not sure of the extent of his malice, but the empty air behind the mask, behind the fancy dress, may be perilous to breathe.* How many had stumbled into convivial traps, spoken too loosely, and been jailed or executed for it? The layers of intrigue at court—in any of the four capitals cross-beaming power across the Empire—were all politeness and honeyed compliments, while spies thrived. What did the Briton say? That Decimus wanted to "find out things" from people. On whose behalf, it remained to be seen.

An amiable nod was how Aelius agreed to the change of subject. "I have reason to believe I may have acquired an original Roman helmet from Teutoburg Forest."

"Now, *that's* intriguing!" Decimus sat up, all ears and a simper. "How do you know you haven't been duped by the seller?"

2 December, Saturday

Notes by Aelius Spartianus, continued:
What Curius Decimus says is true. Mediolanum is a city of merchants, of handlers of goods, and artisans of all kinds. While in Rome one has the impression of being the guest of a noble old woman whose house is the repository of all that is sacred and official, here one feels that if one has no money, one doesn't count at all. Although the mint was closed in the days of Our Lord Aurelian (Restorer of the Army), business keeps thriving, and one still currently finds coins in use that were minted here, and in great quantity.

When I left after dinner last night, against promise of giving Decimus the opportunity to view my Teutoburg acquisition, I found my way back to the barracks without trouble. After all,

compared to Rome or Alexandria, this is a large burg, but everything is built sparing no expense. Seldom have I seen such lavish
use of marble and porphyry on columns for private use, although the floorings, from what I could judge, generally do not
compare to the mosaics I saw in Sicily, and the figures on them
are rather stilted. The porticus maximiana, as they call the porticoed avenue I took yesterday to Decimus's place, is instead a
masterpiece of architecture, a glorious terminus into the city
from the Aemilian Way. It flattered me to recognize that on the
triumphal arch, in painted relief, our campaign against the
Egyptian Rebellion is illustrated among the wars fought by our
rulers to secure the Empire. The Pyramids in the background
are finished in gilded detail, and some of the cavalry weapons
are appliqués of gilded bronze, so realistically rendered that you
can recognize our long swords and even the devices on our
troopers' shields.

Under the colonnades on both sides of the street, bookshops
and jewelry stores alternate with sellers of fine dyed cloth and
expensive spices. I must visit the bookshops. Which reminds me
I must take down some of the prices encountered in Mediolanum,
higher than elsewhere in the Empire. Aside from Nicanor's expensive books, I recall noticing that silk sells for 15,000 denarii
per pound, a full one-fourth above the governmental fixed ceiling of 12,000 denarii, or 48,000 drachmas. Since death or exile
is contemplated as a punishment for exceeding the ceiling, I can
only deduce there's connivance on the part of city administrators (and although I am not telling on anyone, as Decimus
would have it, I must find a way to inform His Divinity without
appearing to be critical of his colleague's rule).

In the large northeast district newly enclosed in the urban
walls, south of the barracks are the so-called Herculean Baths.
Built in Maximian's honor, they're splendid in excess of their
size, which is median. A handsome statue of Hercules in the
cold-pool hall shows the god leaning on his club: The veins on

the figure's hip and the knots on his weapon are so skillfully carved that you would think them flesh and wood rather than Greek marble. A smaller version of this work is in the barracks' shrine, also dedicated to Hercules.

As a soldier, however, above all other things I admire Mediolanum's walls, because they have one advantage over Rome's, in that a river or canal runs all around them. It dictates—even limits—the circumference, but makes the defense more secure.

Compared to Egypt, crime is scarce, so they tell me. There's no report of marauders infesting the waterways or houses broken into, and even murder is rare. According to Decimus, a Mediolanum brick manufacturer would only be murdered for a question of profit. "How do you know he was not killed for profit in Treveri?" I asked. Anyhow, here the streets are considered secure after hours, except in those districts—the small river harbor, the leather- and cloth-making quarter—where brothels and drinking places thrive. Of course, I consider exaggerated prices a form of stealing.

In sum, one has the impression that everyone in Mediolanum owns or runs a business; folks are rushed and not particularly friendly, and if I think back on Egypt—how people there take life in a cyclical, philosophical way—and compare it to the bustle of folks at this city's gates, all contracting with haulers the cheapest transport of this or that good, I realize how different the Empire really is. Worlds away, in fact, from the frontier I have known since my young years, where everything was and is a function of the military. There, one's experience is limited to a string of army camps and settlements where all the officers' quarters resemble one another, the officers' wives' parties serve the same food, and everybody knows everybody else.

"May I?" The Briton—his name was Duco—pointed with his freckled hand at the chair across from Aelius and, having received an assent, sat down at the table. "One doesn't often see officers writing, in these barracks. I suppose Curius Decimus is right in calling us boors. How did it go last night?"

"An excellent dinner."

"And the company?"

"Also."

There was no telling whether fact-finding was limited to court officers, so Aelius chose not to let out more than he had to. The truth was that the after-dinner conversation had taken an odd turn after he'd mentioned the helmet acquired from the German antiquary. Given that the Roman commander at the time of the military disaster was Quintilius Varus, son of one of Caesar's murderers, Decimus had said something humorous, to the effect that Varus had disgraced the family more than his father. "You could also say," Aelius had replied, smiling all the same, "that he elevated betrayal to an art. Through his military lack of skill, Varus betrayed Augustus, his emperor, as his father had betrayed Augustus's father."

But Aelius had no reason to be rude to the Briton this morning. So he thanked him for ensuring that his Guardsmen and himself had such good accommodations, and invited him to join him for lunch if his duties allowed. Duco shook his head. "I'd like to, but I ended up being officer of the day again. The colleague who was supposed to do it today has gone off in all haste. There's been a murder at the Old Baths, as we call them, and riots are reported throughout the Circus and Palace area."

Having just jotted down flattering words about safety in Mediolanum, Aelius was taken aback. "Is murder so rare here that mobs protest it in the streets?"

"No-o-o." If Duco found the observation naive, he saw no reason to laugh at it. "But the victim happens to be the judge who sits on the proceedings against the Christians, and he was everyone's darling. A squadron of Palace Guards had to disperse the crowd in front of the city jail, as they wanted to drag out those awaiting judgment inside. Too bad in a way, because popular justice would have hastened the process at least."

Aelius cleaned his pen with a bit of soft cloth. "This judge, is he a man called Marcellus?" Having replaced the pen in its case, he blew over the papyrus sheet before rolling it up.

"Minucius Marcellus, yes. The Legal Turtle, as his colleagues loved to make fun of him. You heard of him?"

"Only in passing." His writing kit gathered and put away in a leather bag, Aelius stood, and the officer of the day with him. "Where are the Old Baths?"

"I wouldn't go there now, there are bruises and worse to be gotten. Wait until the mob is bloodied a little."

"Thank you." Aelius laughed. "I've broken up disturbances before. My men and I held the main entrance to Alexandria's harbor during the Rebellion. We'll get our anti-riot gear on and go take a look."

"As you like." Duco gave him directions to the murder scene, suggesting a detour that would put a cavalry troop at an advantage. "Do you happen to have another password in mind, since I'm stuck here?"

"Yes. How about the one used by one of Septimius Severus's predecessors: *Let us be soldiers*?"

3

The riot was reported in the southeast district of the city. There the Old Baths—Balnea Vetra, in the local speech—stood not far from the city prisons, on an irregular small square that went by the name Gallic Meadows, the two establishments set in roughly facing positions.

Duco said that well outside the Palace's perimeter, the Palace Guard formed a protective loop stretching from Porta Vercellina to Porta Ticinensis, that is, cordoning off the entire southwest quarter of the city along the two ancient perpendiculars. "Imagine Mediolanum is a square cut in four parts. You'll find the bottom left segment sealed off by horsemen, more than three thousand feet worth of steel."

"Who is facing the mob, then?"

"The police, probably the firemen. We can't send more than a handful, as most of the garrison is out for maneuvers."

Aelius's Guardsmen—thirty-two in number, the usual subunit of a cavalry wing—were trained to ready for battle on a moment's notice. It was a good thing, too, because in the time it took Aelius to alert them, a request came from the Palace to send all available units to Gallic Meadows. Thus the wearing of anti-riot gear, which in his mind had been only a commonsense measure, became a prerequisite. Quickly the Guardsmen reached the stables, threw covers and saddles on their mounts, harnessed them with hackamores (to keep them from opening their mouths and running away from the bit), and buckled leather chest guards and chamfrons on the horses' faces. Themselves they fitted with middle dress, a kit between escort duty and battle gear that included quilted blow-proof jackets under leather corselets, battle helmets with cheek pieces, and kerchiefs with the regiment's colors tied around their necks. Aelius did the same, so that in record time they headed out of camp following Duco's instructions to bend left at the "place where washing is done in open air vats" to reach the city prison, not far from a secondary gate called Posterula Mariana. Here they would face the prison's blind side wall, where it was unlikely that rioters would congregate. The added advantage was that side streets were not paved, so that the clack of hoofs would not give the riders away—a useful anti-riot trick given that, unlike other units, the Guardsmen's horses rode to battle metal-shod.

As Aelius and the Guardsmen approached Gallic Meadows, the street became crooked, flanked by low constructions housing meat shops; these were barred shut or in process of being locked up by frightened shop boys. To the left, a lane opened like a crack between walls. Duco said it eventually led to the Jewish quarter at Porta Ticinensis, and there must be considerable nervousness there.

Duco's instructions said that ahead, around a narrow elbow bend, the street was supposed to widen as it neared the square. Humming sounds and a disorderly clash of voices—the noise of all crowds—came from that direction. Aelius lifted his right hand, with the extended forefinger biding his men to halt. At a pace, alone, he rode to the corner and looked. A wider pavement, yes, but given the curve, not enough room to charge. More shops. People pressing and running everywhere. That looting was going on was clear by the traffic of carcasses from the meat shops: The left side of a split hog, pink-white-red, heavy with fat, navigated like an obscene boat above the sea of heads; skinned goat carcasses with their opaque staring eyes bobbed over shoulders. Aelius hardly recognized the policemen among the tumultuous crowd. The street and square beyond were a sea of agitating bodies and dead meat. Duco had been right about the blind wall of the prison being unattractive to rioters, but he had not considered the lure of well-stocked food stores.

Across the square, what resembled an improvised fortification of overturned carts, market crates, benches, and whatnot made him at first think that the authorities had set up an enclosed area to protect the prison. By the movement on both sides of the barricade, however, Aelius understood that the mob itself had built it in order to have a free hand while it attempted to enter the jail. Bloody-faced and limping, some policemen staggered away from the melee, stumbling on sausages and blood pudding mashed underfoot. It was impossible to gauge what was happening inside the prison: For sure, its bronze-studded doors were being battered with wooden poles, such as are used to lay a foundation in marshy soil.

At the other end of the square, the Old Baths attracted no attention, even though the respected Judge Marcellus had been assassinated between those walls.

"You had better have a plan, Spartianus."

When unexpectedly Curius Decimus joined him, having come from behind at a trot, Aelius thought two things. First a question: *Why is he not with his colleagues manning the Palace?* And then the answer to himself: *because his house by Porta Romana stands, as the crow flies, less than a thousand feet away from this mess.* Decimus tensely greeted him with a wave.

"I do have a plan. Before it reaches the Jewish quarter, where does the narrow lane back there lead to?" Aelius asked. He listened to the reply, then wanted to know, "Is it wide enough, and can I take a right from there?"

Soon, one by one, the Guardsmen were filing between house walls barely far enough apart to let a horse through, as if riding down an oppressive canyon, exiting into a surprisingly wide, paved avenue running parallel to the street they had taken. It seemingly parted the district in two, marking the edge of the Jewish quarter on the opposite side. From left to right, the pavement streamed with people seeking the square, but one hundred or so feet down to the left, the avenue was still empty, and there was ample space to line up and maneuver. Aelius directed his Guardsmen there.

In the square, the riot continued. Outnumbered and defeated by the mob, the policemen could not relieve those inside the prison building; bare- and bloody-headed, powerless, they mostly let themselves be shoved here and there in the thick of screaming men, and the battering on the doors continued with good chances of succeeding.

Without haste Aelius rode down to join his troop, nearly at the head of the avenue. The Guardsmen had lined up in three rows of ten abreast, with the two noncoms at the ends of the first row. Lifting their man-tall oval shields, they waited for an order to start banging their swords on them. Aelius looked at the shadows under the handsome horses, like puddles or swatches of cloth between blue and gray. The men ready to attack, the tumult, those shadows about to unravel like wind-torn rags: It felt like Egypt a few years earlier, except for the difference in temperature and light. There, an attempt to usurp the throne was at stake; here, as far as he could tell, only rage against the Christians for a judge's murder. But the thrill, the dancing in place of the excited mounts—that was no different. If Decimus was watching from somewhere, Aelius was not aware of it, and did not much care.

At his order, in a double-time rhythm slow at first, then accelerating, the advancing Guardsmen filled the avenue with the clang of metal on metal edges. Speed increased to a canter, then to a trot. The clack of hoofs on the pavement awoke a dry echo, like rocks knocked against one another at the start of a landslide. A chance glancing back, more than the noise, caused the outer fringe of the mob to see the troopers: First one, then another of the rioters looked and shouted; the mass of men began to undulate as others heard the alarm and looked back. Something like a shiver was transmitted from one side to the other of the crowd, but those protected by the barricade did not stop their battering. At the distance of sixty feet, Aelius gave the order to charge, and the next ten feet were literally leaped by the horses spurred into a gallop. The yellow-black of kerchiefs and shields shredded into a blur; the clacking sound grew hard, sharp, ringing, until the thunder of metal under the heavy animals and riders shook the avenue.

Aelius rode ahead, and for all the speed and haste, time seemed to elongate and dilate around him. He was conscious of details as if standing still—a hand, a face, the corner of the building ahead; he recalled Egypt and Armenia and every other place where he'd charged, wedged in the secure hold of the four-horn saddle. He even noticed a few black shiny strands in the gray braid of his horse's mane, just before rumbling into the square.

In the square, panic had struck at the sight of the approaching Guardsmen. A breech in the wall of backs and legs ensued, but also a rain of things pelted from the sides, rocks and reddish things, and great shouting everywhere. Aelius's mind kept reasoning in that oddly dilated time, like a calm wheel. Had there been Christians among the rioters—not the case, since these were people come to lynch Christians—they might have resorted, as they did in Alexandria when they backed the usurpers, to throwing themselves on the ground, because horses will not charge supine bodies. But they weren't Christians, and they were running. Those on the other side of the barricade kept battering the doors. Moments had gone by, no more. Aelius halted, harshly pulling the reins to let the three rows of Guardsmen trundle around him to part the crowd like weeds under the scythe. He galloped back the space necessary to take a run-up, and, whooping to incite the horse, he wedged it and himself where his Guardsmen had made the void, leaped over crouching backs, over arms folded on heads and faces, over the cart, knees tight to the animal's flanks, landed without sliding on the flagstones. He did not even have to lower his sword. Showing it unsheathed and ready to strike sufficed to cause the wooden poles to fall from the hands of those by the doors. Before him were open mouths and wide staring eyes, ferocity becoming fear on the faces, rocks and red bricks making arcs in the cold air. Past the steam from his horse's nostrils, Aelius saw one of his horsemen, squarely struck, lean over and only remain mounted because he was wedged in the saddle.

Then time regained its speed, and this was like every riot, every urban battle. The mob ebbed back; the backing up and awkward turning
around formed a whirling motion like a slow vortex in a herd; the barricade crumbled like a weak dike in the current. Suddenly it became a
rout, with folks scuttling into doorways to escape the charge, flattening
themselves against the walls, uselessly attempting to climb through
grille-covered windows, being corralled by the horses into the crooked
street; nearness and lack of space brought a shock of animal chests on
human shoulders, heads. The Guardsmen forced what was like a cork
of bodies at the corner where the crooked street angled tight; there was
a fierce moment in which the horses nearly forgot their training and
reared against the human wall. Trusting his troopers enough to let
them conclude the operation, Aelius did not follow them.

When he vaulted off the saddle and removed his helmet, the cold of
day was like water splashed on his skin. Opening only enough to show
a livid face—a prison official, surely—the bronze-studded doors
yawned little by little. The building appeared inviolate. White with an-
guish, those who had been manning its entrance walked out. Prison
guards followed, armed with clubs and short swords. The battered policemen were already removing the barricade, and silence stretched
above everything as it did every time after a battle or a riot. Sounds
themselves seemed to have been trampled into silence. Several bodies
remained on the ground, most of them still moving, although there
had to be a few dead, as always.

A deep trench at the wider end of the square, half filled with water
that had either rained in or seeped up from the ground, marked yet
another construction site. To excavate it, flagstones and paving slabs
had been dug out; rocks, bricks, and other improvised projectiles came
from there. Aelius saw wooden shafts, like those used to batter the
prison's doors, stacked to one side; a few feet away lay a series of tall
columns and ornate capitals, waiting to stand in a building yet to be
erected. The Palatine Baths, Aelius had heard from Decimus the night
before, to match catty-corner the great ones across town.

The Old Baths were what interested him now. He walked toward them, a small building of brick and a peculiar, creamy limestone Aelius recognized as the porous Tibur stone of the color and appearance of mountain cheese, liberally employed in Hadrian's immense villa outside Rome. They'd been, he saw from a glance at the plaque by the entrance, private baths a citizen had bequeathed to the city a generation before, along with money for their upkeep. In fact, the building resembled old-fashioned army camp baths, longer than wide, unadorned.

Inside there wasn't much light; the windows were small, high up in the thick walls. The vaults were cement and stucco, with no ornament except for that wavy pattern one often saw on stone coffins, recalling the shape of the sweat scrapers athletes used after oiling their muscles. A scratched sentence on a service door was in Greek, a verse Aelius knew but could not at once identify. *Woe, woe, look, look! Keep away the bull from the heifer.* Room by room, odor of sweat, wet towels, shoes, a perfume that had the same tangy aftertaste of Theo's spice shop in Antinoopolis. The latrines opened to the left, a semicircular row of holes, with a bruised policeman kneeling with his head low over one of them. Cold room, tepid bath room, a sharp left into a long, narrow room for the hot baths; beyond, the closed door of the sweat room.

Minucius Marcellus, Duco said, had been killed in the hot pool.

In the six hours since the murder, the hot pool—an oversized marble tub below ground—had been drained after the victim's removal. Pink puddles on the floor reflected the twilight in the spot where the bloody corpse had been laid before being carried out. Water had been tracked everywhere; on the wall closest to the pool, the bloody imprint of a left hand probably only pointed to the fact that one of those who had fished out the corpse had then rested against it.

It was perhaps significant, perhaps not, that no one had sought refuge from the disorder in the Old Baths. Aelius stepped out of the hot room, walked the small building in all directions, had the terrified serfs (North Africans who had been huddling in the basement) show him the two-feet-wide service passageways in the main walls, and the access stairway to the furnace room below street level. What he was looking for was only vaguely sketched in his mind, like the scribbled Greek verse whose author he could not recall.

When he walked out, the nip in the air took his breath away. His Guardsmen, riding two abreast, calmly returned to the square from the crooked street and regrouped. At once Aelius informed himself about their well-being, hearing that but for the trooper stunned by a brick and a few bruises, there were no casualties. At the point where the same crooked street met the square, Curius Decimus sat straight in the saddle, accompanied by two officers—twins, so similar that side by side they gave one the odd impression of seeing double.

"That was a nifty action," Decimus said, in a tone that sounded like the opposite of a compliment. "The bastards ran as far as my house, trying to escape through the city gate. I had my house serfs cudgel them back toward your men, and the police are making arrests."

Aelius patted his horse's neck. From the saddlebag, he took out his round cap, and put it on. Decimus made a polite gesture with his up-turned right hand. "Commander, let me present to you Gaius Dexter and Lucius Sinister, colonels of the Palace Guard; gentlemen, Commander Aelius Spartianus, lately heading a thousand-strong mounted regiment at Nicomedia. The Ioviani Palatini, was it not?"

"It still is." Aelius answered the twins' salute. "I am only on temporary special assignment as a historian."

Hands folded on his right thigh, with the reins loose in his grasp, Decimus surveyed the signs of rioting in the square. "The good people of Mediolanum amaze me at times. But you may be sure the shop owners who suffered damage during the disturbance will be more severe in asking for prosecution than any of us." He spoke to all, looking at Aelius directly. "This was just an excuse to make trouble, you know. They say that, with the times being as they are, the temptation to loot is overpowering. I say it is bestiality as well. Anyhow, the Palace ordered that the watch be doubled around the grain storage, and the city gates will close an hour early tonight."

"What happened, exactly?"

Decimus raised his eyebrows. "*Exactly,* I doubt anybody knows."

"There must have been provocateurs in the crowd."

"Why? An interruption in the trials against the Christians is enough to enrage any right-minded community."

Aelius glanced at the officer who had interjected the words, the twin called Dexter. It was more or less the opposite of what Decimus had just said, but it only mattered in terms of whether the riot was a sign of more generalized discontent or a brutal protest of the loss of a prosecuting judge. "In my experience," he replied, "after a disorder, everyone declares that someone else started it; that he was dragged along by someone he knew, and so around and around, until it comes to those who were dragged along by people no one knows."

"I thought you served at the Palace in Nicomedia, not in the streets." Dexter was young, pale, and dark-haired, and close up his jaw drew a line ever so slightly longer than that of his twin, to whom he was otherwise identical. He did not talk out of spite, not consciously at least. The cities were filled with officers at the threshold of maturity who had only served in command posts and could hardly conceive of life in the field.

"In Egypt I fought the rebels of Domitius Domitianus and Achilleus in the streets. It comes in handy in case of riots."

Dexter breathed in, so that his nostrils crinkled nearly shut. Curius Decimus half-smiled. "So, Commander—were any rioters hiding in the baths?"

For the first time this morning, Aelius felt a jab of irritation. "No. Only one of your city policemen vomiting his heart out."

"Pity—what are we coming to. Good help is as hard to find at city hall as it is in one's house." Decimus slapped the reins on his thigh, a flop-flop sound in the silence of the square.

During the rest of the day, at bookshops and in archives, wherever an interlocutor gave him the impression of wanting to discuss the event, Aelius inquired about Minucius Marcellus. It was half a step above idle curiosity at this point, a way to occupy time in Mediolanum while awaiting an answer from His Divinity.

To all reports, the judge seemed much happier dead than he did alive. The melancholy cast on his face, his principal characteristic in the minds of those who knew him, had been smoothed out by death, and if he did not quite smile, he looked serene at least. Somehow, it appeared as though death had freed him from a consuming care, a fact that should put at ease the hearts of his fellow citizens.

Nevertheless, aside from the riot at the prison, outrage in the city was enormous, and perhaps sincere. Marcellus had been in the process of trying a number of Christian clerics from the city and the outlying areas, accused of refusing to give up their holy books and of associating despite prohibition. Because he was a patient, thorough man, the trials he presided over tended to last a long time. One of those rare professional judges that notwithstanding a long career do not seem to lose faith in human nature, he'd only lately begun to admit his sadness at confronting "pertinaciousness and perversion" in the courtroom, as he put it, "every day the gods send to earth." His sentences were masterpieces of attention to legal detail, impossible to appeal; what was surprising was their mildness. In the two years since the multiphase edict against the Christians, which Galerius had wanted and Maximian was more than happy to apply in his portion of the Empire, the capital sentences issued by Minucius Marcellus were rare. Even the most liberal-minded intellectuals agreed among themselves that those who had finally been put to death had it coming, if nothing else for trying the patience of the court to such an extent.

Not only that: It was commonly agreed that Marcellus's private life was as impeccable as his public behavior. He did not drink, did not eat meat, had read Seneca's *Moral Epistles* a number of times, with profit, had been married to the same woman for over fifty years; his children and grandchildren were all well matched, occupying important posts throughout Italia Annonaria. Exemplary to the point of ridicule among his acquaintances and colleagues, he had never kept lovers or concubines, did not owe or lend money, possessed an honest wealth commensurate with his long service. In such a money-oriented, pragmatic city, he was not for sale, and his virtues—admired by all—made many uncomfortable. Thus even "the last man anyone should want to kill" could be at the same time sorely missed and a welcome absence.

These generally positive comments were what Aelius heard from those to whom he spoke well into the evening, and even after his return to the barracks from downtown. Of course, he had not yet asked Decimus, who might have a completely different view regarding the victim, if for no other reason than to sing out of the chorus.

True, the military considered Marcellus a little (or a lot) too indulgent in his sentences against the Christians, some of whom were former soldiers. "But you can't have everything in a judge," the Briton pointed out to Aelius. "And besides, last summer he ruled in favor of the army when it came to a dispute regarding additions to the barracks' retaining wall."

Aelius let the sentence go through him before even realizing there was a small, interesting detail embedded in it. "Do you mean a dispute regarding the building contract?" he asked.

"Yes, precisely. We ordered bricks from Modicia, northeast of here, and when they arrived, traveling first by waterways and then on wheeled transportation, a good part of them were nicked or broken altogether—below quality at any rate." Duco sat in his small office with his feet propped on a stool, circling his freckled thumbs. "The owner of the brickworks tried to maintain that he had no control over the way the transport was effected—this was in fact done care of the military. Our commander argued that if bricks are worth their salt, they do not fall apart just because they are placed on a barge or a cart. Minucius Marcellus listened to both sides without comment, with his usual calm, and then ordered a third party who was in the business— the brick business, I mean—to select one of the bricks taken at random from the lot and report to him. Well, the expert was not long in declaring that the firing process was defective—too low or too high a temperature in the kilns, I forget now—with the result that the final product was friable and structurally weak. There was no argument afterward: The brick supplier was made to return the advance the army had paid him, and not only that: He was also fined and had to refund us for the delay in the construction."

Aelius leaned against the doorjamb. He'd gotten a bruise, likely from a rock hurled full force, on his outer right knee, and under the trousers his leg was becoming sore; it felt a little torpid. "Who was the defendant in the trial?"

"Oh, a man called Fulgentius, from Modicia. You would think he could not stay in business, after the story of the faulty bricks came out. Clients who had bought material from him in the past followed suit, literally. But he paid up and went back to work as if nothing had happened, selling the overstock of bad bricks to rural areas where there aren't smart city lawyers or judges."

"And the brick-making expert Marcellus appointed: Who was he?"

"Not from these parts. A fellow who happened to be at Mediolanum for business but had no connections whatever with the local manufacturers. That is why the judge chose him."

"He was not from Augusta Treverorum, by any chance?"

Duco replaced his feet flat on the floor. He shrugged his shoulders, palms held flat upward. "I couldn't tell you. The officer at the engineering department might have the information, though."

The brick-making expert called in by Minucius Marcellus was not Lupus, but turned out to be one of Lupus's competitors for the large bid on the annex and tribunal at Treveri, the man from Mogontiacum who, according to the naked old bureaucrat Aelius met in the baths up there, "had lost by a hair." The ruling in the *Army vs. Fulgentius* case had stirred discontent among local brick-makers, to the point that their northern colleague had been manhandled at his exit from the courthouse. Under army escort he'd been taken out of Mediolanum. "As far as we know," the head engineer told Aelius, "he continued without further incidents his journey back to Belgica Prima, and that was that. As for Marcellus, he received some unpleasant anonymous threats, which were ascribed to the brick-makers."

Coincidences of people and places were not unusual in areas close to the frontiers, especially when army suppliers were concerned. The same trademarks returned across wide distances, and one could wear in Africa body armor made in Mantua, or trousers sewn in Segovia. Still, Aelius found it an intriguing detail, that brick-making should figure among the judge's last sentences, as it did in Lupus's murder. It did not make sense, not quite. The connection was hazy and thin, even though something so solid seemed to constitute its foundation. A *connection?* No, a window revealing a possible vista; a background to the events that included brick-making, or the men making the bricks, or possibly their relations with the State: He could not begin to tell.

But the *Army vs. Fulgentius* case was three months old. Marcellus's assassination had to have another reason. Eyes on his paperwork, the engineer concluded that he could see no apparent logic to the murder, as it did not remove a martinet or a corrupt civil servant. "I've heard of judges killed before, Commander, but they were thorough pricks, or thieves, or both."

3 DECEMBER, SUNDAY

In the morning, rain came and went; the wind had grown cold. From the tower balcony, the sight of the mountains was impeded by low clouds. Pigeons huddled in gray clusters on the lee side of the many roofs over the Herculean Baths, south of the camp. Aelius's knee hurt more now than during the night, which he'd spent mostly awake; he limped back inside to reread the draft of a second letter—not counting the message about Maximian's refusal to receive him—he'd been jotting down for His Divinity.

... I am mindful, Domine, of your encouragement when my pursuit of historical research in Antinoopolis became against my intentions a criminal investigation. A few months since then, as I report on a separate addendum, another violent death has marred my travels. Perhaps I am making more of it than

there is, but the person and rank of the victim—a judge from an eminent Mediolanum family—justifies my boldness in trusting that I have Your Divinity's permission to find out who the players may be in the ugly deed.

For the rest, having begun work on the biography of Severus, whom they call Septimius Severus, I am greatly troubled as to the approach I should take regarding the life and deeds of this famous prince. The sources and documents I have gathered thus far (including Herodian) indicate him as a man who during his reign continuously had to defend himself from enemies within and without the Empire. Yet the mode in which he took vengeance upon those who had fought him, after they were defeated, goes beyond what good Roman sense would term exemplary. Indeed, on many an occasion, not only did he have the enemy killed and his body dismembered and publicly exposed, but he also exterminated his family. Thus he behaved with the senatorial class (I counted at least thirty-five senators among his excellent victims), thus with the citizens of towns and provinces deemed by him less than faithful, not necessarily supportive of his adversaries. I am mindful here of the words spoken by the deified Trajan and the deified Hadrian, your forefathers in the sacred purple, regarding clemency toward those accused without certain proofs. And while as Romans we value above all the safety and well-being of the State, at the same time, it appears to me, we should wonder to which level we are willing to lower ourselves before behaving like the enemy we abhor.

Severus had two sons (Geta, and especially Bassianus nicknamed Caracalla, his eldest), who were monsters. Julia Soaemias, a woman of his family renowned for her beauty and intelligence, bore the likes of Elagabalus. And yet the selfsame Severus embellished the City, rebuilt the frontier towns and settlements destroyed by the barbarians in the previous years, and was an excellent commander of troops. How am I to handle the story of his life?

*While for the deified Hadrian I confronted the pure genius
and brilliance of the man with his occasional acts of cruelty and
mutable character, here I am faced with a prince whose hands
are bloody thousands of times over. All lights and no shadows
do not make for a distinguishable relief, as stonecutters teach
us. In darkness, no portrait is visible. Thus, I remit the judgment to Your Divinity's wisdom, as I wish to tell the truth without troubling the readers' minds, or besmirching the name of
Caesar that Our Lords Maximian and Galerius bear with such
honor.*

In the officers' mess hall, Duco and the engineer were eating breakfast.
They were still talking about Marcellus's death, and how elsewhere in
the city the rioters had succeeded in emptying bakeries and even as-
saulting private homes.

After an exchange of greetings, Aelius said casually, "Speaking of
houses, where did Judge Marcellus live?"

Duco glanced up from a porridge-like blob of boiled wheat in his
bowl. "Nowhere near the places that were attacked. Why?"

"I thought I'd go pay my respects to Marcellus's widow."

It was not entirely true, but the Briton had no reason to suspect ul-
terior motives. He deferred the question to the engineer, who said,
"Actually it wouldn't be bad if someone from the military went. Marcellus's suburban estate is half an hour south of Porta Ticinensis, at the
second crossroads past the public arena. The lady's name is Lucia Catula. Would you present the Maximiani Juniores corps of engineers'
condolences for me?"

"I will."

Duco planted his spoon in the thick meal and watched it lean over
slowly without touching the edge of the bowl. "Mine, too, if you
would. Bringing a couple of Guardsmen along would not be an excess
of prudence, I think."

Again, Aelius said, "I will," because he agreed that it would not be
excessive prudence.

———

"Forgive the confusion, Aelius Spartianus. We were having some work done in the garden."

Lucia Catula apologized as if this were a simple courtesy call, and she had to justify the to and fro of masons Aelius had crossed to reach her door. He had his own turn at apology for coming unannounced, and once they had abided by the etiquette of the case, he followed the lady to a well-lit little parlor.

She wore no jewels. Her white hair was neatly arranged, not a wisp out of place. That she had hastily applied makeup on her cheeks was hardly a mark of vanity, this Aelius understood well; on the contrary, it meant to conceal from the visitor's eyes the paleness of her grief, inappropriate to her status. She graciously accepted the offer of sympathy, and listened to the guest's words (that he was Caesar's envoy, saddened and concerned about the crime) without interrupting him. When she spoke, her voice was like water running in a small, smooth conduit that descends ever so slightly. It trailed down without affectation, because she was surely tired. Aelius wondered whether she had wept—whether status and dignity allowed her that much.

"You understand, Commander Spartianus, that if a judge or his family had to take seriously the threats against his person, they would stop living. Minucius Marcellus had received hundreds of threats in the many years of his work. He would not go as far as my dear departed father-in-law, also a judge, who during Philip's reign collected the insults and menaces against him in a booklet he distributed to friends under the rubric *Honesty's Recompense*. Marcellus merely ignored those messages."

"Did he ever express fear for his life?"

"Never. Perhaps because he was not afraid of dying."

"The prevalent opinion is that it may be a Christian plot, given the trials your husband sat on."

Catula's crimping of lips, far from being a full-fledged smile, indicated polite disagreement at hearing something silly. For a moment, she reminded him of her namesake cat, but without the cat's air of self-satisfaction. "If so, they will soon be disappointed by his successor. No, I do not believe it was the Christians. We had some among our serfs when I was a girl, and unless they have changed their ways since then, they would not resort to murder."

Aelius kept to himself the fact that he'd seen violent behavior among Christians in Egypt and elsewhere. *What, then?* He wanted to urge her firmly, but it would be the wrong approach. The softness of her speech forced him to keep his voice below normal tone as well, and he limited himself to saying, nearly under his breath, "As a daughter, wife, and daughter-in-law of eminent judges, Lady Catula, you have probably formulated a theory of your own."

"I am sorry, I haven't."

Behind her, through a window open despite the cold day, laborers among the flowerbeds shouldered piles of bricks on flat wooden supports, for some unidentifiable addition to the low walls, altars, and fountains already in the garden. If her unwillingness to elaborate had come as a headstrong refusal, Aelius would have found a way of insisting, driven by suspicion that she knew and did not want to tell. But Catula's serene lack of curiosity in that regard sounded genuine, as if she had not even begun to want to know, dropping mundane concerns much in the way someone lets a handkerchief fall on the ground.

"I heard that the local brick-making industry was unhappy with the judge's sentence regarding the army barracks, three months ago."

"Ah, that." Lady Catula lowered her eyes briefly. They were light blue, a peculiarity Aelius had noticed in men and women of this part of Italy. "Yes, they are a tight brotherhood, but the same can be said of other groups." The care he took in concealing his attention to the hauling of bricks outside kept her from making a connection between his words and what he saw. She added, without in the least changing her tone, "Judge Marcellus was disliked by conservative circles, by some in the military, even by a few of his colleagues. But dislike is often accompanied by grudging admiration."

"Forgive me: If someone entered the Old Baths to stab your husband to death, I see more grudge than admiration in the act."

"It was probably a madman, to be pitied in his delirium."

Whether or not anyone was to be pitied, the new judge thought otherwise. Serfs and free-born personnel of the Old Baths were seized without trial and quietly put to death outside Porta Ticinensis, where the chosen execution place was. Aelius found out accidentally during his return to the city from Marcellus's estate. At the crossroads closest to the arena, he overtook a police detail, and as the officer at the lead recognized the Guardsmen who'd broken the riot, he made conversation at once. Yes, yes, well, it'd been one of those sudden orders that come once in a while. It was done now. "See Nemesis's temple, Commander? There's a whole set of burial areas back there." The policeman indicated a vague direction of bogs and thickets. "Which'll make it easy on those who have to dispose of the bodies." The charge—Aelius didn't even have to ask—was failure to provide security, with more than a hint at possible collusion with Marcellus's killers. "The Christians, that is."

"Those executed, were they interrogated beforehand?"

"What for, Commander? They were Christians from Africa, the worst of the lot—violent, fanatical. Eh, the days of Minucius Marcellus are gone: It's back to lop the head first, and then ask questions. May he rest in peace, but I like it better this way." With a sidelong glance at the raised flap of Aelius's saddlebag, the policeman laughed a strangled little laugh. "You carry along for good luck one of the projectiles the rioters threw at us, I see."

It was actually a brick from Marcellus's garden, unobtrusively taken along as he left, without the workers' knowing. Aelius let the policeman's comment fall, forcibly closing the flap over his saddlebag.

If there was one thing more efficient than the imperial postal service, and even quicker, it was the system by which employers and servants communicated with one another. Aelius had not been back at the barracks an hour before a man sent by Lady Catula asked for permission to speak to him. Duco, who had the day off and was itching to visit a girlfriend across town, offered his colleague his office as a private meeting space. "I don't care if you mess up my papers," he joked. "They can't be more disorderly than they are."

Off went the Briton, and in his place appeared, led by an orderly, a gray-haired, well-dressed fellow who had all the marks of one who has risen from servitude because of his intelligence. His greeting to Aelius was ceremonious but not fawning, and the moment he began to speak it became obvious that it was a habit in Marcellus's household to converse in whispers.

"Protasius is the name, Commander Spartianus. I was Judge Marcellus's freedman, and he honored me with his trust. Let me tell you right off that with his death the great city of Mediolanum has lost one of its brightest lights. Our public and private horizon is made dim by his demise. Lady Catula bade me be open with you, all the more since I was among the first to see Master dead. With Virgil, let me say that reliving the scene would be for me *infandum renovare dolorem*—renewing unspeakable grief. But if you're Caesar's envoy, and a wellminded man, I am at your disposal."

Sitting behind his colleague's desk, Aelius could tell by Protasius's stare that the spread of tablets, pens, and papers did not meet the visitor's idea of a well-run office. Automatically, he began creating some order on the wooden surface. "I thank the lady for sending you. You must know that I showed an interest in the murder scene."

Protasius took one of those deep breaths that unwittingly become tremulous, what remains after weeping. "It was one of those sights that stay with you, sir. First thing in the morning, before work, the judge could always be found at the baths. No, never the new ones—and not the ones at his villa, either. Always Balnea Vetra, yes, the small ones at Gallic Meadows, not far from Posterula Mariana. He was in the habit of sitting in the hot pool because he suffered from cramps in his legs, and warmth loosened his muscles. As you have seen, the room in question is internal, fairly private, because no more than two people can fit comfortably in the pool at any time, and more often than not the judge soaked alone. The Old Baths were never considered fashionable, and after the opening of the Herculean establishment, they nearly fell out of use. Now and then, especially during holidays, lawyers and state workers frequent them, because they can have some peace and quiet there. Sir, may I ask how old you are?"

Aelius, who had thus far listened attentively, only pretending to set aright Duco's mess, found himself staring up at the older man, who stood before him with hands clasped. "I'm thirty. Why?"

The brusqueness of his answer did not affect Protasius. "Forgive me, Commander. Your face is a young man's, but the white hair—at my age one stupidly longs for interlocutors as battered by life as one is." It was an odd justification, but to all appearances the real one.

"Won't you sit down?"

"I'd rather not, sir. Bad back. Anyhow, returning to my unfortunate master: Having been stabbed so that a vein in his neck was lanced, what with the heat that accelerated his heartbeat, what with the precision of the blow, he must have bled to death very quickly. Did he thrash about? Did he try to crawl out of the pool? Did he cry for help? No, no, and no. His valet and I found him sitting there composed, in what seemed to have become a cauldron of blood—a scene from a Greek tragedy. What am I saying, from one of Seneca's gory plays. The young valet passed out, and I myself became violently ill. You know, I don't like circus games because I can't stand bloodshed. I close my eyes when animal sacrifices are performed. I made wide detours if I know that executed criminals are exposed in this or that square. Terrible, it was."

"I noticed that the barrel vault of the room is so low, steam collects on it and falls back on the floor. Given the early hour, was the space around the pool already wet?"

"Oh, yes. They start the furnace much in advance. I did look around for footprints, Commander, but none were discernible. Upon leaving the room, it would have been sufficient for the killer or killers to dry their bare feet—who wears shoes in the baths?—with a towel at one of the two entrances, and they could have stepped away without leaving traces. It could have been a client walking in from the street, although at daybreak even the cold pool, the only one to be frequented somewhat regularly by civil servants and officers of the prison guards, is generally empty. The serfs working in the furnaces were all accounted for at the time of the murder, and so were those who man the wardrobes, the masseurs, and so forth. But there's many of them who come and go doing errands."

Aelius saw no point in informing Protasius of the executions outside Porta Ticinensis. The whole city would know before long. "Is there a possibility that Marcellus knew his assassin, and let him approach without suspicion?"

"I haven't a clue. The judge knew so many people! More often than not, he would fall asleep as soon as he sat in the hot tub. He was a bit hard of hearing and had a heavy slumber. Anyone who'd wanted to surprise him could have done so." Protasius seemed to read the question in Aelius's mind. His long head, with patient, distant eyes that gave it a horsey look, moved from side to side in a disconsolate denial. "Marcellus desired that none of us in the household raise our voice on account of his infirmity. He read lips, but that would not help if his eyes were closed. As a matter of fact, the bath attendants told me they left him asleep, seated in the water as usual. I heard what's being said about Christians being responsible for the crime, Commander, but I don't believe it."

Well, Aelius thought, *this is finally getting somewhere. These educated freedmen are wound up like tops, and have to stop twirling before you can see their colors.*

"I'd be grateful if you explained why, Protasius. Lady Catula in no way holds it against you, but she did inform me that you used to be a Christian yourself, before squaring things out with the authorities. Are you not one of those the Christian hierarchy brands as *lapsi*?"

"Those who have fallen out, yes. I certainly hope it will not be counted against me during this conversation, Commander. I had my good reasons for abjuring, and believe it or not, they have nothing to do with fear of legal proceedings."

"What was the reason, then?" Side by side, Aelius lined up Duco's many stylus pens by length, creating a Pan pipe on the desk. "I'm only asking out of curiosity." *He's a powerful family's freedman, and knows it. Look how unconcerned he is to speak of such things, in times of religious prosecution.*

"Unless you are familiar with some of the Christian texts, Commander, you cannot understand. Let us say that it had to do with a discrepancy I perceived between the teachings from Christ's mouth and the way things are run by the clergy these days." Protasius blushed; it was a strangely revealing reaction in a controlled old man, which pleased Aelius. "I read the classics. I didn't come to Christianity unprepared as do urchins and old widows."

"I am not familiar with Christian texts, but suppose you give me a quick course in the organization of the sect. For example, the word you used, 'clergy,' derives from the Greek."

"Yes, *kleros.*"

"It means a drawing of lots, does it not?"

"Precisely, and by extension, the allotting of a portion—God's portion. Those men who are God's portion on earth."

Aelius made a lopsided octagon out of Duco's pens. "Does it mean the Christian hierarchy is drawn by lots?"

"In the way an election to office is a kind of lottery, yes. The presence of the faithful—the will of the people, if you wish—is necessary to the process of investiture." Blood left Protasius's cheeks, slowly, as liquid evaporates from a cloth. "It is a kind of monarchical structure, based in Rome as you no doubt are aware, even though many bishops from other imperial cities wield great power. Marcellinus held last the office of pope, that is, head of all bishops, until his execution on October 24. Word has come from Rome that he showed some hesitation and fear during his trial, but having repented, he readily accused himself and suffered the capital punishment. Despite this, in Rome, and in Mediolanum as well, some Christians consider him a *traditor*—a betrayer of the faith, which puts into question his past decisions and even his ordinations. Great confusion could arise from this, as the Christians are all but united."

October 24. Aelius scattered the pens with a slow sweep of the hand. The same day he'd concluded the investigation in Egypt, and the one hundred seventy-fourth anniversary of the Boy's death in the Nile. The youthful image of the deified Hadrian's favorite, melancholy, rose before him like an unlikely mirror to his different anxiety and solitude.

"Now for the local hierarchy." Protasius was taking seriously the indoctrination. "It includes bishops, presbyters, deacons, and subdeacons. Bishops and presbyters are priests, but not the deacons, who are at the bishops' service. Lectors, deaconesses, widows, and virgins are not ordained as such, but they fulfill auxiliary duties in the Church. Then there are other roles, such as those of healer by laying on of hands, exorcist, and so on. Those clergymen ordained by the laying on of hands receive the Spirit, or Grace. But deacons in some places are more powerful than bishops."

Aelius knew he'd been slumping, because the chair squeaked when he sat upright. "Did you ever meet a lady from Laumellum—perhaps a deaconess—born as Annia Cincia, now called Casta, who travels with a supposed miracle worker?"

"No, sir." The freedman raised one eyebrow, glancing upward as if to search his memory. "But I did read about her in an episcopal letter when I was still in the superstition. Bishop Maternus, head of this city's congregation, used the story of the noblewoman's conversion as an example of how the drawing of lots—the *kleros*—can extend even to the lesser among us."

"The lesser? She is of noble birth—why, I heard it from relatives of hers."

"I meant that she is a woman."

Aelius set the pens in a star pattern of unequal rays. "And what about him, Agnus the fire waker?"

"He's said to be pious, celibate, severe. She follows him as his servant, ministering to women when required." Protasius lifted his forefinger to his lips—no, to his nose, or to both, indicating a need to be on the lookout, or to keep a secret, or both. "I think the clergy envies his success in preaching, and even more so the wonders he does. If what is said of him is true, not since the Apostles have such miracles been seen. I don't know what to think in that regard, not having seen his works. But the gossip that malicious tongues have put around regarding Casta's virtue is belied by the fact that the Christian hierarchy does not allow immoral men or women to spread the Word. Had Casta even been widowed of two husbands rather than one, she would have not been accepted by the Church."

Idly, Aelius considered that Casta was a much lovelier name than Annia Cincia. He wondered how old she might be, and why Decimus had said, *She was a beauty once.* Perhaps she was a beauty even now. The thought distracted him from the matter at hand; visibly, perhaps, because Protasius resolved to conclude the lesson for the day.

"In sum, Commander, I betrayed no one, turned in no one. I did change my mind. My good master, who had never imputed religious wrongheadedness to me before, did not charge me with cowardice afterward. He, who read Christian texts in order to understand how to judge those who lived by them, reminded me that before his permanence in Rome the apostle Peter himself was an apostate not once but three times over."

"Really?" Mention of the City interrupted Aelius's reverie. "In Rome I was shown by my guide a spot in Gaius's circus, where this man Peter is said to have been executed during Nero's reign. But my guide—an Egyptian—was not very trustworthy, so I don't know."

Out of prudence or disinterest in the topography of Rome, Protasius did not comment either way. "Now, tell me if a man of such wisdom and generosity would be killed by the local Christians. Minucius Marcellus was the best thing that happened to them."

They chatted for a while longer, in the rush of autumn rain that came through the window like the sound of a distant waterfall, with the dripping of eaves closer in. Then, when the freedman had been already dismissed, he turned back from the door so vivaciously that Aelius was surprised by the reaction. "If I were in the authorities' shoes, Commander, I would knock on the door of Fulgentius Pennatus, brick-maker from Modicia. I saw the threat he or his sent to my esteemed master, and there is no doubt in my mind that he is guilty, or involved at any rate."

Awkwardly Aelius dropped in his lap one of the pens he was laying to rest after playing with them. "Lady Catula told me the judge showed the threat to no one and disposed of it at once."

"Well. He told me to dispose of it at once. But 'at once' does not mean I could not lay my eyes on it as I held it over the flame. It read like a threat."

"Are you sure?"

"My Greek is *very* good, Commander. And the paper came from Modicia."

"Really. How can you tell?"

"As a secretary, I make it my business to be familiar with writing material. Now, there's a papyrus manufactory in Modicia. They import the raw material from Egypt and process it locally. The workers themselves are Egyptians, although the owner is a local man. The paper they produce is recognizable because of its texture. You might know that when the bark is stripped off the papyrus stalk, the inner fibers—they're technically called *philurae*—must be delicately separated from one another. Afterward, the resulting stripes are plaited crosswise, again and again. Lime-water is used to wash the paper, which is then pressed until it's ready. *But*—at Modicia they do not use the innermost vegetable fibers, as they ought to. They sell those to another paper-maker in Ticinum, for the production of *charta regia,* 'royal paper' for state documents. In Modicia they use the second-best fibers; not quite those outer layers you make packing paper out of, but second-best. The result is pompously called *charta niliaca modiciana,* Modicia's Nile paper. The threat Master received was scribbled on a piece of such paper. And who else but Pennatus held a grudge against him in Modicia?"

"But that was three months ago."

"How little do you know Italians, Commander. They serve vengeance very cold on their plates."

Aelius stood from his chair. "Well, then! The brick-maker must be investigated and, if it's the case, denounced. Lady Catula—" Protasius's expression alone interrupted him, as the freedman would never dare doing so in words.

"Dear sir, *there is no proof.* The word of a freedman whose master has died does not hold up before the court as well as that of a brick kiln owner and contractor, with many friends ready to support him. Working with a judge has made me all too aware of the limitations of illations such as the one I presented you. Mistress is not interested in prosecution anyway, and I wager that Judge Marcellus's successor has already decided who is guilty."

4

An immense cloud occupied the northern sky, rising from the mountains. The road to Modicia left the city through Porta Nova, a new gate nicknamed "Golden" even though there was nothing gilded about it, only because the next gate over was known as "Silver" on account of a place called Argenta, to which it led.

Paved for the first six miles, the road ran lower than the surrounding countryside, fairly straight in a north-northeast direction, among mulberry trees and other deciduous plants, some of which still retained a few leaves, especially the plane trees, with pale spots of peeling bark spotting their smooth trunks. The peeling bark made Aelius think of the freedman's words about the paper manufactory, a piece of Egypt so far from the Nile. As a boy on the frontier, he'd used paper-thin, curling plane bark to write on and to make small boats and wristbands. His father wrote in his letters that he'd planted plane trees around the house, but surely Aelius's childhood recollections had nothing to do with it. During his dinner with Decimus, he'd jested that his family "had broken his arm" to make him study with the best teachers. He had not said that—in a different context but in the same year—his father had literally broken his arm, punishing him for a small infraction.

Grackles fussed in a shrub growing out of a funerary monument along the road. It was a fig tree, actually, stunted by the northern weather, that had pushed its way up between the steps and now barred the monument's door. If the fire waker ever decided to call back to life the inmate of that burial, he had better be ready to hack away the plant to let him come forth. Simpering at the idea, Aelius admitted that aside from the unkempt graves, the signs of abandonment of the countryside that he had noticed elsewhere in the Empire were not so obvious here. Still—from the saddle he could see them even riding along the sunken road—farmhouses looked reduced in purpose and use, windows on their upper floors barred shut, the better part of the properties left fallow at a time of sowing. The upkeep of irrigation ditches seemed less attentive than that of the canals in the city; weeds strangled the wooden floodgates, blocking them in an upright position so that—should early winter rains fall, as they always do on northern plains—it might be impossible to control the overflow.

NOTES BY AELIUS SPARTIANUS:

One arrives at Modicia by way of a road post named Sextum, after a travel of about fourteen miles. The place—halfway between a village and a small town—is built on the banks of a navigable little river called Frigidus. The river does not seem as cold as the name suggests, carries a limited amount of water, and flows southward. Across a bridge of some pretension there lie Fulgentius Pennatus's brickworks. Another brickyard, a mile before reaching the town, belongs to a different owner (more about him later). As for the paper manufactory, it stands not in Modicia proper, but on the bank a bit north of the community, a place where mills and a small fish-shaped island enliven the site. Uninterrupted woods rise just beyond, although I am told that farms and small settlements are to be found in clearings here and there, lived in by folks who still speak a Celtic dialect and "are none too swift" (Protasius's words, not mine).

Despite the ravages of the Alamannic attack years ago, the area seems prosperous. A man who gave me directions to Pennatus's brickyard bragged that he makes a living dowsing for money and silver buried by folks who died during that invasion. Thus, the loss of some makes the wealth of others, but who knows how many of these small treasures go unclaimed!

The self-important Fulgentius Pennatus, whom I met at his brickworks, has the face of a toad, and his complexion is nearly as lumpy and gray-green. The spitting image of a procurer in Nicomedia, whom in the old days my colleague Tralles and I kicked roundly for his bad habit of beating the girls.

Every time we encounter the look-alike of a man we once found unpleasant, we have to be particularly attentive not to transfer to him the antipathy we felt for the fellow he resembles. I'd have succeeded in keeping equanimous this time, had Pennatus not grumbled as soon as I stepped into his office that I reminded him of a German colonel who tried to wheedle money out of him. Such conceit, and the way he showed himself annoyed with me, my visit, and my words, made me right away suspect he has protectors on high, well above his colleagues in the brick-making guild. As it turns out, it is so.

Replying that, thanks to the latitude my charge from His Divinity grants me, I am allowed among other things to look into criminal cases I judge of some peculiarity, I posed such questions as I thought appropriate. Usually, the sole mention of my position as Caesar's envoy strikes as lightning in a haystack. Pennatus, toad that he is, stayed perfectly cool.

To begin with, he denied any knowledge of the judge's violent death, which is only marginally possible, Modicia being less than two hours from Mediolanum. But let us assume that I traveled faster than bad news. Every inch the businessman, *the brick-maker prevented my next question by letting me know that unless I have taken leave of my senses, I would not go as far as suggesting he has anything to do with Marcellus's end.*

One thing he added makes sense, however: that if he planned to eliminate the judge, he would not have sent him a threatening message beforehand, something he boldly admits having done. Whether or not he assumes the message was kept by Marcellus (I did nothing to disabuse him of the opinion), with impeccable logic Pennatus maintains that he contented himself with venting his anger at Marcellus through the written word. As to his whereabouts on the day of the judge's murder, he says he has half of Modicia ready to account for him. I believe that's the case; it would be the case, probably, even if his fellow townsmen knew he had gone swimming in the Old Baths at Mediolanum on that day. "What about the other half of the town?" I asked, and Pennatus answered that the other half "doesn't count for nothing."

Such haughtiness is becoming more and more frequent, as the distance between the haves and the have-nots increases throughout the Empire. And to think that the Maximum Prices Edict was written to limit the accumulation of wealth in the hands of a few! When I remarked that hired killers can be sent to do one's dirty work from anywhere, Pennatus grew openly provoked. It was then that he informed me he is friends with the city prefect (not a good thing for me if it's true, as the prefect is known to be extremely close to the Palace), and that if I didn't measure my words, he'd make sure a vibrant protest would reach His Divinity's desk. It isn't this that troubles me so much, as I am reasonably confident I could explain my reasons to Our Lord Diocletian; but the local authorities could make my stay in Italia Annonaria very uncomfortable. Not yet satisfied, Pennatus threatened—it must be his favorite sport, when he isn't producing faulty bricks—to put investigators at my heels, to "find

*out why a soldier shows an interest in matters not of his compe-
tence."*

*Rather, he told me, I ought to take a look at Minucius Mar-
cellus's politics, and at those who opposed them long before the
trials against the Christians began. "You think you are so
smart, when you haven't been here enough time to know who
outsniffs whose doorjamb in Mediolanum after someone else
has marked it with his piss." Why these merchants have to be
so crude, I am sure I don't know. But I can be crude with the
best of them, thanks to my elective profession, and so replied
that I have a nearly uncanny ability to tell by the height of the
mark the measure of the man who has been doing the pissing,
and nothing I'd seen thus far worried me too much. I was bluff-
ing, naturally, since I had no idea of what Pennatus meant.
What doorjamb? What politics, and who is involved? Protasius
says that conservative circles disliked Marcellus. If I only knew
what "conservative circles" means these days. Pennatus is not
the one to ask.*

*Our Lord Diocletian brought back peace and order to the
Empire, and politics of any kind is out of place. "It is extremely
dangerous to be in politics these days" was the last comment the
brick-maker regaled me with, adorned with a quip about the
relative height of my own mark on the doorjamb.*

*He is not the type one can soften up with words, being one of
those men who love confrontation and receive physical gratifica-
tion from an argument. I know only one other person who dis-
plays such a hankering for verbal contrast, and that is my old
Nicomedia flame, Helena. So, whatever Pennatus meant by the
judge's "politics," I was unable to pull it out of him. I left the
brickyard after as inconclusive a meeting as I can think of, saving the impression that he is a crooked merchant and a bully,
but likely not a murderer.*

*On the northernmost wooded island on a bend of Modicia's
Frigidus, where I stopped to take a look at the paper manufactory,*

a crew of fullones *from a nearby clothier's were dying wool in great vats. The dye was madder, and even from a distance, the liquid in the containers resembled blood. I understood what Protasius meant when he said that Judge Marcellus, dead in his bloody pool, reminded him of the scene in a Seneca tragedy.*

The towering cloud had hardly moved at all when I regained the road. Even after I passed Modicia's bridge, leaving behind the clay beds that give it its name, the vapors were still motionless over the mountains, as if the peaks themselves produced moisture, and this gathered into clouds above them. I don't know the wind currents in this region enough to predict what cloud-capped mountains portend, but there is always a sense of imminent change in a thunderhead. Something tells me not to inquire directly of Curius Decimus regarding politics in Mediolanum, of the conservative kind or otherwise. Indeed, there is no need to bring up the subject with any of the locals— least of all with the officers at the horse barracks, who talk far too much.

Riding back, I recalled that I promised Decimus to show him the antique helmet I bought at Arae Flaviae. He has—what else?—a forebear among those who died in Teutoburg Forest under Quintilius Varus's ineffectual command. I am also taking along the humble brick from Marcellus's garden, just to see how he reacts.

That evening, the ancestors' room seemed warm when Aelius walked in from the street, because a freezing norther had risen outside. In fact—this time he noticed, being less dazzled by the elegance of the surroundings—mildew stained the bottom of the walls, around the floor where humidity seeped despite all. A draft from the window agitated the drapery in front of it, and its invisible fingers tried to nip the lighted wicks in the lamps.

The helmet he had placed on the studio table was of the kind used for parades and cavalry exercises, the *hippikà gymnasia* beloved in earlier years. Decimus, who had scoffed until this moment that it was probably a fake, and that Aelius had been taken in by an unscrupulous vendor, changed his expression when he had it in his hands.

"It had fallen in a bog," Aelius explained, "and that is why it is so well preserved. The man found it in the process of saving his hunting dog from the quicksand. Succeeding when the animal had nearly gone under, he felt something else in the mire, reached for it, and here it is. He told me that completely preserved bodies are occasionally pulled out when peat is cut from the dryer areas. Flesh, clothes, weapons: All is kept intact by a sort of tanning process."

"And that's all the eternity any of us can hope for."

During the stops on his trip southward, Aelius had buffed and polished the helmet himself. Now the hinged construction—a true helmet molded for the skull, with a short crest mimicking feathers, and tritons facing each other above the visor, attached to an elaborate full-face mask—shone with the paleness of steel and silver, the eye slits seemingly twinkling in Decimus's hands. He turned it this way and that between his dark fingers, observing it in the light of the closest lamp.

"There's the owner's name punched inside," Aelius said.

This, too, Decimus looked for eagerly.

"The vendor told me he found an officer's arm in the same bog, with bracelet and rings still on it; he hoped to sell the whole, except that the limb soon decayed in the fresh air. As we read about the battle in Dio Cassius and Velleius Paterculus—"

"How much do you want for it?"

"It's not for sale."

Decimus kept the helmet on his side of the desk, in a jealous grasp. "You have no forebears among the ambushed Romans."

"No, but for all I know I might have some among the auxiliaries, six cohorts and three cavalry units of whom were slaughtered. My mother's people were from those parts."

"This is not a Germanic or Pannonian name, punched inside."

"Vonatorix is not exactly a Roman name, either."

"How much do you want for it, Spartianus?"

"It's not for sale."

The mask, molded so as to cover the entire face, represented a youth with curly sideburns and an expression of absorbed serenity, as if he were thinking of something pleasant and secure; a narrow chin and chiseled mouth, the virile ideal in Augustus's day, gave it a sensitive air of adolescence preserved. With a pouting grimace that buried his lower lip under the upper one, regretfully Decimus watched Aelius wrap the helmet in soft leather and replace it in a canvas bag. "I hope you'll change your mind."

This not being a formal dinner, they remained in the studio to chat. First came the story of Decimus's heroic ancestor, chief of staff under Varus, like Varus a grief-stricken suicide in the face of disaster. His portrait sat on the shelf with the other family members, staring out of a gloomy black marble face with silver-leaf eyes. From this, the conversation progressed to Marcellus's death, the riots, and—on Aelius's part—the coincidence of having brick-makers figure one way or another in the murders at Treveri and Mediolanum.

Asked about his opinion, Decimus smiled slowly. He joined his hands, palm against palm, and tapped their edge against his mouth, as if giving himself time to think. Still smiling, he let a suspended moment go by. The signet ring on his left hand, bulky and antique, formed a shiny gold spot on the swarthiness of his skin. It was the sole ornament on him. Compared to the regalia worn by the Palace Guard and officers as a whole, it seemed self-effacing moderation, but Aelius believed otherwise. *These aristocrats,* he thought, *they wear old gold like their names and titles. The precious metals and famous, inherited names are consumed by the passing centuries, but do not lose luster because of it. How many of them are left who can actually claim their primacy as Romans? Entire clans have died out one hundred years ago already, other families have few or no sons, and—unless they are stopped—the Christians will claim more and more aristocrats as celibates and virgins. My seven nephews and nieces have a better chance to reproduce, and stand to*

generate a myriad imperial soldiers and civil servants, none of them Ro-
man.

Decimus removed the hands from his lips but did not cease smiling. He said, "It must be true that when an object is too large for a room, folks risk not seeing it. I am surprised at you, Spartianus, who don't belong to this batch of shop-owning burghers. Naturally *they* would understand nothing unless there's money at the bottom of any enterprise, including crime. But you! Leave the argument about the bricks alone. It's patent, the sole party to have a valid motive to kill Marcellus is the extreme fringe group of the Christians. Why? Because even a lenient judge is still a judge, and will pass judgment. A sad reality worth pondering, how often the harshest prosecutors are respected for their dourness and go unscathed, while the nice fellows with a sensitive heart are made to pay."

"It seems to me like cutting one's foot to spite the leg, on the Christians' part."

"Well, do not expect me to join the procession of those who sing the praises of the dear departed: I did not like him. And I don't care who killed him."

Decimus's last statement, unrequested, was pronounced without animus. The coldness in his tone—like everything else about the man—had a touch of artificiality, something he might well try to pass off as superficial disregard, but was not. In fact, while it implied the opposite, such iciness gave Aelius the impression that a man like Decimus could maintain his composure even when he cared enough to kill.

"Truly, I don't see why you insist on the matter of the bricks," the host added after having wine served, with a choice of cured meats "from Parma and Mutina, where they know their hogs." Holding a small slab of ham on a serving fork, he took out of it an even smaller bite. "Saying that bricks somehow form a connection between the killing of that Lupus of yours in Treveri and our esteemed judge's end is like trying to link a mutton shoulder to a pheasant thigh, simply because both animals get slaughtered for meat. If you wish to penetrate the not-so-shady world of brick-making, why don't you stop by my estate north of Sextum? I own clay beds and kilns there, and if I can say so myself, the *figlinae* of Manius Curius Decimus—an ivy leaf and palm branch as trademark devices—built half of those grain depots whose workers are so stupid as to fall into the bins."

Yes, Aelius knew. He had ridden by in the morning and, mistaking them for Pennatus's brickworks, had inquired of the laborers and learned the name of the actual owner.

Decimus was about to say something else, but his mouth clamped shut. His attention, until now alternating between Aelius and the food, migrated to the corner of the studio table, to the object his guest had taken out of the canvas bag and laid there. Irritation tweaked the tightness of his lips. "Well, what do you want with this, and where did you pick it up?"

"In Judge Marcellus's garden."

Decimus coldly lifted his eyes from the brick. "And what, if I may ask, were you doing there?"

"Paying my respects to his widow."

"That old biddy. Why?"

"Isn't it generally done, among civilized people?"

"Yes, but you never even met Marcellus, and his murder is hardly your concern. Unless you want to count the fact that you broke up the riot at the prisons and went uninvited to the crime scene." Decimus swept the air with a bored, dismissing wave. "Collect bricks for all I care, see what you can learn from them. Before fantasy runs away with you because I sold construction material to the judge, you should also know that it was my brickworks that won the horse barracks contract when Pennatus lost it."

"I knew that already. And also the contract for the works near the Old Baths. Along with rocks and clumps of dirt, it was your bricks that were hurled at us during the riot."

"So. We're back to your being either stupid or a tad too clever,

Spartianus. There's something about you that goes beyond a historian's snoopiness."

Aelius stared at the brick. He wasn't sure why he had brought it
along, much less shown it as if it were a proof of some kind. Noticing
Decimus's mark on the construction material near the Old Baths, and
then in Lucia Catula's garden, he'd limited himself to making a mental
note of it. Still, he'd asked the head mason for one of the bricks at the
villa. Only later had he learned that Decimus was the proprietor of
the brickyard south of Modicia. Pennatus had deepened his interest,
spitefully speaking of conservative circles and their dislike of Judge
Marcellus.

But it was hardly enough, simply because his host did not mourn
the judge, and had described Casta's late husband as a conservative, a
man after his own heart. Now Aelius was even more confused. He
could only hope that the urbane aristocrat would take his move as idle
woolgathering about the crime.

In fact, "I do think you're stupid," Decimus said, with the appeased
air of one who has solved a lesser problem. "Put away your brick, it will
lead you nowhere. As far as the Christians are concerned—strike them
hard, I say! If the sender of the murderer is among them, justice is
done; if not, it will keep the abominable sect from committing aberra-
tions later. Believe me, if the Public Thing"—in conversation, Aelius
had noticed he referred to the government in those terms, as *res
publica*—"had from the beginning exerted its rightful authority over
those scoundrels, we would not have come to the point that our cities
are rife with Christians. In three centuries they have spread like oil in a
hot pan: If you move the handle, oil runs to coat the whole bottom of
it. Thank goodness there are still the peasants in the countryside who
stick to traditional beliefs. It is a sad state of things that we have to depend on boors as champions of right-mindedness, the *bona mens* that
made Romans who they are." Decimus poured more wine into the delicate silver bowls, at least as antique as the Teutoburg helmet. "Were
you aware that in the mountains northeast of here Christian clerics

and other such interlopers are fair game, and the moment one of them shows his sorry face in the village, he risks being lynched? I have seen a couple of them hanging from the trees myself, while going to see some property I own north of Leucum."

Aelius put away the brick. The act seemed silly to him now; he was surprised Decimus seemed to have been put in a better mood by his faux pas. Was he not, after all, the officer Maximian used to find out about visitors? He'd played into his hand easily enough. There was no putting a patch on things, so Aelius might as well try to play stupid to the end. "We don't know what the new judge will decide," he said, "but isn't it true that a hasty sentence may cloud the waters? If Our Lord Maximian had wished for more severe legal action against the Christians, he could have removed Minucius Marcellus at any time. And if the sole result of a mild judge's removal is a recrudescence of the prosecution, I fail to see how the Christians will gain from this murder."

Decimus made once more that waving gesture, back and forth. "*Cui prodest*—the great question. As if an assassin always had to have his own benefit in mind. Even in money-grabbing Mediolanum, someone may be placing higher things before his advantage. Maybe Marcellus's own bonhomie caused his fall. You know they have an apocalyptic literature, these Christians, whereby the end of the world is advocated: They might seek to hasten their own destruction."

"So, someone murdered Marcellus for a higher cause: but which one? They say he was not involved in politics and shook it off himself like a duck does with water. On the other hand, this religious prosecution is all about politics, you know better than I. Rome has never been intolerant of foreign cults, and Christianity isn't the first antisocial sect to penetrate our borders. But it is admittedly the most pernicious and resistant. I say that whoever killed the judge for a 'higher principle' did it for a political motive unknown to us."

"It may be. Whoever it is did us all a favor."

There was gratuitous cruelty in Decimus's words and a contemptuous, mean edge in his tone that made Aelius forget his good intentions and his tact. The last question he planned to ask—the question he had specifically decided *not* to ask—slipped out of him

"Yes. How do conservative circles feel about Marcellus's death?"

Decimus pressed his lips tight. Not a clamping of the mouth this time but its disappearance into a slit. Unlikely dimples formed in those hollow cheeks. He seemed annoyed, or to be pretending annoyance, as if the question were impertinent or should seem so. When he spoke again, his words came out flattened, ironed by the tightening of lips.

"I don't know what time you rise in the morning, Spartianus, but I am an early bird. I will bid you good night, and retire."

6 DECEMBER, WEDNESDAY

On the matter of Christian responsibility, superficially obvious, Aelius chose to suspend judgment for now, but three days from the murder, the city as a whole seemed to think like Curius Decimus. Indeed, any serious investigation was immediately vitiated by the fact that Marcellus's auxiliary judge, overjoyed at seeing his way to promotion unexpectedly cleared, felt the need to show himself quick and fierce in prosecution. All the Christian clergy and laymen awaiting judgment in the city prisons were tried en masse in those three days, and all of them condemned to death.

It was not unheard of, but in contrast with the mildness of previous proceedings, the sentence affected Mediolanum in an odd, sated way. Booksellers said it was a good thing, if lacking in procedural elegance; officers at the cavalry barracks drank to the new judge's health, but through the side of their mouths whispered that the days of having to pay bribes were back. Archivists sniffled, took this or that document down from the shelf, and observed that hasty trials made for less paperwork. Decimus exulted, to the limit of good taste for a man of his style and measure.

As for Marcellus, his body was cremated at the family *ustrinum*, and the ashes laid in the Minucii monument on the road to Ticinum. Lucia Catula took care of all details, from the inditing of gladiatorial games in her husband's memory to the distribution of charity to orphan girls. She freed the house slaves according to Marcellus's will, sent thank-you notes to those who had attended the funeral, and amiably consoled the judge's friends. By midday on Monday, she was dead by her own hand.

Aelius learned the news on Wednesday morning, from a junior officer who came early to the barracks and climbed to his tower room to knock. One of the Palace Guards manning the inner halls of Maximian's residence, he introduced himself as Ulpius Domninus, a friend of Decimus's. "Chamberlain Aristophanes requires your presence at court, Commander."

"At what time?" Up already, and about to leave his small quarters, Aelius stood with the messenger on the wooden balcony, buckling his belt. It was unconscionably early in the day, especially by bureaucratic standards, so the answer came as a surprise.

"On the double. I will wait for you below, and accompany you myself."

Aelius watched Domninus speedily go down the stairs. The summons gave him pause, a reaction just below a sense of alarm. He breathed in slowly, slowly exhaled, taking in the view as if to set himself solidly within place and time. Overnight, the norther had brought clear weather and a hard frost. On the barracks grounds, stable attendants broke the layer of ice in the watering troughs; troops assembling for roll call let out rhythmic puffs of condensed breath. Roofs on the covered passages would not begin steaming until the sun gained strength, but already the camp cats followed with tails straight up the soldier carrying out kitchen scraps; they, too, had a small trough laid out for their food, and Aelius watched them scratch and tumble to establish their eating order. From the tower, the mountains had the speckled blue color of lapis lazuli Aelius had seen in Persian markets, after the war.

Below, "I took the liberty of picking up your mail," Domninus said in a colorless voice, handing him two rolled and sealed letters. "Your mount is ready at the camp gate."

Aelius caught a glimpse of Duco, who looked out of the mail room and made an obscene gesture behind the messenger's back. It might be out of personal antipathy, but more likely it meant that he'd been forced to give up the letters, whose distribution was under his care today.

Not a good sign. The eunuch Aristophanes, Greek as the playwright whose name he bore, but (according to Decimus) possessing none of his humor, had the second-highest power in Mediolanum, whatever else hierarchy disposed. A belated decision by Maximian to receive His Divinity's envoy would unlikely require such haste, so it had to be something originating in a chamberlain's office, where all intrigue traditionally thrives.

Domninus, sporting a full beard, but only in that sense out of fashion, led the way to the camp gate in a uniform weighed down by embroidered purple strips. That he did not wear the fussy fringed cape of his rank might mean that he, too, had been thrown out of bed to run this errand. As soon as they were mounted, Aelius placed the letters in his saddlebag, and although one came from Thermuthis and the other from ben Matthias, he would not give Domninus the satisfaction of seeing him rush to read them.

In fact, he asked no questions as they rode the half-empty cold streets. It was when they crossed the avenue leading to Porta Ticinensis—the avenue Aelius's Guardsmen had devoured to charge the rioters—that Lucia Catula's death was brought up. Making a diversion and taking the long way to avoid the Jewish quarter, Domninus pointed vaguely in the direction of the Minucii's suburban estate and reported that hours earlier the old lady had cut her wrists on her wedding bed, wearing her wedding-day jewels. *"Never in fifty-two years have we been apart for more than three days,* she left written. *We will not be apart for more than three days now.* Nobody does *that* anymore. Pure class act. I wept when I heard."

"Sad news for the Minucii."

"Yes, especially since her soft little husband hardly deserved the sacrifice."

If further inquiry was expected, Aelius refrained from making it. He slipped the comment among the things worth recalling, and with his heels touched the horse's sides to ride a couple of steps ahead of his colleague. *Kind Aelius Spartianus,* Lucia Catula had told him Sunday, by way of a dismissal, *as far as I am concerned, the punishment of death ordered after a death is only more death, even when it strikes the guilty. I will not attend any trials regarding our tragedy. We met briefly, you and I, but it moves me that—having no obligation to do so, not having known in person my beloved Marcellus—you brought your respects, and your disquiet for an assassination that seems without a reason. You asked me then whether I had a "theory" of my own, and I answered no. I still say no, but sometimes we search afar for something which is very near.* She had quietly closed the door on him then, preventing explanations.

A click of the tongue, and Domninus overtook Aelius's mount and looked back over his shoulder. His hairy face, pale with the cold of the hour, was framed by the outer bastions of the Palace as if by a cascade of interlocking bricks. "The chamberlain wishes to be addressed as *Eminence.* Make sure you do."

"He's equestrian rank, is he not? Isn't *perfectissimus* the appropriate title?"

"You'll call 'most perfect' the chief *speculator, Spartianus.* The chamberlain goes by *Eminence.*"

So, the head of criminal investigation would attend the meeting. Why? Without a particular reason, it set Aelius's teeth on edge.

"Credentials, credentials."

The Greek singsong accent was no doubt something the chamberlain affected, as administrators were perfectly schooled in Latin. He received in an office at the end of a long corridor paved and wainscoted in black marble, mirror-shiny like the hall Emperor Domitian had constructed in the old days to discourage sneak attacks. Left by Domninus at the threshold of the corridor, Aelius had walked to Aristophanes's door under the escort of his right and left side reflection. It was true, no one could approach from behind and not be noticed, but Domitian had been assassinated all the same.

Inside, he faced a curly-headed man wider than he was tall, looking larger because of the reduced size of the office. Other than its resident and the ornate chair he sat in, the room contained a desk that judging by its dimensions must have been built in place. The disproportion might want to impress, but it only struck and unbalanced the visitor. Of the chief investigator, there was neither hide nor hair, although palaces were known to have spy holes to watch and listen unseen.

"Credentials."

Aristophanes followed his words with an urging gesture of the hand, fingers curling back and forth. Aelius handed in his credentials, along with a letter of presentation from His Divinity that specified the variety of his official roles, and the privileges attached to them.

Thus far in his travels, the sight of the senior emperor's seal had sufficed to open doors and cow the mighty. The impatience with which the chamberlain unrolled the letter and ran his eyes over it suggested a different response. Standing in the small space between the edge of the desk and the door, Aelius set his face to the lack of expression that makes an envoy what he is, but was careful to capture all of Aristophanes he could. A loose yellow blouse, clasped by a pin at the neck, covered a yellow tunic to the ankles. Stuck in the sandal-like slippers worn by state officials, his meaty feet pulled the weave of the socks like sausages stuffing their casings. The face perusing the letter had a double—no, triple—chin, the cheeks pushed up to the chamberlain's eyes with pink rolls of healthy, unveined fat. Aelius had dealt with state eunuchs before and knew they came in all sizes; this was obesity due to being a sedentary glutton, not to castration.

"Why are you still in Mediolanum?"

It was a predictable question, whose answer Aelius had had time to anticipate between the barracks and here. "Historical research, Eminence."

Aristophanes stared at him above the imperial letter. "Not awaiting His Divinity's instructions before continuing your journey?"

"That is a given, Eminence."

One of the bejeweled hands relented its grasp on the letter, so that the paper curled back up into a roll. "Yet you have become involved in other than reading the shelves."

"How so?"

"The most perfect gentleman at the lead of the city *speculatores* has protested to this office because of your interference in the matter of Minucius Marcellus's death."

This was less expected. Aelius had not gone as far as imagining a collaboration from that quarter but assumed that his actions would not be challenged. "Has the most perfect gentleman protested it or *pointed it out*, Eminence? Your Eminence readily sees that a specific clause in my credentials authorizes me to look into crimes that seem to have political implications and to report directly to Nicomedia."

Letter and credentials were slowly placed in the middle of the desk, so that it was unclear whether Aelius should take them back or leave them there. "He protested it," Aristophanes specified. "There is nothing political about Marcellus's murder, and besides, sentences have already been issued against those responsible. I believe the expression is *the case is closed.* But because this office is concerned that no misunderstandings arise among officials, Commander, an interview with the chief *speculator* has been set up for you next door. I am confident you will both profit from it."

"Next door" was often a misnomer in an imperial residence. Here, it was nonsense. In the time it took a polite but disgruntled Aelius to retrieve his papers, an eager young man in a secretary's knee-length smock materialized at the threshold to serve as a guide. Hands clasped, elbows at an angle, he led the way through a maze of corridors and stairs that might well zigzag back to a room sharing a wall with Aristophanes's office.

"Go right in, Commander."

Here the space was nearly excessive. Four desks, shelves, and chairs did not begin to fill it; a detailed city map on sheepskin stretched on the wall behind the principal desk, on the corner of which sat a middle-aged man in army trousers and boots.

"You made His Eminence get up two hours early," he said.

"I came when I was bidden, *perfectissimus*."

Papers handed in. "A-elius Spar-tia-nus. You pronounce it with a *z* or hard *t* sound?"

"A hard *t* sound."

The chief *speculator* did not give his name. But however he was called, Aelius had in his twelve years of soldiering learned to recognize a man risen from the sordid ranks of police informer to the role of interrogator, and on from there. There was nothing wrong with the process, of course: It all depended on the reasons for promotion. A short gray bristle covered his skull, too short even for a soldier, and only a little longer than a wrestler's. He'd lost the thumb of his right hand. But with that animal-like paw he easily received, opened, and held Aelius's credentials at arm's length to read them, so perhaps he was left-handed, or else had well adapted to his mutilation.

"Caesar's envoy." He read moving his lips, pronouncing the words under his breath, as Aelius's own father had always done. "All the way from Aspalatum, by way of Treveri." He raised his voice in the middle of a whispered sentence, still reading.

The observations required no answer, so Aelius stood with his eyes to the wall behind the *speculator*, scuffed by the backs of chairs under the large city map. Whoever used the three empty desks was supernumerary, or so orderly as not to leave traces of work in progress in his absence. The bullish gray head stayed low on the papers, spelling out words.

"Well, Spartianus," was the final judgment, "you may be Caesar's envoy or Jupiter's envoy or Jupiter's cupbearer, like Ganymede. There's a division of labor in place, offices and duties are ordered and assigned, and nothing I read here tells me you have a say in investigation or the application of the law *in Mediolanum*. Mediolanum is where we are. There is nothing political about Judge Marcellus's murder, and any action you may take in that regard from now on will be overstepping your boundaries."

"With all due respect, imperial envoys may only receive orders from Our Lords, His Divinity's colleagues."

"*If* their credentials are locally accepted, Commander. Since yours were not, and neither were you received by His Serenity, you're just another army colonel on temporary duty, and we've got more of those than fleas on a dog." The papers were given back gruffly. "We're not in Egypt here, we don't let outsiders teach us our jobs. And we scratch our fleas off when we itch."

Aelius thought of a couple of ripostes—one foolhardy at best—neither of which could undo the bureaucratic knot tied before him.

He was left to his devices in finding the Palace's exit. Past the second set of marble halls he crossed, Decimus stood with a pale green stalk—dry fennel, it seemed—in his lips, arms crossed, resting his back against one of the columns of the antechamber where Aelius had waited the first time. "Let me guess: You did not convince Aristophanes or the *most perfect* Sido of the validity of your claim."

"I prefer not to discuss it."

"It only means you will have to stick to your historical research while awaiting His Divinity's letter."

Aelius's mood did not improve when, upon his return to camp, he was informed that regrettably his lodgings would be no longer available after the end of the week, given the arrival of a new unit in the barracks. The best he could do was receiving assurance from Duco that letters to his attention would be forwarded to him upon request wherever he should find new accommodations. "That asshole Domninus *made* me hand him your mail, Aelius."

"You outrank him."

"But I don't out-ring him. He carried a signet ring from Aristophanes—which admittedly isn't too difficult to obtain, given that the eunuch has more rings than fingers. He'd wear a fat one on the other body piece, too, if they hadn't snipped it for good."

"What do you know about Domninus?"

"Not much." The Briton fluttered his right hand, to indicate idle moving about. "He runs around with Curius Decimus, mostly because they served together, I think. Although Domninus's sister was Decimus's first wife, or maybe his second. Say, are *you* married?"

"No. Are you?"

"I get married next month. I'd invite you to the ceremony, but I don't know if you'll still be here, and there won't be much to it anyway. She's eleven, so it'll be three or four years before we can get down to business. Her father will sign the contract, and that's that." Duco glanced at the letters in Aelius's grasp. "I noticed one of them is addressed in a girl's handwriting, so I thought maybe it was from your spouse. Egyptians make good wives, I heard."

"If you can convince them to marry you, yes."

The letter from Thermuthis had been mailed on October 30 in Hermopolis, across the Nile from her brothel by Heqet's temple. Aelius opened it first, climbing to the privacy of his room to read it. Protasius, he thought, would approve of the refined paper texture, of the elegant, slanted Greek script.

Thermuthis to Legatos Aelius Spartianus, abundant health and greetings:

Why is it, Aelius, that I get myself into these tangles for you? You're no different from the other junior officers who spent a fortune on my girls during the Rebellion. At least, that is what I tell myself, although your couth recommended you above the mass of blue-eyed randy fools who made me rich.

Anubina, about whom you asked that I keep you informed, is now physically well. The contagion following the river flood has left the province of Heptanomia, and only in Alexandria are some cases still reported. However, the loss of her husband and young son still ails her. Her usual courage and her embroidery business will be the cure, I wager, and of course the care for her daughter Thaesis. (Aelius noticed the madam did not refer to the little girl as "*your* daughter," and had to wonder whether it was the writer's choice or Anubina's refusal to admit she was his.) *I regret to say she is not as beautiful as Anubina was when her own mother sold her to me: She will grow up rather flat, I think, and excessively long-legged. But enough of that.*

Your Egyptian girlfriend is smart, Aelius: She sees through my questions about her well-being and will not tell me more than she wishes me to relate to you. So it has to be because I like uniforms and what they contain (and those little games the two of us played before you met her), that I have out of the goodness of my own heart taken my promise to you further. In return for some small compensation, her neighbors report to me that she never speaks of marriage, nor of leaving Egypt to join her man. She wants sons, she says, which is the only oblique encouragement I can give you at this time. Does she speak of you? No, I must confess, neither to me nor to her neighbors.

But it may be an intentional freeze, a delay she chooses to see clearly into her own desire. Imagine, thinking of Anubina, one of your poets' verses came to me: "There hides and shines within an amber drop / the honey bee, as if by nectar caught." I may be turning sentimental after all, something I swore never to do.

All for now, dear Aelius. If in your travels you should pass by Placentia, do stop by Felicitas's house behind the Capitolium. She's a dear old girl and knows her business. May the gods, especially our beloved little Frog-goddess Heqet, watch over you and keep you hale: Wise, I fear you never will be.

Written by Thermuthis in her chambers at Antinoopolis the

first day of Athyr, the vigil of the Kalends of November, with a full moon.

Thermuthis was not one to lie. Anubina simply took time. Good. In her circumstances, it was the right thing to do. He'd wait also, and then write to her directly. Out of the letter, Aelius chose to latch on to that sentence—"she wants sons"—as the sole significant, promising one.

Ben Matthias's message, on the other hand, took no special interpretation. He was on his way to Mediolanum, he wrote, and once there would be available if needed at the Faunus's Fortune inn by the circus.

I plan to spend the Saturnalia in Mediolanum. Call me a fuddy-duddy, but gift-giving holidays always put me in a good mood.

By now, with all your courtly duties, you have probably forgotten all about Lupus's lamentable double death in Treveri, but—just for fun—without going into details I can supply you with a few tidbits about his supposed reviver Agnus. Know then that he headed east once he left town, and considering that the climate is not favorable to Christians on the frontier, as Our Lord Galerius applies the letter of the law more stringently than his colleague in the purple Constantius, some believe he is seeking a martyr's death.

His sidekick Casta was reportedly manhandled by soldiers at a bridge checkpoint in Argentorate. A rough obligatory passage, that one. When I went by myself recently, they searched for coins even inside my beard. True to her name, Casta escaped with her virtue, or most of it, even though with the excuse of looking for undeclared goods they forced her to strip naked. How do I know? I will tell you if and when we meet in Italia. It goes without saying that the soldiers must not have been aware of the duo's religious beliefs, otherwise we'd be minus two healers.

Lupus's murder, in the words of the local head of criminal police, is a deep mystery. Which, in my experience of speculatores,

*merely means he doesn't have a clue about motive or culprit.
My tooth is poisoned against him because of his behavior toward my son-in-law: but more about that when we meet, as I
will not dirty my pen writing of the brutal son of an impure sow.
I wish you all good things, et cetera.*

*Written by Master Baruch ben Matthias at a bedbug-ridden
roadside shack its Roman owner dares calling a* mutatio. *If this
is a horse-changing station, I am a Gentile. No date, because I
lost count.*

Aelius irritably put away the letter. If intimidation had been attempted
with him here at Mediolanum, he could only imagine how the authorities had dealt with the Jewish supervisor of a Roman citizen's brickyard. And as far as Casta went, the guards' behavior at the checkpoint
was unheard of, unless she had not disclosed her aristocratic rank:
Christians could legally be roughed up, of course, but ben Matthias
suggested neither she nor Agnus had been recognized as such. What,
then? His guide in Rome, Onophrius, had told him tales of holy
women of the Christian persuasion dragged by soldiers into whore-
houses and stripped before the rowdy clientele. Why, he'd pointed out
to him the door to the small brothel at the head of Domitian's racetrack, where "a virgin thus offended had by divine miracle become in-
stantly covered by a mane of blond hair to her feet." He rather doubted
that was what his Jewish correspondent had in mind when writing that
Casta had escaped with most of her virtue.

7 DECEMBER, THURSDAY

"I didn't know you were looking for a place to stay. Does it mean you
are moving to downtown Mediolanum?"

Aelius heard Decimus's voice as he left the central Mall's real estate
office. The Roman stood mounted a few feet away, bound to or returning from some official duty, it seemed, with colleagues; among them

were one of the twins, unclear whether Dexter or Sinister, and Ulpius Domninus.

Looking at the latter, Aelius said, "As I am sure you heard from Palace gossip, only the time needed to conclude my research in the archives, and to receive further instructions. Still, the quarters I occupy at the barracks will be needed for the new mounted troops colonel, and although they're not throwing me out, I think it's appropriate that I seek another accommodation."

"I see." With a nod, Decimus separated from his colleagues, who continued in the direction of the old mint, and dismounted. "Anywhere in particular?"

"I'm considering the recently built condominium near Porta Argentea, the one with a fountain on the front."

"That one? It was constructed with Pennatus's bricks. I wouldn't stable my horses in it."

"Then I'll find a flat in the Palace district."

"And pay four times its value? If, as I imagine, you're traveling at the government's expense, you shouldn't be extravagant." Decimus said it lightly, in mock censure. "It so happens that last week a tenant of mine left the annex to my house—the part you did not see, oriented toward the downtown. If you're interested . . . I like to keep the place rented, because there's talk of widening the street it looks on, and the city fathers could easily ask for the application of eminent domain on an empty wing."

Aelius refrained from answering. The coincidence, he did not know what to make of. And he was not so much evaluating the opportunity of an association with Decimus as he was wondering about the relative distance from the barracks, where his Guardsmen would remain. But the Palace district was even farther off, and it was true that they did ask a fortune for an efficiency. His colleague perceived the hesitation, and capitalized on it.

"It has a separate entrance, comes furnished and with house staff, has small but perfectly appointed baths. And I just redid the crawl space, so there is hardly any mildew."

"I'd like to see it first."

"Well, I happen to have the keys on me."

NOTES BY AELIUS SPARTIANUS:

Went to see the place Decimus is renting on Vicus Veneris. It'd be a miracle if it weren't musty, I thought, because the north side looks over a canal. The water all but touches the outside wall, and only the fact that it will freeze soon will keep moss from creeping up it. For the rest, it may well be that it is nearly four hundred years old, as its owner says. There's scarcely any marble used in the thresholds, the floors are plain white mosaic, and the baths are built on the scale of men shorter than where I come from. Doors are low, windows small. But except for a small malfunction of the heating pipes, correctable in two days' time, everything is in top condition. The house serfs are so retiring and discreet that I wonder who last rented these rooms.

In the bedroom, the sole decoration on the black walls is a painted frieze, very old, perfectly done. The frieze represents erotic scenes among dwarfs and baboons, with the occasional crocodile trying to bite off sensitive body parts. The location is Elephants Island in Egypt, on the upper course of the Nile. I recognize the buildings and the rocks, the rapids, and the herons flying above them. Smaller guest bedrooms, unadorned, would be useful to place a couple of my Guardsmen within calling distance. His Divinity bade me do it wherever I travel, for the dignity of my charge, and for security as well.

All in all, I am inclined toward accepting Decimus's offer and renting the place. Privacy is ensured by the fact that the door connecting the annex to the main body of the house is not only locked, its keyhole has been sealed.

The narrow street on which the annex looks, made narrower by the open-air canal, owes its name—so says Decimus—to a small shrine of Venus the Blessed, no longer standing, or alternatively, to the brothels that once lined the pavement. Elegant apartments are there now, but one can tell the old use by the large windows at the sides of the doors, where girls would sit on display behind the grids. Such houses still exist everywhere on the frontier.

Today the gladiatorial games in Marcellus's memory begin at the Circus. Already folks are swarming to the southwest of town, bundled in shawls and even quilts, because it's sunny but quite cold. It's odd that the weave and pattern of some of those garments reminded me of clothes woven at home when I grew up. The old historians (Posidonius, Strabo, and others) say that the Celtic tribe of the Boii, after disastrously failing to conquer this part of Italy seven centuries ago, retreated to the Danube. Does that mean that we Pannonians share ancestry with these peasants from Italia Annonaria, who still dress like their un-Romanized forefathers?

Later today I will confirm with Protasius my attendance at Lucia Catula's funeral tomorrow morning, and then bed for the night at the Faunus's Fortune Baruch ben Matthias spoke of. It is an inn patronized by foreigners and those who work in the arena, owing to its nearness to the Circus and the city walls. There, I may be able to gather hearsay about Marcellus's murder and the upcoming execution of the jailed Christians. For them, fifteen in number, the sentence is to be carried out in less than a week in the Circus itself.

From Decimus, who treated it as if it were no more than an interesting piece of gossip, I found out that Lady Helena, whose son Constantine is best friends with Our Lord Maximian's heir Maxentius, is expected to visit from Aqua Nigra, where she reportedly enjoyed the mineral springs. This confirms what I had already learned in the few days I spent at Aspalatum back from Egypt: She is extensively traveling on the Danubian frontier, where many veterans remember her as mater exercituum. And although the role of "mother of the troops" no longer applies after her repudiation, men of my father's generation adore her.

They remember when she rode alongside Constantius in an offi-
cer's cloak, reviewing the troops. Reports are that she occasion-
ally brings her son along, which makes me wonder whether
there is more than nostalgia to Helena's tour. She comes alone
to Mediolanum, at any rate.

The darkness of the room swallowed all sense of direction. Made
deeper by the shuttered small window and a moonless night outside, it
was—if not safety itself—as close to safety as a soldier was likely to
come. Yet the dark, measurable as long as the lamp had been burning,
dilated unbroken to immense dimensions. Aelius felt less at ease in it
than he had bivouacking along Armenia's highlands and ridges, with
the Persian enemy within earshot. Watches on desert nights had been
less void. He listened, lying on his side. He listened as if one could listen to the space around, sounding it for extraneous shapes, because
emptiness he'd long ago learned to sense. If he felt a presence, he was
unable to gauge it. It was not a noise, nor lack of noise. Not a noise
from the street.

Out of the three better cubicles in the small upper floor, only his
had been taken for the night. There were supposed to be no late visitors, no servants that he'd asked for. Aelius listened, holding his breath,
feeling as if muscular tension would give him away by taking up more
space around him. Step, floor tile, wall brushed past. Sounds on these
he knew, and his mind said no. Rustle of clothing, creak of leather, the
friction of metal on sheath: For years his life had depended on recognizing those before they became full sounds. He told himself, listening, that he'd never given a second thought to camping alone at the
edge of hostile territory, or within it; had he not been the only overnight
inhabitant of Hadrian's abandoned city-size villa, which Onophrius
feared haunted?

He listened as if the boundless dark of the night, flowing in through
the inn's walls and out again, extended all around to the edges of the
earth, and yet his ear should alert him of what his instinct *felt*. The
door could be five or five hundred feet away, the stairs a mile to the

south, or the distant north. Flint and oil lamp, another continent. Floor tile, wall brushed past. No. Step. Step, maybe. No.

The odor of someone who'd come in from the outside, and had crossed the street at a place where mud pooled. That place, slick square of paving, presented itself to him with the clarity of a hallucination, a spot just so, which, coming here, his horse had disdainfully moved left to avoid. The waning light of day had slapped a gray-blue eye of reflection in the watery mud, and the neutral, dead odor of dirt had drawn an unlikely, faultless line from the street to his nostrils. Aelius could only go by that faint trace of mud, not an intruder's smell. Nor could he tell how many.

Jumping out of bed would create a storm of covers pushed aside, and he was not one to crawl under them to the foot of the mattress, making himself small to offer a minor target. Motionless, Aelius waited for the moment before a blow, when by necessity some rustle would signal it to him. What noise does an arm rising make?

A motion perceived as it crossed the dark above him. Aelius stopped the blow about to come; the following one became caught in the quilts, glanced off the boiled leather of his army vest. Aelius bound the sheet around the attacker's arm, pulling him in. The man became unbalanced and fell forward across the bed, at which time Aelius knelt up to hit him with his joined fists. To the right of the bed a blade bounced off, clacking on the floor, but it was Aelius's army knife, recognizable by sound, slipped out in the confusion from where he kept it under the pillow. The other blade in the quilts, wherever it was, could be as dangerous as if still wielded. Bodies surged together—his and two more—grappling blindly without a word, fists and kicks ungluing from the tangle what was needed to strike.

Then a truncheon or something like it struck at random. His wrist seemed to explode into sparks with pain. Aelius kicked hard; the wall gave out a hollow sound when the man's body slammed and bounced off it. His wrist hurt and white sparks kept crackling up from it, but it was not his wrist only. Aelius saw himself precisely—precisely— digging his heels into the horse's side as he went over the barricade at

Gallic Meadows, over the rioters' upturned faces and bending backs, and yet this time he did not land squarely, reining in the mount, but went capering forward head first. Head first. He'd seen troopers die that way during charges. Head first against the hard paving stones. Head first. Amber and honey flowed on him, as they had on the poem's prisoner insect.

5

Notes by Aelius Spartianus:

What I felt on my face during the attack was blood and not honey, but sweet and sticky all the same. The bed, as I saw when I came to shortly, and fumbled about for the lamp, resembled Caesar's toga on the Ides of March. I did not bleed so profusely, nor had I tracked gore out to the hall, not having left the accursed cubicle where I let myself be surprised. To this moment, I have no recollection of having used my army knife (I do recall it falling on the floor, instead, out of my reach), but the blade was stained nearly to the hilt, so I must have. Blood, as I say, had been tracked up to a certain point of the hall, where it stopped, in the middle of the wooden planking. The hooded cape one of the two fleeing attackers had been wearing lay still where it had fallen. Madder red army cloth, but not an army cut. The first impression was that a badly wounded man had reached a certain spot and hesitated there, before dissolving in air (see below).

The blow to my head had broken the skin, that's all—I received worse knocks during basic training. Even when I had the wound attended to, the rift in my scalp merely hurt and pulled.

It is my truncheoned right wrist that worries me, because—even though no bones were fractured—I feel it useless as far as effectively fighting with it (and even writing, for now at least—I am dictating this). The Circus's physician was the closest available; summoned by the innkeeper as soon as the commotion got everyone up, he confirmed the relative smallness of my problem. Would he speak otherwise, when he is used to caring for charioteers with broken backs and run-through gladiators? With his exclusive style of bandage, he assures me, not only will my wrist ache less: In a week's time it will return to full motility. We'll see.

Matters would have gone differently had I not been wearing the anti-riot vest (a whim on my part, choosing to sleep with it on). The knife blow deeply sliced the leather, but had it met flesh, I wouldn't be here to speak of it. Still in the quilts I used to grab it from the attacker's hand, the blade is common, bone-handled, was filed down to a razor's edge. The innkeeper assures me that he "sleeps with one eye and both ears open," so he called out the alarm as soon as he heard the scuffle. It's the sole thing that accounts for the fact that I wasn't finished off, unless:

1. *They realized I was the wrong victim.*
2. *They did not want to kill in the first place.*

Anyhow, as far as I can reconstruct the events of the past night, they went something like this:

—*3rd night hour: Spartianus retires to Faunus's Fortune inn, by the Circus; he occupies alone the second floor.*

—*9th night hour, more or less: Two men attack him, and a brief scuffle ensues; attackers are interrupted and/or choose to escape, one of them wounded.*

—*10th night hour: Everybody is up, night watchmen are summoned, and also the physician.*

—*Through the 12th night hour: Inn and the surrounding streets are effectively searched (see below for details).*

—Balance: Good judgment and poor judgment mingled in my behavior. In fact, while I wisely presented myself as an anonymous army colonel to the Faunus's Fortune, I decided at the same time against having any of my Guardsmen stay with me.

The abovementioned innkeeper, a man from the lake country north of here, fears repercussions. As soon as the confusion abated, he stood there groveling and swearing he did not know how such a thing could happen—as if public inns were ladies' sewing circles! "But your lordship knows how, when there are games, folks come from all over, especially if there's no charge. Judge Minucius's widow did things the grand old way, giving out money to all those who attended."

I, who had meanwhile solved the small detail of the vanishing blood, was doubtful about a random attack by occasional thugs. "How many would know of a trapdoor in your roof?" I inquired, and, holding before his eyes the hooded cape I'd found, "What can you tell me about this piece of clothing?"

He replied it is "homespun found anywhere around the city." Which is possible, given that Mediolanum produces government-issue *sagum* cloth, and fabric below standard is probably sold cheaply on the civilian market. According to him, the trapdoor leads to a low attic where wine was kept and fruit used to be laid out to season, but due to dry rot and vermin, the practice was discontinued a year ago. Habitual customers knew of its existence. He pointed out that the nails keeping the trapdoor shut had been yanked out, or rather hammered out from above. This could have only happened before I retired for the night, while the cheers and racket from the nearby Circus would cover more than hammering.

As the innkeeper came downstairs with me, to a ground floor still crowded with customers and serfs detained for the time being, the night watch came in to report that a man's body had been found in the washery not far away, by the round end of the Circus. So out I followed them, in the dark that still sealed the district, with a fierce wind channeling along the towering race-track wall, and a mercilessly clear sky.

The man, in undistinguished civilian clothes, leaned over the edge of the open-air tub, with his head underwater, as if he'd dragged himself to that point to die. But the physician, following at my request, declared after a quick exam by the light of the torches that he had reached the spot alive and drowned, possibly because he'd swooned, falling with his face in the water. "Could he have been forcibly held down?" was my question. The physician, who along the way had paid close attention to the amount of blood dripped by the fugitive on the street, answered that it was possible, but given the hemorrhage it would have been easy to finish him off. The wound, we saw, had in fact reached him under the rib cage, an expert blow from below with a half-turn of the blade. It's the sort of stab-and-twist wound I have inflicted in combat, but not exactly the casual blow I am likely to have given during a scuffle in the dark.

It was one of the night watchmen in our group who recognized the dead man once his face was illuminated. His words, which I reproduce faithfully, were, "If it isn't the shop boy at the Greek butcher's, under the Circus's arches! A brain the size of a lentil. To participate in an attack against an official, he must have had even less sense than I thought."

As for me, no trace of the other attacker having been discovered, I am beginning to form a hazy idea of this incident. It is now close to the end of the first morning hour, and something tells me I will receive visits soon.

In the crude morning light, the head of criminal investigator Sido looked more menacing than it had inside his office; a Minotaur's head,

Aelius thought, bull-like, with a neck as wide as his nearly shaven skull, roped with muscles. Judging by the way his eyes bulged from the orbits and were bloodshot, the steam room flush was still on him.

He came by with two *speculatores* at the pearly edge of sunup, to ask what happened. As no one had summoned them, and this was a routine case not requiring their competence, Aelius searched their faces for smugness or satisfaction. But they were only hard, seamed faces one would not want to sit across from in an interrogation room. They were already informed of the man's body found at the washery.

"Some stags ran off last night from a bakery by Porta Ticinensis." Sido used the slang term for runaway slaves, fists on his hips, looking up and down the alley in front of the inn. "Coincidentally, we caught all but two."

"I doubt my attackers were slaves. They lowered themselves with a rope through a trapdoor from the roof to the upper floor, which is why I did not hear them climb the stairs. Trained well, because they made no perceivable noise across the planking between the hall and my bed. I couldn't be so stealthy myself."

Sido wetted his lips. The meaty, pink point of his tongue, too, resembled a ruminant's, as it layered moisture on the mouth. "Slaves are stealthy by definition. Besides, houses are crowded on this alley, as you readily see, so attackers could easily walk from one roof to the next. Impossible to discover where originally they came from. Why, the corpse at the washery has got a cheap ring on him, low-grade bronze or copper, no bezel, just a button-like decoration. They make them by the thousands on the Danube."

"Well, he wasn't from the Danube but from the butcher's stall down the way. And one of the two at least had crossed the street at the head of the alley, coming to the inn. I smelled the canal mud on him."

"There's canal mud everywhere in Mediolanum."

Whether excitement or the able care received was responsible for it, Aelius felt no pain whatever in his head or wrist. But he fretted. He watched Sido's bulky figure lean against the inn's wall, where a brightly painted, merry goat-footed Faunus entered a nymph from behind. "It seems to me, sir," he said, "that an attacker of mine should have had more marks and bruises on him. I did defend myself."

"Perhaps you punched the other, or did not hit as hard as you thought, with the dark and all." Sido spoke with his arms folded, a stance that made his shoulders look huge. "The hale one must have pulled his wounded cohort up the rope, through the trapdoor, across the roof, and down the side of the trellised house one block from here. There are bloodstains between the trellis and the washery. Once abandoned because of his weak state, the man died. Let us not seek complications over a random nighttime attack in a disreputable inn. You escaped with your life, and in such lucky cases, as they say, the rest is sauce over a good steak. If there is news about the matter, you will be informed."

NOTES BY AELIUS SPARTIANUS, CONTINUED:

I am not convinced. It puzzles me that a perfect fool was some-how convinced to participate in a risky assault on a random victim, and that I did him in without having recollection of it. Besides, it is true that blood stains the pavement from the trellis to the washery, but I detected no blood on the trellis itself, nor any evidence on the ground of displaced roof tiles, dirt, or other matter from the eave above.

No sooner had Sido left with his associates than I hurried to the butcher's stall under the Circus's arches, opening for business just then. When I arrived, the butcher was foaming at the mouth. Ranting to himself that his shop boy was nowhere to be found, he used colorful expressions the lightest of which are reported here. "The son of a whore, I will split him in half! I've got ten hog carcasses to cleave and he doesn't show up! He didn't even sleep in his cot, son of a bitching whore," and so forth.

As he'd begun a threat aimed at the bastard who delayed his employee, I thought I should say, "You're looking at him, butcher."

"Legatos . . . Strategos . . ." (I notice how I rise in rank exponentially when civilians try to endear themselves to me.) Turning and seeing my colonel's uniform, the Greek butcher all but made me chief of staff, changing his tone and his tune. "I meant nothing by it, sir. It's just that I can't understand what you'd want with that no-good idiot of mine." Before I could answer, some perky spirit returned to him. "But if he's committed some fool thing or other," he specified, "I'm not paying for it. Before the law he's a freeman employee, so do with him as you please."

"It seems I did."

After I concisely reported the facts, the butcher gave himself to trembling and muttering in Greek. With another about-face, he swore up and down that his boy was big but harmless, a bumbling idiot who kept his old mother (I expected the old-mother detail) by an honest day's work, gladly running errands for anyone who'd pay him a copper. "The brain of a flea, my lord! Wouldn't know how to climb a roof to save his life."

"But he can cleave ten hog carcasses."

"Under supervision, high lordship. Strong, but so clumsy I had to make sure he wouldn't smash the cutting block in two."

This was all very interesting. I showed him the knife used in the attack, and he seemed not to recognize it. "Not a butcher's knife, with this file job that thins out the blade. Apart from the excessive smoothing, they make them like this in the valleys west of Lake Larium."

"Well," I said, "did your freeman at least tell you last night whether he was to run errands for anybody before morning?"

The butcher acted as if my question were extravagant. "No, but he wouldn't tell me nothing ever, exalted Commander: He was unable to speak from birth."

With that intriguing additional detail in mind, I walked

back to Faunus's Fortune, where I am determined to spend a second night. Head of criminal police Sido, minus the speculatores, was standing on horseback at the street corner, where his shadow drew long in the rising sun. Waiting for me, obviously. And whether he referred to my returning to the inn, or to my initiative to inquire at the butcher's, his sole words to me were, "Do you know what 'cease and desist' means, Commander?"

In his room at the barracks, where Aelius had come to gather his books in view of his move to Decimus's annex, Duco listened, and said he did not like the look of things. His red eyelashes were so thin that his eyes looked like worried rabbit eyes, set in a worried-rabbit freckled face in general. "A nice bump," he remarked, "and it's a good thing it bled. Blows to the head that do not bleed are dangerous."

"It may be a nice bump, but it makes me furious. It makes me furious that they surprised me in my own bed."

"Whom did you inform that you'd spend the night in that hole? And *why* did you, in the first place? Holy Diana, you could have shared my quarters. Bumpkins and Jews stay at the Faunus's Fortune, not officers!"

"I had my reasons to stay there. And I told no one. Not a great idea in retrospect, but I did not even tell my Guardsmen."

The Briton cracked the door open, looked around the balcony, and pulled the panel shut again. "If it's the *speculatores* you ran afoul of, rank won't help you much."

"I know. In Egypt the police were on the take and more brutal than highway robbers. In Europe, in a capital city, I assumed things were different."

"Don't make me talk, I get in trouble enough as it is. All I can say is that Sido is not one to forget a wrong: even a perceived wrong."

With the excuse of supervising the serfs sent to take Aelius's luggage, Curius Decimus stopped by to see him in the officers' mess at noon.

Holding a kerchief to his nose in disgust, as he said, at army greasy spoons, he made it clear that news of the attack had made the rounds in Mediolanum. "Had you stayed at my annex, none of this would have happened."

"I'd have stayed in your annex, had the last-minute trouble with the pipes not delayed things."

"*What?* I will pass over the fact that you seem to suggest some kind of involvement on my part. But suspicious tenants annoy me, and I will require three months' advance rent."

"And I will be thankful to you if you do not put words in my mouth, Commander. I imply nothing, and said exactly what I meant: Trouble with the heating system delayed the start of my tenancy."

"Jesus, how can you eat in this place?" Decimus waved the bunched kerchief in front of his face. "What do they serve, hog feet in fish sauce?" He laughed, showing his small, stained teeth. "Why did I say 'Jesus'? I don't know, Spartianus, it's a Christian exclamation. I find it droll. In case you change your mind about tonight's lodgings, I can put you up in one of the guest bedrooms."

"No, thank you. I will come as agreed tomorrow at the fourth morning hour, bringing a three-month rent deposit." Aelius was beginning to feel the sting of the wound on his scalp, and his right arm and shoulder had grown progressively sore. His colleague's disdain of the food and drink encouraged him to finish his watered-down army wine. "Say," he added, to provoke, "I have it from a traveling correspondent of mine that your lady relative incurred a regrettable incident at a checkpoint in Belgica Prima."

The news, briefly explained, did not appreciably alter Decimus's humor. "As far as I am concerned, it's as if she ran away with the acrobats, when she became a Christian. She deserves the respect due to a rope-walker, or a juggler." He stood from the bench with the same derisive smirk he'd allotted the mess hall. "If I weren't due back to the Palace, I'd indulge in expressing to you how completely and utterly I will ignore her plight if the former Annia Cincia is arrested at any checkpoint for her superstition."

9 December, Saturday

Just as she had chosen to disregard the customary interval of seven days between death and burial in her husband's case, so did Lucia Catula leave instructions for a private funeral as soon as possible after her demise. Its final act took place Saturday morning at the family *ustrinum*, a fenced-in area where a permanent dais was set for the cremation pyre. Its garden, planted with cypresses and bloomless roses, lay adjacent to the Minucii's monument, not far from their estate on the road to Ticinum.

The small funerary complex looked upon a wet meadow stretching between the suburban arena and a time-worn, gloomy temple of Nemesis, while in the back it bordered a modest private property. Smoke rising from the consuming pyre all but concealed the latter's view, but Aelius could now and then discern a low tiled roof among the shiny evergreens. Hadn't Decimus said something about Casta's retaining a small property in this neighborhood for her aged nurse?

The thought intruded idly until the end of the rites, when, having taken leave of Catula's grieving sons, Aelius did not at once take the road back to the city. A hazy sun, the color of a debased coin, glared between clouds enough to light up anonymous spots across the fields, pale tracks and lanes intersecting and bordering estates. Closer in, a narrow track, crowded by dry gorse and other weeds, departed from the *ustrinum* to reach a wayside miniature shrine, then doubled back, skirting the garden with the evergreens. Aelius followed it on foot, leading his horse.

At the southwest horizon, above sparse shrubs and thickets, a chain of azure hills formed a crisp edge against the clouds. Above him, the last smoke from the pyre stretched into a false ceiling, but the stench of charred flesh rarefied. Ahead, from the small enclosed garden, laurels had escaped by dropping their seeds over the fence, so that here and there, as he approached, the lucent dark green of their shoots broke the pallor of winter grass.

Yes, this was the only property matching Decimus's description of the nurse's house. The first domestic sound Aelius heard from the inside was the squeak of a door, then the hurried latching of it. No voices, no watchdogs barking. Unafraid, a crow heavily took flight from one of the laurels. The shuttering of windows clattered next, one after the other, as if the distance between them were covered in palpitating haste.

The overgrown path to the little one-floor house led to a wooden crossbar gate, chest-high to a man, linking the ends of an even lower wall. Unpainted, plain, it was the gate to an old woman's unkempt garden. So concluded Aelius, looking past it without attempting the latch. In a mosaic of black and white pebbles, on the ground just beyond the gate, an improbable watchdog with pointed ears and a hanging jaw pulled at a line of black pebbles, mimicking a chain. CAVE CANEM, it read: *Beware the Dog*, but the *c* in CAVE had fallen out, and now the word AVE all but welcomed the visitor.

Aelius lent his ear to other perceivable sounds from within. Nothing but the slam of one last door came. Old women, scared and forever on the lookout for thieves and soldiers and male visitors in general! Stripping a laurel leaf from the closest branch, he mashed it between his fingers to squeeze the scent from its fibers. The motion made his wrist sting, but he kept fingering the leaf, holding it near his nostrils. The scent was green, bittersweet; a scent of well-kept wardrobes, victory crowns, and days when a murdered man's wife is laid to rest.

Back in Mediolanum, Aelius made one last stop at the barracks to check his mail and to take leave of Duco. The Briton handed him with due respect the purple envelope just delivered by courier. "From His Divinity's residence," he said. Only after Aelius scanned its contents and put it away to reread it at leisure did Duco say there was worrisome news. "Trouble brewing on the frontier."

"What, has the new unit transferred in already? I haven't seen evidence of it."

Duco shook his head. "The officers came in advance, while the troop will be here before nightfall. They were attached as a mobile cavalry wing to the II Adiutrix legion, patrolling out of Aquincum the Vetus Salina–Lugo border road. So they would know what goes on. Not sure whether we're talking another full-scale raid, but the signs are there. Informants from what used to be Dacia report large movements of armed men—few families, no elders in tow—from the Centum Putei area."

One Hundred Wells—Aelius had heard the place-name many times. "My father used to be stationed there when we still held the province. Was there when I was born. It's on the road to the old capital, no?"

"It is. And if the hostiles followed the watercourses downriver—any of the watercourses—they could have started out as far as the farthest steppes of Barbaricum." Duco lowered his voice, speaking behind his cupped hand. "Patrols have been wiped out in such numbers, they're starting to choose them from units that speak no Latin, so they can't ask too many questions."

"Well, we might have to go to war, eh?"

"*We?* I don't know about you, Aelius. Our men, very likely. I could smell a rat when we were informed at the last minute of an entire unit coming from the East. The Maximiani Juniores will be sent in their place, I bet."

Aelius had heard alarming rumors of tribes on the move at Aspalatum, weeks earlier. Instructed by Diocletian to keep the information for himself, he'd said nothing, and neither did he speculate now. "What's the name of the unit coming in," he asked, "and who leads it?"

"It's the Ala Antoniniana Sagittariorum Surorum, under Julius Saphrac."

"Syrian bowmen. But Saphrac is not a Syrian name."

"No, his mother was an Alan chieftain's daughter. His father's from Pisa."

LETTER FROM HIS DIVINITY TO AELIUS SPARTIANUS:

It pleases us that your mission to Constantius Herculius, our brother and colleague in the imperial purple, was so well received in Augusta Treverorum. We are likewise well pleased, dear Aelius, that your travels are proceeding without complications.

You have done well by inquiring of us regarding the treatment you should give to the life of our predecessor Severus. Because in our earlier years we ourselves were faced with rebellion and intrigue, we understand both the necessity for harsh measures against usurpers and hotheads, and the value of forbearance after victory.

Concerning the quality of Severus's sons, be guided by this question: Are monsters begotten by monsters? What about Commodus, who stained the imperial name: Was his father not the most pious of princes, Marcus Aurelius Antoninus, who made of philosophy the weapon and support of his rule? What of Caligula before them, who—although a son of the excellent Germanicus—did not hesitate to bestow senatorial rank on his horse, and shamed the institution of marriage by betrothing his own sister? Did not the Father of the Country himself, Octavianus Augustus, sire the wanton Julia?

Coming to the question of vengeance versus pardon, there is no denying that Severus much exceeded, not only in our opinion, the strictness that his very name and role required. Severity should not become license to rule as a tyrant. Still, this prince's generosity to the army, whose organization he laid out as a stepping-stone to important careers, should be counted in his favor, like his great building projects in his native Africa, on the Danube, and elsewhere.

If, all said, in Severus's life shadows still be more profound than lights, Aelius, so be it, because a portrait is not such if it does not resemble the sitter. The majesty of Rome does not fear the fact that occasionally her princes have been found lacking in

virtue. Without tarrying over sordid details that will not im-
press a sordid audience, but may scandalize the pure reader, we
encourage you to tell faithfully the life of the noble Severus, hon-
oring truth and history.

Because news of your reception at Mediolanum by our
brother and colleague in the imperial purple Maximian will
likely cross this message, Aelius, we reserve our further orders to
you until a later date. Stand ready for them. Know meanwhile
that it pleases us to hear of your inquiry into the strange events
preceding and following the brick-maker's murder in Belgica
Prima. We encourage you to persevere, to keep us abreast of
your findings, and, time permitting, to learn more about the su-
perstitious practice of so-called resurrection operated by Agnus
or Pyrikaios or fire waker, as he is also known. It is precisely to
stem such senseless beliefs that we have to exercise dour disci-
pline on the Christian sect.

Written at Salona, the vigil of the Kalends of December, 30
November.

As expressly stated, Diocletian's answer had been sent before he received Aelius's report of the failed mission at the Mediolanum court.
Still, at a second reading, Aelius had to check his disappointment over
the vacuum that lack of specific instructions created around him, vis-
à-vis Maximian and Sido's *speculatores.* His Divinity's confidence in
his investigative pursuits was the most encouraging element, although
he might have to underplay his official role.

He waited until the day, grown cloudier and chilly, declined toward
evening. The half-empty city streets were run through by a norther
that tasted like snow, and when Aelius crossed into the Jewish quarter,
he met hardly anyone around. Mediolanum's gates would close one
hour from now, which left a span of time sufficient to run his errand
and return.

Thickets shrank into the dim distance already; bogs were undistinguishable from wet meadows and fields. Riding past Nemesis's temple, closed and gloomier at this hour, Aelius told himself by way of an excuse that few things like the locking of doors and windows in a soldier's face get his dander up. What reason could possibly bring him here again, other than compelling Casta's old nurse to open and let him in? More likely than not, the servant knew nothing, concealed like an owl in what remained of her mistress's wealth. Aelius had no specific questions to ask her, no curiosity beyond the crossing of her threshold. Unless he wanted to see the rooms once owned by Decimus's distant cousin, on the vague assumption (or hope, who knows why) that she was as beautiful as her marble forebear in the ancestors' room. The thought crossed his mind. It might be also—no, not outrage exactly; pity, maybe, for the woman stripped and insulted as she traveled eastward with her teacher, who claimed to call up the dead but could not stay a soldier's rude hand.

A last touch of light hesitated in the air when Aelius unlatched the gate and walked the brief space of the overgrown garden to the door, in a whirlwind of dry leaves. One of the two narrow windows on the facade was closed; the other, half shuttered, showed the glimmer of a lamp inside. The glimmer came and went, so it was probably an oil lamp hanging under the inside porch, open to the wind.

To make sure the old woman heard him, Aelius took out his army knife and used the handle to rap on the door, metal against the metal knocker. Nothing, not even a fleeting sound, came in reply. Bringing his ear close to the wooden leaf, he only heard more acutely the rush of wind in the laurels. A series of energetic raps—which he would have to justify if this were after all the wrong house—was finally followed by a grumpy, suspicious voice from behind the door. "Who is it?" Unlocking, unlatching, a sliver of space unhinging between one panel and the other. "What d'ye want?"

Aelius had to lower his eyes to make out a shadowy wedge of wrinkled face, peering at him. He asked, "Is this Annia Cincia's property?"

"No, mine. What's that to you?"

"Let me in."

That was all it took for the old woman to let out a strangled yelp. "Help, thieves! Killers! Murderers! Help!"

Aelius expected the frantic try at slamming the door once more, and promptly drove his right boot into the crack. With his knee he pushed the panel back by degrees, without exerting too much pressure, because it was after all a diminutive old woman struggling to keep him out. He overcame her easily, entered, and closed the door. "Don't speak nonsense. Can't you see the uniform?"

She did look, squinting in the semidark. Far from seeming relieved by the sight, she fluttered back like a ruffled bird. "Then you're the guards, you're the guards! Somebody help!"

At one glance Aelius took in the old-fashioned space: low columns surrounding a little open-air court, the solitary oil lamp hanging from a hook under the porch, no other exits. "I am not 'the guards,' goose."

"Then you're the head of the guards! Help, neighbors!"

There were no houses within hearing distance, and had there been menservants around, they'd have shown up already. Aelius watched the old woman run around in a patter of slippers, arms waving over her head. She was just making noise out of fear. "Stop screaming." Quickly sidestepping her, he put himself in her way and she ran into him, not even chest-high to his size, a sack of cloth and bones. "I am just visiting, woman." He spelled it out calmly. "No one means to harm you."

She spat at him in a passion. Her fists rained on him, weak and rabid, pummeling his sides; Aelius would have laughed, were he not embarrassed at the way things had turned out, but was just as close to growing angry.

"Issa, that is enough."

That someone else had spoken was unexpected. Aelius looked under the porch in the direction of the voice, and let go of the servant for the time it took her to grab a garden rake and land it on him, ineffectually, to tell the truth, like a combative chicken unwilling to give way.

The woman who had spoken stayed in the shadow; it was impossible to judge anything about her except that her voice was young and well-bred. "Do not strike, Issa. They have found me."

A dull clack of wood on the flagstones alerted him that the rake had been dropped behind him. Out of the shadow he faced, Aelius perceived the stretching forward of feminine arms slackly crossing at the wrists: thin wrists, pale under the lamp, emerging from dark long sleeves so far as was necessary to manacle them.

The motion of surrender unsteadied him. Aelius felt as if the evening had turned a page and was now another evening, strange and unknown, belonging to someone else's destiny, and to another man. "Lady Annia Cincia!" He said the words half asking, half confirming them to himself.

"That is not my name."

"Tonight it has to be, *domina.* It makes a difference to my visit." His other self (whose evening it now was, new and untried) introduced himself, bowing his head as officers greet ladies. Aelius as he'd been until now hung back, stupefied. Her presence, her smallness, her severity troubled him. "I thought—reports say that you were traveling east."

The pale wrists stayed crossed, but her arms lowered slowly. "Who sends you, Commander?"

"No one. That is—I am acquainted with your relative, Commander Curius Decimus."

"A relative, but no friend of mine."

"Well, he does not send me, either. I am here of my own accord, simply because—"

"Caesar sends you: You are Caesar's envoy. I was told your name. You sought me at Treveri already. Why?"

Through the corner of his eye, Aelius caught the furtive movement of the old nurse, giving him wide berth as she went around to join her mistress. "Because of the fire waker."

"He's not here. He preceded me eastward. Are you to arrest him?"

"Why, no."

Time had stopped. No invitation was made to seek one of the few rooms opening on the court, nor to light other lanterns, or simply

move away from the darker and darker porch under which they
stood. The moribund oil lamp swung from its hook. Thanks to it or
to imagination, Aelius at one point caught the glimpse of a cheek in
a severe head covering, and in another moment, a sparkle of eyes
such as sometimes dark women have even in the shade. Not until
now had Sido's order to "cease and desist," and stay away from investigation, sounded welcome to him. He heard himself precipitously
tell Casta of his desire to meet the miracle worker, of Lupus's murder
and other such disconnected bits, linked by inquisitiveness and
nothing else.

Nothing else? *Others* kept watch. Suddenly, the thought that gendarmes or soldiers patrolling after dark might see his horse tied outside the garden and grow suspicious distressed him. He should not
stay, for the women's sake. In order not to renew their alarm, Aelius
finished what he was saying, and then added in a sedate voice, "It may
be unsafe for you to remain here, *domina.*"

"God will provide."

"Allow me to wonder about that. There are twelve Christians awaiting execution in the Gallic Meadows jail."

"I know."

"They stand accused of killing Judge Marcellus."

"I know that as well." Her voice was mild, secure, unafraid. "Christians are taught not to lie: Should you ask me, I could not tell you that
Christians are innocent of Marcellus's death, because it would imply a
knowledge I do not possess."

"It matters little, their days are counted." When Aelius stepped forward to take leave—not planning any contact, even the touching of
hands being unthinkable without an aristocrat's permission—she re-
coiled with a half-turn of the shoulder, head averted, sinking back into
the dark, a figure like Alcestis, the mythical bride called out of the
realm of death. He said, "It's best if I leave. As you are to me the *claris-
sima domina* Annia Cincia of the senatorial class, Pupienus's widow, I
can only apologize for my intrusion and assure you no one will hear
from me of your presence here."

She answered nothing, made no gesture of acknowledgment. Stepping away, she subtracted herself from his sight, noiselessly, like the phantom bride in the myth.

"Now go," the old servant told him gruffly. Before stepping out, on the threshold Aelius thought of his schooldays, how as a youngster he'd chosen to write the essay: *Why should Thanatos have relinquished Alcestis from Hades on the strength of her husband's love?*

When the door closed behind him, a last translucent ribbon of sky piercing the western clouds told him how little time had in fact passed. The rest was clouds, darkness under the laurels, cold wind. His horse's patient click of hoofs where it waited, tied in the back, brought him back to himself. This was his old evening again, Aelius's evening. And it would be Aelius's coming of night.

It had begun to snow when he rode through Porta Ticinensis, just as they were pushing it closed.

At the head of the Vicus Veneris, lights and smokeless torches in their brackets formed a fiery necklace along the wall of Decimus's house. Far from taming the illumination, wind and the twirling snow made it more fantastic, a fairy-tale splendor that was nearly blinding after the dark districts Aelius had crossed. He led the horse around the corner, to the paved piazza by the main entrance. The space was crowded with elegant litters manned by hooded, burly slaves, horses were being stabled, and the doors opened to a bustle of guests. The noise of a party flowed from the severe entry hall, bright with lamps and braziers, where ceremonious butlers stood in their holiday clothes. More than a party, it seemed a traditional, grand Roman feast, judging by the scented to and fro of handsome freedmen in short furs, the girls' squeals from the inner halls, the music and laughter.

The head of Decimus's staff waited for him at the annex's doorstep, quiet and dim in comparison. He informed Aelius at once that a bath and change were ready if he so required. "Master inquired whether you were in, Commander, in case you wished to join the feast."

"What is the occasion?"

"Master's birthday, and an early start to Saturnalia."

The calling out of the alphabet, shouted from inside, loudly betrayed the repeated birthday toasts to each letter of the host's full name. "M . . . A . . . N . . . I . . . U . . ." The girls let out high-pitched little cries, no doubt because glasses were flying around, to be smashed for good luck.

Aelius unclasped his army cape. "Bring my thanks, good wishes, and regrets to your master; I am tired and not well."

Three hours later, the party was still raging beyond the wall that separated the wing from the main house. Litters and slave teams had all left, so Aelius assumed that guests and entertainers would spend the night, or stay up until morning. He'd bathed at leisure, read, started a reply to Thermuthis, and now sat in a cozy little library, thinking that Anubina had been "dancing at men's parties" (Thermuthis's words) for six months when he'd met her. The fact would not ordinarily keep him from dinners where girls sang and danced naked and slept with the guests; tonight the idea was unsavory, even though he was not as tired or unwell as he'd said. Head and wrist hurt a little, that was all. Celebrations jarred him, at the close of a day and evening that threatened to change things in more than one way.

The autobiography of Severus, which he'd been marking in anticipation of using it as a source, had long since become a jumble of words escaping attention, and Aelius set it aside. Closing his eyes, with an ear to the cheers of "Long life!" he saw the smoke of the funeral pyre rising from the *ustrinum,* the overgrown path behind it, Nemesis's temple. Broken images from the day just past and from other days rose before him like flashes in the dark.

Tedium turned to irritation when music and the rattle of tambourines grew to a pulsing rhythm, popular in Egypt and a must at officers' parties. Four beats always repeated, with emphasis on the third, increased in speed to create breathless expectation. Anubina, dancer that she was, disliked the tune. For the same reason, during the Egyptian campaign Aelius cringed whenever he heard it, unwilling as he was to accept that she had been auctioned off at the sound of such music. Men, she'd told him, had lined up to touch her between her legs to make sure, probing her carefully advertised virginity as far as the madam allowed, until a wine merchant from Alexandria bid an extravagant amount of money to uncork her, as he put it, in front of the company. "But afterward I was drunk, Aelius, so I don't remember much. I don't even know if it hurt."

In the Rebellion, the merchant had sided with the usurpers and raised a militia, and those facts—not counting in Aelius's eyes as much as his private grudge, those days—supplied the unhoped-for, honorable justification to cut his throat in battle. He'd never told Anubina, but Thermuthis knew, and it was the only time he'd seen the brothel-keeper afraid of him.

Thus the festive noise vexed him because of his Egyptian memories. But Aelius would lie to himself if he didn't admit that he was thinking, too, of the other woman, standing in the dark of the lonely house between the temple of Nemesis and the arena where her companions would be executed soon.

10 DECEMBER, SUNDAY

In the morning, no sign of life came from the main house. Aelius had finally fallen asleep, he who never let go during a poolside rub, under the kneading of a big-handed masseur on Decimus's staff. He awoke at the usual time, after strange dreams of forcing doors only to meet with other doors, each of them promising a wild party beyond, and then opening on darkness and silence. During breakfast, he learned that Decimus's birthday was actually not until January, but he had decided to celebrate it early, "along with early Saturnalia."

"Does he anticipate his birthday often?" Aelius asked the compunctious freedman.

"No, sir. This is the first time."

Along Venus's Street, the snow cover lay nearly untracked. Water ran murky and slow in the canal, between crisp rims of white. Above the roofs of the old brothels, the morning sky shone cloudless, and sun would melt the snow by midday at the latest. Faint sounds of harness from around the corner indicated to Aelius that the first party guests readied to leave. It would be a race between the sun and the feet of litter-bearing slaves, wheels, and hoofs for the mashing of snow, he thought.

Within the hour, the Guardsman he dispatched in civilian clothes to the Circus came back to report that the butcher's stall under the arches had not opened for the day. Shop owners nearby gave different versions, two of which were privileged: He'd been seized for the role his idiot employee had in the night attack at Faunus's Fortune, or he'd run off to avoid arrest.

"Any clue to an upcoming return?"

"None, sir. The fishmonger two shops down says ten hog carcasses were hauled away yesterday evening at closing time, and that was the last they saw of the butcher as well. None of the merchants will say more. Going toward Faunus's Fortune as by your orders, instead, I ran into an unanticipated commotion just before reaching the inn. Children tossing snowballs had chased one another in the narrow spaces between houses, it seems, and stumbled upon a dead body."

Aelius had been dressing to go out and now stopped with his fingers on the bootstraps, frowning. "Not the butcher's!"

"No, sir. One of the idlers said the dead man was a known face, a branded thief. Run through the chest as far as I could tell, and not yet or no longer stiff, apart from the effect of the cold. I overheard that a group of Jews was the first to come by after the children, but hurried back to their district, to avoid trouble. By the time I arrived, the gendarmes were removing the body and let no one stand near."

"It seems an even worse neighborhood than I thought." When Aelius buckled the belt on his tunic, his bandaged wrist sent a sparkle of pain to the elbow. "What about the Minucii *ustrinum*: Did you check the paths around it for tracks?"

The Guardsman confirmed. "Aside from the main road, where the

snow had already been driven and stepped upon, there was no disturbance anywhere around. No human tracks around the arena or the
temple of Nemesis either, only the trail of a fox."

With two of his questions answered—regarding the fate of the
butcher and Casta's safety—Aelius planned his day around a visit to
the Jewish quarter, officially to browse through used-book shops. In
fact, he meant to look for Baruch ben Matthias. His Guardsman reported that the Jew had checked into the Faunus's Fortune the night
before, alone. Local relatives, however, had come to greet him in the
morning, and he'd gone off with them and his luggage.

Curius Decimus had bags under his eyes, looked not one but ten years
older, and said his head felt "as large as the feather-filled balls girls kick
on the beach." He met Aelius already mounted, as he wearily climbed
into the saddle to reach his post at the Palace, late as it was. "Why
didn't you come?" he asked with a yawn. "It was a smashing party—
they'll be talking about it long after we're gone."

Aelius wondered at the meaning of the comment, whether it signi-
fied the memorable quality of the feast or something else. "Was it a
spur-of-the-moment idea, celebrating the holidays before their time?"

"Yes. Didn't you hear the scuttlebutt? Rumors of war precipitated it.
We were notified that several of us will be leaving for the frontier
soon—most of the friends you've met already." Decimus adjusted the
issue fur cap on his head, smoothing the hair on his temples. "You
must have known it was in the air, coming as you did from His Divinity's summer seat. Was it why Our Lord Maximian would not receive
you? In any case, the barbarians are rambunctious again, and it sounds
like a threat that we had best not ignore. So—call me superstitious—I
decided to celebrate early and share the unbeatable triplet of dance-
cunt-wine with the friends I love. Riding my way?"

"Only to the end of the street. Is there a scheduled time for moving
out?"

"No, and we aren't yet mathematically certain that officers of the Palace Guards will go. It stands to reason that Our Lord Maximian may want to contribute with the flower of his troops."

The ironic tone was out of place in a man in Decimus's position. Aelius took note. If it was Maximian who set up this jaundiced officer to do his fact-finding, no wonder his guests rushed to proclaim their loyalty to the State; the trap was too visible to be stumbled into. But Aelius did not have to pretend to speak as he did. "We're in the business of war, whatever uniform we wear."

"True, true. Nothing like an honest-to-goodness barbarian raid to make Marcellus's death and your investigative itch seem puny and out of place."

What would he do if he knew I met his cousin last night? Aelius discreetly avoided staring at his colleague's blighted after-the-feast looks. *Would he insist on hearing where she hides? Would he turn her in?* Keeping the information to himself gave him a pleasant edge this morning.

"The *perfectissimus* head of criminal police, Sido, has already pointed out the inappropriate nature of my curiosity." He allowed himself to grin. "He seems to think it will suffice to make me quit, even without the barbarians' help."

Decimus gave him a spiteful look. "Don't smile just because you have nice teeth." At the head of the street, where they parted ways, he replied to Aelius's farewell with a careless wave, leading his horse down the opposite direction.

"You're asking me? Little old me? I'm just a poor Jew."

"You're a Jew, but not a poor one, not by a long shot."

Finding ben Matthias had been easier than expected. His name was well known in the Jewish quarter, and after satisfying questions from a number of menacing young men, word of mouth brought Aelius to the right doorstep in a dead-end street barely wide enough for a man to stretch his arms out. Presently they sat facing each other in a smoky little kitchen, going through the routine of claiming to have happened here by chance on one side, and to be surprised that anyone would ask him for information on the other.

Ben Matthias framed Aelius's inquiries about Lupus's case in his own perspective. "Well, I am not happy about it, if that's what you mean. My son-in-law spent some uncomfortable moments explaining in detail to the local *speculatores* where he was, and with whom, between the time he left work in the evening and the early morning when he went to awaken Marcus Lupus. Only because he has friends in high places who are willing to vouch for those in low places who vouched for him was he able to prove that he was not involved. My daughter, who's expecting, gave us all a scare by having fainting fits. As for Lupus's brother, Commander, I wish you hadn't asked. He was one of the worst, pouring insults on Isaac only to remove suspicion from himself. *They're Germans,* I told Isaac when he went to work at the brickyard, *I don't trust them. Can't you be a supervisor for somebody else?* But, no, he had to work for Lupus, damn him to Gentile hell."

"And now?"

"And now, I don't know and I don't care. The family will grease the right palms to quell rumors and inherit Lupus's wealth, which I'm sure they feel they deserve. After all, they showed the world how disinterested they were, after they hired the fire waker to resurrect their relative the first time around. The most visible result of the entire business is that even a moderate like Constantius has lost patience with the Christians. Miracles create unrest, and besides, he's listening to those who accuse the fire waker of black magic. He and his girlfriend Casta fled barely in time, being charged now with conjuring evil spirits against Lupus to make him ill, faking a resurrection, and then killing him out of their 'hatred against humankind,' the time-honored charge made against Christians. The price is being paid by the Treveri church fathers, who have been arrested en masse."

Aelius studiously removed his cloak. "Black magic is nonsense. Philosophers say it does not exist."

"Right. And I believe in one God rather than in a bunch of divinities. Most people beg to differ, Commander. I am telling you, I left Belgica Prima a week after you did, and made sure I shook the dust off my sandals. Ugh, I *wish* it were dust. It was snow, and plenty of it. We have it good here in Mediolanum by comparison."

Studying his guest, ben Matthias did not indicate how he'd learned that Aelius had preceded him in the Italian city. Aelius did not ask, knowing that the Jew had his sources. "But what about yourself?" Ben Matthias spoke up with a smirk. "It ought to flatter me that you seek me out. However, much as we collaborated, shall we say, while in Egypt, you're not so enamored of my presence that you would stumble here without a specific reason. Or was it all you wanted, hearing about the investigation in Treveri?"

"Yes and no." Not to show the stitched cut on his head, even though the room was warm, Aelius kept his cap on, and the right cuff pulled over his bandaged wrist. "You've been here only—what? A matter of hours? But you're one to keep your ear to the ground, so I will ask you whether you heard of Minucius Marcellus's death."

"Ha! Who hasn't. He ruled in favor of the Jewish community in a case over water rights, so they told me all about his murder at breakfast. I'm shocked to hear it. Still, it's a good thing he was prosecuting Christians and not Jews, else I'd be packing from here as well." Ben Matthias stood to kindle the fire in the open hearth. "I can tell you right away that more than one man was involved, but probably no more than two. One would be watching out for other visitors and bath serfs, while the other did the judge in. Was the murder weapon found?"

"No. They might have rinsed it in the hot pool, and smuggled it out as they brought it in."

"Did they search for it around the Old Baths?"

"They said they would, but I wonder if they did. When I went inside, I saw a bloody imprint on the wall, rather smudged. At first I assumed it belonged to one of those who lifted Marcellus out of the

water. The serfs I spoke to—before they were so speedily beheaded—
denied that any of the baths staff leaned against the wall, but who
knows. His freedman Protasius did not touch the body at all. It could
have been the killer who propped himself up after stabbing his victim.
If it's true, why would he do that? The murder of a slumbering old
man cannot have been too strenuous."

"Maybe the murderer is overweight, or suffers from vertigo." Ben
Matthias was joking, because Aelius's confidence in his sleuthing skills
flattered him and amused him at the same time. He waved the burning
tip of a wooden stick as if it were a brush. "Maybe he stumbled because he had a limp, and had never heard that the fire waker could
make him whole. Hands differ from one man to the next, but a
smudged imprint isn't much use. Did all five fingers leave a mark, at
least?"

"Yes."

"Right hand or left hand?"

"Left hand, I'd say."

"You could be seeking a left-handed man. Or not. Are the Old Baths
of the type that allows men and women to use them at different
times?"

"No, too small. Only men may use them."

"Well, there goes my idea that the weapon could have been hidden
somewhere inside and carried out by a woman accomplice at a later
time. Are you sure you want to keep your cap on? You're sweating."

"I'm fine, thanks. No, no one could have taken out the weapon after
the body was discovered. The baths have been closed to the public
since the murder. And nothing the gendarmes found on the premises
could be linked to the culprit."

"What do *they* think about the hand imprint?"

"They're so dense as to say that it was Marcellus himself who left it.
It's unclear how he could do so, given that he was stabbed in the water
and did not have time to do anything but give up the ghost."

"Policemen—you've got to love them."

Aelius shook his head. "I said *gendarmes,* Baruch. The criminal police isn't saying a word about its investigation, and even warned me to mind my business."

"Is that why they sent a couple of hoodlums to knock you over the head at Faunus's Fortune?" Smiling in his beard, ben Matthias pointed to Aelius's cap. "I had the cubicle where you slept at a discount, because guests are scared of spending the night in it. It seems that ruffians fall from the sky around that inn. Early this morning, while I was coming here with some relatives, I saw that someone had been thrown from the roof down the interspace between two houses."

"So, you were one of those who first saw the body: I should have known. Why do you say he was thrown down? He could have been stabbed on the ground."

"No. A freshly broken roof tile had landed on him, and others lay smashed under him. I say that he was left dead or dying on the roof the other night, and the snowfall caused him to slide and tumble down."

"That's impossible! *Two* men attacked me, and I can't have stabbed both without remembering."

"Perhaps you stabbed neither one of them. In my old fighting days—don't ask for details, as my archenemies were the Romans, back then—I found myself once or twice in the unpleasant condition of having to *silence* my companions after an especially delicate mission. Beastly unpleasant, but has to be done. I don't think the fellow on the roof was supposed to rain down before the spring."

"You may be right." Aelius tossed his cap on the window sill. "Until then, the butcher's boy would be blamed officially, and who questions the reasons of an idiot? He was probably only hired to stand watch and provide a useful corpse after the deed. That's why I detected no blood on the trellis: The poor fool had never climbed to the roof in the first place. Counting him, there were three, and only one was supposed to return. But why go through all this trouble and not slit my throat at least?"

"You're Caesar's envoy. It would not look good. And all you did was try to meddle in the *speculatores'* open-and-shut case of Marcellus's death. For now." Turning his back to the hearth, the Jew rubbed his hands. "At least, that's all I imagine you did. It was supposed to appear as a random aggression to the world, but give a specific message to you. I may be off course, Commander, but if the criminal police had for whatever reason killed the judge, they would not have hesitated to cut you down as well."

6

Notes by Aelius Spartianus, written on Monday, 11 December, Feast of Agonalia:

After listening to ben Matthias, the question of the murders appears to me even more intricate than I surmised. On one side we find the victims: Lupus, "resurrected" by Agnus the fire waker and supposedly friendly with the Christians, and Marcellus, whose sentences against the Christians were believed by some to be too mild. On the other side, someone who killed Lupus, and someone who killed Marcellus. Why do I want to see a connection between these two deaths? Apparently there is no logical link.

Some coincidences do exist: One of the brick-makers underbid by Lupus helped with his expertise Marcellus's ruling against the fraudulent Modicia brick-maker. The latter sent a threat against Marcellus. Am I missing something, or am I making this connection up, as Decimus says? Speaking of Decimus, he is related to Agnus's assistant Casta but anti-Christian, conservative, and no friend of Marcellus's.

On the surface, it appears that animus against Christians may lie behind both murders, especially as they are suffering the consequences of them. And yet there's the accusation of black magic against the fire waker, and Christians were convicted of planning the judge's death. Even Casta does not discount the possibility, or at least she is not willing to say her fellow believers are innocent. Although no real proofs were brought against them, and the sentence was hurried at best, this in itself does not guarantee the innocence of those soon to die in the arena. What else does Casta know? How do Christians behave, when confronted with the choice between telling the truth and exposing one of their own? She was ready to surrender to the authority of the State, represented by me in her eyes. It's like the Christians not to resist arrest—they elude it at most. Why? Baruch ben Matthias says that the church hierarchy in Treveri was effectively decapitated. The same is happening in Mediolanum. Cui prodest, in Decimus's words? Only possible answer for the moment: the conservatives, who have long been preaching the elimination of these zealots.

Anyhow, the Jew promised to keep me abreast of any rumor filtering out from the Christian community: Is there a group this formidable rogue has no friends or informers in?

Taking advantage of the holiday, which keeps gendarmes and police busy downtown, this morning I rode by the Minucii's monument and ustrinum. I was bound to the arena, curious to see it close up. I was, like all officials in town, sent a reminder to attend the public execution of the Christians, which is to take place on the fifteenth. Because that date, marking the sowing-time feast of Consualia, is what the priests call an endotercisus dies, unfavorable morning and evening, but favorable at midday, the execution will take place at noon. If a snowfall does not intervene, it is likely that the show will take place as planned.

There's an army saying that goes, "The world is not so large that you can ever be sure you won't meet someone you know." Imagine when you go to a neighborhood visited before! Paying her respect to Marcellus's and Lucia Catula's ashes, as it seemed, Casta's feisty old nurse stood at the edge of the funerary area. I recognized her by her diminutive size. All bundled in black, she resembled one of the witches Horace speaks of in his verses; were I superstitious, I'd have stayed well away from her. Instead, I approached and, after praying to the Manes of the dead couple, looked at her meaningfully. She did not return my stare. All she said was, "She's gone. Gone gone gone," with such malicious satisfaction that only fear of me must have kept her from bragging about the way her mistress managed to escape. To be sure, if Casta is headed eastward, she will try to avoid the cities of Brixia, Verona, and Vicentia, following the road to Aquileia in order to avoid the mountain passes out of Italy. It will be the same route the army, and I, too, will follow in a month as we travel to the frontier. His Divinity's second message has in fact reached me, yesterday afternoon. It acknowledges without comments His Tranquillity's refusal to receive me at the Mediolanum court, and directs me to leave the city as soon as possible, when chosen Mediolanum units will move out. This is according to my wishes. During my few days at Aspalatum, after sailing back from Egypt, I did in fact ask that he look favorably on my intention to return to active duty. One long year and a half has passed since my return from a military campaign. I may be "you people" to the likes of Curius Decimus, but feel so strongly my love for Rome that leaving the intrigues of civilian life for war sounds more exciting.

Duco, who anticipated the date of his wedding contract, invited me to meet his bride and family. The little girl is scarcely older than Thaesis, Anubina's daughter—and mine, unless Anubina swears to me that someone else fathered her. Meeting her for the first time, my red-haired colleague seemed less than taken with her betrothed. The girl's mother, however, is a florid woman with all the attributes that may make a Briton (or a Pannonian, for that matter, or a Roman) anxious to enjoy his marital rights with her. I told Duco that the little girl will

probably resemble her in a few years, and he cheered up consid-
erably. A personal parenthesis: Several weeks have elapsed since
I enjoyed a woman's company (my good Stoic teachers' euphe-
mism for what I first did with heart in mouth in a little brothel
at Poetovio, with my father waiting outside to keep an ear on
things). I believe myself rather good at controlling my passions,
but temptation is what it is. Perhaps I should have joined Dec-
imus's party—some of the girls I saw stumble out of his doors in
the morning were authentic beauties. Still, Mediolanum is a
place where Venus must feel at home: I am confident about my
opportunities for lovemaking. Having heard from colleagues
that Constantine's mother, Helena, will be here in a couple of
days frankly makes my desire more acute, as a few years ago she
was an accomplished lover, and to all reports she is still beauti-
ful and man-crazy.

This afternoon I am off to the Palace, where I asked for an
interview with the head of criminal police. That well of all gos-
sip, ben Matthias, hinted at multiple layers of entanglement
and competition among imperial offices and their holders, but
from the outside they certainly give the impression of a wall as
solid as those surrounding the city.

Perhaps Sido was satisfied that Aelius had followed procedure in order
to be received by him, or else he was in a good mood. He freed his spa-
cious office of the underlings who occupied the other desks with a curt
"Out," then gave a pleasant nod to the visitor.

"How is the wrist, Commander? Are we on the mend?"

"Yes, thank you."

There was no chair on this side of the desk, likely because the majority of those brought here had no hope of being treated as guests.
Sido came around the paper-strewn table and stood at arm's length
from Aelius. He was armed, an unusual detail in a man of his rank, in
a secure office, within such a well-guarded imperial residence. A blade
narrower than, but as long as, an old-fashioned army sword emerged

from a plain leather sheath at his belt. Its ivory handle was actually closer to a sword's grip, carved in the shape of an eagle's head and feathery neck.

Careful not to stare at the weapon, Aelius explained he had come to hear whether there was news about his attackers. "I appreciate your assurance that I would be notified. Still, what can I say, I am anxious to hear your professional evaluation." Saying the words without sounding sarcastic was something he had practiced in his bedroom several times upon awakening. Sido's suspicious gray eyes searched his face, although composing his features to serene neutrality had been Aelius's second exercise.

"It's a rough area around the inn," the policeman said, rocking on the fores and soles of his boots, relaxing enough to clasp his hands behind his back. Why not? He had no reason to fear, since Aelius had been thoroughly searched not once but twice before reaching this office. "They fish corpses out of the canal now and then, Commander. Men with assignments like yours may come to see themselves as privileged and distinct, and assume that what befalls them is also special. Believe me, despite our efforts on behalf of the good citizens of Mediolanum, what happened at the Faunus's Fortune happens virtually every night in one or the other of the city's inns. Even if we should find a connection between the branded thief and the attack against you— well! A thief is a thief, and does what thieves do. When we climbed to look for traces in the attic, we also checked the roof above. No corpse lay there at that time. How do you explain it?"

I don't, and I think you're lying, Aelius said to himself, without elaborating. "Those who first saw the body say his neck was broken."

Sido looked behind Aelius; he made a sign to someone standing at the door, or out in the hallway—a dismissive wave that meant things were under control. "Affirmative. The fact that my men did not discover him during their search, the morning after the attack, tells me he had nothing to do with your accident. And even accepting the possibility that he ever was on the roof, clearly he slipped and killed himself by falling. Happens to the best of thieves."

Ben Matthias, in his brief examination of the corpse, had recognized an injury to the neck that might or might not derive from a fall. *They could have snapped his spine on the roof all the same* had been his comment to Aelius. *Someone, though, stabbed him in the stomach beforehand, and I wager it was his blood that you saw in your bed and on the floor.*

It was not a detail Aelius found wise to share. He took note of the policeman's silence about the stab wound. "The body," he said, "could have been artfully wedged on the roof until the snow displaced him."

"Not necessarily." Sido reached for a piece of paper on his desk distractedly, placing it flat and even with the edge of the wooden surface. Either he loved order, or else he needed a moment to adjust his expression to the lie. "The interspace between the two houses is small, and full of garbage. A perfect place to conceal someone killed down the street, in a neighborhood where folks tell the authorities nothing if they can help it." He glanced up at Aelius, who in turn was wise enough to be found staring at a corner of the office. "Why do you insist that there is a connection between this corpse and what happened to you?"

Aelius had had just about enough. He would rather Sido admitted his role behind the attack, because rough play—even within a inch of killing—is admitted between men of action. "With all respect, *perfectissimus,* I suggest a wild hypothesis of mine, namely that there were three confederates, two of whom actually participated in the assault. One of these two, the branded thief, was killed right off to eliminate a possible witness, and soon after the same happened to the butcher's boy, who kept watch by the trellis below. The third man escaped."

A small muscle pulled the skin under Sido's right eye, contracting and releasing. "Excellent!" he visibly forced himself to say. "That is *clever*! Now we have *three* criminals, two of them being too few for a victim like Caesar's envoy. If it weren't fanciful nonsense, I'd ask you to consider the possibility of lending your deductive abilities to the State, joining the *speculatores.*"

The joke made Sido regain his good humor. When he amicably

placed his hand on Aelius's shoulder he must have felt the stiff hardness of his muscles, no matter how the visitor tried to pretend calm. "You flatter me, *perfectissimus*," Aelius managed to squeeze out of his tension, "or at least I think you do. Is there any word on the Greek butcher, the employer of the man I seem to have killed?"

"None. But a slimy Greek is a slimy Greek: You can be sure he won't be found, Commander."

I bet I can, Aelius thought. *You'll make damn sure he's never found.*

His powerful grasp still on Aelius's shoulder (he could break the bone in a quick, single move, there was no doubt in his mind), Sido accompanied him to the door. "Do stop by if you have any other suggestion for us. You and I will see one another at the execution, won't we? We both owe it to the judge."

12 DECEMBER, TUESDAY

"You will not refuse me again, Spartianus. I forgive you for snubbing my birthday, but tonight I celebrate the vigil of Tellus's day, and Mother Earth is a goddess none of us can disagree about."

The invitation to dinner, so affably and straightforwardly presented, left little room for Aelius to wiggle. He promised Decimus he would come, bought an illustrated copy of Eliodorus's *Ethiopian Tales* as a birthday gift to him, and attended the elegant get-together in the company of those Decimus called *amici quasi fratres*, his brother-like friends. The officers Aelius had already met were there, plus three more, whose scrutiny of him went beyond the mild curiosity they could feel for Caesar's envoy.

If reclining on dining couches was becoming a thing of the past, here it represented only the first of a series of traditional ceremonial features. Finding himself between Decimus and Ulpius Domninus on the middle couch, the place of honor known as "the consul's seat," confirmed to Aelius that his assignment was acknowledged. The menu followed the ancient division of entrées (Decimus had chosen flounder from Ravenna, pond-grown pike, and peacock eggs), three main courses (boar, hare, pheasant), and sweets (preserves and honey apples). Warm and cold wine, mixed with water and honey by handsome boys, was passed around in goblets from the Rhineland, intricately decorated with outer reticles of spun glass, wishing long life and happiness the Roman way: BIBE VIVAS MULTIS ANNIS, VIVAS FELICITER.

Throughout the reception, chatter seemed directed in subtle ways. With the excuse of the coming war, and of going east, much was made of each guest's background and career, travels and acquaintances. Aelius watched Decimus direct his friends in the choice of food and drink like a chorus master, and waited his turn with the unease of the outsider among men who know each other through family, education, service in the same unit.

It was not the self-consciousness he'd felt when first seeing Rome from the Aurelian Way, so overwhelming that he'd spent the night outside the walls, but rather insecurity, provoked by this game that was midway between braggadocio and the male marking of the post Pennatus the brick-maker had spoken of in Modicia. Thankfully laughter and idle comments interrupted the telling of this or that campaign experience. The twins' assignment to the same command made for a hilarious comedy of errors that included a general officer's wife; Decimus's own disastrous encounters with Caledonian cuisine peppered his tale of harsh frontier duty.

When Aelius's turn came, the uneven attention paid by the guests to one another's stories became a nearly uninterrupted silence. Eyes rose toward him above half-empty plates, full glasses; men who had seemed tipsy took the keen posture of listeners. Sarmatia, Egypt, Armenia, Persia, the days at court: Decimus encouraged him to speak of those experiences no differently than he'd done with the others. Yet, and it was more than an impression on Aelius's part, his telling attracted a scrutiny that only politeness separated from a test. The sense of being evaluated remained with him even after repeated toasts put an end to the comparison, when the cheers to emperors and army units became maudlin wishes to faraway courtesans and girlfriends, and boy lovers for those who had them.

At the close of dinner, the host's absence from the table for the se-
lection of more wine created an odd parenthesis that made more acute
Aelius's feeling of exclusion. Ulpius Domninus opened it, the way one
takes up an old conversation about something that continues to puzzle. "Nothing doing, gentlemen. Our Decimus keeps the secret so well,
I say we abandon our bets, or else put the *speculatores* after him."

"Why?" Lucius Sinister, who had drunk more than the rest and
struggled to stay propped on his left elbow, patted his couch like a cus-
tomer asking for another glass. "We could add Spartianus to the wager
instead: He makes good money as Caesar's envoy, I'll bet."

His brother, next to him, laughed in his glass. "If *we* haven't found
out in years, how's a newcomer to figure it out? You don't even know
what we're talking about, do you, Commander Spartianus."

Answering that he didn't, or a self-conscious protest against gossip,
would accentuate his otherness. Aelius said nothing, with the result
that he heard of the mystery anyway. It surrounded Decimus's daughter, whose existence he had never even mentioned to Aelius. She was
fabled in the officers' imagination as very rich and proud, being the
sole heir, of such beauty that her father kept her locked up like Danae,
so that neither man nor god could take her, so learned that it would be
shameful for a woman to exhibit similar knowledge in public.

"Some of us think her name is Plautilla," a tanned man called Vivius
Lucianus said for his benefit, "because Decimus's first wife was called
Plautia. Some swear it's Portia. We just don't know. She probably lives
in another city, or here under another name. He won't say, and we can
only wonder."

"Why is it necessary that you know?"

Aelius's words snipped a tense rope. Ulpius Domninus laughed.
Had a provincial recruit put his feet on the table, he wouldn't have
looked more amused. "What do you mean, why? We're *curious*. Isn't a
pyramid or a labyrinth or a sealed box there to be forced open? Of all
people, you should live by that dictum!"

Months it had taken Aelius to trace letters, documents, to undo lies
and deceptions, to discover where one sepulcher lay, which coffin to

unseal in order to know the truth. His last mission had shown him the terrible nature of secrets, and not because he'd nearly died in the process. "Forgive me." He tried to speak without arrogance. "I feel no need to unravel this particular secret."

"But would you *tell*, if you unraveled it?"

"No."

After everyone left—even Ulpius Domninus, who tarried longer than the others—Decimus watched Aelius take his cape from the venerable old serf in the cloakroom. "You hold drink well."

"It's not a virtue."

"Not a vice, either. Drinking to oblivion is a vice. Won't you stay a little longer? Talk of old times makes me melancholy."

Aelius found the excuse thin. "It was you who evoked careers and campaigns. We could have spoken of Mother Earth instead." But he did follow Decimus to the ancestors' room.

How does it happen that in the middle of the night men who know one another imperfectly speak more freely than they would to friends? Aelius took it as the next level of fact-finding on Decimus's part. He kept his restraint even when the disproportion between confidence given and that obtained in return grew too large to be of use to his colleague, never mind how tempted he was to reciprocate.

"If you read the founding fathers, Spartianus, you realize how far we have come from our ideals, our original design."

"Well, it depends on which founding fathers you refer to. Romulus and Remus? The Seven Kings? Or do you go back to those who sailed from Troy to found a new world on Italy's shores?"

Decimus wagged his head in denial. Weariness and drink made his face sag; the left eye, particularly, under a lid that wanted to close. He was at the age when men keep themselves up by massage and exercise, but the artificial freshness of the morning does not last. "You know exactly what I mean. The Republic, the people—the *will of the people* intended as citizens. Look around yourself: We have no idea of who or where or how many hundreds of thousands are coming through the borders any one day. You have to strain your ear to hear Latin spoken in most cities." He made a pause, correcting with an apologetic rise of an open hand the impression of contempt he had given. "I don't mean people like you, yours have been romanized for a couple of centuries."

"My mother's folks, perhaps, not my father's. On Father's side I haven't a drop of italicized, let alone romanized, blood. We can't all go back to the times of the Punic Wars like yourself, and know by name all the generations that came in between."

"You see what I'm coming to."

No, it was less than clear what Decimus was coming to. Through the years Aelius had heard similar opinions from civilians, conservative politicians, the occasional urban hothead. Complaints, critiques about the ugly present after the good old days, and the lack of respect younger generations had for their elders. The military cared less in that regard. Integration was a part of its reality, serving together against the common enemy. "I suppose you refer to the composition of the border legions, then," Aelius said. "To the fact that they are often manned by people from the same tribes they're to guard us against."

"Why, Spartianus, in Asia and Africa it's the rule. You fought the Rebellion in Egypt, you know."

"Yes, and we won. If you're pining for the time when everyone was Roman and the enemy dwelled on the next hill over, ten miles off, you have to reduce by much the size of the Empire. To—say—Rome itself and its very first colonies."

"You're telling *me*? Centuries ago, it was my ancestor Dentatus who bowled over the goddamn Samnites, and was awarded a house with thirty-two acres on the Quirinal Hill for it!"

"I like it this way, with half the world in our hands, and the other half trying to become us."

Decimus tightened his lips. His weary mask became fixed and for a moment resembled the ancestral faces lined on the shelf behind him. "That's where you're wrong. They're not trying to become us: They will empty us of our language and age-old customs until we are nothing. Or until we are just like them, which is worse than nothing."

"May I remind you that fourteen out of seventeen emperors in the last thirty-six years have originated in the Danubian provinces? They're Roman princes."

"Roman, my ass. Not even Italian, some of them illiterate."

Aelius felt blood drain from his face, a sign of anger he did not like in himself. "I have not heard what you said."

"Do you wish me to repeat it? Or do you wish me to put it in writing, since you can read?"

Notes by Aelius Spartianus,

written Wednesday, 13 December:

Memorandum: No matter how well you hold your drink, drink half of that.

I came within an inch of striking Decimus, against all regulations and only because drunkenness protected him from the more serious charge of treason. A crash of broken glass caused me to turn as I stormed toward the door, ready to confront him if he tried to throw something in my direction. In fact, Decimus had fallen backward from his chair; he'd hit his head against the corner of the small table where drinks sat, collapsing it and the lamp stand nearby. He lay on the floor with his eyes half closed, in a swoon or a stroke of some kind, I couldn't tell at the time, losing blood from behind the ear. The noise attracted the cloakroom serf, who, aged as he is, ran in to help. He muttered that it happens to his master once in a while, after drinking parties or long wakes. I lifted Decimus's head to examine the wound, an ugly glass cut that needed stanching. His head lolled like a dead man's, and although his eyes were open, I doubt that he saw me or anything else.

The house physician took it from there. When I checked on Decimus's condition this morning, they assured me that he's

*better, yet forgetful of everything that happened after the arrival
of his dinner guests.*

*At midday, while I was reading the autobiography of Severus
(like all self-celebrations, much in need of exegesis and critical
commentary), I received an unexpected visit by the Minucii's
freedman, Protasius. After seeking me in vain at the barracks,
where Duco directed him to my new address, he came on his
own initiative to ask whether I have any influence on the Mediolanum judiciary system. I answered truthfully that I have none.
Besides, Marcellus's successor has left for the winter holidays,
and the fate of the Christians detained at Gallic Meadows is
sealed. For all his protestations of having left the superstition
behind, Protasius clearly feels for his old fellow believers. Losing
the leaders of the local church—the bloom of the* kleros, *as he
calls them—will in his judgment cripple the movement for years
to come. I replied that such is in fact the intent of the authorities, even if murder is the official charge.*

*Regarding this, he is adamant: The culprit is to be sought
elsewhere. (Fulgentius Pennatus, brick-maker in Modicia, remains his chosen villain.) He did admit that two out of three of
the Old Baths serfs, already executed, were reputed to be Christians. "Couldn't one of them have killed your master?" I asked.
He stayed mum. When I tried to walk him through the moments before and after his discovery of the judge's body in the
hot pool, Protasius gave me a description as vague and emo-
tional as the first time. He looked for footprints, uselessly. He
took ill. When I mentioned the bloody imprint of a left hand on
the wall, he gave me a blank look. Was he so overcome with grief
and dread that he did not notice? It's possible.*

*Keeping as neutral a tone as I could, I then inquired about
the working relationship between Minucius Marcellus and the
criminal police. He defined it as "correct on both sides" but in
no way amicable.*

It always makes me uncomfortable seeing an old man,

whatever his status, standing while I sit. Protasius and his bad back, however, stood before me throughout our conversation, at the close of which we stared at each other for a long, embarrassing moment. I was thinking that the Minucii's house is not far from Casta's refuge, and wondering whether the freedman knew anything about her brief visit; he looked back as if on the point of sharing some information. Did he read my mind? He told me that, recollecting my interest in the fire waker, he has been looking into his old papers and found nothing. (I bet he's cleaned his drawers of religious drivel, these days!) However, he added: 1. That Agnus thundered against Judge Marcellus in a fiery brief to his Mediolanum fellow believers, and 2. that he could obtain a copy of what he calls a "pastoral letter" written by Agnus to the Christians of Aquileia some time ago. Would I be interested? I said I would. While he spoke, pain, worry, pity, any or all of those affects were on his face. On mine, I venture to say, were my usual curiosity and a less than spiritual concern, a mixture of the impression I received from the (beautiful?) deaconess, and the growing, worldly anticipation of Helena's arrival late tonight.

14 DECEMBER, THURSDAY

"Fresh from the baths—I can smell how clean you are."

Flavia Julia Helena had not changed in the two years since Aelius had last seen her. She had never been beautiful, thus time used her with a courtesy not granted to great beauties. So, at least, thought Aelius, who had studied the portraits of the empresses of the past. Augustus's wife and Hadrian's wife, and even Severus's Syrian bride, had gone from being delightful girls to frowning matrons, if sculptors did not lie; and it was unlikely that they would portray them as uglier than they were.

The former imperial concubine Helena, gray-eyed, with her rich hair still dark and lustrous, a swimmer's body, and long-fingered hands, maintained what attractive looks presumably she had always had. Judging by her outfit, she still spent a fortune on clothes (Constantius paid the bills to make his repudiation of her more palatable), and even more on jewels. Once Aelius had seen her wear so many drop-shaped pearls that she had seemed to him the goddess Artemis Ephesia, with her many pendulous breast-like ornaments from neck to waist.

Upon meeting him at court ten years earlier, she had considered him one of the handsome young officers who habitually caught her eye, and made him pine for days before taking him to her rooms. Off and on, they'd been lovers for a summer, although he was not the only one, of course, she was giving herself to. And if Aelius's father (and not only he) said he remembered full well when Helena served drinks in her family wine shop, she was an emperor's former concubine now and—unless gossip was altogether mistaken—stood to be a usurper's (perhaps an emperor's) mother soon. No doubt she was here to further her son's imperial bid.

In the elegant inn outside Silver Gate, where she had stopped overnight, they embraced and kissed on the cheeks, then on the mouth, and when Aelius pulled back at last "out of elementary prudence," as he said, Helena lightly gave him her permanent address in the city. She was here to see her old friend Curius Decimus, she said, and a few other acquaintances, over the holidays. "You know," she added, wagging a finger at him, "back then I chose you because you were attractive, not because you were smart. Smart men are as rare at court as anywhere else: Why should I be looking for one of them in Nicomedia? I haven't made up my mind even now whether you're smart or not. And I haven't decided whether I'd want to have a lover who's even marginally as intelligent as I am."

"Well, I am obliged. The next thing you'll tell me is that in Nicomedia you meant to check my teeth and hoofs before choosing me from the herd, but in your kindness decided to spare me."

"Oh, I had your teeth checked, and—well, not your *hoofs*, exactly. Do you recall the military physical you underwent when first called to court? It was not required, but I thought it'd be nice." She laughed. "I have size requirements, and such. Why do you look embarrassed? You men do the same the moment you step into a brothel, or gossip among yourselves about your girlfriends, to hear who's narrow here and big there. I heard my share in my teen years." *My teen years* was Helena's way of referring to her past as a wine-shop maid, even though Aelius had heard her once or twice say *my apprenticeship.* "You say you know Curius Decimus: I can tell you about him, for example."

"No, thank you."

She stroked his cheek with her knuckles, back and forth. "You do outsize him if not outlast him, but he has a couple of tricks you haven't—unless you learned them in the meantime. Stay away from him, Aelius. He *is* a smart man, and there's no telling what he might do with his cleverness. And don't trust him, he'll seduce you. No, not in *that* sense, in a political sense." She stepped back. "Now go. I have to change, and my girls are so clumsy, they're useless."

Aelius watched her open a trunk, leaning over it with a rather seductive posture of buttocks and hips. "Wait. What about this matter of outlasting?"

She spoke without turning, elbow-deep in frothy cloth. "Uh, nothing, nothing—you *were* a baby after all. In a hurry."

"I'm not in a hurry now."

"We'll see. I'm staying a few days, so it's possible—" Helena did not complete the sentence. It was her way of speaking, he remembered. She would keep her options open by hinting at a probability without saying exactly what it could lead to. Her voice trailed into a "hm-hm-hm" sound of suspension, leaving a blank space for her interlocutor to fill. Aelius decided it was best not to tell her he was staying at Decimus's.

She flung around veils and light cottony stuff. "You're one of the few I stayed friends with through the years. I want you to know I did feel sorry for your mother, having you in my clutches for that whole summer."

"She never even knew."

"Do you think so? A mother's heart is a mother's heart, Aelius. She feels everything her child needs, and does." Helena turned, suddenly impatient. He couldn't tell whether she was giving in to impulse or voicing a well-pondered decision. "Come by this evening: I'm bored. Nearly all the mineral springs I visited were full of pious temple attendants and priests, with the nasty habit of keeping an eye on you. I haven't had a man in two weeks." She tossed a black, sheer fabric over her head, and when it fell lightly down, draping over her, she stood covered to her waist, visible as behind a dusky haze. "I had to make do with a dull officer from Spain who was at Aqua Nigra to cure an infected ear, and wasn't half-happy with him. Aside from his ear, I mean." Kissing him through the veil, she unbuckled her knees, so that he had to pass his arm around her to hold her up. Her tongue moistened the cloth. "I'm sure I don't know how you manage to do without, during a long campaign."

Aelius felt her tongue with his. Alcestis, the poem said, climbed from the underworld veiled in black. *And the veil was both / impediment and invitation.* "I had good teachers, Helena."

"Good teachers, my foot." She squirmed behind the delicate barrier. "Ten years ago you'd already had your education, and it didn't take me long to bring you to bed."

"You made me wait a week."

"Did I?" Her hands moved wisely between them, finding no resistance. "I wonder why. It's sweet of you to remember."

With two fingers, slowly, Aelius pulled down the veil. Her face emerged white, clean; the small wrinkles at the sides of her mouth seemed to him added perfection. "I wore down the floor in front of your apartments. I'd have brained my roommate, had you preferred him to me."

"Well, the idea did cross my mind, of seeing the two of you scuffle over me."

"Scuffle? We were the best swordsmen in the unit, he and I, so we'd end up hacking at each other. And possibly aiming at the best parts we had to offer, aside from our pretty faces." Helena's touch reached for him so daringly, Aelius had to struggle not to groan with pleasure. "I'll come by this afternoon, if you want."

"Hm, yes. Yes, afternoon is better than evening."

She was unfastening and lifting leather and cloth, speaking over his lips. Aelius began to see everything through a swimming redness, as if she'd worn a fluttering scarlet veil over her. Blood roared in his ears. "I'm not hungry either, so—that is, I could come by, I don't know, Helena, even before lunch." The throaty silliness of his own words came as from someone else, because he had come hoping this would happen, was happening, and speaking was entirely out of place.

"Before lunch, what an idea. But it wouldn't be worth your while going home and then hastening back to my place . . . what if we say it's before lunch right now?"

They'd played a similar anxious game the memorable first time in Nicomedia, in a room where there was no bed, only carpets covering the floor from wall to wall, and the cushions Helena had always been fond of. Carpets and cushions abounded here, too, and there was even a bed in this transitory room.

The first time with her, rain was coming. Nicomedia's sky was black at midmorning; wind pushed doors open and shut, made the drapes billow into the room. From the cushion under her, Helena ran a red strip of silk between her thighs, shiny and narrow, as if emerging from that desirable place; she pulled it slowly up to her belly, navel, between her breasts, to her neck. It seemed like a precious wound cleaving her in two. I knelt beside her and took my clothes off with a blind need to cry, trembling to enter her before the rain came.

Crouching naked on the bed, Helena held her breasts, letting her nipples show between her fingers. In most other women, let alone women her age, the coquettish pose would have been ridiculous. In Helena, it was seduction and promise of more seduction. She said, "Aelius, you know I'm right."

"No, I don't."

"You do." Forenoon, noon, and afternoon had gone, dark crowded at the small window, and once more she began to pull down the sheet from him. He stopped her, but kept his hand on hers. "Constantine is the smartest of them all, Aelius dear. He can't be wasting time waiting for the old men to die or to give up, to have his chance. Maximian has no intention of retiring, whatever he told you. He will plot with his son to retain power, and then there's bound to be war, because Diocletian will never allow his co-ruler to hang on to the throne."

"I'd rather not think of it. I've seen the Rebellion in Egypt, and it lasted me a lifetime."

Helena slipped under the sheet to his side. "So, you see that we need a strong man." Kissing and blandishing began again, only on her part at first. "Let Constantine know you care, right now, and you'll both benefit."

Angry at her as he was becoming, Aelius kissed her back, and was already close to not minding what was being said. "You wouldn't be asking me if you thought Constantine could make it on his own. I doubt that my benefit is what you have in mind, or that it's where your heart is."

"Well, so you think, darling. But if you *are* Constantine's friend, there's no telling what you might end up gaining, once he's on top."

"Your son will have to come up with a better reason than not wanting to bide his time, Helena. There's a system in place. He has to re-spect it."

"But, Aelius, Aelius, once a man's on top . . ."

Which was more than a suggestion for the business at hand.

15 DECEMBER, FRIDAY, FEAST OF CONSUALIA, SOWING-TIME FEAST
The glass pane deformed the view. Through its imperfect surface, the

glare of morning filtered green. The sun rising from the mist over
the fields dilated into a pale, watery opaqueness marking the east (the
roads, the border, the frontier). Aelius turned to Helena, seated at her
dressing table.

She pinned her braid up, fastidiously pushing in the wisps of hair
that escaped her knotted, shiny crown. The fact that she had here and
there a pale thread of a steely color—not quite a gray hair—made her
more interesting, more curiously desirable. From her composure, one
would not suspect she had not gotten out of him what she wanted, except physically.

"Whom do you have these days?" she asked, looking back from the
mirror. "I know you haven't gotten married, but whom do you keep?"

Aelius turned to the diminutive window again. Tying his belt, he
was ready to go. In two hours the executions of the Christians would
begin, and he had promised Duco he'd ride with him to the arena. "No
one, in the sense you imply," he answered. "I see women."

"Women. What does *that* mean? Whores, ladies, wenches from
across the border?"

"Not the last."

"Oh, come, Aelius! You're being difficult because you don't want to
tell. It's not anyone at court, otherwise I'd know. Two years ago you
used to woo Ignatia at Nicomedia."

"I don't want to brag, but she actually wooed me."

"Successfully?"

"So so." Regret, or melancholy at least, already carved a piece out of
Aelius's morning. Anubina's name was buried so deeply in him, he
would not pronounce it for the world. "Whom are *you* keeping?"

"How impertinent, from a man who turned gray at twenty-five."
Helena made faces as she put on her makeup. "When I become a
Christian, I will pray for you and your sins."

"Well, Helena, if that day comes, the underworld as we know it will
cease to exist: Tantalus will be able to reach his meal, and Sysiphus's
rock will tumble under his push."

"I wouldn't be so sure, if I were you."

"Yes, of course. If the dead can be resurrected by a charlatan, anything can happen." Aelius was laughing, which was the sole reason why Helena did not grow cross.

When she stepped into the light from the window, her eyes, circled in sooty black, shone like silver. "You just thank your fortune that you're a good-looking fellow, Aelius Spartianus."

"Yes, and I respect the privacy of ladies."

At all entrances of the arena, temporary altars had been set up to ensure that all in attendance would toss grains of incense coming in. The measure effectively kept out Christians and most Jews, but not secular Jews like ben Matthias, whom Aelius glimpsed in the crowd. The old freedom fighter carelessly dug in his nose before catching some incense with the same fingers and sprinkling it on the fire.

"It's the usual thing, when they decide to put up one of these shows in haste," Duco grumbled, pulling the fur cap down to his frostbitten ears. "There isn't a lion to be had in all Mediolanum, and those they sent for at Ticinum, they wouldn't give us. Lions don't do well in this kind of weather anyway, not to speak of tigers. You watch, Aelius, it'll be one of those lame shows that drag on forever, until soldiers are ordered to hurry things up. Saphrac has been told to send a handful of his bowmen. Well, no, they do have some animals. Three bears were brought from Germany by the army last fall, but one of them took ill and died. So they're down to two bears and thirteen Christians."

"Twelve, you mean."

"No, I mean thirteen. There are thirteen spelled out in the program. Look."

"I thought there were twelve arrested for Minucius Marcellus's murder. Who's number thirteen?"

Duco said he didn't know, and neither did he notice his colleagues' agitation. When they reached their seats, Aelius stood up again nearly at once, saying, "I'll be back in a moment." While he battled the flow of people to the closest exit, he saw Helena and Decimus step together into the next sector, acting the old lovers.

The guard Aelius asked said he didn't know, either, but his noncommissioned officer might have names and identities of the condemned. It was not so. "I don't keep a list here, Commander," the noncom explained. "I can tell you there's seven men and six women altogether. One was added at the last minute."

"Who is it? Man or woman?"

The noncom raised his eyebrows. "Do you have a preference?"

Not as long as it isn't Casta. "I am a precise man," Aelius insisted, "with an erroneous program in hand. It piques me that programs are changed without the public's knowledge."

"It's a man, a Greek. Implicated in an assault against an official. Anything else, sir? You *do* know there's only two bears instead of three."

NOTES BY AELIUS SPARTIANUS:

Ordinarily I have no difficulty watching executions. The instructive relevance of public punishment does not escape me, because even those who attend for the worst reason (watching human suffering) understand the message that breaking the law results in swift and dour redress. In my philosophy, pain is inevitable and not to be fled. It is the sight of intemperance in the face of death that disturbs me, as a soldier and as a man.

The unfortunate Greek butcher, whom I regret not having warned to flee after his idiot shop boy did what he did, struggled horribly but at least was killed first. To my judgment, the spectacle of women bound hands and feet, trying to crawl away from wild animals, was especially unpleasant, and a punishment I deem unworthy of our legal system. I was told they were the wives of the Christians arrested in the wake of Marcellus's death. Charged with no direct crime, they chose to follow their men into prison and into the arena, no doubt deluded by the babble their priests write about the glory of martyrdom, and

how their god hands out crowns of roses, and beasts recoil before
the holy.

One of the poor creatures succeeded in getting her wrists and
ankles free—unless the executioners decided to tie her loosely to
add to the viewers' thrill—and started running about, screaming like a madwoman. Not young, fear gave her unsuspected
energy, as we read happens during fires and earthquakes. She
tried uselessly to climb the wooden bulwark that separates the
arena from the first row of seats. She hammered at the wood and
begged those above to help, with the sole result that people tossed
down apple cores and garbage and incited the bears to pursue
her. One of the animals, goaded by a soldier, did before long trot
in her direction. Dull as bears can be, it approached her swinging its head, then lost interest, because those still tied up had
been mauled in great part and twisted on the ground, attracting
it by the smell of blood. For some time this ugly ballet continued,
made worse by the woman's ceaseless cries for help. When she
was finally reached by the beast (I am ashamed to write this),
her bowels were loosened in the extremity of her terror, and even
from the relative distance of my seat was the fouling of her white
clothes most visible.

At this, the crowd roared. Only some of the women, from the
highest rows where they sat with the serfs and foreigners, at last
began to protest. Nothing could be done to save the victim at
this point. Even so, it was a good while before she stopped howl-
ing and contorting in the bear's clutch. Her death made the
beast completely disinterested: Even it had had enough! With a
last sweep it pushed the limp corpse from itself and turned to
those who still waited to be finished.

To my left, as I drew back in my seat, I noticed that Duco was
looking down at his knees, red to the ears in excess of his natural
color. Sweets and drinks were passed around to Aristophanes,
Sido, and the Palace Guards in their box not far from us. Decimus's colleagues stuffed themselves, especially Domninus, who

*stretched his legs over the seats Decimus and Helena had left un-
occupied at some point during the show.*

Ben Matthias, who'd been sitting with the foreign merchants, in their presence indulged in ceremonious oriental greetings, touching his chest and lips. Outside the arena, in the dispersing crowd, he waited until his companions were out of sight and then winked at Aelius. "I am honored that you desire to ride back to town with this humble funerary art entrepreneur, exalted Commander. Pfui." He made the act of spitting. "This mealymouthed talk is *terefah*."

"Unclean, that is? What we just saw goes beyond filth." Trusting his well-healed wrist, Aelius vaulted into the saddle. He had no desire to join Duco, headed somewhere for a drink, while a conversation with the Jew could come in handy.

"And gladiatorial games are all right, eh?"

"Gladiatorial games, I don't mind. It's a completely different thing, Baruch."

Ben Matthias rode a nervy mule. He said little while they filed past the double row of sepulchers flanking the road to Mediolanum. His careful eye evaluated sculpted lintels, carvings; twice he opened index and middle finger of both hands at a wide angle, joining them at the tips to form a frame, through which he could examine the monuments. "Passable decoration, shoddy inscriptions," was his comment.

"Good news for you, no?"

"I hope so." Changing his voice to imitate the pitch of a tour guide, the Jew pointed at the city gate they would reach soon. "The Porta Ticinensis, also known as Palace Gate. Here you may admire the angle tower and westernmost entrance to Mediolanum's walls, where the racetrack forms an additional bulwark with its magnificent mass. Notice its farther end, where the starting-line towers reach the sky. Prepare for the avenues elegant with government buildings! At the other end, modest inns are crowded. Here the noise on racing days is deafening with cheers and the clatter of chariots making the tight curve or running disastrously into one another. The inn called Faunus's Fortune, especially patronized by Jews with business in Mediolanum, was recently the scene of a treacherous attack—"

"Baruch, quit it. I need some information."

"Oh, very well." Ben Matthias wrapped a scarf around his neck. He gently smoothed the curly beard under his lower lip, dividing the strand down his chin. "I understand that you and Lady Helena got together last night, euphemistically speaking. Did you know that for a time she had a Jewish lover in Nicomedia, and liked him so well that she asked her next lover to undergo circumcision?"

Clearly there were Jews among the staff at Helena's temporary quarters, Aelius thought, a little amused by the disrespect. "I assure you I wasn't that boyfriend, Baruch," he replied in good part. "What else can you tell me?"

"About what, Helena, Mediolanum, or politics? Ah, the three of them. I should have known. It is a sad day when screwing a woman does not suffice to make her *reveal* her reasons for letting you do it. So, I assume you are not acting officially, but only out of your own curiosity."

"Why?"

"It makes a difference to what I would or would not say."

"Without compensation, that is. Let's say I am acting purely out of curiosity. No orders from above or anywhere else."

They had come to the busy crossroads in front of the gate, an intersection so representative of its kind that it was commonly called just that, *quadruvium*. Those returning from the arena in wagons climbed down to seek the nearby smoky eateries and open-air sausage stands. Mangy dogs collected swift kicks in return for their begging; still they crouched expectantly in the fat odor of deep-fried pork rind that pooled above the area. Even fashionable litters, curtains drawn against the cold, the noise, and the smell, were stationed by fish-fry stand and wine shop.

Ben Matthias drew back his lips in disgust. Whatever criticism he was about to utter died on his mouth at the sight of his companion, busy buying fried pork in a cornet of greasy papyrus. He breathed out only after the historian began tossing it piecemeal from the saddle to the pack of stray dogs.

"I hope you won't touch me with your hands afterward, Commander."

Aelius glanced over. "I'm still waiting for information."

"Well, let's see. Rumor has it that Helena got it into her head that she will be passed over by no other woman, wife or daughter-in-law. She cannot do much now with Minervina because she just gave Constantine a son, but there's no telling how long the marriage will last. During her mineral springs tour—trust me, I have it from very reliable and very close sources—she tried to seduce every officer and politician she thinks might further Constantine's posturing. She even fucked Maximian's son in hopes he'll take second seat to her offspring."

With a kerchief from his saddlebag, Aelius wiped his hands thoroughly. Winding the reins around his left wrist, he turned the horse back toward the gate. "All this I could surmise on my own, Baruch. What else?"

"Well, they say that whoever killed the much-lamented Marcellus also tried to kill Caesar's envoy."

"Oh?"

"And that the weapons used in both cases were dipped in poison, so that—should the wounding fail—the toxin will work its way through the veins and cause the heart to rot." Ben Matthias took on a look of pious concern. "In your case, if the truncheon they used to knock you out was poisoned, you can expect death to come eventually—say, in a month or so."

"You're making this up."

"I swear I heard it said. Others say the fire waker wants you dead, so he can publicly resurrect you during the feast of Saturnalia, and convert the masses. That he shifts shapes like Proteus, can be in several places at the same time, and is in Mediolanum right now."

What nonsense, Aelius told himself. If the Jew was not lying on purpose, though, he might be reporting distorted rumors about holy people of the Christian sect passing through. It sickened him to think of

Casta after what he'd seen in the arena. Was she really "gone gone gone," as her old nurse said, and safe? And the story of the slow-working poison! No. There could be no such thing . . .

"Enough, Baruch. I want you to check on somebody."

"It will cost you."

The incoming flow of people called for a presence of gendarmes and soldiers at the gate. Aelius nodded at the noncoms who saluted as he passed right through. When the Jew was held back and like everyone else had to identify himself, he did nothing to help him, smiling in his saddle. "While you prepare the bill," he told the Jew as they joined each other again, "keep in mind what *I* know: Although officially a 'funerary art specialist,' as you term yourself, you sign contracts and hold the strings of a dozen different activities. All of them licit, you publicly say, so you 'care not a whit if government agents come to snoop.' I doubt that you don't care. You keep abreast of what happens in the city so thoroughly that someone must whisper information to you several times a day. How's that for counter-information?"

"Average. Whom do you want me to check on?"

7

Aelius Spartianus to Thermuthis, greetings.

I am in your debt for the good news you gave me about Anubina's physical health, and wish you the happiness of the holiday season. Know that even in faraway Mediolanum it is possible to meet officers who have fond memories of their stay in Antinoopolis, because of your hospitality. Indeed, a colleague named Lollus Antiates bids me to convey his warmest affection to you and to Demetra and Thenpakebkis (if I spell her name correctly).

Regarding Anubina's desire to have sons, it goes without saying that, had she not refused my offer of marriage, she would likely be with child now. I do not understand why she does not want to tie herself to me. You have known her longer than I, so I entreat you to explain her behavior to me. As for your difficulty in speaking directly of these matters to her, I believe none of it. You do not carry the name of the Nile's poisonous snake without a reason, Thermuthis. Your wiles are endless, and your diplomacy comparable to those. Speak well of me to Anubina, and particularly insist on the fact that her sons by me would be well provided for and handsome, too (if I may). Her life, as well as her daughter's, would be such as ladies lead.

*Thus I anxiously await further news. In the meantime, I re-
new my wishes of good health and fortune to you, send greetings
to your brother Theo, and ask you that you address your next
letters to the military mail exchange at Savaria, as it will ensure
delivery wherever I may be.*

*Written in his rooms on the Vicus Veneris (so appropriate an
address for a recipient such as yourself), in Mediolanum, Italia
Annonaria, on the festive first day of Saturnalia, the XVI day of
January's Kalends, 17 December.*

18 December, Monday

"I am not one to apologize." Decimus stood at the threshold of the annex when the slave doorman drew back, head low, to let Aelius see who
came to visit after dark. "May I come in?"

Aelius dismissed the serf with a nod. "It's your house."

A sprinkling of snow dusted the cape Decimus had thrown on to
step around the building. He said. "I thought you should know that
His Tranquillity decided to accept your credentials. You have an audience with Aristophanes tomorrow at the third morning hour."

It was unexpected and overdue, but good news. Still, "Why was I
not notified officially?" Aelius asked.

"You will be. I heard it this evening as I overtook Aristophanes in
one of the hallways, talking to his secretary." Decimus removed his
cape and shook it. Nothing but infinitesimal melting bits fell from it to
the floor. He sounded less cocky than usual, or simply not in a bantering mood. "The chamberlain is considerably worried about the way he
received you the first time."

"I see."

The annex opened directly on a small reception room, dimly lit.
Wicker chairs around a low table and the family altar in a wall niche
comprised the severe furnishings. Aelius invited his colleague to sit.
Arms folded, he himself remained standing.

"How is the heating system working?" Decimus inquired.

"Fine."

They had not seen one another for three days, during which the week of year-end celebrations in honor of Saturn and the harvest had begun, bringing cheer and partying, processions and masquerades. In truth, Aelius had avoided his colleague. Now his lack of encouragement, devoid of open hostility, left Decimus little choice. "I get exasperated at times. It's a trait in my character," he grumbled to justify the bitter mouthful that had to follow. "I should have shown respect for the pride you take in your accomplishments."

Aelius stood by his chair. "You don't have to patronize me."

The words were deserved. Decimus reacted to them as one acknowledging the critique, one step below accepting it. "I cannot drink to oblivion as I used to, that's all."

"Then you ought to be careful of the company you keep at drinking parties." It was not the tone Aelius had planned to use in case this conversation should take place. He had meant to ignore the incident and let time roll until the day the army units would depart from Mediolanum; if not, to dismiss the matter as briefly as possible. However, he discovered an edge of anger under his own words, or vexed righteousness. "Whether or not this is an act you put on to test the loyalty of your colleagues, I don't care to be put to the test or be clumsily led onto political ground in hopes I'll stumble. I have been at court off and on since I was nineteen, Decimus: I know the etiquette and the gossip mill, how to respect the first and avoid the second. It may be only a character trait, but my loyalty is unquestioned. You won't catch me off guard."

Decimus had been listening with small, growing signs of impatience. His eyes slid around the twilight of the room, searching corners and objects he knew very well. "Everybody is caught off guard eventually."

"Not I."

"We both have stitched wounds on our heads to prove the opposite."

"Let us not compare the circumstances in which we received those wounds." Aelius came around the chair and sat in it. At the other side of the three-legged table, Decimus must have exhausted the amount of goodwill he had in store for others. Tapping the armrests, he seemed torn between the desire to leave and an inclination to continue the conversation from a different vantage point. In a provocative voice, turning landlord from guest, he said, "*Futuisti puellam meam,* as the poet put it."

Aelius would not let himself even blink. "I could say the same. Helena was my lover as much as yours."

"Well, never mind who screwed whose girlfriend, I am not particular that way." Staring at each other was leading nowhere. Decimus kept at it only because he did not want to give Aelius the satisfaction of lowering his gaze. "Like her Trojan War namesake, Helena will cause men to kill one another on her account, and not only her account. I urge you for your own sake to stay away from her."

"Interesting you should say that. She warned me likewise about you."

"Spartianus, even bedding her isn't safe—although it's damn pleasant, I must admit."

"I promised not to discuss her."

"Really? She thrives on having her lovers compare notes. Believe nothing Helena tells you, even as far as your bedroom abilities, or anyone else's. She always brags about another man in your presence, and hopefully about you to others."

It was another trap in the grass. Aelius stood figuratively in front of it, evaluating the danger and choosing not to step forward.

His colleague mistook it for uncertainty. "What are *you* doing here?" He spoke as if the apologies were due to him. "You come as an imperial envoy, and then you stay, ask questions about matters unrelated to your official business . . . Mediolanum is not so large that such behavior would not be noticed. After your mission to Rome the past summer, officials were arrested here as elsewhere in Italy, the last ones only a week before you came. People suspect you are an *agens in rebus,* but if you are an undercover operative your cover is a bit short."

What nonsense. This is the result of ease and boredom in cities like this. "I do not have to explain my position in Mediolanum to you or anyone else, Decimus. Think what you will."

Decimus continued to tap the armrests, a sequence beginning with the forefinger and ending with the small finger. He darted glances here and there, avoiding Aelius's face now. "So, you're coming east as well," he said.

"I have my orders."

"The names of the officers transferred to the frontier are posted at the Palace, that's how I know. The specific units are rumored to be assigned soon. I am not sure whether it's a prize or a punishment: What about you?"

"Orders are orders."

"Oh, that is enough, Spartianus! I will not have you act as if you swallowed a broomstick. Men who go to war together ought not to behave this way with one another."

Aelius took a deep breath. "That is generally true. So behave as the good comrade at arms, and accept that I will see Helena tomorrow."

"Where, at what time?"

"None of your business."

19 DECEMBER, TUESDAY, OPALIA, FEAST OF WEALTH

At the second morning hour, an obsequious lesser official from the chamberlain's staff came with the summons for Aelius. He'd have waited around to provide proper accompaniment (he had six soldiers with him), had his charge not insisted on coming with his own escort.

A consistent snowfall deadened all human sounds in the streets. Faint lapping noises came from the canal where water met small tangles; belligerent sparrows raised a chirping clamor on a windowsill where they fought over crumbs or seeds sprinkled for them. The clean odor of snow, well known to Aelius from his childhood, acquired from place to place a flavor of burning coals, saplings and sawdust used as kindling, soup boiling in iron pots. Odors related to home and women, in his mind.

But Helena was no doubt still asleep at this time, perhaps alone, perhaps not, and sleep kept her from worrying about this wrinkle, that small sag, the all-important smoothness of her inner thighs. Casta— did what? Brave the weather, sit in a hostile guardpost, pray to her god, think in an offhand way of the officer who'd come to the little dark house near Nemesis's temple. In her blue house outside the city gate, or in her Antinoopolis workshop, Anubina had been up for two hours at least. His mother, the soldier's wife and mother, since before dawn. Aelius impractically hoped one of the four at least was thinking of him at that moment, as he thought of them.

Crossing the Jewish quarter toward the Palace district, he ordered the head of his Guardsmen to carry a message to Baruch ben Matthias. Streets, slippery and mushy in turn everywhere else, had been swept as one approached Maximian's residence; soldiers and Palace Guards stood stomping their feet at corners, in doorways. The canals flowed threateningly high where snow had been dumped into their beds from the pavement

In his diminutive office, Aristophanes was wearing green this morning. The color made him appear underripe, compared to the mellow gold he had worn during the first interview. The embroidered ovals on the front of his tunic represented archers and horsemen, stitched in black with silver thread detailing armor and weapons. Egyptian needlework, Aelius recognized. Anubina's shop produced such minutely decorated appliqués, sold separately or already sewn to fabric.

This time the eunuch made sure to be found standing. His relatively little feet, stretching the cloth of his slippers, supported a mass that was all courtesy, but without apology. As if the first interview had involved two different men, and they were seeing each other for the first time, Aristophanes asked for credentials. No irritable repetition this morning; no urging of the right hand accompanied the request.

Aelius played the game. Direct orders to accept the imperial message had come from Diocletian, that much was certain. It might or might not mean that he would be received by Maximian after this encounter. Likely not, which saved everyone time and embarrassment.

"His Serenity will view the brief from his colleague and brother in the purple, Commander, and will be pleased to issue a response on Wednesday morning." Surprisingly, the Greek accent had all but gone from the chamberlain's speech. Forgetfulness? Admission that pretense was no longer useful? Under the button nose, his mouth drew an upward crescent in the fat of the cheeks, short of a smile.

Aelius bowed his head. "I am grateful to His Serenity for the consideration."

Maximian's bitter reluctance to renounce the throne held with his senior colleague for twenty-one years was understandable. According to His Divinity's irrevocable decision, in less than six months courtiers, bureaucrats, and hangers-on in Nicomedia, Mediolanum, Treveri, and Sirmium would lose their jobs or have to reinvent themselves to please the new imperial foursome. Their clients would tumble in turn, and if the professionals—among these the legal experts and regiment commanders—were expected to retain their posts, loftier heads would have to seek new resting places. The cadres of the criminal police stood to change as well. Overnight, Aristophanes's and Sido's positions were made unsafe.

The meeting with the chamberlain lasted the time necessary to agree on the time on Wednesday when Aelius could return for Maximian's official answer. Acceptance of Diocletian's terms was out of the question; still, much can happen to an imperial envoy even in a few hours. To err on the side of prudence, Aelius planned to send a message to His Divinity before the afternoon.

After the sense of disorientation of his first visit to the Palace, he was starting to make sense of the labyrinth of halls and corridors. There was a sense to the maze: According to the rank of the officials housed therein, marble, travertine plaster, or bricks lined the walls. Name tags on doors, number of guards at the threshold, presence and quality of carpets spelled out the usual self-importance, but May would sweep like a flood through those fragile claims to fame.

At the head of its corridor, the door to Sido's office was open; through it, Aelius saw his empty desk. According to Decimus, Aristophanes's secretary had suggested that the head *speculator* himself convey the news of the summons to Aelius. Aristophanes had pondered the question a moment before saying no. But Sido knew of the change in policy, clearly, and was perhaps more dangerous now than when his position had been unassailable.

Turning on his heel to resume his winding walk toward the exit, Aelius collided against two Palace Guards. They had silently come up behind him, despite the echoing vaults that magnified sounds. "Commander." Just short of hooking his arms in theirs, without explanation they escorted him back to the threshold of Sido's office, hugging his disarmed sides with their thoroughly armed hips.

As though conjured up by magic, Sido was now sitting at his desk. Alone in the room, he acted as if he'd just heard Aelius coming, or simply happened to look up from his papers at this time. His bullish head and menacing bundle of muscles set themselves into a posture between vigilance and aggression.

Delivered by the guards inside the office, Aelius forced himself to mouth a proper greeting.

"Are you in a hurry, Commander?"

"Not particularly, no. I was seeing myself out."

It was hardly true. Aelius had purposely made the diversion in order to look the head of criminal police in the eye. In the past days, under friendly pressure, he'd made Duco the Briton admit what else he knew about him: namely, that Sido took bribes from army purveyors and suppliers. Because of it, the fabulous contract for the construction of the walls (miles' worth of bricks, mortar, iron brackets, ashlar) had grown like bread dough full of yeast. "Sido is tied to the brick business, to the lead pipe business, to the army mule business—you name it, Aelius. See why I say that I get myself in trouble by talking? Do not tangle with him."

Presently the police official pushed himself up from the desk with his knuckles and surged from behind it. "Why leave? Come forward."

If it was meant as an invitation, the tone of it resembled an order. Aelius checked himself for anger. Finding none worth noting, leisurely he detached himself from the guards and walked one more step into the office.

"Closer, closer." Sido's bristly head occupied the center of the Mediolanum wall map, marking the place where the old mint building used to be. "Come closer. You have to see something."

Had Aelius not known better, he'd identify the oblong metal box on Sido's desk as a tureen used to serve fish; Decimus's pond-grown pike had been brought to the table in just such a container. "Closer, Spartianus." When the pot was uncovered under his nose, he saw that salt was packed tightly inside it, under the thinnest veil of brine, and he sensed an indefinite smell of pickle rising from it.

"Here." The chief of criminal police was handing him a stylus from his writing kit. "Look in the salt."

A scooping motion, and Aelius exposed a severed human hand. Wrinkled, pale things that had been fingers formed its inert, blue-nailed appendices.

"Did you think you were the only one who noticed the smear of a bloody hand in the room where Marcellus was murdered? The good thing about the Old Baths is that they require a small staff, and you can quickly run a check on them."

Aelius kept his eyes on the tureen. He felt no disgust—not exactly, given his battlefield experience: malaise, rather, ominous and uneasy. "So, it belongs to one of the slaves who were taken and executed right off." Saying it, he set aside the stylus. "Am I right?"

"No. It belongs to the judge's secretary, the former Christian Protasius. His fingers and the span of his hand matched the smear on the wall."

Malaise came suddenly close to disgust. *He knows the smear could have come from anybody's left hand.* Aelius told himself the words, taking one rigid step back from the desk. *He knows the bloody stain could belong to anyone who'd helped fish Marcellus out of the pool.* "I was under the impression that the Christian clergy was found guilty of the crime," he observed.

Sido took the stylus back. He pricked the dead hand with it, squirting brine around it. "*He* was the one who actually killed the judge. But who do you think enlisted him to commit the crime? Once a Christian, always a Christian. Their leaders take all the decisions for them."

The blue-nailed, pale fingers, shrunken as they were, resembled a woman's fingers. Aelius took another, less steady step back. "Well, I presume this settles the murder case."

"Right." Deliberately, Sido brought the tip of the stylus near his lips and tasted it with his tongue. "I am being transferred to Siscia." He pronounced the sentence, so unrelated to the conversation, as if it were a disgruntled logical corollary to it, implicating Aelius somehow.

"You're fortunate," Aelius commented. Looking away from the obscene savoring of the metal tip became necessary for him. "Iron mines, the weapons factory, the army mint. It's an excellent assignment." Even with his attention on the city map, the spearing of the severed hand was quickly upgrading disgust to nausea. "With your permission," he added, "I have errands to run."

Sido let him salute and start to leave before saying, "Rest assured, Commander, this is not the last we see of each other."

"It hardly ever is, in public service."

"You worked against me."

In theater dramas, the audience shuddered hearing such phrases, pronounced in a hollow voice by the actor playing the ghost or the vengeful god. In real life, the accusation turned Aelius around as if he'd been shoved. "I? What motive would *I* have to work against you?" Never mind that he could think of several reasons, all sufficient.

Sido stood behind his desk, dominating the center of the large empty room. His fists pressed on the wooden surface, giving the impression that with a sudden impulse he could propel the heavy piece of furniture forward, to bowl down his interlocutor. "You will not be forever His Divinity's historian, nor his envoy."

Who knew what palace intrigue was behind Sido's transfer. Surely it had not been done on account of his corruption, much less on the suspicion that he'd planned the attack at Faunus's Fortune. Aelius saw no point in contradicting him, either. In Treveri, Constantius had mentioned his interest in having a scholar on his staff, now that he'd rise from vice-emperor to head ruler. Aelius had reserved his answer until after May 1, because, as he'd said, "Until then Diocletian is my emperor. I grew up with him, and need to serve him to the last."

To Sido, who continued to scowl at him with his fists clenched, he could only tell the truth. "I assure you I had nothing to do with your reassignment, *perfectissimus.*" Choice of words, tone, posture: All three were under control. His eyes—Aelius knew himself well—had the confident, smiling cruelty of the soldier answering a challenge.

Ben Matthias did not want to talk indoors. "Let's walk toward the synagogue," he said. A hooded fur cape made his bearded figure resemble a sly character from myth. Ulysses, Aelius joked, and the Jew laughed. Snow began to come down again, in large wet crystals that fell heavily in straight lines. Compared to the celebrations elsewhere in the city, the Jewish district was quiet, despite the fact that it was a holiday season here as well.

"The men you asked about, Commander—Curius Decimus sees them often. Vivius Lucianus, Ulpius Domninus, and a man who goes by Otho and claims to belong to the Salvii clan, another called Frugi— all I know about him is that he's fat. Plus those two, the twins. Dexter and Sinister, the only ones who are not aristocrats by birth, but are— I am assured by friends who lived in Rome—pure urban stock, plebeians from way back whose father was knighted by Aurelian."

"And what do they do?"

"You ask too much. I'm a smart Jew, not a magician. They're officers, you're an officer: What do the likes of you do when they get together?"

Aelius ignored the question. "They are all assigned to court, aren't they."

"No. Otho is a liaison to the weapons manufacturers in Ticinum.

It's a club, nothing secretive about it. Cato's Sodality, they go by. Have their bylaws and calendar, meet for lunch or dinner at their respective homes, by turns."

"Cato the Elder, or the Younger?"

Ben Matthias shrugged. "I don't know. Does it make a difference? If I read Roman history correctly, they were two conservative pricks, both of them."

At Decimus's dinner, no mention of a club had been made. The appearance was of an occasional get-together among Roman-born colleagues. "Any gossip about their politics?" Aelius asked. "My sideways inquiry at the barracks made everybody clam up."

"No politics that would land them in trouble. Decimus is believed to be a high-level imperial informant, but so are you."

They had come within sight of the synagogue, a smart building at the end of an alley that had private houses on both sides. Neither shops nor public places opened their doors on the narrow pavement. Ben Matthias winked. "We're like Decimus's friends, Commander: We like being among our own. The tenements belong to the synagogue and are rented to people we know."

Aelius nodded distractedly. "Anything else about Decimus?"

"He was involved in a litigation with his relatives over an inheritance seven years ago, Judge Marcellus presiding."

"*Really.* Won or lost?'

"Lost. You'll find the acts deposited at the tribunal."

Aelius's sudden interest was so overt, ben Matthias smirked widely in the grizzled bush of his beard. "See why one can't be friends with a Roman? You gossip and spy on one another. No, I haven't inquired further into the court docket. I'm doing this for free, remember. In other news, my son-in-law sends me word that a scandal that threatens to turn ugly is rocking the city of Treveri. Already several people have been arrested. Isaac himself has taken his wife and gone out to the country. But he has good lawyers, so we hope that all will be resolved as far as they are concerned."

"Is it still about the brick-maker? Does it involve Lupus's heirs?"

"It involves Lupus himself! Several individuals, from physicians to gravediggers, are being prosecuted for lending themselves to the trickery of Lupus's resurrection." Because Aelius had halted to listen, ben Matthias took him familiarly by the elbow. Away from the snow, they stood under a projecting eave. "The brick-maker's relatives are fighting to show themselves extraneous to the affair. They now swear it was Lupus, on the occasion of an illness, who asked that the fire waker be called to his bedside."

"Does it make a difference?"

"It does. However the Christian healer managed it, Lupus did get better. Then he and Agnus hatched a plan to pretend Lupus's death, preparing an elaborate mise-en-scène that would fake a resurrection from the dead. The advantages for the fire waker's career were self-explanatory. There aren't too many holy men, even among the Christians, who can claim such success. As far as Lupus, the idea was that his brickyard would turn popular after he became famous as one who came back from the dead. So there goes the value of my first-issue bricks."

"Leaving out the particulars, it's exactly what I thought had happened. What proofs are there that Agnus maneuvered the deal?"

"An anonymous letter, showing by the wealth of details that it was written by one of those directly involved, reached the prosecutor's office. It seems that even among the Christians the occasional traitor crops up—Agnus must have stepped on one of his comrades' holy toes. Thank goodness Isaac's name appeared nowhere on the letter. The upshot is that Agnus the charlatan is being sought, and—by association—so is his female assistant. And not only in Belgica Prima, where they were last seen. Warrants for their arrest are being issued for other provinces of the Empire as well."

"I see." Aelius resumed walking. He thought of the morning when he'd ridden to Lupus's brickyard, of the veiled women crouching in the wet fields, waiting to see the man brought back from the dead. How he'd looked at them, and they at him, covering their faces. Sounding more indifferent than he felt, he asked, "What role did the deaconess play in the mise-en-scène, do we know?"

"According to Isaac, her name is not directly mentioned, either. The letter is an invective against Agnus's hypocrisy and legerdemain, but Casta *is* Agnus's close collaborator, so . . . Why, even Constantius, who's had such a soft spot for the Christians thus far, ordered the heads of their movement arrested for questioning, on the principle that, if you cannot catch the thief who runs away from you, you catch the thief who's at hand. Trust me, once the authorities lay their hands on them, the fire waker is as good as thrown to the Circus's beasts; and as far as his girl is concerned, they won't stop at stripping her naked this time. I stop here, Commander. Have to go back to work."

"This is all well and good, Baruch, but it doesn't tell us who poisoned Marcus Lupus."

"What does it matter? Send what you owe me to my quarters." Drawing the furry hood closer to his face, ben Matthias made something between a nod and a bow of farewell. "Like bakers, let me add to the dozen a thirteenth bun for free, although I don't for the life of me see why I should bother to warn you: Leave things alone. I haven't come this far in life without being able to smell danger in the air. There's danger here. I can't see its shape, but somehow I perceive its slithering motions. If you thought enemies lurked in the shadows in a sunny place like Egypt, think of how much longer the shadows are in the northern provinces."

Mediolanum's courthouse rose in the Mall, overlooking the Main Hinge, one of the two first streets from the original layout of the city. Because of the holidays, few employees were present. It turned out to be an advantage for Aelius, because they let him search the archives by himself. The building was unheated. Aelius had to walk back and forth as he read this or that list of dockets tied to property and inheritance rights. The good folks at Mediolanum seemed rather litigious when it came to money. Under Decimus's name, four different disputes were listed: *M. Curius Decimus vs. P. Curius Livianus* (two disputes);

M. Curius Decimus vs. Publilia Otacilla (his third wife); *M. Curius Decimus vs. the Estate of C. Pupienus.*

A meager bucketful of coals in a brazier offered the sole relief from the cold of the high-vaulted court archives. Aelius stood with his back to the warmth, reading with growing interest how, claiming an intricate web of entitled family relations, Decimus had tried to prove that Pupienus's widow, Annia Cincia—"barely of legal age, and ill advised by fanatics"—could not dispose of the vast property left by her deceased husband "in favor of parties not connected by blood." The dispute had dragged on for months, at the end of which Minucius Marcellus had ruled in favor of the young widow. The list of property was extensive: from a large house in Laumellum to the villa in its suburbs, complete with fish pond, working farm, horse paddock, pasture and woodland; from private and business rentals in Mediolanum to other pieces of land across the region. All this, presumably, had been given by Annia Cincia to the Christians and, after the beginning of the religious prosecution, was among the real estate confiscated by the State.

That was a small detail Decimus kept for himself, in telling his distant cousin's story. Aelius wondered what, if anything, the late Protasius might have had to report about that dispute. A member of the conservative aristocracy scarcely fit a killer's profile, but a loser's grudge over an adverse ruling was still the most credible explanation for Marcellus's death. Hadn't the Christian hierarchy supplied a useful scapegoat? Decimus's slipping away from the execution at the arena, with the excuse of Helena's company, took on a disquieting new meaning. True, the timing was delayed. Seven years is a long time to nurse murderous discontent, except that Pupienus's inheritance might have seemed not wholly unrecoverable until the recent expropriation of church goods put it back in discussion. Aelius was replacing the dockets on the shelf when his eye fell on a slim document that had escaped him. It, too, was under Decimus's name, and it concerned an act of interdiction of his daughter, Portia, aged twenty-two, "for moral degeneracy."

In a thoughtful mood, he left the tribunal under a thick snowfall, less wet, adhering to everything. Protasius had given him as a city address the rented rooms where he stayed while Marcellus's heirs decided what to do with the family villa. It was nearby, behind the government mint—an edifice closed for the past several years. Walking by its nail-studded bronze door, Aelius thought there was little chance it would open again soon; today, most of the currency needed to pay the army was minted directly in the Danubian lands.

No point in asking whether the poor old freedman had left messages for him before his death. Gloomily Aelius continued on his walk to the exclusive flat, midway between the Mall and the city theater, where Helena had her chambers.

Helena was still dressing for the day. She dismissed the girl who combed her hair and finished the task herself, driving ivory pins into the shiny braid circling her head.

"You did not tell me you were staying at Decimus's! I am so provoked, Aelius, I don't think I want to see you."

The spearing motion of her hands unpleasantly reminded Aelius of Sido stabbing the severed hand. "I wasn't the one who told him I knew you."

"But he mentioned you to *me,* dumb calf!"

"When? While the rest of us watched the execution of the Christians?"

"No, it was when we had dinner together, afterward. Last year we left each other so badly, I decided we needed to talk. Not to patch things up." Helena raised her voice spitefully, to make sure Aelius would not come to such a conclusion. "To give myself a chance to be a little more civil, since I broke a couple of his antique vases during our final disagreement. I was on the point of poisoning his candied apple a little, by saying I was here to see an old flame." She pointed at Aelius with little jerks of her forefinger, as if piercing the air. "But he beat me to it. 'I have a guest at my place,' he said, 'whom I'm surprised you didn't take to bed in Nicomedia: tall, fair, blue-eyed.'"

"There were hundreds of us with those characteristics," Aelius broke in to say. "How did you know Decimus meant me?"

" 'He's His Divinity's historian,' Decimus said. It annoys me no end to think that two of my lovers room together and can compare notes."

"Gentlemen wouldn't dream of such a thing."

"Ha!"

They lunched alone, at a table so small their heads could touch if they only leaned forward. With a mixture of comradeship and co-quetry, Helena told him of her heartache for someone she'd seen at court, so Aelius would know that she had made her diplomatic rounds there, too.

"How high up?" he asked.

"Close to the top."

"Close to the top there's a eunuch."

"A eunuch, and a gray-eyed brute."

"Not Sido!"

"Why not Sido?" She aped his surprise, then smiled. "He reminds me of Constantius when he was young. And he's *political.*"

"If you can trust him."

"I trust none of the men I sleep with, Aelius. They wouldn't sleep with me if they were trustworthy." She took tiny bites from a green olive, exposing a little at a time the stone within. "Take yourself. You, I'm friends with, but I cannot trust you."

"Because I say that your son has to wait his turn? His Divinity has already—"

"His Divinity, His Tranquillity, His Serenity—His Idiocy! They're *old men,* Aelius."

"You wouldn't say such dangerous things if you didn't trust me, Helena."

"No, it's true. I trust you, but it bothers me." She tossed the dis-carded olive pit his way. "Anyhow, it is a dreadful waste of hale man-hood, this marching to the frontier."

"You know about that, too, eh?"

Her gleaming eyes held him. "My darling, I *will* be an emperor's mother. I have to know what goes on."

NOTES BY AELIUS SPARTIANUS:

Events and revelations are overlapping so quickly that I cannot tell whether they are unraveling or becoming more tangled. One constant runs through everything: Namely, Christians are suspected and accused regardless. It is a characteristic of sweeping prosecutions to ascribe to the enemies of the State all crimes, even those that rightly pertain to other culprits. It is said, and Suetonius warrants it, that in Nero's day the Christians were accused of setting the Great Fire in Rome. Without going as far as Suetonius (who suspects the Emperor himself of burning down the city to rebuild it anew, or for other reasons of his own), it is plain to all those who visited the overcrowded districts of the world's capital that accidental fires are likely to start without human intention. Not long ago, the imperial palace at Nicomedia suffered a devastating fire. Christians employed in the building crews were logically suspected and prosecuted accordingly.

Applying the edicts against the Christians in Treveri as in Mediolanum hardly needs excuses. I am not inclined to see the mark of zealous servants of the state (not even the speculatores*) on Marcellus's murder and the subsequent destruction of church leadership in this city. A venomous and acquisitive aristocrat, on the other hand—*

Lupus's case is even more complicated. It does not trouble me that it brings into question the good faith of the fire waker, hailed as a holy man. It would not be the first time that a charlatan conjures up tricks and is unmasked. Lupus's assassination afterward troubles me, because it appears as it's a crime committed to silence him. But why should Lupus tattle on the holy man? A man whose affluence is due to his status as a miracle recipient would not threaten to publicize the deception he willingly lent himself to. So perhaps it all comes down to a conspiracy among relatives, to inherit the wealth; or among Lupus's competitors, who feared the "resurrected man" would have a supernatural edge with more than a credulous brick buyer when bidding against them.

The fact remains that Agnus was nowhere to be found when Lupus's body was discovered. He "skipped town," to use ben Matthias's term, leaving his female assistant to risk her neck in his place. Had I not alarmed her by looking for her at the Solis et Lunae address, she'd have probably stayed behind and been captured. If the fire waker continues in his chicanery, Casta will have to take care not to fall before he does.

20 DECEMBER, WEDNESDAY

The following day, at the Palace the presence of military men had increased twofold. Headed for this third interview with Aristophanes, Aelius limited himself to wondering why—he would not indulge his curiosity until he had in hand Maximian's acceptance of abdication—and dispatched a waiting courier to Aspalatum with the brief. In one of the outer courtyards, it did not take long for him to learn that the specific commands and assignments were being communicated today to those leaving for the frontier. He himself found out that his old thousand-man cavalry unit awaited him in Mursella. The city of Savaria was the army's gathering point, and from there the campaign would be launched without waiting for the spring, a sign of haste that indicated the gravity of the danger.

The officer called Saphrac, recognizable in the uniform of the Syrian bowmen, was talking to a small crowd of colleagues from the Maximiani Juniores barracks. Duco introduced him to Aelius, and soon they were all discussing the coming war.

Saphrac was pessimistic. "Before leaving for Italy, we suggested to the civilian authorities the withdrawal of colonists and settlers to a minimum of thirty miles from the military road and the frontier itself.

It was not taken well, although the governors of Pannonia and Moesia agree in principle. Families have cultivated the land, built houses; they regard the settlements as their permanent home. But it won't be. High as the birthrate is in our border provinces, it is much higher in Barbaricum."

"During the Persian campaign," Aelius said, "even on the Euphrates we heard widespread reports of westward migrations far to the east. Entire peoples, not hordes, moving from places farther away than Bactria and Paramisos, beyond what Alexander conquered. I don't know how true it is. Or why, those lands being so rich, their inhabitants ought to be seeking Europe."

"I can tell you it isn't as you say." Saphrac gesticulated and looked like any man born and bred in Italy, except for his eyes, elongated and foreign. "Or, rather, it is true that countless tribes are pressing westward, but they aren't settled peoples. They are mounted nomadic groups living off their herds and constantly on the move. They want nothing of the culture we have, only plunder. If we're wise, we'll buy them off, because we surely cannot stop them all."

"Well," Duco intervened, "many of the tribes beyond the frontier can be brought to reason."

"We cannot be fooled by those who dwell closest to our frontier; they've lived alongside us long enough to become half civilized. My mother's uncles have encountered wild foreigners in Bactria who were like nothing they'd seen before: They pack meat under their saddles and eat it raw. Their women give birth riding."

"It seems a little excessive. Giving birth, I mean—"

"Duco, my uncles saw a child born on the saddle before their very eyes. The mother steadied herself by keeping her feet in metal hoops those people use to secure themselves while on horseback." Saphrac clapped his hands in scandalized amusement. "Can you imagine, tangling your feet in hoops hanging from the saddle? What would happen to cavalry tactics? Only barbarians can come up with such inventions."

21 December, Thursday, Divalia, Feast of Secret-Keeping

Notes by Aelius Spartianus, continued:

In the face of war, I keep thinking of Lupus's death, Marcellus's death, and the fire waker. Am I forsaking all sense of proportions? What if a charlatan killed someone to protect his secrets, what if an old judge was cut down? It would not be the first time. Why does it bother me? The authorities in Germany and here are satisfied that, following the first arrests, justice will be done—I am the only one still thrashing about, not accepting that things went as they say. Ben Matthias smells danger, but by his own admission folks of his race have good reasons to smell danger.

How wrong it is to say that dead men cannot speak! Poor Protasius is more useful to me in death than in life. A serf brought me a letter from him yesterday afternoon, while I wrestled with the vexed historical question of the influence of Severus's wife and sister-in-law on imperial politics. In order to peruse it in peace, I left Decimus's property for a private little drinking place. There, I read confirmation that my landlord fought bitterly to keep Pupienus's inheritance from ending up in the Christians' hands; so much so that his relations with the Minucii, until then exemplary and affectionate, were abruptly severed after the adverse sentence. Decimus opposed Marcellus's reappointment as a judge, even alienating from him the support of influential Roman families connected to him by clan. Now, that's something to keep in mind!

Regarding my other request to the late Protasius (that he secure for me an illustrative piece of writing by the fire waker), the letter contained none, but today the same secretive young serf from the Minucii household came at the first morning hour, bearing a basket of apples.

I was up, and judged it an odd time to deliver a Saturnalia

*gift. So, like Cleopatra, I bravely stuck my hand among the fruit
to seek, as the poem goes, "what lurks amid the luscious
bounty." Unlike the queen, who met the asp's fangs, I felt an envelope under the apples. In it was the pastoral homily by Agnus,
also promised to me. Apparently sent from Placentia, where he
preached and performed cures at the time, to the then thriving
Christian community of Aquileia on the border between Italia
and Illyricum, the homily is lengthy and heavy with admoni-
tions. The serf also related Protasius's last message to me, that I
"enjoy the fruit and leave none of its contents for others to pick."
Hence I will destroy the homily after reporting below the ele-
ments that give me an idea of the fire waker's personality.*

*"Beloved brethren in Christ, whose fortitude is according to
prophecy tried by the hands of impious men and the wiles of the
Evil One, answering your request for instructions on how to prepare for the supreme trial and suffering, our love and ministry
compel us to instruct you accordingly."*

*Here follow mindless suggestions on how to tempt a judge's
patience by refusing to answer, or ever repeating the sentence "I
am a Christian"—these tactics I have myself heard in Egypt,
and confirm that they are infuriating. Below, Agnus finds his
first target.*

*". . . And what to say of those blind men who give themselves
wholeheartedly to the impious practice of military life? Do they
not make of murder and plunder their daily business? Do they
not carry standards representing obscene gods and beasts? Better
that they should all perish in the upcoming wars, so that their
bloodthirsty race will be extinguished forever! As the blessed martyrs Julius the Veteran, Dasius, and Expeditus have proven, the
army holds nothing but temptations for the Christian. Much
preferable is the crown of martyrdom . . . [et cetera]*

*"As for the teachings of Plato, Aristotle, and Plotinus and of
the devil-driven liars who go under the name of Epicureans and
Stoics, it is precisely the pretended morality of their instructions*

that makes them perilous. In fact, while they teach probity of life, they extol the false gods whose stories, known to all, even to schoolchildren, are abominations of lechery and fornication.

"The army and false teachers are to be avoided, but of all the dangers from which Christian men must guard themselves, women are the worst. Their bodies are pits of perdition. Being monthly defiled by filthy humors, weak-minded, and prone to all irrational beliefs, they rank below ignorant boys and barbarians who cannot speak Greek or Latin. Their sensuality is a fluid that attaches itself to the eye of men and clots their ability to see, which is why Eros is represented blindfolded. Forget not that the first created woman dragged man into sin!"

I will disregard the rest of the text. As it is readily seen, several categories fall under Agnus's theological ax. Never mind that he calls as a witness to his argument against women a deity like Eros, whose authority he ought to reject. One would never believe, reading such self-righteous pomposity, that the selfsame fire waker does not mind stooping to chicanery and falsehood.

It makes me laugh that Helena threatens now and then to become a Christian. How would she like being termed a "pit of perdition"? Such disregard for women convinces me that should Casta be arrested or put to death, Agnus would not consider it much of a loss to himself or to his superstition.

DECEMBER 23, SATURDAY, IX DAY BEFORE THE KALENDS OF JANUARY
"Leather trousers. Does it mean you're off on a campaign?"

"It doesn't mean I ran out of woolen trousers."

"Where to?"

Aelius wouldn't say. He nodded in the direction of the headstones lined against ben Matthias's wall. "Good business for you, in any case."

"Don't make me more cynical than I am, Commander. Besides, any threat to the Empire is bad for business." Ben Matthias hooked his thumb in the apron tied to his waist. "It is true that I have developed this

nifty method of setting five stonecutters in a row: The first only dresses
the front of the headstone; the second roughly chisels out the panel
where the portrait will be; the third carves the basic portrait—male or
female, military or civilian; the fourth cuts the standard inscription,
leaving the name blank; and the fifth workman adds words or features
when available."

"Clever." Pacing around the room, Aelius looked at the sketches and
models. "And *my* headstone, the one you carved at Confluentes?"

"I left it there, as an advertising sign for the franchise shop." Super-
stitiously the Jew touched his groin. "It'd be bad luck if I presented you
with it as you prepare to leave for Barbaricum. May I interest you in
waterproof, sunproof shield paint?"

"If you have black and yellow, *that* we could use." Aelius stopped in
front of a finished bust. "A portrait of His Divinity? It's a speaking likeness of him!"

"Thank you."

"But it looks as worried as he does."

"*Exactly*. What an artist is trying to do these days is to convey the
pathos of life, Commander. Already in antiquity, the Greek Skopas understood that a soldier-ruler like Alexander had to be represented as in
the thrall of Fate, an Achilles-like figure of doomed beauty. Why do
you think the great Macedonian is represented with his head turned to
one side, his gaze uplifted to look anxiously above him, as if an eagle
or a god were sweeping over him? Such was the way the ancients
thought they should represent the chosen nature of the hero. These days
we have a more controlled way of conveying the drama of individual life.
To my mind, the face must show the furrows of thought, worry, responsibility. If the face is too young to be marked—I am thinking of
Gordian III, or the beastly Elagabalus, who died in their teens—it has
to appear marked nonetheless, because our mind shows the weight
and wear of existence long before the body follows suit. Two, three
quick horizontal lines across the forehead, commas at the sides of the
mouth. The eye must be open, staring ahead. I want to impress a
frozen quality of expectation, and at the same time the resolve that one

needs to look trouble in the eye. None of the bending and twisting commotion so beloved in the days of Marcus and Antoninus, when marble coffins were a squirming confusion of embattled men and horses, maenads, drunken satyrs, carved nearly in full relief to better gather dust." Ben Matthias swept his hands all around the granite head, quick gestures of removal and cleansing. "Less, less, less. Simplify! A few telling lines are all you need."

"Simplicity is a virtue in most endeavors, I find." Aelius looked around the workshop. It was a time for farewells. Already the approaching date of departure made objects and sights strangely extraneous to him, a phenomenon he'd observed in himself before. Commonplace things and their details became new and alarming. In fascination, he stared at the way dust from ben Matthias's apron convulsively sought the outdoors when he stopped on the threshold to look at the clear day.

"You see that my workshop is outside the Jewish district. As a Jew, graven images should be an abomination to me. As an artist, they seem to me the only thing that stands between me and the forgetfulness of death. I carve them out of anxiety and the desire to ensure that my work stays, and lasts. It's like this, Commander. You go to war with your great armies: What will remain of you all? Tales by the fireside? History? You may write your own history, to make sure the tale is told correctly; but will it be your version that remains, or your enemy's?"

The correspondence between his feelings and ben Matthias's words made Aelius thoughtful, on this side of sadness. He said, "If I am not mistaken—I am scarcely an expert in the field—Jews trust in the permanence of their own scripture, without the need of graven images."

"Please do not ruin my exposition, Commander. We're not engaged in theology here. Simplicity and permanence. I favor porphyry and granite, because they are nearly indestructible, and because they are so difficult to carve: You *have* to simplify your portraits."

The farewell to ben Matthias was characteristically short and ironic. The Jew said that "one never knows, Jews are like parsley, to be found in all dishes on all tables." They might see one another even on the frontier, if Aelius happened to stop at Intercisa. "Why not?" Aelius answered. "I have friends among the First Thracian troopers stationed there."

Parting from Helena was even easier. She was head over heels about Sido, she confessed; kissing Aelius on both cheeks, she told him to behave himself and not to forget what she'd told him.

"When we were making love, or at another time?"

"Impudent dog, you know very well what I mean." She bit his earlobe with a last kiss. "Remember what I said about a man on top."

As for Curius Decimus, the occasions to meet him had become fewer in the last week Aelius spent in Mediolanum. His colleague was away, visiting relatives and whatever else in the region. The evening of the second-to-last day he came to visit, with the excuse of returning the three months' advance rent paid for the annex. "You scarcely stayed here three weeks. It'd be indecent to keep the sum."

"The government is grateful," Aelius answered. But he was smiling. "Won't you come in?"

"I was hoping you'd ask."

As before, they sat in the wicker chairs facing one another. Incense had been burned recently in the wall niche of the family altar; its oily scent did not escape Decimus, who openly approved Aelius's act of devotion. "It's good doing it now and then. These walls don't get enough old religion."

Aelius looked at him. The mask of politeness and disdain fit less well on Decimus's face after the drinking bout. Comments on his colleague's remark were unnecessary, and accordingly he said nothing. He discovered that he had very little to say to Decimus, in fact. The court dockets, Protasius's words, and his own observations formed a twin image of the man, much more sinister and reliable than the finicky disguise sitting here.

"Now it's the time of fear, isn't it?"

Amity as a wicket hiding the trap, again. Aelius heard the words go inside him like spikes, as if he'd stepped in despite his vigilance. "But I am not afraid," he said slowly.

"Yes, and you never stumble. I know." Decimus smiled with his ugly little teeth. "We are to travel together, serve together—the truth is to be told once in a while. Even in your pan-Roman army, Aelius Spartianus. Officers and gentlemen seek their likes' company before a campaign, and open their comradely hearts."

"Are *you* afraid?"

"I don't know what fear is."

And that was how they opened their hearts to each other.

Afterward, Aelius stayed up until late. Decimus's visit had interrupted him while he readied to unseal a letter from home, whose handwriting at first he did not recognize. Now he opened it and saw that it had been sent a month earlier. From post exchange to post exchange, it caught up with him now: That was hardly a novelty. What surprised him was the sender. Never before had news come directly from his mother. The tone and style of the writing revealed a capacity to articulate he had not suspected in her. He knew she was literate, but all communication (scarce, to tell the truth) that through the years had come from his parents had been written and signed for both by his father. In fact, only because he was "still under the weather," as Aelia Justina put it, did she put pen to paper to let her son know how things were in the province.

She referred to another brief that must have gotten lost in the mail, in which work being done on the family's retirement home was probably mentioned. It all confirmed an ominous mood of expectation in Pannonia and elsewhere on the frontier.

> . . . *Everyone is fortifying his house these days, Aelius. We are all aware that what happened forty years ago could happen again, and are not about to be found unprepared. Everywhere masons and carpenters at work; one could say there are no unemployed in this province. Itinerant mosaic-layers and stonecutters make a splendid living. They are mostly Italics from Aquileia and*

Gradus, some of them former soldiers who understand the needs and taste of military settlers.

The army closes an eye on the fact that ours is an independent civilian response to potential threats from the outside. Each man a soldier, a citizen-soldier, if you will, each house a garrison. The style, as you will see when—the Gods willing—you come to visit, is fairly uniform. It includes two or four projecting towers, second-storied usually, which double as granaries and places to keep dry fruit and farming implements. Once those doors are locked, an attacker would have to fight just to get inside. Of course, light suffers from these arrangements, and quarters are somewhat cramped; but we are all glad to do our part, as we see it as an additional border line to protect the Empire. The Roman-style villas are much more relaxed, and more beautiful, with their open porches and gardens with canals and fountains. But there are hardly doors you can lock in those properties, and—if life should put us to the test—we will see what we will see . . .

31 December, Sunday, eve of the Kalends of January

Outside Silver Gate, the one-legged beggar hobbled from across the street, leaning on a makeshift crutch. At the head of the bridge he sat on the cobblestones against the parapet, to keep out of the direct wind. Pieces of ragged, unidentifiable army clothing covered his nakedness; his one foot wore an ill-fitting boot over a toeless knit sock. His right stump, tied into the threadbare cloth of his trousers with a string, was severed above the knee.

Blue with cold, he cut a miserable figure when he first eyed Aelius, who was approaching on horseback at a walk and looked his way.

"Charity for a man who gave his all to Rome, and was crippled in the war!"

Aelius clicked his tongue for his horse to halt. "Which campaign?"

"Armenia, most honorable Commander, and Persia after that. I was at Daphne near Antioch, when we took the Persian king's harem . . . I was there when we entered Ctesiphon. Charity for a soldier!"

"What unit?" His back to the fierce wind, Aelius leaned from the saddle to drop a coin in the man's hand.

"The Bear Standard troopers, Ala Ursiciana."

A second coin followed. "Your colonel?"

"Ah, Commander—" The beggar caught Aelius's attention, and kept his palm expectantly open. Frostbite on his knuckles and fingertips cracked and bled under a crust of filth. "That's the man I lost my leg saving, when he fell and couldn't pull himself out from under his dead horse. A hail of arrows rained on me while I ran back for him. Twice he urged me to save myself, and twice I was wounded but would not cease my efforts." The coins clinked in his hand, asking for more. "You should have seen me."

Aelius simpered. "I should have seen you, all right. *I* led the Bear Standard troopers at Daphne and Ctesiphon."

"You—and—and did you not fall from your horse?"

"I didn't fall once during that campaign. And we call our horses *mounts*."

The beggar hung his head. The meager skin of his neck reminded Aelius of a turtle, but even turtles were less malnourished and cleaner. "A man has got to eat, Commander."

"That's true."

"No one wants to hear you lost your leg under a wagon wheel. It sounds *common*. And in the streets it's damn cold this time of year." The hand stayed reluctantly half-open. "Now you'll want your coins back."

Aelius looked ahead, at the span of the bridge. He blew air through his lips as men sometimes do when they're doubtful or annoyed. No one was coming from the other end, and behind him, he saw that people were busy at the market stalls. He unclasped his army cloak—first-rate weave from Aquitania—and stretched it down to the beggar. "Ask soldiers what unit they served with, before you make up tales."

Incredulous, at first the beggar wouldn't take the cloak, but seeing the officer's impatience he grabbed it and jealously wrapped himself in it twice, pulling his hale leg under it to keep it warm.

"May the gods give this back to you tenfold, Commander."

Aelius smirked. "It'd be too large a cloak."

Aelius had made it a rule not to sleep in his own bed (whether it be at the camp, barracks, or other quarters) the night before starting out for a military campaign. Inns, friends' houses, occasionally even the open air would do. And he had to be alone, much as others went to drinking parties or sought the company of a woman, or caroused the night in brothels, stumbling out in the morning with their eyes full of sleep, not thinking.

He had to think clearly. Having written his testament on the vigil of his assignment to Egypt at the time of the Rebellion, he faced less pragmatic concerns. It was a stage that followed the estrangement from familiar objects. Already he walked around the annex like a foreigner who has never seen the place. Even the riotous charm of the figurines painted above his bed, the Egyptian dwarfs and baboons, surprised him anew; it made him wonder what in the end was habit, if he could so easily forget it. Then came the conscious exercise to make himself familiar with those things around him, and the realization that closeness to objects, textures, shapes in one's bedroom could haunt one's resolve to separate from them, perhaps forever.

Whenever possible, Aelius packed in advance and sent his things ahead, not to have to review them with the perspective of their becoming objects of a dead man, like the helmet found in the northern bog. Who could ever know what the man who had worn it thought, the night before setting off for the march through Teutoburg Forest? Aelius imagined how the man set aside the ornate helmet, wrapped it carefully, anticipating the wearing of it. Had he thought of the helmet when he'd been killed, as they said often men do strangely think of this or that domestic or paltry object of theirs before dying?

A fellow officer mortally wounded in Armenia had asked for his neckerchief before dying, with such angry insistence that they had gone to fetch it, useless as it was, and he'd died sucking on it, like an infant. The image had remained with Aelius with a kind of embarrassed horror.

A week before, he'd written a short note to his parents, informing them that he was leaving for the frontier. Now, on his last night in Mediolanum, his different place was an inn near the barracks, where his Guardsmen were also ready to leave.

II

FIRE

8

N otes by Aelius Spartianus:

Whether one takes the northern route or the southern one, only one province (Noricum in the first case, Dalmatia in the second) separates Italy from Pannonia to the east. And, far as they seem to those who remark on their frontier state, the four administrative units that form Pannonia lie only one-third of the way between the Italian Alps and the maximum European extension of the Empire, having its terminus at Byzantium.

Pannonia—whose name is said to derive from the woodland deity Pan—is a vast land of plains, forests, lakes, and high mountains. The inhabitants are also called Danubians because the Danube forms the region's outer limit, and to the great river's spirit have long been devoted the peoples who live on the rich, continuous length of its banks. Physically, male and female Pannonians are tall and sturdy, fair rather than dark, gray- and blue-eyed, resistant to fatigue and bad weather. Their natural pride is tempered by patience and goodwill, which makes them excellent recruits and valuable officers. Their women are modest, honorable, and fertile.

Shortly before my birth Our Lord Aurelian—Rebuilder of

the Army—saw the wisdom of abandoning the unmanageable Transdanubian lands forming the province of Dacia. Thus an enormous territory, conquered about two hundred years ago by the deified Trajan and Hadrian, reverted to Barbaricum. Ever since the days of those two warrior princes, and through the reigns of Septimius Severus and his otherwise abominable son Caracalla, the fortified border we call Limes, or Limit, has become a continuous frontier consisting of river, ditch, stone wall, watchtowers, blockhouses, barracks, and full military camps, connected by rapid-transit military roads and fortified bridges, and strengthened by the occasional counterfortress on the enemy bank.

Those of us who are natives of Pannonia and Moesia, provinces sharing the same geographic area, depend on Greek and Roman historians for the narrative of our own antiquity, which goes back to before the times of Alexander of Macedonia, six hundred and more years. It appears that our blood is Celtic; more, that the tribes (Boii and Scordisci primarily) that form the ethnic core of the population are not native at all, but came, as I have remarked elsewhere, from Gaul three centuries before Julius Caesar (indeed, my own paternal ancestors are Boii, who settled a vast territory called Boii's Mountains, Boihaemium, or Boihaemia, commonly called Bohemia). Having failed in their foolhardy bid to attack Rome, those Celts escaped eastward to settle along the Savus, Dravus, and Tibiscus rivers, tributaries all of the great Danube. Still in their barbaric state, they fought the natives and among themselves.

Nine years after Julius Caesar's death, his heir Octavian Augustus occupied the Pannonian capital of Siscia, and for the following fifty years the region alternated between peace and impossible revolt. Under the deified Vespasian and his sons, Pannonia saw a permanent assignment of legions, and the first organization of the Limit, from which the great Dacian campaigns of Trajan and Hadrian would be launched. Marcus

Aurelius, the philosopher prince, wrote his Meditations *while in Pannonia, dying soon of the Great Plague that all but depopulated the Empire one hundred twenty years ago. Severus and his dynasty brought unprecedented prosperity to our region. Between then and now, barbaric raids, warfare, and two Pannonian-born emperors (Decius and Probus) typified our history. Seven years ago Pannonian soldiers, reputed the best in the Empire, were chosen to fight the victorious Persian campaigns.*

Presently Pannonian cities and peaceful settlements face an array of threatening hostiles from beyond the river: Quadi, Marcomanni, Goths, Sarmatians and their Roxolani allies, Gepids, Suebi, Vandals, and more.

It made sense that, if the Danubian provinces were their goal, in order to avoid the higher mountain passes between Italy and the east, Agnus and Casta had separately sought the low road. Traveling the same route with his Guardsmen and the units from Mediolanum, altogether the strength of a thousand soldiers, Aelius retraced the fire waker's possible itinerary. Pons Aureolus, Bergomum, Brixia . . . At every stop, if there was an occasion, he asked about the state of inquiries on religious charges. In Bergomum he was told of a riot among the "orientals," that is, Christians and Jews, on account of a false prophet and his claims. No word on who the prophet might be. Two men had been killed in the disturbance, and arrests had been made among the Christians.

Two more dead, and arrests likely to result in the death penalty. By this time, whatever role the itinerant preacher might have played in fakery, incitement to riot, and even murder, Aelius's desire to expose him had grown past curiosity. Beyond His Divinity's magnanimous permission to "*learn more about the superstitious practice of so-called resurrection operated by Agnus or Pyrikaios or* fire waker, *as he is also known*," he wanted to confront him face-to-face. The likelihood of such an encounter ran against all odds, but when, during an overnight stop at the army post in Brixia, he heard details about the Bergomum

riot, Aelius was certain that Casta's teacher had been involved somehow. The controversy centered on a sick boy, son of a Jewess and a
lapsed Christian, whose healing in Treveri had been differently reported to the local Jewish and Christian communities. Cross-charges
of chicanery and claims of a miracle had resulted in violent disorders.
Out of the incident, for the first time, Aelius received a description of
the fire waker: more than one, in fact.

It came in the form of a report by the commander of the unit dispatched from Brixia to Bergomum to quell the riot. Although supposedly the healer had passed through recently, the soldier had not seen
him in person, but interesting details about him had emerged from
those who had. The impression was of a man absorbed or distracted
by ideas; he did not look at an interlocutor directly but "as if searching
above the other's head, or to the side of him, for presences or signs."
He let no one touch him, no one come closer than five feet to him. He
slept alone, and no one saw him eat or drink; many believed he never
partook of anything, "being somehow maintained by the flame of his
own spirit." Long-haired and unkempt, he walked barefooted regardless of weather or terrain, yet his feet did not appear wounded or worn
by his wanderings. His nakedness no one had seen, either, past his
hands and feet and head to the neck, because he wore a long-sleeved
tunic, black in color. This, according to one description. Others said
that he was in no way distinguishable from other men, wore everyday
clothes appropriate to his age, trimmed beard, short hair. How else
could he pass unobserved through provinces where the authorities
were on the lookout for religious fanatics?

The report mentioned no assistant, female or otherwise, a circum-
stance that only confirmed that Agnus and Casta traveled separately.

The army's advance across northern Italy continued, at the mercy of
weather that alternated between blizzards and clear days of breathtak-
ing cold. Curius Decimus and his Mediolanum friends formed a tight
group, nearly impermeable to the rest. Whenever they arrived at one of

the army towns or forts en route, they had errands to run and acquaintances of their own to see. Occasionally, Aelius sought the aristocrat's company.

Because his personal relations had thus far been characterized by
remarkable openness of intents, Aelius was at first troubled by the idea
of frequenting his colleague because of his suspicions of Decimus regarding Marcellus's death. Life during an army march being what it is,
however, soon he was telling himself that polite officers could hardly
avoid one another. For his part, Decimus seemed singularly pleased
with the development: even amused. He likely credited his own brilliant company for Aelius's change of heart. True, at the beginning he'd
remarked, "There's a distinct scent of smoke in the air. Where's the
fire?" But Aelius pretended not to understand.

South of Lake Larius, on a spectacular morning of bright sun, when
the chains of high mountains to the north were blinding with snow
like a barrier of mirrors, Sido and a retinue of *speculatores,* fur-caped,
overtook the army units at a trot. Gravel and bits of ice shot around
under the horses' hoofs. One of the twins—Dexter or Sinister—barely
kept his mount from shying. He cried out loud, "Son of a whore!" in
Sido's shimmering wake.

"A *lucky* son of a whore," his brother, half-laughing, specified contemptuously for the benefit of their colleagues. "I say it's a timely thing
that Marcellus croaked before bribery charges made him lose his police post."

Aelius, who was riding ahead of the group, fell back a little, to hear
more. All he caught was Decimus's repartee, in a merry voice. "Why
credit Sido with killing the judge? Give credit where credit is due."

Nothing was added, but the Romans laughed as if it were a joke.

VERONA, 7 JANUARY 305, SUNDAY

As sometimes happens, the letter his mother had sent before the one he
had already received reached Aelius on the sixth day out of Mediolanum,
in Verona, where the army stopped to get supplies and equipment at the

local weapons factory, and was then delayed a full night because of a snowstorm.

Aelia Justina to Commander Aelius Spartianus, love and greetings.

Dearest son,

I am writing to you in hopes that these lines will reach you wherever you may be, and find you well in body and spirit. It is primarily to make you aware of a fortunate event that befell us that I communicate with you without waiting for your father's slight indisposition to pass.

You remember that when your father acquired this property six years ago, in anticipation of his retirement, he did so through the estate of a distant relative, who died leaving no legal heir. He was in turn the nephew of that Resatus whose property was destroyed by the barbarians forty-four years ago, during the war that devastated our province, and the man and his entire family exterminated. Such was the disorder in those sad days (I remember well, although I was a child), the burned and collapsed house was left in the state it was in, with the corpses inside where they had been murdered. There was a story in the settlement that Resatus's house was haunted, and in fact we children were not allowed to go play around the ruined place. Not only that, even the stretch of country lane that had once led to the unfortunate place had the reputation of being visited by ghosts, both at noon and in the middle of the night. Now they are all buried in a spot which is at the very corner of our property. No doubt you remember it, because you used to hunt lizards there, and badly scraped your knees there once, falling from Resatus's monument.

At the time of the invasion, your maternal grandfather served at the Ala Nova camp, and my sisters and I grew up here. I perfectly recall old man Resatus and Blanda, his wife; less their children, who were older than I. But Blanda I can see in front of my eyes today as she was then, on the day we girls brought fresh eggs to her as a gift to thank them for some courtesy they paid to us.

Well, about two weeks past—it being the anniversary of the attack so many years ago, which I always observe by bringing the appropriate libations to their graves—I was wondering to myself whether these graves, which we kept as carefully as if they had belonged to our own parents, will receive similar upkeep after your father and I are gone. An old woman's thoughts, you will think, but there are days when I look at the workers laboring on our house and grow superstitious, lest some misfortune should befall us or our children. In fact, at times it seems to me that I can imagine a time when none of these settlements and communities will be left, and either the woods and the animals will take over again, or new people, strangers or barbarians, will dwell here in our place. And I cannot help thinking, what—if anything—will they think when finding the solitary brick or discarded jar or whatever else that marks our passage in this place? They will know neither our names nor what mattered to us, whom we loved, what we cared for, what gods we believed in and revered. But such are the thoughts that come to mind when one sits down to consider what I write below.

In the process of enlarging the house (we decided to build a porch and add two towers in front, to protect the property), some changes have to be made. Yesterday, before the workers came to start digging for the addition, your father said he was going to cut the shrubs to clear the men's way to the front of the house. They are—were—my favorite shrubs, so we had words over them, and after quite a row, a sudden rain made your father give up his intent for the time being. It was getting dark, too, so we went back inside and, without talking to one another any further, soon went to bed.

Now, who should come to me in my dream but Blanda, looking precisely as I recalled her. It seemed to me that I heard

*knocking on the door, and found her on my doorstep, smiling.
In my dream I did not recall that she was dead, you see, so it
seemed natural to invite her to come in. I wanted to show her
how we rebuilt the place that had been hers, and how well
we took care of things. She, however, would not enter, and bade
me not to embrace her. "Only," she said, "make sure that before
the workers come tomorrow you dig under the pear tree that
casts its shadow over the little stone table in the garden. I hid my
good things at its foot, they were never found, and I want you to
have them."*

*Imagine how I felt, as I have heard that prophecies and the
departed do come sometimes during sleep, but I never expected
it would happen to me. Wondering how she knew of our work
on the house (but that is silly, as the dead supposedly know all
things), I thanked Blanda and asked her again whether she
would not like to come in and sit a moment. She kept smiling,
repeating that she would (or could) not enter, but rather that
my husband would be soon bringing her a pair of earrings,
which she described in detail.*

*Well, dear son, this morning I awoke greatly confused. When
I shared my dream with your father, he took it as a woman's
sideways manner of admitting that I was wrong about the
shrubs, using dreams to justify myself. Out he goes bright and
early, and starts digging—first the shrubs, then precisely where
I told him from my dream, under the pear tree. He has grown
corpulent in the last couple of years, so I advised him not to
strain himself, but as he never listens, I quit insisting after a
while. Believe it or not, two spans down in the earth, his spade
struck something hard. It was metal, a strongbox of some kind.
He kept digging, more and more furiously, and at one point told
me to send away the serfs and everyone else, which I did with
some excuse.*

*To make a long story short, he pulled out a box such as valu-
ables are kept in, and when we opened it, with some difficulty,*

we found a set of silver vessels and two gilded cups, plus a small treasure in gold coins from the days of Our Lord Aurelian, and a few lady's jewels. Among these, fully recognizable, was the pair of earrings described to me in the dream. Your father went crazy with the find, and of course I was pleased, too, as they will make good gifts for you children.

The only thing I am not sure about is Blanda's words about your father bringing the earrings to her. I don't want to be such an old woman and begin believing in all kinds of omens . . . Anyway, I suggested to him that we dig an inconspicuous little hole as close as possible to the lady's burial place, and place the earrings inside it. But my heart is not at ease. I tell myself that it is just because your father, who caught cold after sweating so much while digging, is running a fever this evening. As soon as he recovers, I will feel much better.

Be well, my dear and only son. I pray Magla, Mammula, and the Pannonian Mother Goddesses to watch over you always. Written in her own hand at Aelius Spartus's property in the Savaria district, province of Pannonia Superior Savia, on the 19th day of November, XII day from the Kalends of December.

It was perhaps the longest exchange his mother had ever had with him, in words or in writing. Aside from the strangeness of the letter's contents, Aelius appreciated the difference between his father's short and badly written notes and this attentive, lively, smooth way of communicating. He delighted in it. Why had she let him speak for her all these years? *I am much more my mother's son,* he found himself thinking, *than my father's.* News of the old man's indisposition was secondary compared to the discovery of Justina as an interlocutor.

The following night—they'd left Cadianum behind, and taking advantage of clear weather the units had proceeded farther than they usually would—they were caught by dark still at a distance from the closest usable quarters. Pitching tents was no easy task; but it was accomplished. The officers sought shelter here and there in farmhouses, except for Aelius and Curius Decimus, who decided to rough it in the ruins of a homestead dilapidated by past wars and abandonment.

It was one of those decisions taken by mutual accord, no reason given. They built a fire, munched on hardtack, and talked of things that apparently had nothing to do with the unrevealed aims each of the two had for the one-on-one conversation.

Decimus took the long way in, discussing philosophy. "You say—with Seneca, if I am not mistaken—*in regno nati sumus,* by which I understand you to mean that one way or another we are from birth in a world that enslaves us with its rules. If it is so, Spartianus (and let us admit it, Seneca did not let his philosophy get in the way of his enriching himself and even becoming a tyrant's advisor), then I can only reply that no one can force us to remain in such a world."

"True. But if every virtuous man took the way out, wouldn't it leave the world precisely to the sinful and the evil? I say that, conscious as we are of the difficulty of the situation, we have to face it, and do our best."

"I was not thinking of suicide. Did I ever tell you what Mediolanum's nickname is? Fat City, because it produces so much, and so many goods pass through its gates. It is like an immense heart and intestine rolled into one, pumping and excreting. Hardly what I'd call a city with republican ideals. Yet there is a reason why my friends and I regularly met in Mediolanum, Spartianus. As a historian, you no doubt remember that before the Ides of March, nearly three hundred and fifty years ago, Brutus held office in that very city. The Republic kept breathing there even after it ceased doing so in Rome."

Aelius was careful to keep his attention on the fire, to show only so much interest. "It is, I assume, to Brutus the republican that you are referring, not to Brutus the assassin."

"The *tyrannicide,* you mean." Decimus laughed. "Brutus was one individual, not several actors sewed up inside one skin. Quintilius Varus, he who led the owner of your beautiful helmet to die in Teutoburg Forest, was the son of one of the Caesaricides. Why, one of my maternal ancestors was at Brutus's side on the Ides of March. 'Assassin' is such an ugly word: We don't use it in my family."

Aelius's answer, whatever it was supposed to be, did not reach his lips. He crouched by the fire and through the corner of his eye watched his colleague tease the flames with a long stick, whose tip burned bright. Was Decimus circling around the matter of murder, challenging him to make an issue of it in regard to Judge Marcellus? His statements were meaningful, political but not only that. Insecure, shifting darkness crowded in from the corners of the room, a sooty dark like a presence. Through the rafters, the precipitous starry sky seemed wholly black, as if a sackful of burning twigs and logs were capable of turning off the heavens. Decimus's words were a kindling and waking of the fire as well. Whatever the pretense or desire to provoke, they also stirred and needled a concept of freedom Aelius's Stoic teachers interpreted so literally as to justify the taking of one's life before dishonor.

Decimus read lack of critique in his silence. Lazily whipping the flames, he said, "Take Pertinax and Macrinus, historian: Did they not have a hand in freeing Rome of the monsters Commodus and Caracalla, becoming emperors in their places? There will always be well-minded officers who gather—*gather*, not plot—to dash down the tyrant and save the country's honor. They will always be at risk of being discovered, accused, tried, and executed. Death in battle is not as noble as execution at the hand of a tyrant." The stick in his hand incandesced without catching fire. "You can't possibly approve of the way Rome is run these days."

Weighing his words, Aelius found them difficult to handle. "Why, was Rome better governed in the days of the Republic? Social wars and civil wars abounded then. Powerful men had powerful private armies, which held sway over the City and its territories. *They killed with impunity.* I believe we invent a virtuous past in order to compare our present unfavorably with it. Nothing I studied in the great historians' works points to the excellence of the 'good old days,' Decimus. There were outstanding men in the Republic, as there are now. It may simply annoy you that never as now have men born of low state achieved so much, and climbed so high."

"That, too."

The wind outside circled the building like a wolf, seeking a cranny to force its way inside. The sound was low-pitched and insistent, a sound of night watches and standing alone in one's boots and cape. Aelius thought that there had been other times when, sitting with someone else, discoursing, he had suddenly felt detached from the moment and the spot. *It's because I am used to not belonging, not becoming attached*, he told himself. *Because, contrary to the man who sits across from me in his bitterness, I have no glorious string of ancestors tying me here and there, entangling me to Rome like a fly in a spiderweb.* And he pitied Decimus, as soldiers occasionally are shot through by a painful sense of man's misery. It seemed to him that in his severity and pride, his colleague was struggling in a cocoon of spider spittle, unable to set himself free. Yet such a man could find not one but ten different reasons to justify murder, Aelius was certain of it. Making him stumble into a confession was another matter, and a risky one.

14 JANUARY, SUNDAY

They crossed from Italia Annonaria into Noricum in mid-January. Aquileia, Concordia, Tergeste, Emona had each required digging out before continuing the journey. In Aquileia, where Christian presence was said to be strong and pervasive, Aelius picked up the fire waker's trail thanks to an overnight stay in a barracks not far from the city jail. Greek-speaking Christians awaited trial there, after contravening the law by associating and making use of their forbidden holy books. Agnus's writing, hidden by Protasius in the basket of apples, had been sent from Aquileia, so Aelius was fairly sure he would hear more about the healer. He did, although not from the Christians.

The officer in charge of the jail was more talkative than his charges. Agnus had led a congregation in town years earlier, without controversy until the daughter of an official had converted to his superstition. "She had a line of wooers from here to there," the jailer explained, "and to her father she was the apple of his eye. She turns Christian one fine day, starts fasting and mortifying her flesh, will listen to no reason, and within a year or little more she wears down like wax on a taper and dies. You can believe her father went after the Christians, even though in those days they were given a chance to grow like weeds. Agnus, of course, had already moved on to preach elsewhere. There's been an open arrest warrant for him for years. Two weeks ago, informants told us he was rumored to be in Aquileia, passing through. Well, we thought, we'll be damned if we let other girls of ours go pining after his magic tricks. We move, make arrests. Too late. Goes by 'fire waker' these days, eh? That's good to know."

"I don't understand why the official's daughter let herself die."

"Why, Commander? Because to Christians women are the spawn of the evil spirits and must punish their sinful bodies. Have you heard of anything more ridiculous? Women have no brains—their bodies is all they have!"

Emona was the last army town administratively attached to Italy. Its location on the Amber Route gave it already the cultural flavor of the Pannonian region; dialect, hefty walls, and square donjons said frontier, whatever else shops and urban amenities led one to believe. Aelius jotted down his impressions of the place.

My Guardsmen were allowed to take the evening off for their religious practices at the local Mithras shrine, because this cult, related to that of the Unconquerable Sun, thrives from here to the Danube. The shrine is in the basement of a building next to the place where Decimus and his friends—"the Romans," Duco calls them—were having dinner together. Close to midnight, the head Guardsman came to see me as I sat up reading; according to my orders that I be briefed about anything out of the ordinary, he reported overhearing a loud argument among my urban colleagues. Not news, exactly. If they drank as I've seen them do in Mediolanum, it's a wonder they didn't smash the place up.

Across the border, past the Savus River and a road station by the telling name of the Tax Collectors, the next city of some importance was Celeia, "Gate to Noricum." Accordingly, the army units made an official stopover to offer sacrifices for a good beginning and end of the campaign. They arrived at sundown, with an eastern wind that cut like a blade and forced men and beasts to seek shelter. The officers requisitioned an inn outside the western gate, too tired to eat or do anything else other than sleep.

15 JANUARY, MONDAY

Duco was shaking him. Aelius turned in bed, heavy with slumber but already alarmed.

"What, have I overslept?" he muttered.

"No, it's wake-up time, but there's trouble." The Briton was not yet dressed. In the faint light of his lamp, his red hair stood up like quills on a porcupine. "One of the Romans is dead."

"Dead? *How, who?*"

"It's the one they called Frugi. He slept two bunks from me. He just won't wake up. I didn't hear a thing, Aelius."

Aelius was putting his trousers on. "Well, we're all dog-tired." He'd been dreaming an odd combination of faces and events, forgotten as soon as he'd opened his eyes except for the fact that Anubina and Casta figured in it somehow. "Who else is up?"

"Otho and one of the twins."

"Decimus?"

"Still asleep."

"Go wake him up—no. I'll go." The floor planks felt cold under his bare feet as Aelius hastened to the other room. Like the one where he'd slept, it was square, large enough to contain four or five bunks. Decimus awoke only after much calling and jogging. He listened to the news with his feet out of bed, half-seated. His eyes were glassy. "Bullshit," he replied, and gave a disbelieving, mumbling laugh.

Within moments the men were up, in different states of undress. Ulpius Domninus felt his dead colleague's congested neck and face.

"He's cold. Must have died shortly after we retired. He doesn't seem to have struggled, so it must have been a sudden thing, a stroke of some kind. Who spoke to him last?"

Otho raised his hand, without opening his mouth.

A few hours earlier, each of them had retired to the first bunk he happened to stumble on. Duco, Decimus, Frugi, and Sinister had taken the room closest to the stairs; Aelius, Vivius Lucianus, Dexter, Otho, and Ulpius Domninus the next room, connected to the first by an open doorway. Aelius looked at Frugi's fat body, stretched out on the anonymous mattress. Of all of Decimus's cohorts, he'd been the least colorful, an obstinate man of few words, even during the party when everyone had bragged about his career. He was the one who'd said Decimus's daughter must be fabulously rich.

"Who's keeping watch downstairs?" Ulpius Domninus looked at Aelius while he asked the question. "Your Guardsmen?"

"Yes. I vouch for them personally. Why?"

"Just asking."

Summoned without being given a reason, the Guardsmen confirmed that no one had entered the inn after the officers. The intact snow cover around the building proved the fact. Four men had alternated in keeping watch; the second shift had begun only an hour earlier.

"This is a bad thing twice over." Duco interpreted everyone's thought. "A colleague dead, and a *very* evil omen for the campaign."

"Yes, without counting that the gendarmes may delay us all." Decimus had been yawning in his cupped hands, so widely that his jaw seemed to come unhinged. He said the words between yawns. "Spartianus, you said you vouch for your men in person."

"I do. What of it?"

"Don't misunderstand me. I am thinking what half of us at least are thinking: Frugi is dead, and getting the city authorities involved won't bring him back to life. Hell, we don't have the fabulous fire waker here, do we?"

"We should at least get a medic here, to make sure it was a natural death."

Had Aelius dropped a large stone in a puddle, his colleagues wouldn't have drawn back more automatically.

"What?" "What are you saying?" "Are you out of your mind?"

Decimus quelled the voices with a slow semicircle of the right hand in the air. "You offend all of us here, Spartianus, including yourself. Poor Frugi ate and drank to an excess; those of us who knew his family can tell you his father died of a stroke in the Senate, his uncle seated on the latrine. I say we give him a chance to show us one last courtesy by not delaying our march. Who is familiar with the city?"

The twins, Otho, even Duco seemed relieved by Decimus's proposal that Frugi be dressed and carried outside while it was still dark. Otho had served in Celeia two years earlier and suggested a small settlement outside the western walls, a mile back.

"It's all brothels. The whores are Egyptian and Syrian—I promise you they can fuck a man to death."

"Don't speak nonsense."

"Why, Aelius—can you vouch for Egyptian whores, too?"

Ulpius Domninus intervened. "Spartianus is right, I don't like it either."

Decimus took his boots from his bedside and put them on. "Well, there's two of you, and four of us. Five if you count Frugi, who'd never want to delay our progress toward war. Spartianus, since you want no part in it, send out your Guardsmen before they see us bringing our friend downstairs."

It went without saying that the sacrifices offered in the morning at the army post shrine were somber and had an undeclared reparative nature. Frugi's body, found by gendarmes at daybreak behind the brothel known as Red Priapus, was considered a casualty the prostitutes could not account for, but an accident all the same.

NOTES BY AELIUS SPARTIANUS, WRITTEN ON 26 JANUARY:
Our march continued along the military route Celeia-Poetovio-Sala-Savaria. We camp outside Savaria tonight, and tomorrow our units will separate after a brief ceremony downtown. The

Palace Guards and other soldiers from the Mediolanum garrison will head southeast to Herculia and then cross the border at Intercisa. I meet my troopers at Mursella by way of Basiana, and as far as I know, will follow the Marus River upstream from Arrabona into Barbaricum.

Ever since Frugi's death, I have been observing my Roman colleagues. Is it my impression, or is there a level of anxiety within that group? The haste with which a friend's demise was handled troubles them, I think. Ulpius Domninus seeks my eyes now and then, he who was the most disdainful of Decimus's cohorts. He wants to talk, but does not dare. Decimus keeps a close watch on his companions; they eat and quarter together without exceptions. Duco is left out by them, and even with me he opens up less than he used to. Do we secretly suspect one another for what happened to Frugi, not being so sure that it was a natural death? But what could possibly be the reason for any of us to kill such a colorless colleague?

The weather has been strange at best. Italy has a reputation for mild winters, yet it dumped snow on us from Mediolanum to Tergeste. Noricum and Pannonia are synonymous with the bad season; still, we've encountered only one snowfall since leaving Celeia. I can't conceal that it all feels like home, or as close to home as anyplace can feel to a soldier. My father served in all the principal posts of the region we are crossing; my mother, while still married to her husband's older brother, lived everywhere on this frontier. Their retirement home is less than forty miles west of here, on the foothills of the heights that stretch toward Scarbantia.

At Poetovio, seat of the procurator Augusti *and accordingly busy in all things bureaucratic, we crossed the bridge into Pannonian land. There we stopped to offer sacrifices at the hillside temple of Jupiter, overlooking the well-laid streets fanning down to the Dravus River (with a brief personal halt at the shrine of Isis and Serapis, to leave an offer for Anubina and Thaesis).*

Sala, on Lake Pelso, has become sprawling with vacation homes. Contrary to what Mother wrote, these aren't fortified at all; even the least aggressive of attackers would have no trouble plundering them. Who would have believed that I would catch Agnus's scent again in a resort town?

The local gendarmes were on the lookout for him, "a dangerous Christian charlatan with a public woman in tow." So they said when we filed by at the checkpoint. I observed that I knew the fire waker's companion to be a victim of superstition, but not immoral per se. Am I to assume the two of them have reunited? If so, it can be very dangerous for Casta.

Dinnertime. After ignoring me for days, Curius Decimus asks the pleasure of my company; the pleasure is all his, but I agreed to join him. I transcribe below, for its drollery, the dialogue preceding the invitation.

Decimus: "Do you have children?"

Myself: "I think I have one."

"You think?"

"Her mother won't say for sure."

"It's rough when you have no heirs."

Especially when one disinherits his only daughter on moral grounds, I told myself, recalling the docket I saw at the Mediolanum archives in his and Portia's names. Still, I answered. "Well, I'm in no great hurry, but I plan to have them. If my sisters are an indicator of the family's ability to perpetuate itself, I will have no problem in that regard."

Only local wine, cut by the appropriate amount of snow water, was served with different kinds of boiled fish; the dishes' elegance was ensured by abundant "sauce of the allies," a flavorful blend of spices and mackerel blood.

Decimus was in a quizzical mood. The room he'd taken for the night, not far from the campground, had the plain looks of a rental, yet the table had been set with his fine tumblers of spun glass from the

Rhine, silver underplates, and embroidered cloth. "From Antinoopolis," he said, as if Aelius had not recognized the minute stitches decorating the cloth's border and napkins. "Didn't you tell us you served there during the Rebellion?" As was his habit, Decimus tore small amounts of crumbs from the bread bun before him and idly played with them. "On the subject of rebellion, I suspect that our common friend Helena has spoken to you about her son's dreams of greatness. Something in her attitude, during an intimate moment, made me think you might be inclined toward supporting her motherly ambition."

"Helena loses her head when she's under a man, you should know that."

"A little crude, but I assume it means no."

"I never mix politics and lovemaking."

"Yes, yes, and you never stumble, and you're never caught off guard." Decimus rolled his eyes. "I told Helena the same, that I wouldn't support Constantine if he were the only pretender to the throne."

"He's not even a pretender, Decimus."

The Roman watched him with his head bent, nearly resting on his left shoulder; he was making a small ball out of crumbs, smoothing it between his palms. "You should understand once and for all, Spartianus, that I do not gather information for His Serenity, as so many of my stupid Mediolanum colleagues seem to think. I would do nothing for His Serenity beyond my duty as a Palace Guard officer. I don't even like His Serenity." Quickly, in a voluble fashion, he pressed words hard upon that sentence, not giving Aelius time to reply. "The fact remains that, whatever Helena's dreams are, a vacuum of power will form as soon as the sun goes down on May 1. Maximian will only pretend to pass the power to his dauphin Flavius. Constantius is sick and has a few months to live at most. I tell you, it's going to be played eventually between Maxentius and Constantine, and it will be bloody. You know this as well as I, whether or not you play hidebound for reasons of your own. *No!* This is *not* treason, Spartianus! Do not infuriate me with such sanctimony."

The ball of crumbs, shot by the pinch of Decimus's fingers, made an arc and fell into Aelius's tumbler. Aelius watched it sink in the wine; before it had time to dissolve at the bottom, he grabbed the glass and violently tossed the contents on the floor.

Decimus grinned. "Oh, at last. At last a reaction worthy of the name. What I am telling you, dear colleague, is that soon enough we'll all have to make a choice, because there are mighty changes coming. Or do you want to sit like a twig in the middle of the political hearth, waiting for the conflagration to consume you?"

"And I suppose you have pondered the question extensively, Decimus."

"For *years*."

"Coming to what eminently traditional conclusion?"

"Phew, tradition." Decimus sipped from his tumbler, smacking his lips. "You have no idea what the word means. *Dicunt Homerum caecum fuisse.* Not only does tradition say that Homer was blind, it perpetuates other bits of information we can't check against the facts, or patent untruths. If we had to believe tradition as you intend it, you should have found one-eyed men and men with their faces in their bellies in Upper Egypt, toward the sources of the Nile. And I wager you found no such thing. *My* sense of tradition is another thing altogether. You, like all outsiders, have no traditions, and can only waver from gullibility to distrust."

"Whom, in particular, am I guilty of distrusting?"

"Me. You met Annia Cincia last month and did not tell me."

Aelius was warned by a tingle on his face that he was growing pale. "You tried to *ruin* Annia Cincia with your lawsuits, as you ruined your own daughter."

"Ha! What do you understand, you pup."

They ate the rest of the dinner in near silence. Aelius felt bruised, irritated; the reasons why he did not leave the table confused him. Traps he'd been trying to avoid snapped around him, and in order not to stumble he did not move at all.

At one point Decimus stood, squaring his ring-laden hands on the finely embroidered cloth. "A coward, you're not. I *challenge* you to follow me without knowing where we are going."

Outside the night was as dark a wolf's gullet; a mile off, the camp's few lights trembled sunken in blackness. A bitter wind blew from the north, where the stars seemed to be resisting being torn from their fixed places.

The road Decimus took on horseback, followed by his colleague, glared like a spill of milk for the moment a serf stood with a lantern at the door, then it, too, went black. Gravel clacked under the hoofs; distant trees gave out sad sounds of crashing water. Aelius rode without thinking, because he'd been challenged and because curiosity drove him on. Logical thoughts were snatched from him as soon as they were formed, as though the wind were cleansing him of prejudices and easy truths. Childhood terrors, long forgotten, inhabited the darkness and those angry sounds of northern forests. He recalled, out of his credulous past, the tale of the faithless bride who follows her night visitor into the pit where dead animals are thrown, and where he turns into the skeleton of her vengeful dead lover.

Decimus said nothing, but appeared to know the road very well. He turned at one point, where the trees grew closer to the verge, and their heads in the wind made a sound as of bellowing great bulls. The gravel became deeper; hoofs slipped now and then. In the woods the darkness became nearly unbearable. When it broke, without warning, the clearing seemed to shimmer with light. But the moon had only risen above the horizon. Before and below them, in a dale, a villa sprawled, its terraces and porches lacquered white by the moonbeams, like an enchanted place, or the land of the dead.

Decimus spurred, reached the villa first, and was dismounting when Aelius joined him. In the shade of the moon, nothing was visible of the facade; nothing was heard beyond the moan of hinges when the door opened.

Inside, it was a Roman-style home with an elegant hallway. Decimus lit a lamp, exchanged a few whispered words with someone, through the crack of a side door, and kept walking toward a flight of stairs. Aelius followed with a singular tightness of his heart, holding his breath. A fresco of Eurydice being rescued from Hades flashed at his side, undulating in the wake of the lamplight. Orpheus looked back, anxiously. The mythical bride, veiled, stepped back with a rigid gesture of the lifted arms, palms upturned, like one who falls irremediably into forgetfulness. The idea—the certainty—that Decimus's fabled daughter lived here caught Aelius like a cold flame.

Decimus did not say, "Wait here," but proceeding without permission seemed improper. Aelius stopped on the threshold of a chamber, large for a bedroom, whose darkness was mitigated by the lamp his colleague brought in. At first he judged the bed empty, nothing but a bundle of quilts. A rich bed, gleaming with carved ivory and gilding, in a space carpeted and warm.

Setting aside the lamp, Decimus leaned over the mattress, and the bundle of quilts moved. A *thing* was lying in the sumptuous bed. As it stirred, Aelius made out its misshapen head, a forehead bulging and swollen at the sides, a skull all lumps, barely covered by scarce, hanging hair. The lower part of the face formed one tumor-like swelling that was more than a chin, high and gross, so that flat nose and lips were squashed and scarcely visible between those bulges. The head hung on the creature's chest, heavy and sleepy-eyed like a newborn cat's. Short, childish arms hung from her shoulders; the hands were large, long, and white. When she was raised in a sitting position, the hands began moving slowly, ceaselessly; inarticulate sounds came from the sunken mouth. Decimus petted it, unaware as the creature seemed to be of endearments. Only the food—sweets—placed in front of her seemed to cause a reaction, and she reached for it without using her hands, trying to lap it directly from Decimus's hand, but the shape of the face would not allow her to, and she grew furious. Hands flapped inert; the formless head struggled against its own weight, helpless squeals coming from within it. Decimus placed the sweets into her mouth then, one at a time, calming her. Seated on the bed, he combed down the stringy, thin hair over her ears, cradling the monstrous head against his chest.

When Decimus left the room, noiselessly pulling the door closed behind him, Aelius had gone to stand a few steps down the corridor, leaning against the wall with his arms folded and his head low over them. He said nothing while his Roman colleague passed in front of him, lamp in hand. Nor did he speak when Decimus, halfway to the stairs, turned back. "If you come a moment to the library," he invited him, in his usual bantering tone, "I'll lend you an insufferable panegyric of Severus by a Syrian poet." And because Aelius still would not react, he let out a mean laugh. "Well, are you coming? We have a war to fight."

During the ride back, in the face of Aelius's muteness, Decimus chatted on, acting as if nothing had happened. The wind had fallen. Human prattle chafed the silence of trees and fields all around, otherwise unbroken. Unbroken, too, was the dark, after a long, smoke-colored cloud hid the rising moon.

"I can hear your mind turning like a millstone." The well-bred voice of his colleague reached Aelius' ears. "You've been thinking about it ever since we had dinner. Why torment yourself in ignorance? I can tell you where the fire waker is: in Barbaricum. If they're still together, he and my distant cousin should have crossed over between Carnuntum and Ala Nova this afternoon at the latest."

Aelius opened his eyes wide in the night. "What do you mean—how?"

"Just what I said. How is her business. I haven't given up on the idea of laying my hands on the property she so inconsiderately gave to the Christians, thanks to Judge Marcellus. So let's say that during a brief meeting in Mediolanum I lent her what she needed to buy her way out of Italy, and out of my thinning hair. They'll catch her, sooner or later."

"You have no morals whatever."

"Morality is for peasants and romanized yokels like yourself."

SAVARIA, CAPITAL OF PANNONIA PRIMA SAVIA, 27 JANUARY, SATURDAY

Aelius slept hardly at all but was lucid in the morning. Riding into Savaria, he had to admit that an ample footnote to his biography of Severus would have to concern the rebuilding of Danubian cities after the Marcomannic Wars. Savaria's wide, well-paved streets, the aqueduct and baths, the governor's palace and the glorious temples—these were welcome sights after the nearly monthlong march. Adjacent to the thriving quarter populated by merchants from Aquileia was an affluent Jewish district, where Aelius had agreed to deliver a couple of business letters to one of ben Matthias's endless relatives and pick up messages and letters come for him from the Jew.

Ben Matthias's associates had no mail for him, but at the city's military post exchange he found a note from his mother, waiting to be picked up by the next courier and delivered posthaste. *Your father is not getting better,* it read. *I sent for your stepsister, sisters, and their husbands. If at all possible, do come.*

Time was tighter than it had been during the march. The ceremony and parade in the governor's presence, the official parting of the units for separate assignments at the border, would take most of the daylight hours. His regiment, the Ioviani Palatini, quartered two days away at Mursella, but a cohort from his old Persian campaign cavalry wing, permanently attached to his unit, had come to town to meet him, and the Guardsmen had already joined them at the city barracks. Hastily, Aelius penned a reply for his mother, explaining that moving out toward assigned positions took precedence. He would come as soon as he could get away. As his next delivery address, he gave the army fort at Arrabona, less than two hours from the frontier.

At the third morning hour, the units met for a common sacrifice at the provincial altar—*ara Provinciae*—and the taking of omens from live victims. The omens were favorable, but Aelius (and his colleagues, too) knew all too well that clean, ruddy, healthy animal entrails were kept on hand by priests for such occasions. The *praeses* himself, in his governor's regalia, witnessed the assigning of standards, eagles, and dragon-headed windsock banners to the soldiers, lined along the street that led from the Mall to the eastern gate.

Beyond the walls, since dawn a widespread haze had been rising from the northeast like a white tide, as if the enemy across the frontier were building its own rampart against the brightly arrayed, formidably armed foot soldiers and troopers.

30 January, Saturday, III day before the Kalends of February
The post commander at Arrabona had been his father's colleague during Aelius Spartus's last assignment, and the first thing he told Aelius when he came to report with his regiment, was, "A messenger came early this morning from your mother, Aelius. I've known Lady Justina thirty years, and I have never known her to be overdramatic. She was especially anxious that her message reach you, as your father's condition has worsened, and she fears for his life. Three days will not make much difference to your departure for Barbaricum, so I suggest that you go home and see to your family business."

9

"Husband, how wide open is the house,
How the keystone collapsed from the door!
And now who will look after us anymore?
And now who will speak for us anymore?
And now who will protect us anymore?
And now who will take care of the children anymore?
Oh, good of a lifetime, my life!
Who will tell the family, my husband?
Who will cry with you, my husband?
Who will walk with you, my husband?
Who will visit your grave, my husband?
Oh, good of a lifetime, my life!"

His mother's lament through the open door, and the fierce clap of hands at the end of each verse, filled the air like a bird's mournful call, like the dry sound of axes in the woods. No one was there to welcome him in the entry room; no sign that he'd been overheard came from the inner house. Only when his shadow, long in the rising sun, poured itself across the floor and reached the threshold of the bedroom did the high wailing stop at a peak, as if the voice itself had been cut.

Groaning sounds still came from within, and women sobbed, but Justina walked out drying her eyes. She pinned her hair back in a severe bun, which was her habitual way of wearing it. How ritual her complaint and bitter recriminations had been, how overlaid on her grief, was obvious by the way she resumed her army wife's lucidity.

She did not say, "You have come late, too late," or any such thing. She embraced him and then kept him at arm's length, holding his hands, to take a good look at him. "You have gone gray," was the other expected comment she could make, and did not. As a matter of fact, Aelius remembered, his mother seldom said the obvious, or commented on what was under everyone's eyes.

"Did you have a safe trip?" was the first question she asked. And with her right hand lifted, mildly she bade him not answer with an apology for his obvious lateness. "You must have had your reasons," she only added.

From the bedroom, the sounds of weeping came fainter, long, tremulous, a sign that the paid mourners were beyond the violent stage of the wake. Alerted that the dead man's son was about to enter, they stood from their kneeling positions around the bed. Their faces, bruised with their own blows, scratched with their nails until blood ran, were like those of women possessed. Chunks of hair yanked from their heads were strewn over the old man's body. And to the body they spoke in one voice. "Here comes Aelius, your son, your only son, who is visible to you but not to Death." From a brazier where boughs burned slowly in a bed of embers and incense, letting out an acute perfume, they lifted sprigs and sent a cloud of smoke in Aelius's direction, making him invisible to Death. "Here he comes, the keystone and the door that keeps the house safe."

Justina watched her son look at the body. Seven small coins had been placed on the old man's eyes, mouth, hands, and feet, to pay for his passage to the other world; the one on the mouth represented an offering from his wife, the two on his eyes from the son, those on his hands from the daughters, the two on his feet from the sons-in-law.

The mourners stood by the bed to receive their compensation.

Justina placed a coin into the cupped hands each one held out, kissed them on both cheeks, had them kiss her back, and then passed around what remained of the funeral feast in small baskets, as no piece of bread or chunk of meat from the ritual dinner must go lost or uneaten. "The rest I have given to the beggars," she whispered to Aelius. Only after they had all left with thanks, and with sidelong looks at the son who had come late for his father's death, did Justina gesture for Aelius to follow her into the kitchen. There the hearth was unlit, ashes strewn over the logs and embers to make sure that no flame burned in a dead man's house. A single glass full of wine and a loaf of bread sat on the table, as the ghost would return overnight to drink and eat a last time, while the family spent the dark hours elsewhere.

She said, "Three nights ago I dreamed of picking up green saplings, which as you know is a bad sign. The following night I dreamed that I was folding white sheets—another unfortunate message." Placing her right hand on the upturned palm of his, she touched his chest with her forehead. "He asked for you, and I told him you were on your way."

Aelius kept his lips tight. It was difficult to read his feelings, even for him. He let his mother's words go through him, breathing slowly.

She lifted her hand to his cheek, holding it there as she did every time they met after a long time: an affectionate way of checking her son's face against her memory. "I walked into each room of the house, and told every object that your father was dead, and held a mirror to each thing of value so that its image may follow your father into the other world. And we counted out loud all the properties and animals that belonged to him, so that through their names they, too, may follow him to the other world."

From the back door, she pointed to the first house where they'd lived after retirement, a small farm at the farthest end of the estate, now only used when grandchildren and friends came to visit. There, where she and her husband had awaited the refurbishing of the villa, she'd brought the linen used during their early years together, the old pots and pans, bedclothes, and the marriage bed, which she would never use again. "When you marry, Aelius, take your bride there. Make your first son there."

How he had undervalued her, Aelius thought. Justina was like a fixed star, small in the dark but a reference point for everyone and everything in the family. "Your sisters and their husbands are at Savaria to seek lawyers." He heard her say it as a matter of fact, without rancor, only making him aware of it. "Father was too superstitious and too attached to life to make a will, so now your brothers-in-law insist that they be repaid for the million sesterces each of the three of you loaned him when he bought the property."

Aelius discovered when he opened his mouth that the sound of his voice was new to the house, that he'd never said a word since coming. "Father paid us back the three million within six months' time: I was *there*."

"Gargilius and Barga claim otherwise, son. At six percent interest, in five years it amounts to over two million six hundred thousand they claim between them: more than half the value of the entire property. Half of which, according to the Law, should go to you. It robs you of more than half of your inheritance."

"As far as I am concerned, it robs you of all of yours. I want none of it. Mother, my brothers-in-law serve in provincial offices here; they have good stipends, and so do I. You certainly will not come out of putting up with Father for thirty-five years with only a fraction of his property." He spoke with his face averted, not out of shame but because he did not want her to see the bitterness on it. "We all went off or married as soon as we could, but you had to stay."

"They're looking to sell."

"They would have to win the case first, and they never will. What is their plan, to make you move in with one of them? I will not have you settle for hospitality at army post quarters; it is not fitting for a colonel's widow to reduce herself to being a guest of her sons-in-law. As for the silver and money cache discovered thanks to your dream, it all belongs to you by rights."

Of all Aelius had said, one thing seemed to resonate with her. "I traveled for years." She spoke with her hands in his, feeling the calluses of sword-wielding. "Followed your father wherever the army brought us. You were all born in different places, and those who died as babies are buried in a stretch of borderland that goes from Oescus to Castra Regina. Five years since retirement, and in five years we finally built a stable life, grew a garden, had our serfs and animals. I have no desire to move again, even less to keep moving. There are times, Aelius, when I think that only death allows you to stay in one place."

Seen from the back door, the hills Aelius had climbed as a boy drew a line that like all the heights from here to Noricum ran from northeast to southwest. Their highest point, he recalled from the days of his father's assignment to Savaria, afforded a panorama of the army camp, the city, dark forests, and farther down the plain, to far-off Scarbantia and Lake Pelso Superior. Close by, even under the snow cover, the work done thus far to lay out a formal garden amid the vineyards showed the abundance of well-earned retirement, even in these hard times of inflation and war. In the clarity of the western sky, Aelius conjured his father's face, thinned out by death, emptied of passions, the large body that for more than forty years had served the State and ruled the family. He thought he should say what he did.

"I could pretend that I came as quickly as I could, Mother, but it is not true; I had no intention of traveling faster than a horse could carry me on a regular day. Father did everything he could and more to set me up in the world, and to heighten my chances of success. For that I am grateful, but I did not love him, and I can't pretend now. He was brutal with his soldiers and with us. Did nothing to cultivate his god-given soul or to recognize the god-given intelligence in his wife. You earned his inheritance by your patience and love: I did not, because I never loved him or respected him. In my career thus far, I have encountered half a dozen men who were fathers to me more than he ever was." Piles of bricks to be used in completing the corner towers drew his attention, red against the snow. "As for my brothers-in-law, let them do as they will. Let them hire lawyers and try to cheat you and the Law. You will come out victorious, and they will have to come to your door with the respect due to you, as will my sisters and their brood."

Justina seemed suddenly tired. In the two days since her husband's death, she had no doubt taken care of everything. Now that the family had gathered, her energy was flagging, or else she dreaded the disagreement. "How does it happen, Aelius? Those who most look like us physically are least like us. You resemble your father, and even more so your uncle, although you're more handsome than they ever were. But inside—and it isn't just because of your education—you resemble none of us, except myself, a little. I wonder if that's good or bad, because I worry so much, I *feel* things, and these times aren't kind to those who feel. Your father was what they call a good husband: He never brought his lovers home, never made a house serf pregnant, regularly sent money when he was away, and built a career. I never wanted for anything material. You were the apple of his eye; I do think he secretly hoped to the last that you were, or would become, involved in intrigue, that you would seek power as others who soldiered with him did. These are the days when the throne is open to all, he would say. You don't know how many times I shuddered at the thought that someone would overhear us, and ruin us all—ruin *you,* and your chances of advancement." She stood at his side, tall, a solid woman with graying blond hair, clear-skinned. "Or perhaps he did it for himself. One son who'd survived childhood: He bet everything on you. For all his overbearing, he knew his limits. In you, he saw the stuff that he'd glimpsed in others who climbed very high since the days they soldiered with him."

"He was wrong in giving me to the care of philosophers, then."

"Tell me, how long will you stay?"

"I leave early tomorrow." Aelius realized he had not asked for details about his father's death, nor spent more than a dutiful moment by the body. When he did inquire, and Justina told him how the illness had progressed, he listened passively, with his mind still on the fraud concocted by his brothers-in-law. Then something his mother said made him pay keen attention.

"Toward the end, Aelius, when he realized that no physician was likely to save him, your father began listening to anyone who promised that his health could be restored. Lately he heard through one of the neighbors' serfs—a dull woman who is always mumbling to herself—that there was a man capable of working miracles in Savaria. He threw a terrible fit when he was told that a trip in winter would surely kill him. So we had to bundle him up and take him out of the house in a snowstorm. He only went a couple of miles before he had another attack, and was dead by the time we crossed the threshold again."

What had ben Matthias said? "I smell danger." Aelius heard his mother's words and suddenly knew that the curiosity first kindled at Lupus's bedside had taken him across half of Europe to this doorstep, that his father's death was somehow part of a game that linked him to the elusive saint or charlatan. Could danger follow him even to his mother's house? He asked the question only because he felt he should.

"Who is this miracle worker, and where is he now?"

"I think he goes by the name of 'fire waker,' Aelius. His given name, I don't know. The mourners heard he's moved on from Savaria to Contra Florentiam, where the commander's wife is said to suffer from an issue of blood."

Contra Florentiam was a counter-fortress built on the other side of the Danube, over two hundred miles from here. If Agnus sought to cross over, it was improbable that he'd choose such a place; more likely he'd headed for Ala Nova or Gerverata, due north. After his mother's comment, Aelius felt like a hound that picks up the scent again. Glimpsed before, suspected, unrecognized, the likelihood of Agnus's guilt in the deaths at Treveri and Mediolanum flashed before him like the red tail of a fox running to cover, or a tongue of fire. For a moment he did not know what to do with the intuition; it blotted out the reality of this visit to his parents' home, and only Justina's touch on his arm kept him anchored to his duties as only son to a dead father.

He went back inside, and for a time stood alone in his father's bedroom. The burial—inhumation as by family tradition—was set for the early afternoon. Before his kin, neighbors, and military representatives from Spartus's last assignment began to arrive, Aelius would have time to go see the district judge in Savaria and return. Accordingly, he rode out.

For a week, widow, family, and serfs were to avoid crossroads, because the dead man might attach himself to them when instead he had to be able to continue on his way. Already a path had been traced in the snow around the place where two lanes—one of them leading to the property, the other to another retiree's house—traversed each other. Such crossings, however, abounded between here and Savaria. Twice, as long as his mother could see him from the door, Aelius did avoid the intersections, but the third time he went right through. Soon he was passing by the newly prepared family plot along the military road that from the belt of estates went to the settlements, and from those to the great river.

SAVARIA

The original of the quitclaim document had been lost during a fire at the courthouse two days earlier. This was the first thing Aelius heard from the judge. The second was that all but one of the witnesses who signed it had since died, and as of last report, the survivor had left for remote duty in northern Britannia. Aelius kept his copy at Nicomedia, and as far as his brothers-in-law, they claimed of course to have none.

He was in a disgruntled mood when he left the magistrate's chambers. His incidental inquiries about prosecution against the local Christians confirmed that a number of them had been detained or executed. No miracle workers figured among them, no women. Any claims of miracles or strange deaths in town? The court employees looked at him as though he had two heads. No, or at least they'd heard of none.

There was just enough time left to call at the cavalry barracks, where Duco was stationed with his troops in anticipation of transfer to the front. The Briton did not expect to see Aelius in town; informed of the reason, he gave him his condolences and invited him to a drink. Over a beer, they agreed that weeks of armed reconnaissance, skirmishes, and patrolling in Barbaricum would pass before the units would join in a strike force at the end of winter. Besides, the first seventeen days of February were *nefasti,* and no campaign—unless unavoidable—would be initiated.

After the beer took the edge off the talk of war, Duco reverted to his chatty self. "I didn't tell the truth in Celeia, Aelius," he said half apologetically. "I did hear something the night Frugi died. The floor squeaked a little, only enough to make me realize that someone was tiptoeing from one bunk to another . . . to Frugi's. I've been in the army long enough not to pay attention to what men do when they sack out in the same place. I mean, you know."

Aelius blinked, which was the only sign of impatience he gave. "I *know* what you mean. Were there sounds you identified? Did it sound like a conversation, or what?"

"All I heard was the rustle of sheets, a groan, and a whisper. Because of what I thought it was, I turned over and covered my head. When we all got up after his death, it seemed embarrassing to mention it. And anyhow, since Frugi died of a stroke—" About to take another sip, Duco put down the mug slowly. "He did, didn't he?"

"Who was it, Duco, can you tell? Think of the disposition of the bunks in the room."

The Briton would not answer directly. Finishing his beer came in handy as the excuse for a troubled interval, and alternative doubts of his own. "Why would Decimus get up in the middle of the night to check on a colleague? It's not like Frugi was sick the evening before."

Again that feeling of hunting close to the prey. Aelius glimpsed tracks, sensed a whiff in the air, but it was a different quarry he was after. Or else the quarry, unrecognized, that had always been there. The stupor in Duco's eyes warned him not to go beyond what he'd already said. *I knew we should not have dumped Frugi,* he thought, *without verifying that he died a natural death.* To his colleague, he only said, "I have to go back for my father's burial. Take care of yourself. I'll see you across the border, whenever."

At Aelius Spartus's estate, after the interment the family gathered in the large dining hall, the best room in the house. Sighing, Aelia Belatusa passed her hands in circles over her belly. She was close to her term, she announced (as if they couldn't tell), and would stay with Mother to give birth. She'd only had daughters thus far, but "If it's a son," she said, "we'll call it Aelius Spartus. I felt it kick when I leaned over to kiss Father: I think it'll be Father reborn."

Her sister and half sister exchanged a spiteful look. "What are we, strangers? Between the two of us we have three sons."

"No." Calmly Justina interposed herself. "The name Aelius Spartus is reserved for your brother's first son."

"The way he's going, Mama, you're not going to live long enough to see Aelius's first son."

"Belatusa, I intend to live long enough to see Aelius's *grandson*, thank you very much."

Aelius caught the conversation walking in from the garden. He had until now kept an eye on a nervous real estate agent, brought by his brothers-in-law from town to look over the property in the company of Justina's head freedman. At Aelius's entrance, blood and acquired relatives turned to him holding their tongues. His sister Belatusa let out another sigh. She waddled to and fro dragging her feet, red-eyed with weeping, and—as when she stood from giving a last kiss to the body— she kept her hands on her loins, arms at a wide angle. Aelius had seldom seen her in a different state ever since her marriage. The other sister, the "young one," had given birth two months earlier and was still thick around the waist. As for Justina's daughter by her first marriage, she'd left husband and children behind to pay her respects and, although she had no claims on the property, to "help with the sale."

Belatusa sat down with an air of exhaustion. "We can all turn gray waiting for Aelius's son, Mama."

Her husband, Barga, laughed. "He's gone gray himself, waiting!"

Barrel-chested, gaudy in their overly ornate uniforms, Gargilius and Barga had not exchanged ten words with their brother-in-law thus far.

"Question is, is he dropping his seed around?" Gargilius answered Barga's joke, taking his crotch in hand. "That's what old man Spartus used to say, 'Aelius isn't dropping his seed around. I wonder what's wrong with him.' That's true, brother-in-law, he did. And he was wondering whether the Greek teachers he got you made you a little *strange*."

Only because of his mother's presence did Aelius refrain from punching him. The intention must have been readable on his face, however, given the way Gargilius pretended a humorous boxing move when Aelius warned him: "Don't raise your voice, and don't you use such language in front of my mother, you ass."

At once the girls got in the middle of it, noisily, especially Belatusa. It was a good thing that Justina's freedman came to announce that the real estate agent was ready to depart and wanted a word with the men in the family. Barga and Gargilius rushed to precede Aelius outside, where the three of them were given a foreseeably lower-than-market-value assessment of the property, should the agency decide to buy.

"You can try to sell on your own, but money is hard to come by these days."

Barga spat a wad of saliva contemptuously. "You bet we'll sell on our own." He cupped his hand to whisper into Gargilius's ear.

"You're the heir," the agent told Aelius. "If there are debts to be paid out of the estate, you had better clear them to get all you can out of the sale."

Aelius saw red, but kept his peace. He waited until the small covered wagon carrying the real estate agent disappeared behind the old firs flanking the gate. He then shoved Barga aside, turned to Gargilius, and struck him squarely on the chin with his right fist, sending him reeling off the porch and into the snow that piled under the treasure's pear tree.

Despite the tensions in the family, the habits and ways of mourning were abided by. The hearth was kept unlit (it would be, for a total of seven days), and copper knives were used at dinner because iron would keep the dead's spirit from partaking. For the night, daughters and in-laws went to friends' houses a mile off; Justina and Aelius stayed with a minimum number of serfs in the little house at the edge of the estate.

In the morning Aelius rose early, but not before his mother. On this clear day of perfect winter weather, she had already walked to the long, army-style stables to oversee the laying out of his equipment and the saddling of his mount, and to place his father's cavalry sword in his luggage.

Aelius joined her there. Without speaking they finished setting things in order, then walked back to the main villa to say their farewells. He kissed her hands when they stood on the front porch, a gesture he reserved for his leavetakings from her.

"Are you really so anxious that I marry?" The need to speak of Anubina pressed within him. He never had, and even now held back, because it might not be the time for that conversation. It all depended on what she would answer.

Justina surprised him. "It wasn't I who sent you by letter the names of those prospects. Your father used my name because he judged it should be a mother's doing, presenting prospective wives to her son. I'd be the last one to impose a mate on a child of mine, even though I realize I am shirking one of my duties."

And so—quickly, because the groom would bring his horse at any moment—Aelius told her of himself and Anubina, of their love affair, and of the little girl who might be his daughter. Justina was quiet for a time. Her fairness in the sunlight made her seem big and bright even in her mourning dress.

"You must understand her, Aelius," she said then. "*I* understand her. She was bought and sold; she belonged to you because you paid money for her. It does not mean you did not love her even then, but no one asked her, did they? Did *you* ask her? Who asked me, when my first husband died? He left in his will the provision that I should marry his brother, your father, and your father readily married me because he was himself widowed and wanted sons. No one asked me. So I gave birth twice in a year and a half, to daughters, and he was already repenting the bargain when I grew big with you." She touched his chest with the flat of her hand. "But then, he never asked you, either, whether you wanted to become a soldier."

"Well, what else could I do? I am a soldier's son."

"And Anubina is a soldier's orphan, whose mother sold her to a brothel. How many took her before you did, against her will or not?"

"But she did marry her farmer husband: It was her own doing."

"More likely than not, because she was carrying her daughter and wanted a man in the house. As for her husband, I know how farmers think: Buying a pregnant mare is buying two horses for the price of one. Didn't you wonder why she had only one other child, in the years you said she was married? Forget the one she lost, those are things that happen. I think she was already claiming her right to belong to herself." With soft sounds the army mount, led by the stable boy, approached on the snowy ground. Justina stepped back, so that her son would not see tears welling in her eyes. Her voice stayed firm. "It's not that she does not want you, Aelius. Anubina wants to be Anubina's, as I wanted to be my own and never could."

When he rode by it one last time, his father's headstone in the low winter sun drew a long, thin shadow. Acquired long before, it represented the defunct, although in his superstition Spartus had not asked that it portray him. It was the stock image of an army officer with the insignia of his rank, sculpted in high relief as a horseman triumphing over a prostrate enemy. Most everybody on the frontier—soldier or no—had such a rider carved on his grave. "The Thracian," it was commonly called. The inscription read DIS MANIBUS AELII SPARTI SIBI ET SUIS. *To himself and his family.* But Aelius was determined not to be buried under the same headstone, come what may.

Notes by Aelius Spartianus, written at Gervelata on 4 February, Sunday, eve of the Feast of Concordia:

Speaking of concord, having failed to hold my temper, I have the little satisfaction of knowing that Gargilius will have to explain to his friends the missing tooth and swollen bruise on his face. It won't stop him and Barga from scheming, but he'll think twice before behaving like a boor in Aelia Justina's presence.

The River Arrabo froze overnight. I didn't remember it so crowded with canes and reeds. When I crossed it before Bassiana it had sealed over so suddenly that unfortunate waterfowl were caught in the ice and died. The Danube reportedly still flows, even though its banks and deeper bends show signs of freezing over soon.

At Arrabona, I heard that Sido has arrived in Siscia and brought his cronies, dislodging the local speculatores to the boonies, including Arrabona. Also, a letter from that amiable scoundrel ben Matthias awaited, the gist of which I copy below:

"Esteemed Commander, I am in receipt of a letter from my son-in-law Isaac, who was completely cleared of suspicion in the matter of his employer Marcus Lupus's death at the brickyard in Belgica Prima. Aside from the consolation that such news brought me, a tidbit came my way I consider worth forwarding to you by special courier. During the investigation, which widened to include the so-called fire waker's activities in Treveri, paupers and ne'er-do-wells came forward (or were pushed forward by the competent authorities) to confess that money was given to them by said Agnus to pretend various illnesses. The most common among these were lameness, epilepsy, blindness, and scabies. The revelation does not directly solve the mystery of Lupus's death but confirms what the anonymous letter said of the miracle worker: namely, that he is a charlatan who lives off folks' credulity. Now both he and his female assistant are sought for murder 'anywhere in the Empire they may find themselves.'

"Here in Mediolanum the execution of Christian leaders has officially closed the case of Judge Marcellus's death. Why then do we hear that the speculatores are still asking questions and looking into things? The name or names of the investigated are closely guarded."

Dated the 14th of January, the letter goes on to ask me, *"Should you have an opportunity to do so in the appropriate circles, kindly consider recommending the army cloth-dyeing establishment of my cousin Judas Hilaros at Intercisa. Good references about his work can be obtained at the command of the I Cohort of Emesa Syrians in the same town."*

Ben Matthias stays true to his bargaining self. What he writes is welcome, however, and reinforces my desire to confront the fire waker, wherever in the Empire (or outside of it) he may be.

After rejoining the regiment, I took a cohort along, as our orders are to seek the Danube's right bank west of Arrabona, passing by Ad Mures, Quadrata, and Ad Flexum. *"Mice," "Square Hall,"* and *"River Bend"* are names that illustrate those places much as I remember them, except that the mice are river rats. Once we reach the place where the Marus River flows into the Danube, we are to cross over and begin reconnoitering; we have good maps and good intelligence of hostile territory from the confluence to the first wide bend of the Marus one encounters traveling upstream. Then it'll be up to us and to my mother's prayers.

Tonight we are housed at Gervelata, an hour's riding east of Carnuntum; sacrifices are to be offered tonight at Nemesis's temple in that city. Curius Decimus and his *"Romans"* preceded us. It is likely that I will be invited to dine with them. My preference would be to see Decimus one on one. At this point I must wonder whether Frugi's death was foul play on his part, and if so, why. I am plagued by unanswered, perhaps unanswerable questions. What else has Decimus done? Could he not be behind Judge Marcellus's death? Could not other incidents that resulted

*in the death of Christians be directly or indirectly his doing,
blinded as he is by his conservative hatred and his lust to ran-
som Casta's wealth from the State? Have I gone entirely off course
by thinking up brick-makers' envious plots, or by suspecting Agnus's elusive person? Is the preacher a charlatan, in fact? Could
not the anonymous letter accusing him of scheming with Lupus
be untruthful? Would Curius Decimus go as far as killing a
brick-maker in Treveri to persecute his cousin and force her out
of the Empire's borders?*

*All I know for sure I do not actually know, but sense. There is
something dark, fearful, and negative about the fire waker. A
charlatan, yes, but what if he were behind it all, somehow? Ben
Matthias's nose for danger and trouble cannot be wrong. Agnus
gives off that scent. Against all logic, I feel pressed to find him,
face him, turn him in if he's guilty, before Casta suffers from her
association with him. A guard at Arrabona told me of several
spots on the river used by immigrants and smugglers to elude
army patrols. If Agnus manages to disappear among the tribes
hostile to Rome (and if they do not kill him after his chicaneries
fail), I could lose him forever. Thus I feel the urgency to track
him down, even though there are so many more important things
in play. I want to see her again, too: Casta, the lady Annia Cincia. She was a beauty once, so said Decimus. It's been only a few
years since then. Why shouldn't she be a beauty still? She means
nothing to me, and yet I may be the sole friend she has. Why?
Because she is elusive, as ben Matthias says, and that attracts
me in a woman? Because her husband died on her, her cousin
Decimus pursued her wealth, her religious teacher let her down?
I am not tenderhearted, but it may simply be because, whether
or not they're Christian, women have a hard time in this world,
and so often we men take advantage of them.*

The frontier was like Helena: It never seemed to change. Despite
the rumors of war, business thrived; one saw the same shop fronts, the

same uniforms, receiving the impression that the same men served
here one year after the next, one generation after the next. Even the
brothels that lined the streets to and from army camps were as always,
with their explicit signs and red drapes across the entrances, the same
bond girls calling out from the doorstep when one went by.

At Carnuntum, both the army citadel and the civilian city were
chaotic with the influx of troops. Aelius found a well-stocked book-
shop, where he secured a copy of Aeschylus's plays. "Brushing up on
your classics?" the seller said amicably.

"No, trying to find a sentence I saw scratched on a wall in the baths,
back in Mediolanum."

Nearly by accident, during the nth inquiry at the courthouse, he
caught the tail of the fleeing fox. On a tip, during a police raid on a
well-known Christian meeting place, a man known as the fire waker
had escaped by the skin of his teeth and, despite all efforts by gendarmes, was reported to have made it across the border. "He can be no
more than two or three days ahead," the courthouse employee told
Aelius, "but who's going to seek him there, Commander?"

"Did he flee alone?"

"We assume. Our informant heard that the fugitive had a female
accomplice, but she split from him somewhere between Ala Nova and
Vindobona."

The two army posts were a day's ride west of Carnuntum. Aelius
had to remind himself of his responsibilities to keep from riding off.
The hook that secured him to the here and now was the ceremony at
Nemesis's temple; even more so, running into Curius Decimus, whose
invitation to dinner Aelius expected and said yes to.

None of the others from Cato's Sodality were present. The room was
small, a private dining nook on the upper floor of an inn run by the
blacksmiths' guild. When Aelius inquired, his colleague answered that
Ulpius Domninus and Otho were with their men at Ala Nova. "The

twins are in town; Vivius Lucianus heads a cohort at Quadrata. They send their wishes."

Whatever Decimus's real intentions were for this get-together, Aelius saw it as an opportunity to make him talk, even if it meant submitting to the usual political palaver on the good old republican days. Asking point-blank about Frugi was inadvisable, but wine might help. There was plenty of local vintage on the side table, and Greek and Italian wines, too. "This is my treat," Aelius said. "The coming of war calls for celebration. I go up the Marus's course tomorrow, and if rumors of a possible intertribal raid are correct, it won't be a stroll."

"I'll drink to that." Decimus did not like the cold weather. He wore a scarf even indoors, and his cloak tucked around his knees. No doubt he had his reason for this meeting, since they had not left each other in the most cordial of ways. "It's a good thing that you're not afraid," he observed after savoring the wine with a smack of lips. "Would you die for Rome?"

"This instant."

"Not *this instant.*" Decimus laughed, refilling his glass. "Not before a well-prepared dinner, Spartianus! Don't your Stoics say, 'If you are sent into exile, stop on the way to have a good meal'?"

"Wouldn't *you* die for Rome?"

"I will." Letting the ambiguous words drop from his mouth, Decimus turned to the side table, crowded with cold and hot plates. They'd asked to be alone, so the Roman served both Aelius and himself. Eating on the frontier meant venison, stringy and flavorful, calling for frequent toasts. At one point, not yet altered by drink but considerably more relaxed, Decimus said, "I assume you realize you are the sole colleague of mine who has seen my Portia."

"Thank you for the privilege."

"Not a privilege: a proof of trust on my part." They drank to Portia, to Thaesis, to daughters in general. "And to the sons I do not have," Decimus added wryly. From a holder containing several little spoons for the many sauces, he chose one and helped himself to a spicy condiment. "Speaking of daughters, you recall what I told you about Constantine's and Maxentius's sure-to-come bid for the empire after May first. It is a fact that through his father's marriage to Maximian's daughter, Constantine became Maxentius's brother-in-law."

"Yes. What of it?"

"Well, in bed I got Helena to own up that she plans to convince Constantine to divorce his present wife and marry Maxentius's sister Fausta. If that should happen, given that his father, Constantius, married Maximian's other daughter, Theodora, Constantine would become—like his own father—a son-in-law to Maximian, but also a brother-in-law to his own father, and brother-in-law to his step-mother; Theodora would become her own sister's stepmother. And as for Constantine's mother, Helena, who slept with Maximian and Maxentius both, not to speak of Constantius, I cannot even reckon her role in this confusion."

"It's interesting, but given that strictly speaking my mother is also my aunt, I cannot say the arrangement is out of the ordinary."

Decimus appeared suddenly annoyed, as if Aelius purposely ignored the hints contained in his argument. "Don't you see? Helena plans to keep Maxentius from fighting Constantine until they both wheedle or kill everyone else in view of the throne."

"It wouldn't be the first time in Rome's history."

"But if Constantine is declared vice-emperor as soon as his father dies in Treveri, Maxentius—who has gotten neither the consul's post nor a miserable generalship—will contend against him, and I wager with his father's help, since Maximian does not want to abdicate. Believe, I know whereof I speak. At the palace in Mediolanum there are open bets on how long His Serenity will stay retired before he claws his way to the throne again. Why, Aristophanes wanted *you* killed as soon as you put your foot in the city, because you bore the abdication command. Only because Diocletian wrote the eunuch a letter holding him personally responsible for your life did he change his tune."

It was possible, entirely possible. "I don't know that any of this is true," Aelius said, not to appear as surprised as he was.

"Judge for yourself. One week before you reached Mediolanum, I was myself given orders to execute you on arrival. Because of that letter, my orders were countermanded no earlier than the morning of your coming."

Aelius swallowed a piece of tough meat. He recalled the first night in Mediolanum, when Decimus had waited for him at a dark street corner, by the brothel where a girl's nakedness was half seen. "Why do you tell me this?"

"Because Rome will be faced soon with two usurpers' rule, or bloody rule by whichever of the two wins. For that reason, it is necessary that you trust me as much as I trust you."

They were coming to it now. Was this the sort of conversation Frugi had been made to hear and comment on, before his sudden death? Aelius saw through Decimus's nostalgia imperfectly, as when fog begins to thin out without lifting. "Honestly, I do not understand the need to reaffirm trust between fellow officers."

"Are you really so dense? We need one like you to do what only one like you can do."

"*You* need me. Who is *you*?"

Seven sauce spoons lay in front of Decimus; one by one, he set them in a row as he spoke. "You come from the same province as Constantine and Maxentius; your father served with their fathers. Helena trusts you." In one sweep, he discomposed the line of spoons. "On my twentieth birthday, thirty-seven years ago, a Roman emperor was murdered by Danubian officers who wanted the throne, and have kept it ever since. Now we run the risk of having Danubians make that usurpation hereditary."

Aelius felt a cringing of the short hair on his scalp. Decimus's voice reached his ears with strange hollowness, as if he were speaking in a wooden tube from far off. In a moment, he went from thinking it an effect of something treacherously poured into his wine to realizing it was soul-fear for hearing what he did.

"So we thought of you, given your declared love for Rome and the way you publicly exposed Rome's enemies as late as last year." Decimus now smoothed the tablecloth with his hand, and the hefty rings on his fingers left furrows in the linen. "The May first abdication ceremonies are to be held contemporaneously at Nicomedia, where Constantine will attend with Helena, and Mediolanum, where Maxentius will be at his father's side. Mediolanum is not a problem, but we need a man above suspicion in Nicomedia." The raking of the cloth halted, started again. "You look a little pale, colleague. Is it because of my words, or because the sole fact of having heard them makes you an accomplice? I can make it formal, and let the walls hear if they have ears: Aelius Spartianus, for the good of the republic which you serve both as an officer and a historian, Constantine and Maxentius must go down on May first. Especially Constantine, who is amassing foreign backers. Please note: Should you entertain the idea of denouncing me, or any of my friends, we will turn all accusations against you and bring proof that you killed Frugi at Celeia because he resisted your plan. We have powerful lawyers, and even more powerful judges on our side."

Aelius could hear his heartbeat pound in his throat, behind his eyes. The ease with which Decimus had poured out what for over a month he had apportioned in bits, letting him see and not see, understand and not, was like the clean cut of a blade. And ben Matthias took Cato's Sodality for a harmless social club! Opening his mouth to speak was an effort. "From what I have seen, you are a handful of nostalgic fools, who will be crushed like grapes."

"Will we? Well, we shall see. More has been obtained with less. We have no revolution in mind, Spartianus. It could never succeed, at this implosive stage of Roman history. We merely intend to attempt a partial restoration. Here, have a drink. You know better than I that entire areas of the Empire are outside of army control, de facto no-man's-land where only nominally the authority of Rome is exercised. Some of these regions are as wide as nations. Some, I wager, will become nations sooner or later."

"You cannot think of succeeding! Whom should such a republic of yours attract? The descendants of pure Romans like yourselves? You wouldn't find enough to populate the place, much less man an army!"

"There's time. Now we go to war, as bidden. Because victory must necessarily be declared by our emperors before May first, it is certain the campaign will be concluded or called off before the end of April." Decimus filled Aelius's glass to and over the brim. "I notice you have difficulty expressing yourself, unlike other evenings. Never mind, Spartianus, I do not expect you to give me an answer at once. There'll be occasion in days to come. Between now and then, you can choose between keeping silent or exposing us and going down as one of the conspirators, with all that it will mean for your dear provincial family; the authorities have no patience with the kin of traitors. No one, not even His Divinity, whose 'our dear Aelius' you are, will believe at a crucial time like this that you associated in blissful ignorance with me and my cohorts as long as you did. Even he, who after all began as an officer and eliminated all rivals on the way to the throne, will think you lie. A letter to him now—if that's what you're thinking—will only be a noose around your neck, and your relatives'. There's—what? Sixteen or more of your immediate family around, young and old?"

Aelius did not recall leaving the inn and returning to Gervelata. He found himself in his quarters long after dark, in a sweat despite the freezing cold. All the questions he'd planned to ask about Marcellus, Lupus, even Frugi, had been wiped from his mind. What was there to ask anymore? Frugi had been killed because he had grown fearful. As for the rest, his thoughts were in a hopeless jumble. He tried to sleep, and couldn't. Sitting up was no better, so he paced the floor for hours. Once he had seen a bear caught in a square pit walk to the corners and slowly back up from them, incapable of turning around. No differently he was going up to Decimus's words again and again, and receding without an about-face, still staring at them.

In the morning he ran a high fever. He concealed it in order not to miss his opportunity to go out into the field, and put action between himself and anxiety.

NOTES BY AELIUS SPARTIANUS, VI DAY BEFORE THE IDES,
THURSDAY, 8 FEBRUARY:

There are gods who watch over us at times of trouble. Before it started, what should have been a routine foray into enemy territory turned into a full alert, due to a night attack on the forward post at Nemorense, far from the fortified bridgehead where we were to cross the Danube. Unhoped-for distraction! There was no time to waste, so my men and I splashed to the other side over rocks and ice and the piled tree trunks the barbarians employed to solidify the ford. The hostiles had vanished as quickly as they had shown up, of course, and for a full day we followed their tracks, to the place where the Marus River flows into the Danube. I knew it to be a wetland, treacherous in the spring and the fall, when rains swell the watercourse and everything around it for miles is nothing but flood land and wet meadows. What I did not expect was to find it only partly frozen, so that while some tracts could be traveled on horseback or at least on foot, leading the mounts by the harness, others were still in the liquid state. A table of gelid water mirroring the sky, studded with large trees whose trunks are more than half submerged. Clumps of canes and water plants make perfect hiding spots, but luckily the temperature of the water does not allow even the sturdiest barbarian to stand in it for long.

Because southern winds have been blowing since Monday, the snow cover had melted in many spots. We could follow the enemies' tracks as well as the signs left by wild animals. Stray dogs following our patrol (there are packs of them on both sides of the Danube) rolled in the yellow grass where badgers and other creatures left their droppings, the old habit of their wolfish ancestors.

On the third day out, by an oxbow on the river, we finally sighted the hostiles. I gave order not to attack at once, determined to ascertain whether we faced a group of scouts, a vanguard, or the front of a larger army. The fever that until then had plagued me (I think two of my captains and all of the non-coms were aware of the malaise, and worried about it) went down with the rapidity with which it had come. I found myself perfectly lucid and well.

By the afternoon we knew that it was in fact a vanguard of one hundred or so, coming from the distant northeast judging from their dress and equipment, foraging off neutral villages and no doubt meaning to report to their chiefs on the readiness of the frontier troops. Mobile troops such as mine, vexillationes capable of setting off at a moment's notice, are all but unknown to them. We attacked at sunset from the west, protected by the low rays that must have reflected like fire on the wetlands and blinded them. We cut through them with vigor. No prisoners can be taken or survivors left alive during such operations. More than once prisoners brought to our side for interrogation found support among barbarians allowed to live in the settlements and turned mercy into a Trojan horse.

In Persia it was everyone's unpleasant habit to cut off the fallen enemy's right ear as a mode of reckoning a victory. I did it myself. We see on the deified Trajan's triumphal column Roman soldiers carrying severed barbarian heads to their commander. As the group we fought against has a mode of hair dressing that involves a braid coiled and fastened over one temple, I had those braids cut and gathered in sacks. Seven of my men were lost in the battle, whose fierceness preoccupies me in view of having to face the same barbarians in the spring. Roman equipment, even some of our better mail shirts, was taken from the hostiles' bodies. The majority of the items, more's the shame, must have been sold on the sly by our frontier troops: worse than losing them on the field of honor!

By dawn on the following day, villagers from the surrounding area were in front of my tent asking for permission to strip the barbarian dead; the elders come from foederati groups, and their status as nonhostile border inhabitants makes them both bold and petulant. I saw nothing wrong in allowing them to make free with clothing and mounts, although no weapons (not even knives or razors) were granted them.

Satisfied with our mission, we began heading back. It is worth noting that beyond the border, the villagers are frightened stiff of us as long as we are there; when we cross back over, they fear the barbarians. That is not new. Rather, I do not like their mood, their half-words; something tells me there may be an uprising planned for much earlier than we expect. My report to headquarters will be in that vein.

Early this morning, on an inhabited knoll at the edge of a woodland, overlooking the river, the gathered elders let themselves be interrogated, but only after promises of money backed with threats. The intelligence gained is incomplete but will provide a few tesserae to the large mosaic. More: These days out, so frantic and removed from the stagnation on the rear of the front, have brought me close to a solution to the murders, against which I battered my thick Pannonian head for weeks. Clues too small and too large to notice finally coalesced, and I could kick myself for taking so long. How far from the truth can a man find himself, misreading all the signals that Fate and his own determination place in his lap? In a purely coincidental way, the Greek verse scratched on the wall of the Old Baths clinched it for me: "Woe, woe, look, look! Keep away the bull from the heifer"—it is Aeschylus's Agamemnon. When I passed by, in my haste to see the place where Marcellus had been killed, I ignored the suggestion implicit in the words from that ancient play. To think that I could recite it by heart once!

The solution, as I have come to it, weighs on me. It is like medicine that leaves a bitter taste on the tongue. Riding to the brickyard on that first morning, it was presented to me, and I ignored it, for the next two months refusing to take it. Had I accepted its sourness, Judge Marcellus would still be alive, and also his wife, and also the idiots who went to their deaths at Mediolanum.

But here we are. Because Nemorense is a watchtower not far from Ala Nova and Carnuntum, and I was in a region facing those localities, I asked my usual question. Describing Agnus and Casta as best I could, I inquired about foreign travelers who claimed to work magic. What did I say about the gods looking over us? The head of the tribal elders answered yes. In his words, a holy man has recently come from the Roman border; he works wonders; his fame has within days spread to the tribes from the Marus to the Tibiscus rivers; sheltering him is a privilege, and the barbarians will let no one harm him or try to take him away.

Thus I understood the fire waker to be hiding nearby, in a neutral village of huts of dirt and branches built below ground, such as—I may add—one still sees in the most backward parts of my own Pannonia. "They can smell Romans from afar," the old man warned me about his barbarian neighbors, to which I did not reply that they won't smell these *Romans: My men are fair-skinned northerners, drink milk as much as wine, and eat a northern diet.*

Need I say that I am going over, with a handful of my Guardsmen?

10

Diplomatic skills, knowledge of the local dialect, and the gift of money were equally necessary for Aelius to gain access to the fire waker's sanctuary. The left bank of the Marus, close to the confluence with the Danube, was pretty much a no-man's-land, where traffickers, merchants, and deserters moved freely, and the occasional Roman patrols were not challenged as long as they left smugglers and women alone. When it didn't snow, and if one proceeded against the wind, typically one smelled hostile camps and bivouacs well in advance of seeing them. The use of hurriedly tanned pelts and large amounts of milk products gave a peculiarly rancid odor to the air. And by the time the wisps of smoke curling into tendrils above the tree line made the hostile hearths visible, usually the army had already attacked.

The location Aelius reached at noon was halfway between a settlement and a seasonal camp. He left his Guardsmen at the outer perimeter, with strict orders not to intervene unless a direct assault was made on him. Once he'd cleared his reasons for being here with the suspicious barbarians who rushed up to him with their barking mongrels, he was allowed to proceed. They pointed to him one of the huts, outside of which a line of bundled locals huddled, hoping no doubt to catch a glimpse of the holy man.

In the semidark interior, Agnus sat with his eyes closed, hands on his knees. Hearing the Latin speech, he opened his eyes so far as was necessary to glance at the visitor, and then rolled his pupils back under the lids, like a blind man or one inspired. If there was surprise in him, he concealed it well. Such a quick rearrangement of features followed, Aelius could not tell what role fear played in them, or spite, or wily interest in this meeting. In any case, the face turned curious and unfriendly. It was possible that superstitious Roman soldiers had already come to seek advice or help, although Aelius's countenance was hardly that of a postulant.

"You are outside the jurisdiction of Rome, Commander."

"Wherever a Roman sets foot, that is Rome's jurisdiction. Aside from that, if you are Agnus whom they call Pyrikaios, or the fire waker, I am here to ask questions, knowing that Christians do not lie, and to confront you with the truth."

"The *truth* from an unbeliever! Are you aware that the good people here protect me?"

"Well." Aelius stretched the extent of his striking power considerably. "The good people here can be cut down." He stood with his right side to the hut's door, ready to react in case anyone should try to barge in. "To start with, tell me what itinerary you and your assistant Casta followed from Treveri."

Once more, surprise was ably guarded. Agnus remained seated like a tribal chief, among the rude gifts these yokels brought him to ask for miracles: jugs of mead, pelts, pieces of bronze harness stolen or stripped from Roman horses and men. "I have nothing to hide. From Treveri, through Germania Superior, I reached Castra Regina on the border. I followed the right bank of the Danube for days before finding a place to cross over. The border is well guarded, if that is your reason for asking, but God was leading me. I met with the deaconess at Astura, where Noricum becomes Pannonia. She was the one who convinced me to follow her to Carnuntum, whose bishop she said had promised to shelter us. There, because of a spy, we were nearly caught by guards. We traveled at night toward the river, and but for Our Lord's help we'd

have frozen to death. At some point outside Ala Nova, we parted ways.
I crossed to Barbaricum. What she did, or where she is now, I do not
know."

"Were you aware, when you crossed over, that your *miracles* had
been exposed as frauds in Treveri?"

Agnus's eyes stayed rolled back and white, with a trembling of
lids. Smoke rising from the hearth in the middle of the hut sought
the hole in the roof. Sunlight rained from above, creating evanescent
blades of smoke as it met with the shadows of branches and posts.
"Our Lord taught that those who truly believe do not need signs and
portents."

"But contrary to your Prophet's teachings, you decided that they
do."

"I know nothing about that. When the power of God flows through
me I am not aware of anything around me. "

"A letter was sent to the Treveri authorities, accusing you of con-
cocting with Lupus his 'resurrection.' There's suspicion that you killed
him when for whatever reason he threatened to talk."

This time Agnus's eyes opened for good. He was a tall man of sixty
or so, and his face had the strange quality ben Matthias had described,
of being forgettable. Beard, length of hair, clothing, everything about
him was ordinary. How many such elders had Aelius met in his life, in
all trades, across the miles? The fire waker's god must content himself
with mediocrity. "I, Commander? I never even spoke to Lupus before
being called to his bedside! I heard of his sad ending after I left Treveri;
it was only happenstance that my departure coincided with the day of
Lupus's demise. During his illness the women in his family approached the deaconess for help, and my heart was moved into acqui-
escing." Down went the lids, and down the corner of his mouth. "I
have no commerce with women. The righteous man's soul fears their
wily tongues. The deaconess is the wall I place between myself and
those impure beings; she is there to shield me from the insufferable insistence of those who trouble my contemplation." The white, veined
hands left the knees slowly, seeking wide-fingered the light raining

from above. "I *am* the vehicle of God's power, because He wants to show the difference between man and woman: a Christian man, a Christian woman—but God's power flows only through the man. How could there be a moment, as Lupus's dead body was shown to me, when in my naïveté I *doubted* my powers? What little faith did I have in the great works God planned for me! I even suspected Casta of setting me up. As if God would let a woman I raised from idolatry serve as anything but a tool in the service of a chosen man. I have to become reconciled with the fact that I am chosen: that it is my lot to perform miracles only Our Lord and the greatest saints have accomplished."

Yes, and have you raised any dead lately? Aelius irritably thought the words without pronouncing them. "Those arrested in Treveri testified they were given money to certify Lupus's death, and to fake his burial."

"I repeat that I know nothing about that. It is true that I had to avail myself of occasional helpers to convince the unbelievers, as teachers use models to illustrate their lessons. What is worse: pretending to heal a false leper, or letting go of an opportunity to convert the crowds? Those who think they'll be healed are often healed: The fire is in them, and it only needs stirring. The name '*fire waker*' illustrates precisely what Christ himself said: 'Thy faith hath made thee whole.'"

A wet log in the hearth hissed. Without flame, a whorl of thick smoke rose from it and filled the sunlit center of the hut. Aelius stepped aside not to lose sight of the miracle worker. "What about those who are not so sure they'll be healed?"

"Why, there's either flame or ice, Commander: There's no such thing as a lukewarm believer. Some are stone cold. I know—I worked with their useless lot for years! Time after time, until the day I met Lupus, I stood for hours in prayer to heal a sore or relieve a fever, to no avail. But the lack was not in me: It was in *them,* as they did not believe. Then, in Belgica Prima, they bring to me a brick-maker's cadaver: I pray in a manner not appreciably different from the others, and the miracle blooms in front of my eyes. He rises and walks again, like Lazarus! His relatives' faith was the kindling, and I was the fire. You speak of fakery, but I tell you, it is an ineffable mystery."

"Not according to the judges in Treveri," Aelius grumbled.

The white hand stayed lifted, each outstretched finger trembling with tension. "What are Plato and Aristotle to the power of God, Commander? What worth has Pythagoras, who holds that women's minds are trainable as men's are? Blasphemy! I have it on the authority of the Apostle Paul. Paul clearly says that man is the image and glory of God, but woman is the glory of man. Man was made directly by God; woman was formed out of one of man's ribs. A clear matter of proportions. Thus a Christian woman's place, in her modesty, is to serve her husband and family and—if she be a consecrated virgin—to serve those who serve God. Thus the relative proportions alluded to by Paul are respected."

"Shouldn't men then have one missing rib in their skeleton, compared to women? I never heard that they do."

The question was ignored. Agnus's left hand went up to meet the other, thumbs joined, catching and breaking the smoky sunlight. "There are physiological facts," he added, head thrown back, lids fluttering, "that prove the truth and wisdom of Paul's statement. In our own scientific tradition, if a woman in her monthly cycle touches wine, it will turn to vinegar. She will fog mirrors so that they become unusable—better, as vanity sits in mirrors like a bitch in her lair—and kill honey bees if she passes by the hive. There's plenty more that, on the authority of the ancients, could be said in regard to such baleful influence, but it all results in the recognition of woman's impurity and unworthiness to be a minister of the faith."

"A girl I lived with in Egypt habitually handled her mirror during her monthly time, and it seems to me that it kept its luster."

The fire waker frowned. Only his right arm remained lifted, hand gathered in a fist except for the forefinger—the theatrical gesture Aelius had seen philosophy teachers and rhetoricians make to mark the importance of the moment. "What do *you* believe?"

"With Epictetus, I believe that the sole thing that truly belongs to me is my will. For me life is a battle to be fought courageously, the cosmos is generated by fire, pain is not to be fled, and equanimity is a chief virtue."

"Is that all?"

"No. I also believe I am a rational animal, with a soul that possesses knowledge of the Good, because in nature there exist what Cicero called 'seeds of virtue,' and the world itself has a cohesive soul. Although I have a bit of trouble letting go of pleasure as intended between man and woman, I realize that the *Logos*—intended as reason—ought to triumph over all irrationality and exaltation."

"Stoicism is only less despicable than most philosophies, Commander. Clemens of Alexandria, one of our profound thinkers, writes that philosophy was for Greeks what the law of Moses was for Jews: a preparation for the coming of Christ. Clemens himself began as a Stoic but saw the error of his ways. Pray to God that you will." Agnus joined his hands reverently. "Now, be so good as to confront me with your *truth*."

Aelius had physically cut men down with less disgust. He said, "I have seen arrogance blind army men and politicians, but your conceit is monstrous. Do you really not know, Fire Waker, that there was no resurrection in Belgica Prima, and the magician is as gullible as his public? *Who* do you think has turned you in?"

NOTES BY AELIUS SPARTIANUS, WRITTEN AT GERVELATA,
11 FEBRUARY, SUNDAY:

My head was reeling and my stomach in revolt by the time I left Agnus. That mountain of self-importance and hypocrisy all but sneered me out of his stinking hut. Had I not been so far from our lines, I'd have cut his throat there where he sat, the sanctimonious prig. In the face of the evidence I presented he denied it, and stands by his role in resurrecting the dead! He claims no moral responsibility in Marcellus's death, despite the inflammatory attacks and maledictions against the judge contained in his pastoral letter, which not even Protasius could justify. When he heard of the many riots and executions of Christians in his wake, he dismissed them as part of God's great plan for him. I left his lair sick at heart, asking myself why, why

*can't he be the murderer I seek, and I'm doomed to keep follow-
ing? Still, the fire waker is a dangerous man, I am convinced of
it: Were he to put it into his head that he can also be a leader of
men, we could have trouble on the frontier. Dragging him before
a court of law would be a move of political prevention, in addition to being an act of justice. Unfortunately, given his apparent
popularity among the barbarians, this time it was not possible
to abduct him with the number of men I had with me. His attitude as we parted was, "Well, what can you do about it?"*

*I plan to do something about it sooner or later. This coming
spring, when we attack in force, if I cannot find a way before
then.*

*No sooner did I return to Gervelata than another duty, at the
counter-fortress of Burgus Aquae Mortae, calls me back out. A
small group of experienced officers is wanted to go out alone, for
a parley with leaders of the Boian and the Quadian tribes, tot-
tering between us and the Sarmatians who breathe on their
necks. A diplomatic duty, but we're to wear mail shirts and full
gear. The name of the counter-fortress, Dead Water's Tower, is
not the happiest, but the frontier has odd names to sell.*

*Perhaps it is my contrary mood that needs lifting: God knows
I have enough worries. A letter from Anubina awaited me at the
post, yet I hesitate to open it, for fear of what she might tell me.
I think I will read it in the field, where events are likely to dis-
tract me if it isn't welcome news.*

*The weather is turning foul, as the winds blow from the
north once more.*

EAST OF BURGUS AQUAE MORTAE, 13 FEBRUARY, TUESDAY,
FIRST DAY OF PARENTALIA, FEAST OF THE DEAD
The snow was small and hard; it did not stick to things and people
but kept turning in the air, doubling the effect of a white mist that

rabidly sought to blind and confuse. Whenever the military road ran
by a clearing, the wind brought pailfuls of dusty ice against the troops
escorting the negotiators. The mounts proceeded with heads low,
looking down, and the men, bundled in kerchiefs and hoods, kept
their faces averted to avoid the sting of the snow. Along the river,
patches of land that had been green until late in the season now disappeared under the squall; a sun so small and ghostly as to seem
transparent sailed above the thin layers of clouds shredding into that
mockery of a blizzard. Aelius had been through much worse storms,
both in and out of Pannonia, but he never took winter weather lightly.
There was no following tracks in this kind of snow, and the only good
thing was that your own mount passed through unobserved. The
southern troopers coughed and sniffled; some of them would be laid
up in the morning.

The four negotiators—Decimus being coincidentally the only one
known to Aelius, and also the senior officer among them—rode
wrapped in their capes, but loosely, so as to be able to reach for their
cavalry swords immediately if need be.

On the other bank, it was unlikely that hostiles were not watching.
Parleys took place in the midst of preparing for war, and there was no
telling which groups or clans at any one time would take part in one
or the other. "Hostiles" was the usual term used to describe barbarians by the army in the field, regardless of the complicated nomencla-
ture of tribes and subtribes that pertained to the crowds pressing on
the border. In stories and from veterans of Aurelian's days, one heard
of how the barbarians would communicate by exchanging animal
calls, but in Aelius's experience that was another veterans' tale. He'd
heard it done only once, and it'd been farther off anyhow, in Armenia.
The sudden silence of birds in the woods, *that* was a signal to mind, as
in nine out of ten cases it meant enemies on the move among the
trees. For the rest, training made him sensitive and alert to what his
senses caught, disregarding no sign but evaluating each one of them
without fear.

By the second morning hour, over waters running black in the ice, the negotiators crossed a fortified bridge to the *burgus,* a three-story tower on the perilous right bank of the Danube.

Appointments with tribal leaders were hardly based on punctuality, yet the Romans' counterparts were late, and then hours overdue. In what had become a blizzard, with mounting impatience, the four officers waited in the counter-fortress. "They don't like entering Roman fortifications," Decimus sneered. "I bet they're out there freezing their rears, expecting us to go meet them in the open. They've done it before. What do you think?"

Aelius spoke only because his colleague asked him directly. "Either that, or they decided against the parley." Facing Decimus after their last meeting he felt a sort of sad repulsion, for the way the Roman covered his insane scheme with self-assured arrogance. "There could be an attack," he added deliberately, looking him in the eye.

Decimus's sneer tightened into a grimace. "I think they're waiting for us to make the first move."

Close to noon, a trooper was sent out to reconnoiter. The woods around the *burgus* had been cleared, but weeklong forests lay just beyond. So called because of the days needed to cross it, the woodland ran nearly uninterrupted from here to regions unexplored, cracked by ledges and ravines, threaded by animal trails that formed the only clues to the maze.

Aelius went to the upper floor to watch the trooper and his mount lose their contours in the spinning wall of snow. Alone in the small room, where the dazzling whiteness of the outside filtered through slit windows, the wait was less oppressive. Eventually, he thought it was as good a time as any to take Anubina's letter out of its cylindrical envelope and unroll it. His eyes met her firm, capable hand, the small, punctilious marks of a woman who takes pride in having learned to write.

To Commander Aelius Spartianus from Anubina, written with the help of Thermuthis to put it into better language.
Dear Aelius, I hope this finds you in good health and happy.

I am well and so is Thaesis, whose greatest friend is presently the dog you left her in October. Sirius is not a very clever animal, but well-behaved and affectionate. Thermuthis says husbands should be that way . . .

The letter went on for another paragraph with the usual update on people and things, but it was the lines below that most acutely caught Aelius's attention.

. . . for the time we lived together, once a month while you were away, at the brothel—not Thermuthis's, the establishment of Isidora the Alexandrian (Aelius could see Thermuthis suggesting that they add the explanation, to protect herself)—*I lay with a man other than yourself. Not a Roman, not a soldier, not anyone you know: every time a different man, as long as he was a farmer or a potter's helper or a fisherman. Not to betray you, but because I wanted to be sure that if I became pregnant, it could not be said the child was yours. You need no such complications, and neither do I. I was a soldier's daughter: I will not have my daughter fathered by a soldier, albeit an important one like yourself.*

Thaesis is too dark, too plain to be yours. Tall, yes, but children grow taller these days. There are half a dozen men in Antinoopolis she resembles. She will go into business with me in three years, and become able to make a living on her own so that she may choose her man freely. Between now and then, she will go to school and learn not only her letters but how to count, and so on. Ladies who are such because of their husbands or fathers are no freer than their impoverished counterparts.

Thus far I have written with Thermuthis's help. Now I add these words in my own voice: May the gods Serapis and Zeus Ammon, Aphrodite-Hathor, and especially our Blessed Lady, Isis, watch over you and keep you. When I will choose a husband I will make sure to ask for your approval. When my sons are born, I will send you news. Please do the same when you marry, and when your children are born.

Written by her hand in Thermuthis's chambers at Anti-
noopolis, the second day of January, eighteenth day of Mechir.

The hiss of the wind through the window struck him with a handful of
snow, as if someone had blown air and ice through a reed. Aelius stood
motionless in the cold blast when one of his colleagues stuck his head
in the door. "Curius Decimus wants you to go out with him. The
trooper reported that the barbarians halted in a small clearing a mile
into the woods; they seem skittish, and to be be waiting . . . Are you all
right?"

"I'm all right."

Below, Decimus had worn his cape again. Lifting the hood over his
head, he said, "They don't trust us. We have to meet them where they
are, or not at all. Since you speak the language, Spartianus, let's go and
see if we can convince them to follow us back here."

Aelius buckled his belt in silence, adjusting the strap across his
chest, where it met the scabbard on his left side. The long cavalry
sword, ivory- and steel-hilted, fell impeccably in line with his armpit.
The precision of his gestures concealed the confused grief he felt for
Anubina's words, whose polite finality he would mercifully have to
contemplate at some other time.

The snow fell more heavily in the courtyard, more perpendicularly
now that the wind was dying down. Once out of the small gate in the
perimeter wall, the officers followed the trooper's fast-filling tracks
toward the dark confine of the woods, and into them. The terrain rose
slightly, stony under the snow; the firs created a sudden dusk around
them. They'd come without speaking more than two-thirds of the
way when Decimus told Aelius, as if there weren't more immediate
matters at hand, "I fear I may have taken the wrong tack with you the
other night." His voice was calm, engaging, without the slightest anxiety in it. Yet his rings and luxurious harness were probably not much
different from those worn by his ancestor as he rode to Teutoburg
Forest.

Aelius, on the other hand, felt a sting of tenseness, just below alarm.

He blamed the thought of Teutoburg and his colleague's treacherous speech for it, not anything threatening them from the woods.

"We are practical men, after all," Decimus went on, "even if we were taught by philosophers. I daresay *especially* if we were taught by philosophers, Spartianus, since for all their brains they seem unable to make a decent living. You will have your benefit from it, if you join us. We are rich. Say the word, and any one of us can give you an estate in Sicily or North Africa, or here in your Pannonian backyard."

"I will see you in Hades first, Decimus."

"Entirely possible." Decimus sniffed the icy air. Under the trees, the snowfall broke into a small sprinkle. He seemed amused by Aelius's reaction. "Is that your final word? Well, that's that, then. I am a man of the world, I can take rejection. We are still colleagues, with a parley ahead of us and a war to fight."

"You don't understand. I am turning you in."

"Ha! And go down with us, along with your family? Think about it."

"I am turning you and yours in."

A mile into the woods, the trooper's tracks had filled completely. The place looked untrodden, primeval. Yet a whiter swatch in the white-and-black of the snowy firs, like daylight awaiting, told them the clearing lay just ahead. Slowly, the officers led their mounts to the edge of the open space, where snow fell thick and even. No one in sight, no sounds. The higher ground at the other side of the clearing was where the barbarians had reportedly stood on horseback. To the left, where the firs grew shaggier and less crowded, a snow-bearing upward draft caught Aelius's attention. A ridge or a drop-off must delimit that side. Silence was absolute but for the low squeak of harness when the mounts moved in place. Excessive, expectant silence. Prudence called them to turn back, regain the *burgus,* and call it a day.

Unpredictably Decimus spurred his horse, causing snow to fly high above its fetlocks. The motion was disorderly for an experienced soldier, which was what Aelius was thinking when he caught sight of enemy riders surging from behind the trees, on their right flank; in seconds, all became fretfully immediate, automatic, grasping and unsheathing the sword and seeking the open to maneuver and fight back, no matter how against hope. In seconds, Aelius perceived no fear on Decimus's part: only cold, gleeful opportunism as he jerked his horse's head by a firm pull of the reins, turned it around in a dazzle of spray, and was gone.

Surrounded in the middle of the clearing, Aelius felt incredibly small, rapid thoughts pop through him: Everything his mind had elaborated until a moment ago had dissolved, not to speak of the complex mountain of reasoning and anxieties of an hour ago; sand running out of a bag, leaving nothing behind. He'd reverted to a brutally quick throng of tiny flashes that were less than thoughts: *Quadians or God knows what—no, not Quadians. They carry Roman cavalry lances. There's no holding them back with a sword. I'm as good as dead.* His life had raced across thirty years to end here. In his anger, he still governed his excited mount, slashed at the closest lance, knocked it off the enemy's hand but could not guard the prod of another spear against his left side; the riveted mail rings snapped only in a small area, enough for the iron point to pass through the breach. He did not feel the pain, only the blow; with an expert pull-and-give of the reins, he brought his mount into a half-turn. Barely avoiding the leaf-shaped lance heads converging on him, Aelius sought a space in the deadly circle that could allow a desperate leap to escape, finding none but spurring nonetheless, at random, because gutting himself against the enemy was better than waiting to be gutted.

Right and left, the slender blades flashed by, glanced off the saddle horns; his mount rammed the wide-eyed, snorting barbarian horses, shorter and shaggier; the counterblow on his right arm alone told him he'd struck hard wood with his blade. Lances become an encumbrance in a crowd. He flew past the long-haired men wheeling around to chase him and headed left.

The ridge was on that side. Snow fell in sheets against the scraggy line of firs; the void behind them created upward drafts and white whirls. Aelius calculated a narrow crevice, a seam in the land that would launch him across it; he incited his mount to stretch for the jump. Snow and rocks flew; the firs went by. His horse saw the ridge yawn and stopped cold at its edge.

Being thrown from the saddle was not the hard part. The hard part was falling badly. The ridge was a deep ravine of exposed rocks; snow boiled upward from its bottom like smoke in a cauldron. Into that cauldron Aelius's sword went capering, and Aelius followed headlong onto the rocks. In the wink of an eye the plunge broke against stone. Black, dismembering pain tore him from consciousness, sucked him into a deeper hole where he went with all that he was, or had been.

Snow stanched the bleeding. It deadened pain. Still, Aelius fell on his knees twice before knowing he was unable to stand, so he lay looking up at the wraiths of snow turning in the air above him, without falling. The ravine was much deeper than it appeared from above. Its edge, toothed with craggy rock his own fall had exposed, seemed a part of the sky. His left shoulder was dislocated, or broken; if he moved, the danger was of blacking out again. In his side was a duller pain where the lance had broken through mail. Thinking wearied him; he limited himself to an awareness that the hostiles were not looking down from above, and it was getting to be afternoon.

When he came to again, evening was near. Aelius had no recollection of having crawled to a protected place at the foot of the ridge, with the confused intent to rest and then seek the low land in hopes of reaching the Danube. He packed snow against the wound in his side, too weak to cover the blood tracks around him, which wolves and bears would smell from the distant dark.

14 FEBRUARY, WEDNESDAY, SECOND DAY OF THE FEAST OF THE DEAD
No sounds anywhere near. Far into the woods, now and then the rumbling call of male deer like men throwing up. Then, sudden, the swish

of birds rising up like the unrolling of a paper roll. From the trailing
branches, excess snow fell with soft collapsing thuds. The sky beyond—
in the intricacy of branches that seemed black from here—was between blue and gold, sparkling, speckled. Aelius did not know how
long ago he'd left the ravine, but since dawn he'd lost his way.

Overnight snow had fallen on him, the kind of snow that becomes
crusty and falls away in crinkly scabs when one shakes it off. Among
the trees, he could see the shimmering whiteness of the flat land beyond the woods, an incandescent whiteness set off by the dark trunks
and dusky trailing branches. No sign of the river, and he was probably
heading west.

Not feeling much pain worried him. It was not a good sign. He felt
lucid, yet on some nights after the exhaustion of a battle or a long
march, he'd dreamed with the clarity of a hallucination. Not feeling
pain could mean that he was lucidly dreaming this, or something else.
In winter, men had been found dead who seemed not to have noticed
the coming of death, as if they were sleeping. Others had to have their
limbs amputated, arms and legs where no feelings, much less pain,
were felt.

When he knelt to stand up, however, pain shot through him like a
second wounding. Aelius fell heavily, striking rock under the snow and
bruising his face. But pain had the merit of telling him he was awake
and alert and blood still flowed through every part of him. If he could
only glimpse a view of the river, detect a sign of Roman presence, the
edge of a military road, an abandoned watchtower, a retaining wall—
the rest would come by deduction. He had a clear idea of the direction
he had to avoid: north. But east, west, south: He wasn't sure about
those. The border was indented, irregular; clearings in the forest mim-
icked the open land on the Danube banks and jumbled one's sense of
direction. Seeking a high point would help, although it'd likely mean
walking away from the river.

Tracks of foxes, young wolves, and wild dogs criss-crossed this and
that snowy space between trees. Cold, need to eat, bleeding: no time
for those. Aelius walked—stumbled, in fact, crawling at times when

pain and weakness made him unable to stand, his left arm useless—
toward the direction where the white incandescence signaled the
opening at the edge of the forest. The deceptive quality of distances in
winter, in the woodland, was familiar to him. He expected to have to
go much farther than it seemed. The clearing seemed to withdraw
from him, to shift to the left, to become lost behind dark firs. The firs
trailed wide like skirts or capes born of the snow, as if tall women in
cloaks went ahead of him. He remembered the tales of the Pannonian
Mothers, the goddesses who appear in threes, or multiply before the
eyes of those who are about to die, a legion of tall women with invisible faces because they are always walking ahead of you. His rational
mind told him that visions of men losing their senses were the origin
of such tales, but it was little consolation.

By and by he did reach the edge of the woods. The intact cover of
snow, now that the clouds broke up and swatches of clear sky appeared, was more than blinding: like a white, silent conflagration that
made him shield his eyes with his right arm. A valley stretched from
left to right, west to east more or less. The land climbed a little beyond
the clearing. More woods crowded on the crest; to the right, the woods
on the low land and the higher land merged, or seemed to do so. Perhaps there was a pass on that side, but no telling whether the thickness
of the forest would allow a passage. Anything—ravine, weeklong forest, impassable river, the foot of high mountains—could be to the east.
Even the great river, the border with Rome.

To Aelius's left, an arm of the forest he had just come through
crowded on the clearing like an army that, having chased him, stood
still waiting for him to die. Everywhere the woods: How many hours'
worth, or days' worth, he couldn't judge. Touching his face to feel the
growth of his beard and reckon the hours elapsed since the ambush
would not help much, either. Aelius was one of those blond men with
glabrous faces; hair grew on his lips and chin thickly but slowly.

As long as the weather held, there was a chance of making it back.
He had flint with him; if he could find dry tinder to start a fire, the
chances of surviving until he could cross the border grew. If not,

determination would avail him nothing. Decimus, Agnus, Casta, Anu-bina, his mother: they would remain names to denounce, or save, or love; his duty was like a red ribbon that might pull him back, if he could only find it.

In the clearing, the snow was more than knee-deep. Crossing it was difficult in the best of conditions. In his state, it could take long enough for the sky to cloud over again and start snowing, by which time he'd have no escape. Besides, the clearing led north. The woods were safer; dying in the woods would be less awful than in the unbro-ken whiteness.

Aelius went back. He knelt and dug with the stiff right hand near the fallen trunk of a tree, seeking dry sticks or bark, until he realized all was frigid or wet, and there would be no fire-making.

Images came and went. One moment it was the copper jar in Anu-bina's house, reflecting the African sun; another, it was a red cloak trailing, trailing, a red cape like the one he'd given the beggar at Silver Gate, or the pale wrists Casta stretched to him from the shade, to be taken in. A part of him was perfectly aware of lying in the snow, of the extremity of his situation. The other was free to move about and be elsewhere; he could see his mother lifting golden coins from the earth, smell the flowers in Egyptian gardens, hear the splash of crocodiles' tails in the Nile. The wind blew in the firs, and should another night find him outdoors, it'd be his last. He thought he saw the hut at the brickyard where Lupus had died, a long line of men and women com-ing to see the miracle man, women who stayed behind and cajoled him, gave him gifts, asked him to tell of his resurrection. They had red ribbons in their hands, like the red ribbon Helena had once passed be-tween her thighs to seduce him. He saw Judge Marcellus in his bloody bath, like Agamemnon slain by his wife; Marcellus had Constantine's looks, and his wife had Casta's face. His Divinity stood in a red cloak, or else it was the beggar who'd predicted him good fortune on the bridge. But hadn't he passed by the crossroads? His father's soul had attached itself to him, and wanted grandsons in exchange for his life. Casta danced like the girls at Decimus's party, and Lupus the brick-maker danced with her. The red cloak came and went, trailing like blood in the snow. At the brickyard, a woman in the bivouac glimpsed him and covered her head. She, too, had Casta's face. The red cloak spread like fire; beneath it, the beggar's bare feet had turned into boots.

A foot turned him over.

The barbarian's face was upon him. The barbarian's eyes, distant and light gray, were all malice and glee.

"Spartianus, son of a bitch."

Worse than a barbarian, it was Sido. He crouched in the snow, calling, "Spartianus, you son of a bitch. Look at me. *Look at me!* Keep your eyes open. Look at me."

The late afternoon sky above seemed blinding, even though stars were already pinned impossibly high over the fringed branches of the dark trees. Wearing belted tunics to their hips, trousers, and boots, the fur-caped, fur-hatted *speculatores* were standing around, a circle of wolves. One of them passed his foot through the bloody snow; another said, "It's a wonder bears didn't come to finish him off."

Sido held his head up. "The last man on earth I wanted to rescue, but it does give me satisfaction." He slapped him roundly. "Tell me if you feel this. God, it does give me satisfaction. Here, drink." Warm wine materialized in a cup, held to his lips. "Slowly, drink. The Roman left you in the lurch, eh? Your mount made it back by itself. It's got more sense than you do."

Aelius had a vague idea that he was shivering. Quilts were heaped on him; they were stirring a bright fire. The chatter of teeth in his head kept him from hearing the words he was trying to say.

"I know," Sido answered to whatever those words had been. "I know. Frugi was my man. The moment news came of his death at Celeia, I knew he'd been killed. I simply didn't know who among you had done it. Then Lady Helena told me you'd infiltrated them to guard her son's interests: I won't let you be the only one she is grateful to." Aelius wanted to say it was nothing like that, but a great torpor was overtaking him. They forced him to drink. "How could you go into the woods alone with Decimus? If the hostiles hadn't ambushed you, he'd have cut you down himself after you threatened him—either way, you weren't meant to come out alive from that errand. Now you've got to tell me where I can find Decimus. He's gone, and you're a witness. If you know where he might have fled, you must tell me, it is your duty to tell." Swallowing the warm wine was so consoling, Aelius was tempted to close his eyes again and let go. But Sido kept shaking him. "Stay awake, don't do that." Someone else rubbed his hands, pinched him.

It took them an hour to get him back to lucidity. Bits of hardtack were handed him, no more than sips of the warm drink. He must have been in a moment of blackout when they'd reduced his dislocated shoulder, because he had not felt the pain, but now he could move the left arm a little, and the ache was considerably less. In the dark, the fire burned high. Sido stood in front of it, a hefty silhouette with arms crossed, listening to what Aelius said.

"Yes, whatever," he interrupted then impatiently. "I don't have time to hear any of that. Murders are another kettle of fish, especially those committed elsewhere. Leave them aside. There's one culprit I want to catch, and that's Curius Decimus. We can't find him. His colleagues were rounded up at Carnuntum yesterday. They won't say where he is, or don't know; I think they don't know, otherwise I would have gotten it out of them. You've got to tell me."

Aelius sat up. Life poured back into him; his wits were rallying at an increasing speed. "Well, I don't know where he is, either."

The closest crossover point to Roman territory was not the *burgus.* From the *speculatores,* riding back, Aelius heard of the raid against Aquae Mortae that followed the ambush. It'd been a relatively small incident, ending with the repulse of the hostiles, but in the confusion no one doubted Decimus's report of his colleague's death. It had been the handful of barbarian negotiators that made the goodwill gesture of informing Roman authorities; they'd witnessed the ambush from the woods where they'd fled, and reported it to the commander at Ala Nova. Sido was there, on Decimus's trail, and had used the information to search for his witness in the barbarian woods. Near Ala Nova, Sido and Aelius forded to safety, several hours after Curius Decimus had left the border for destination unknown.

GERVELATA, 15 FEBRUARY, THURSDAY, LUPERCALIA, FEAST OF THE SHE-WOLF

"What do you think? For over a year I'd kept an eye on Judge Marcellus, who through his vaunted honesty accumulated more threats and antipathy than any accommodating judge I know." The keenness Sido had shown listening to Aelius's report on Cato's Sodality waned into restless lack of patience now that they spoke of other things. "There's no protecting someone all day and all night, especially when he does not care to be protected. When he was killed, it was little surprise. Still, it offered me an opportunity to find out who—among all those who swore vengeance against him—had succeeded. The last thing I needed, Spartianus, was someone like yourself meddling in criminal investigation. Because of your imperial contacts, whether or not your credentials as Caesar's envoy were accepted by His Serenity, you had to be stopped the only way I know how: giving you a lesson, short of killing you. You overreacted; those I hired bungled matters and had to be eliminated. The Greek butcher would have lived, had you not stuck your nose into his halfwit helper's role in the attack against you. You forced me to get rid of him, too, so I added him to the number of the Christians to be executed. One more, one less—who's counting?"

"So now it's my fault if you had me attacked and then had to cover your tracks. But you did not find the judge's killer, did you? You knew it was not Protasius."

"Of course not. It was your traitorous colleague Decimus. His grudge against Marcellus was well known. He had the means of doing it; he provided the bricks and the workers used in the building site near the Old Baths. His men had the advantage of proximity: Any one of them could have done it, and I plan to have them all tortured until the culprit coughs up a confession."

"You're wrong again." In the courtyard of the army post, Aelius supervised the packing of his saddle. Although the wound on his side was a light one, and his sore shoulder on the mend, he'd requested five days of recovery leave in view of the energy needed for the coming campaign—and for other reasons of his own. "You'd waste a jailer's time. It wasn't Decimus, either."

Sido grunted. In his wolf cape, with two wolf's heads falling over his shoulders, he resembled a hybrid creature of the woods, none too friendly. "Rubbish."

"On the contrary. Had you not been in such a hurry to eliminate the Christian slave crew at the Old Baths you'd have found that one of them was indeed Marcellus's killer—but he acted on commission."

"Yes, from Decimus!"

"No, from Decimus's cousin, Annia Cincia."

Sido threw up his hands, causing the wolf's heads to look alive and about to bite his neck. "What? And who's *she*? What does *she* have to do with this?"

"It's a long story. I had it fairly clear in my mind a week ago when I met her old cohort, the fire waker, in Barbaricum. Until then I'd been unsure of my hunches: I still thought Agnus might have been behind it all—Lupus the brick-maker's death in Treveri as well as Marcellus's death. He's certainly self-deluded and arrogant enough to bend events in his favor. But—more's the pity—he is a fraudulent charlatan and a trickster, not a murderer. I heard him out as he slobbered on himself with self-adulation, then gave him my version of the truth. He showed no overt surprise when I explained my theory, so at first I thought he disbelieved it and shook it off his back. Now I venture to say he was struck hard, deep down. His own fire turned against him in the end; he has a responsibility in what happened. On the part of Annia Cincia, or Casta, as she is known, there was instead a formidable series of clever moves, following true feminine tactics. She managed to be where both murders happened, while remaining invisible, and did not hesitate to cause collateral deaths in order to strike her intended victims."

"Rubbish," Sido insisted. "But if so, what was her plan?"

"What *is* her plan, you mean. Let us say that her final intent is to call down the heavy hand of Roman justice on the present Christian hierarchy. Conservatism? No, nothing like that, Sido. The lady is a Christian herself."

"I don't get it." Sido watched Aelius vault with some difficulty onto his horse but would not offer help. "I'm not sure I *want* to get it. If Christians kill one another, they save me the trouble. What I want is Decimus, and the moment you return from leave I expect you to hand me a written, detailed report on these goddamned Roman traitors' harebrained scheme. There'll be time to catch a murderess."

Aelius wound the reins around his left fist. He was thinking of that morning in Treveri, riding to the brickyard, glancing at the pilgrims huddled in the fields. "Not this one. If I think that Fate itself had placed a hint for me in the Old Baths, on that wall where a bored client scratched a verse from Greek tragedy: '*Woe, woe, look, look! Keep away the bull from the heifer—*'"

"What?"

"It's spoken by the mad seer Cassandra, foretelling the king's murder in the bath by his queen."

"I don't know what you mean. You speak in riddles."

"Well, I should have thought that behind Marcellus's death, too, there could be a woman's murderous plan. Not to worry, I will explain all in writing, *perfectissimus*. But unless you get your men after her—and it may be already too late—she'll slip through our fingers as she did before."

There was a road—less than a road, actually, a lane following the bank of a seasonal stream—that from Savaria, in a roundabout manner, skirting two patches of forest land, led over the hills. From there, picking up a trail in the direction of Decimus's isolated villa would be easy.

Still, Aelius did not follow this route. He took a longer, untracked way from his parents' estate, following lanes bordering other properties, along low walls built of stones without mortar, crossing thickets and small watercourses. The last few miles he rode on unmarked land, through a wilderness that had traces of having been cultivated once.

Snow turned to mush under an icy rain; dark fell before his arrival. The serfs let him in without questions, so Decimus must have given them a description of his colleague, and permission to open to him.

The Roman sat in his library, smaller than the one at Mediolanum but, as Aelius remembered from the night when the panegyric on Severus had been lent him, well stocked and cozy. Neat drapes hung before shelves to protect the books from dust. Decimus neither stood nor spoke when Aelius appeared on the threshold. He did raise his eyes. In an instant, the sum of the frantic moments when they'd last seen one another was drawn and resolved; the personal anger Aelius had expected to feel at this time did not materialize. It did not even try to climb to his throat. He did not recall confronting it during the ride here, or in the hours of recovery before it; it simply stayed where it was, so deep and low within him that it might as well not exist.

"There's no getting rid of you, is there." Decimus looked years older—centuries older, Aelius wanted to say, as if the weight of ages impossible to resurrect had crashed on him at once. The attempt to be ironic was like paint on a dead man's face. "Won't you have a seat?"

"No. Sido is after you. He doesn't know where you are, and I don't think his men followed me here. I rode one of our unshod horses, and I'm at my mother's for all he knows. But it's a matter of time."

"Not necessarily." Decimus had been writing, not reading. Letters sat already rolled up and sealed on his desk. "This property is registered under another man's name. The serfs are faithful. Sido and his minions may search the cadastre of the entire region for weeks and find nothing. The fact that you know is the problem . . . for you, I mean. I am beyond problems."

Aelius took the words in stride. He expected them. All in all, it was the reason why not even his political contempt for the man had reason to be anymore. "Have you decided how to do it, and when?"

"Two questions in one, two answers in one, Spartianus: long ago, and tonight."

"Is there any way I may help?"

Decimus made a grimace. For a moment, amusement succeeded in lifting the corners of his weary, downturned mouth. "No, thank you. I'm not exactly Nero, and you're not exactly my merciful freedman. Hand-holding during suicide is tasteless."

"Frankly, I thought you'd seek one of the distant provinces."

"Oh, do not suggest the *provinces* to me, Spartianus. Life in the provinces is not life. I had to put up with Mediolanum for three years, and before then it'd been ages since I set my eyes on Rome. It only pains me having to die outside of Rome, so I am doing the next best thing." Without leaving his chair, he pulled aside the drape behind him. There was no shelf there, only a wall, and a fresco on the wall. Against a black background, like a night sky or a tempest, a view of Rome was illustrated. Aelius recognized the Capitol, Hadrian's massive grave by the Tiber, the circuses and temples. It was painted in a pale gilded bread color, as if it were a cake in the shape of Rome, a great delicacy to consume.

"Do you want me to stay?"

"As you wish."

From a drawer of his desk Decimus took out a surgical scalpel and set it calmly before himself. "Open that cabinet and look inside." He pointed to a low piece of furniture at Aelius's right. "I paid her fare to Africa. You can keep it."

In the cabinet sat a small alabaster portraying a woman, young, large-eyed, with a firm, exquisite little mouth. Aelius recognized who she was without asking, without saying.

"I pursued the bitch, but she wouldn't marry me. Took that old fool Pupienus instead."

"You loved her and were *rejected*—that was your true grudge against Annia Cincia!" When Aelius looked over, Decimus had turned his chair to the painted wall, and the scalpel was gone from the desk.

"Don't speak nonsense. I wanted her wealth."

The motions of wrist-cutting were quick, hardly detectable from where Aelius stood. Decimus did not so much as wince as he did it.

"What about your daughter?" he thought he should say.

Decimus moved his head from side to side. Aelius did not understand if it was to refuse the argument, or because he had nothing to say, or what else. His shoulders were still erect; the neck showed no weakness. "What about *your* daughter?" He echoed Aelius's question.

"She's not mine."

"That is hard."

Until the end Aelius watched his colleague's neck, the lack of tension under the fastidiously arranged hair, and then little by little the straight line of the tendons beginning to sag, the knotty bone between his shoulders protruding slowly as the head began to lean forward, the shoulders drooped. Blood on the floor pooled at the sides of the chair; an imperceptible slope in the floor made it snake under the desk. Aelius waited for the small convulsed motion of the end, a slump he walked forward to arrest. When he lifted Decimus's head, his colleague seemed to stare at him; on his sallowness, death did not show as readily as it would on a ruddy man, but life was gone from the eyes. He closed those, composed the body, and stood there a few moments more before calling the serfs.

Sido and his men were at his mother's doorstep to check on him before dawn, when Aelius had just returned. Justina, already up, received them, giving him time to undress and slip into bed. "My son had his first night of good sleep after risking his life beyond the river, and you come to annoy him at this hour? Go ahead, check in his room, check on his horse in the stables, awaken my newborn granddaughter!"

The insistent mewing of Belatusa's days-old child accompanied the *speculatores* through the house, to Aelius' bedroom. "What is it, has the war started?" Aelius asked, turning on his pillow. Sido himself squelched in the mud to the stables, to examine the army mount and its harness, and found that neither it nor the other horses had been ridden recently. He came back grumpily, passing unawares by the barn where the unshod, weary horse chewed on hay. Mouthing, "My apologies, lady, we had to make sure," he left the property in haste.

III

ASHES

11

There was already a sour, green hint of spring in the air, even though two months at least would pass before the snow would melt. It was one of those mid-February passing thaws, when ice booms as it cracks in the great river, and mounds of wet snow collapse without noise from the roofs. A lukewarm sun burrowed through the overcast sky like a burin through a milky stone; wherever the narrow beam came down, the thing or animal or man touched by it seemed to catch on fire with color, whatever its color was.

Aelius traveled to Intercisa for a number of reasons, professional and private. He was to lead the transfer of a unit of mounted archers from the city to Carnuntum, and it so happened that his mother's lawyer, recommended by the ubiquitous ben Matthias, resided there. Ben Matthias himself, who had gotten good commissions from the army, told Aelius the case was as good as won. "They haven't got a leg to stand on, those hunks of beef." He referred to Gargilius and Barga, rubbing his hands. "To try to rob a widow: *terefah!* But you're wrong in not claiming your part of the inheritance; a man's got to have property."

"At any rate, I sent for my copy of the quitclaim document at Nicomedia. How long have you been here, Baruch?"

"A week."

"It means you already know everyone's business, eh?"

The Jew modestly raked his beard. "Not everyone's. I did hear there was a purge in the army, among your Roman colleagues. They were tight-lipped to the day of their execution, and Decimus is dead by his own hand. Tsk, tsk, Commander: the kind of idealistic harebrained scheme aristocrats come up with. What else? Well, I hear that our *perfectissimus* Sido took all the credit for exposing the camarilla and is mounting Lady Helena day and night."

"Let him: They deserve each other." Aelius knew Helena well enough; her telling Sido that he'd infiltrated Cato's Sodality was not so much meant to save him from trouble as to make him politically beholden to her, officially declaring his concern for Constantine's life.

Ben Matthias misunderstood Aelius's irritation. "Oh, she'll let you into her bed again, be sure." He turned away in disgust from the door when a drover passed by, leading hogs meant for sacrifice to the family gods. "Today I do not set my foot out, there's too much impurity around. Tomorrow, instead, I go to Aquincum, but not for the reason you may think."

"What reason should I think of? I have been at army posts until this morning."

"It's your old bogeyman, Commander—the miracle worker. Gave himself up to Roman scouts at Contra Aquincum and was brought back over the river. For three days he's been held at the city jail, and promises that the wild beasts in the arena will refuse to maul him, blades will fail to cut him, fire will not consume his flesh, et cetera. Folks are flocking from everywhere to see the fire waker's wonder, although I rather think they want to see him cut to ribbons by bears."

"Did he say why he surrendered himself?"

"Am I a fly on the courthouse wall, Commander? I don't have a clue. Maybe he heard he'd been exposed; maybe he chose to save his reputation through a martyr's death, which places him above others and might make him a saint."

"Or else he saw his indirect responsibility in other crimes." Aelius would not elaborate. "Was his assistant Casta with him?"

"Not that I know of. Had there been a woman about to be executed, the publicity would have been louder yet. Me, I'm going to Aquincum to buy real estate—one-third of the town is shops, you know."

By this time Casta had probably embarked at the closest port in Dalmatia, on one of those paunchy ships that plied the Mediterranean waters. That he was not done with her (or she with him) was something Aelius had to come to terms with. She'd not escaped him, in fact: was merely out of reach for the time being. The small translucent portrait of her Decimus had chosen to give him—why?—tied him to her as the means to recognize her face, wherever and whenever.

"Are you still working on the biography of Severus, Commander?"

Ben Matthias's question brought him back to the day. "Piecemeal, but yes."

"I could sell you a fine copy of Aurelius Victor's writings on him. A fair price: I'm losing money on it."

"So, selling at a fair price means losing money?"

SAVARIA, 24 FEBRUARY, SATURDAY, REGIFUGIUM, REMEMBRANCE OF "THE EXPULSION OF THE KINGS"

Yes, the full-fledged campaign would start soon. A movement like a long impatient shiver would go through the long line of forts, citadels, watchtowers, the military road, and men would be on the march across the Danube. Even at headquarters in Savaria, Aelius could feel the squelch of mud under the mounts' hooves, hear the leather moaning on harness, baldrics, straps, the sound of men going to war.

As always when passing by a post exchange, he stopped to check his mail and to send a reply to Anubina, the gist of which was that he understood but did not lose hope of changing her mind. "Think of the sons you and I would have: Wouldn't you rather have mine?"

For him, two letters awaited, neither of them bearing the sender's name and address on the envelope. One of the two was plain, lower-grade papyrus, the other of the finest quality, dyed red. "Who brought these, do you know?" he asked the army clerk.

"Both came with the morning delivery, sir. The courier starts out in Celeia, so they could have been posted there or at Poetovio, or at Sala, or anywhere else in between."

The inexpensive envelope was the one Aelius unsealed first. It contained three thickly written sheets in a quick hand and good Latin. The beginning line made him nearly stumble down the steps from the post exchange, slick with ice.

> *To Commander Aelius Spartianus from the servant of God Casta, blessings in this world and the next.*

He hurried across the marching grounds to the officers' mess hall, empty at this midmorning hour, and sat down to read as close as possible to the window that received light from the courtyard.

> *Esteemed Commander, I am writing this in remembrance of your kind visit to my old nurse's house in December, in memory of Marcus Lupus and Minucius Marcellus, and because your pursuit of the truth, albeit the truth as men construct, and not as Our Lord teaches, deserves a small reward. Arrogance is a sin, for idolaters no less than for Christians. Hubris leads to nemesis. I cannot allow you to take pride in securing my person, but I can satisfy your curiosity now that I am well out of reach.*
>
> *Through our fellow believers, my erstwhile teacher Agnus sent me a message shortly before his capture, detailing what you told him in regard to me when you met in Barbaricum. As a result of your revelations, he decided to crown his dubious ministry by giving himself up to the authorities as a martyr. I am not surprised by his sense of grandeur: It is true to the man. But know that when I first encountered the fire waker, I believed in him. In my despair over my husband's illness, I was ready to believe anything. He seemed to possess the peace of mind I was seeking, the certainty I needed. It was a little sacrifice to sell or give away everything I owned, in order to acquire that peace of*

mind. So little, in fact, that I, an aristocrat, raised in privilege, also offered to serve him. It seemed to me the most abasing, hence the most meritorious, action I could take in God's eyes.

Blinded by trust, it took me many months to realize how small-minded and self-important he was. Agnus's love for virtue was actually love for his virtue, for his virtuous self. His techniques were paltry and transparent: a few herbs, much incense, monotonous chanting and rolling of eyes. People's credulity and the hiring of false cripples did the rest. I had seen better mountebanks in Laumellum as a child. Still, my disappointment could have been tempered by admiration for Agnus's admittedly pure life, had he not held women in such contempt. His pastoral letters circulated widely among adepts, were quoted and abided by. Everywhere they resulted in dismissal of those of my sex from aiding in the ministry, in unbearable restrictions within a Church that claims to honor the woman who gave birth to the Savior!

"Commander, may I get you something?"

The orderly stood by, inopportune as most orderlies are. His mind still on the reading, Aelius stared at him a moment before gathering his wits to say, "No, leave me alone."

You should know that I could have continued serving him, had he not belonged to those in the Church that with the arrogance of Nimrod set themselves before God at the expense of others. Where would Christianity be today, were it not for the women who gave up their husbands, their sons, and even themselves to the true and only God? Were there not more female than male martyrs? Were there not more pious ladies than wealthy men who opened their houses and estates to the persecuted, at their own risk? The Lord is the Lord, Agnus and his would say. But I say, the Lord himself was born of a woman. Was not Mary, Christ's mother, the first minister of this Christian Church? The

*months of her divine pregnancy are an absolute sign of this per-
fect union, and of a privilege no other human being was
granted. Now, if Christ allowed himself to be physically contained in a female body, is this not a sign of the superior holiness
of women over men? Had He chosen so, He could have taken
abode in the seed of His putative father, or sprung fully formed
out of a rock as the followers of Mithras tell of their god. No, He
chose a woman's body as the vehicle for His incarnation.*

*Yet the women's community where you sought me in Treveri,
dedicated to good works and the study of the healing arts, was
closed down because of Agnus's insistence that it was against
God's will. The elders of the Church were ready to listen, in
Treveri as in Mogontiacum as in Mediolanum: Matrons are
deemed useful for the money they will to the Church, for the
embroideries they stitch for priests' robes, and nothing else, unless you count the sons they can raise for the priesthood.*

*I had no money left, no sons, and no embroidery skills. My
own beauty, worthless as it is in God's eyes, militated against
me. Thus I mortified my flesh, fasted until I was ill. After two
long years, however, I decided that this could not be what God
wanted, that this Church is not what God wants. This is why
the arrogant church of these arrogant male priests has to be
shamed, to be shown fraudulent where it is fraudulent. I'm neither a saint nor a chosen instrument, but I will work to change
things.*

The door slammed when two cavalry officers walked in, carrying a
blast of cold wetness from the outside. Aelius turned his head, hearing
them converse with the recognizable cadence of the Roman-born.
Decimus had spoken that way. Strange how Aelius was not ashamed of
having ridden to his lonely villa to warn him of danger, knowing that
his colleague was guilty of planning treason and had left him to die.
He'd been much angrier at other men for much less.

And now, Commander, to the matter of your successful pursuit of the truth, and to the names with which I began this writing: Marcus Lupus and Minucius Marcellus.

You are right, Lupus's miraculous return to life was my doing. It was necessary in view of the letter that I would later send anonymously to expose Agnus's chicanery. The most surprised at the "resurrection" was the fire waker. He purged himself and fasted for three days afterward, to thank God for giving him the power to bring back the dead, when all Lupus had was a banal fever. Arrogance blinded the trickster to the simplest of tricks, to the ease with which you can buy a sleeping potion, physicians, and cemetery workers. Impoverished as I had made myself, I had access to Agnus's huge purse, fattened by the gifts of men and women duped as I had been. He would not defile his hands with money! So all I had to do was use some of it to buy the witnesses, and claim I had given the sum to charity. The holy man was above checking such sordid details.

Lupus, of course, had everything to gain from maintaining a silence that made him suddenly famous and brought business to his brickyard. But he had to die, so that Agnus and his woman-hating colleagues would fall under suspicion. Asking a trusted (and unaware) lady friend to bring Lupus a gift of dainties was child's play. So many admirers and believers queued to see the miracle man! Convincing her to let me lower myself before God by escorting her to the brickyard in the guise of a servant was even easier. No one notices servants. Thus Lupus entertained the visitors until bedtime, and the lady's servant stayed behind with an excuse, hiding in the dark, waiting to seal his room with rags. How useful my readings on the causes of illness and death turned out to be . . . Unfortunately I hadn't enough cloth with me, so I had to use Lupus's coverlet as well: In fact, you noticed the dirt on its fringe. By morning, the rags were gone, Lupus's window cracked open once more. The servant sat among others

*in the bivouac of female pilgrims and believers in the field near
the brickyard and saw you ride by alone at dawn. You looked
over as well, and we were staring at each other when I pulled the
shawl over my head. That is why I could not show myself to you
under the light at my nurse's home.*

*As for Minucius Marcellus, he was a dear old magistrate and
a friend of my family, whose last act of generosity to me was
serving as a victim, so that the misogynist church in Mediolanum could be punished like its counterpart in Belgica Prima.
In fact, who else but Christians would be suspected of attacking
him in the baths, where Christian serfs labored? You lead men
in the field, thus you know how beholden soldiers are to their
commanders, how ready to execute orders. "Casta is less than
dirt under God's feet," I thought, "but Agnus walks with God.
What if a rumor spread among the serfs at the Old Baths that
Marcellus's next trial will be against the fire waker, who thundered against him in his pastoral letters? Would it suffice to
cause an assault?" Christians from the North African provinces
have the reputation of bringing to their new creed the impetuos-
ity of their tribal beliefs. One anguished meeting with them in
one of our hideouts stirred them up beyond my hopes. I only expected a desperate attempt on their part: They much surpassed
my dreams, and killed the gentle judge. Surely Our Lord has a
place not far from His throne for the merciful unbelievers, and
there Marcellus abides now.*

The two cavalry officers sat down at a table behind him. Aelius heard
them order wine, and chat in Greek not to be understood by the mess-
hall personnel.

"You heard about what they had in mind? Yes, it reflects badly on all
of us. Now every goddamned upstart stands to be promoted before we
are."

"Yes, Curius Decimus is the one who bothers me most: Who'd have
ever imagined?"

I do regret the fate of the churchmen's wives, but they made the free choice of following their husbands to a martyr's death. None of us counts much, I less than everyone on earth. The important thing is changing the Church; those wives' sacrifice will be one more step to the recognition of women's role as teachers and ministers. Agnus's downfall is our victory; the dousing of his fire is the kindling of a larger, more brilliant one.

Had you known at the time of our brief meeting at my nurse's home, would you still have kept silent about my presence in Mediolanum? The question puzzles me. You puzzle me, Commander Spartianus. How do you behave toward your own women? Do you honor them or are you like the rest, violent and overbearing toward them? I trust there will be an opportunity for us to discuss these matters, if God sees the good of making us meet again.

By the time you receive this letter, I will be far away but, be assured, working for the goal I spelled out above. With greetings, and prayers to our merciful Lord for your well-being and conversion.

Written by Casta on the twentieth day of February, in a safe place.

Aelius rolled up the letter without haste, without haste slipped it back into its envelope. The fire waker's downfall, he thought, had begun the day of his meeting with Annia Cincia. Maybe her god was greater than Agnus's, not as merciful as she said. Maybe Christians made allowances for trickery and murder to advance their aims. Even executing them was useful to their ambitious design. That firm little mouth, those dainty wrists surrendering from the dark: She would have let him take her off to her death without resisting. He had not done it, yet she did not lie when she'd said, *Should you ask me, I could not tell you that Christians are innocent of Marcellus's death.*

Behind him, the cavalry officers were conversing of lighter things: women they knew, horseflesh. They'd reverted to Latin and cursed a great deal.

The second letter, the one in the costly red envelope, Aelius kept still
unopened in front of him. It was addressed in Greek. He recognized
the handwriting. The sealing wax bore the imprint of an antique ring.
The servant who had entrusted it to the army post no doubt had been
told to keep it for a week before doing so.

Outside, rain had turned to snow and to rain once more. Aelius saw
the grayness of the day when the Roman officers left the mess hall. He
broke the seal.

> *Had you joined me in my desperate venture, Aelius Spartianus,
> I would not be writing any of this. It is because you said no that
> I write.*
>
> *In the two months we knew each other, many things hap-
> pened. Had they been years, I cannot say I would have grown to
> know you better. Is it perhaps because the last weeks of our lives
> became so intense? In Italy and during our travel to the frontier,
> I watched you closely. Amused at first, I watched you for the
> signs of crudity and uncouthness that your wild ancestors are
> said to have raised as a bulwark against Rome. I told myself,
> "His great-grandfathers raped Roman women, sacked cities,
> nailed the heads of Roman officers to the trunks of their fir
> groves. He is one of the trained bears we lead by a chain, forcing
> them by a pull on the ring around their nostrils to dance to our
> tune." And all the while, inevitably, I had to admit that your
> behavior was no less mannerly than that of those I call my Ro-
> man friends. Your Latin speech was not only clear but thought-
> ful and intelligent, if more modern than what I was taught in
> my youth. Your written Greek—I blush at the admission—was
> even better than mine. Hardly the tasks that trained bears could
> be taught to perform.*
>
> *But your essence as a man, seen even from inside the whirl-
> wind of my hopeless conspiracy, was the one element with which
> I could least contend: your sense of history, your knowledge of
> what passed before us, and why it happened as it did. Your*

*familiarity with things Roman that many in Rome—you have
to take my word for it—would envy, if they even realized it is
something to envy. Little by little, against my better judgment,
against that will, even, that you Stoics say is the only thing that
really belongs to man, I came to the conclusion that Aelius
Spartianus—Aelius Spartus's son, whose ancestors were barbarians and slaves—is a Roman. More, that Rome has to be
what you represent, or else she will perish from the earth.*

*As you know I have no sons: None, legitimate or illegitimate,
were born to me. You might say (I can hear you saying it) that it
is the decrepitude of Roman blood, cross-bred to the point of in-
cest and past that point. Two of my ancestors married their own
nieces, and it's fabled that a young ancestress, wrecked at sea as
a child and raised in a brothel, only after being freed and married by her lover realized herself to be his long-lost sister. But
that may be a tale adapted from Plautus's stage play, who
knows. Ancient blood! We have idiots and madmen in our line-
age. I married four women—from the Valerii, the Anicii, the
Fabii, the Cornelii, the bloom of Roman ancestry. And only
from the second did I father one daughter, the one you saw, sole
among my friends. I'd have killed her, you know. Killed her to
save her from her father's absence. But she gave me a second gift
by dying a day ahead of me, after giving me the gift of being
born. You will observe (I can hear you say this as well), "Why
did you not seek a plebeian mate, then, or a woman from the far
reaches of the Empire?" Of course I did, as you and all soldiers
do time and again during your years of service. To my knowledge, not even from my concubines did I beget sons. Thus the
lack is in me, Aelius. Blood and glory and purity and republican
values, generalships and consulships, seats in the Senate, all
ends with me unless I put a remedy to it.*

*You may recall how in Mediolanum, that night that seems to
be so long ago, I invited you to dine at my house, and—hearing
that you hadn't yet decided whether you would accept—I added*

that no one had ever turned down my invitation. Tonight, with things being so different, yet so much clearer in my mind, I invite you once again, and will not accept a refusal. Through faithful lawyers, my available wealth—not the real estate, all sadly to be alienated by the fisc on account of my disgrace—was, weeks ago already, placed into an anonymous trust. The entire sum goes to you, for any of the following reasons you may choose: Because I could think of no one else. Because it pleases me. Or because, even though my attempt to halt the barbarization of the Empire was sacrosanct, it was nonetheless treason, and as you bent neither to my threats nor to my blandishments, you showed yourself faithful and a Roman through and through. My ancestors will turn in their graves less for this than for my dishonoring their name.

Do not trust Sido. Do not trust Helena. Above all, do not trust Constantine.

It is my desire that, in lieu of my son, you pour libations and make all appropriate remembrances of me on the days of my birth and of my death, whenever that will be, on Parentalia's two-week celebration of the dead in February, and on 21 April, the foundation day of Eternal Rome. Salve atque vale. *Manius Curius Decimus, son of Publius Curius Calvinius,* vir clarissimus *of the senatorial class.*

Aelius realized he'd sat at the table a long while, because other officers had filled the mess hall when he looked around. One of them leaned over to say, "Do you mind if I sit here?" Another had not even bothered to ask and was already eating noisily at the other end of the table.

Finding Sido just outside the door did not surprise him. He might have spied him from the window for all he knew. First the head of the *speculatores* spoke some nonsense about going to an appointment with someone, then stayed there with his arms folded, motionless under the eave that protected him from the rain. Aelius decided it was better to give him a chance to speak now and get it over with. So he remained under the same eave, with his saddlebag on the hale shoulder, looking at the drops from the gutter falling to dig a trench in the diluted snow.

"It seems we end this match in a draw, Aelius Spartianus."

"Does it? I didn't know we were in a match."

Sido turned to him. Calmly Aelius did the same, so that they faced each other, careless that rain wetted the side of their bodies under the dripping eave.

"But I'm keeping my eye on you, inside the border and out. Don't you ever think yourself out of my reach. Remember that Decimus left some of his smell on you." Sido touched Aelius's chest, bringing his fingertips near his nose afterward. "I can smell it. And the fly of treason can bite at any time."

"I think I gave proof in Egypt that I am immune to the insect."

"Then let's say that the fire of ambition can be fanned at any time, and the army is a pile of dry wood. You *are* army, aren't you?"

An unintelligent provocation, at a time not made for lashing out. Aelius held his breath, let it go. In May the old emperors would abdicate. Within a year Constantius would be dead, and in the following months Maxentius and Constantine would emerge from the power struggle holding sway over entire armies, drawing barbarian tribes to their side, murdering season after season. The face of Rome itself would be obscured in blood.

This morning, on the marching grounds of the military camp at Savaria, in the province of Pannonia Prima Savia, Aelius could look at the man in front of him and foretell his end, as stupidity always will be crushed in great battles. It was vengeance enough. "I am definitely army," he only said.

Rain melted snow, and a sickly sun wanted to thin out the rain; clouds shredded like veils pulled without mercy. Aelius watched Sido turn on his heel and walk away, squirting mud. He blessed the cleanliness of the coming war. There would be a right moment to take back in hand Decimus's letter and decide what to do about it. For now, it sat in his saddlebag with its flattery and promise of wealth, its warnings, its weight as the testament of a man's soul. Annia Cincia's—Casta's—exquisite little alabaster bust sat alongside it, and both were like tinder waiting for a spark.

GLOSSARY

THE PLACES

Italia Annonaria (Northern Italy)

Aquileia—city in northeastern Italy, important religious seat in early Christianity

Balnea Vetra—the Old Baths in Mediolanum

Brixia—Brescia, city then and now known for its weapons factories (Beretta)

Mediolanum—Milan

Modicia—Monza, city near Milan where Charlemagne's crown is kept

Mutina—Modena

Porta Argentea, Aurea (Nova), Romana, Ticinensis, Vercellina—Mediolanum city gates

porticus maximiana—famous porticoed street built by Maximian in Mediolanum

Tergeste—Trieste

Ticinum—Pavia

Vicentia—Vicenza, still a military town (U.S. Army)

Belgica Prima and Germania Inferior and Superior
(France, and Northern and Southern Germany)

Arae Flaviae—Rottweil, in the Black Forest

Argentorate—Strasbourg

Augusta Treverorum—Trier

Bingum—Bingen

Brigantium—Bregenz
Confluentes—Koblenz
Noviomagus—Lisieux
Teutoburg—forest near Detmold, where in 9 C.E. an entire Roman
army was ambushed and destroyed by Arminius's Germanic tribes-
men
Vindonissa—Windisch

Noricum and Raetia (Austria), Moesia and Pannonia
(region including parts of Hungary, Austria, Slovenia, Croatia)

Aquincum—Budapest
Arrabona—Gyoer
Aspalatum—Split
Carnuntum—location near Petronell, southeast of Bratislava
Castra Regina—Regensburg
Celeia—Celje
Emona—Ljubljana
Intercisa—location on the Danube, about forty miles south of Bu-
dapest
Poetovio—Ptuj
Sala—Zalaloevo
Savaria—Szombathely
Scarbantia—Sopron, near Lake Balaton
Sirmium—Sremska Mitrovica, northeast of Belgrade; the martyr Ire-
naeus was its bishop
Siscia—Sisak
Vindobona—Vienna

Other Geographical Names

Antinoopolis—city, today vanished, along middle course of the Nile
Barbaricum—generic name for the barbarian-inhabited areas outside
the Roman Empire
Byzantium—later Constantinople, today's Istanbul
Dacia—Romania

Dalmatia—Adriatic region of Croatia

Dravus, Marus, Savus, Tibiscus—the central European rivers Drava, Morava, Sava, and Tisza

Golden Spike/Cuneus Aureus—the Spluegen Pass between Austria and Italy

Insubria, Insubrians—today's northern Italian region of Lombardy, and its inhabitants

Nicomedia—Izmir, in Turkey

Tibur—city near Rome, known for its building stone and Hadrian's great villa

THE NAMES

Historical and Mythical Names

Achilleus; Domitius Domitianus—Roman usurpers, defeated in Egypt, circa 296 CE

Aeschylus (†456 B.C.E.)—Greek playwright, authored among others the tragedy *Agamemnon*

Agamemnon, Cassandra—mythical king slain by his wife, and slave who foretold his death

Admetus, Alcestis—mythical husband and wife; she offered her life for his

Brutus (†42 B.C.E.)—one of the murderers of Julius Caesar

Cato the Censor, or the Elder (†149 B.C.E.)—conservative Roman statesman and orator

Diocletian (†316 C.E.)—Roman emperor, great soldier and administrator

Constantine (†337 C.E.)—known as "the Great," first Christian emperor

Constantius (†306 C.E.)—Diocletian's co-emperor and Constantine's father

Galerius (†311)—Diocletian's co-emperor, persecutor of Christians

Hades—god of the underworld, also the underworld itself

Helena—Constantine's mother, later a Christian saint

Maxentius (†312 C.E.)—Maximian's son, usurper and Constantine's rival

Maximian (†311 C.E.)—Diocletian's co-emperor and Maxentius's father

Orpheus, Eurydice—mythical couple: glancing at her, Orpheus failed to save his bride from death

Pentheus—mythical king slain by drunken and possessed women

Seneca (†65 C.E.)—Roman thinker and Nero's teacher (who forced him to commit suicide)

Severus, Septimius (†211 C.E.)—Roman general and emperor, native of North Africa

Thanathos—Greek personification of death

Varus (Quintilius) (†9 C.E.)—Roman general, lost three legions and his life in Teutoburg Forest

Virgil (†19 B.C.E.)—greatest Roman poet, wrote among others the *Aeneid*

Everything Else

Ala Antoniniana Sagittariorum Surorum; Ala Ursiciana; Ioviani Palatini; Maximiani Juniores; Seniores Gentiliorum—Roman cavalry units, approximately of regimental strength

Alamanni, Alani, Boii, Gepids, Goths, Quadi, Marcomanni, Roxolani, Sarmatae, Scordisci, Suebi, Vandals—barbarians of northern and eastern European origin who periodically attacked the Roman Empire between 400 B.C.E. and 500 C.E.

Bibe vivas multis annis, vivas feliciter—well-wishing sentences on Roman goblets: "drink and live many years"; "may you live happily"

burgus—a defensive fortified tower along the Roman frontier

clarissimus, perfectissimus—lit. "most noble" and "most perfect," titles given to the Roman social classes of senators and knights

cui prodest—Latin: "Who gains from it?"

denarius—a basic Roman monetary unit; depreciated through the years from circa 30 U.S. cents to circa 8 U.S. cents

Figlinae Marci Lupi—"the brickworks of Marcus Lupus"

foederati—"military confederates," barbarian tribes allied to Roman army

fullones—"cloth dyers"

Germanicus, Britannicus, Sarmaticus, Persicus Maximus—imperial titles, indicating the victories gained over Germany, Britain, Sarmatia, and Persia

Ides, Kalends—ancient (lunar) Roman calendar subdivisions, indicating midmonth and the last days before the following month

Kislev—Hebrew month, corresponding to November–December

lapsi—"fallen back, backsliding," name given to Christians who recanted during persecutions

legatos, strategos—Greek for "commander," "general"

Manes—spirits of the family dead

mutatio—"horse-changing station"

nefasti (dies)—in the Roman calendar, "negative" days during which official acts were forbidden

praefectus—Roman military title, corresponding more or less to the rank of colonel

praeses—late Roman term for "provincial governor"

sagum—the cloth used for the cloak worn by Roman soldiers, often bright red, hence also the cloak itself

Salve atque vale—"Hail, and be well"

Samnites—ancient Latin tribe, fought Rome at the beginnings of the city

sestertium (sesterce)—Roman monetary unit, ¼ of a *denarius* (see above)

speculator, speculatores—member(s) of the Roman criminal investigation police

terefah—Hebrew for "impure"

ustrinum—a fenced area where the funeral pyre of a family or clan was erected

vexillationes—lit. "flag-bearing," highly mobile mounted units of the Roman army